Goosebumps
THE GRAPHIC NOVEL

MONSTER BLOOD

R.L. STINE

Goosebumps
THE GRAPHIC NOVEL

NEW!
MONSTER
BLOOD
Surprising
Miracle
Substance!

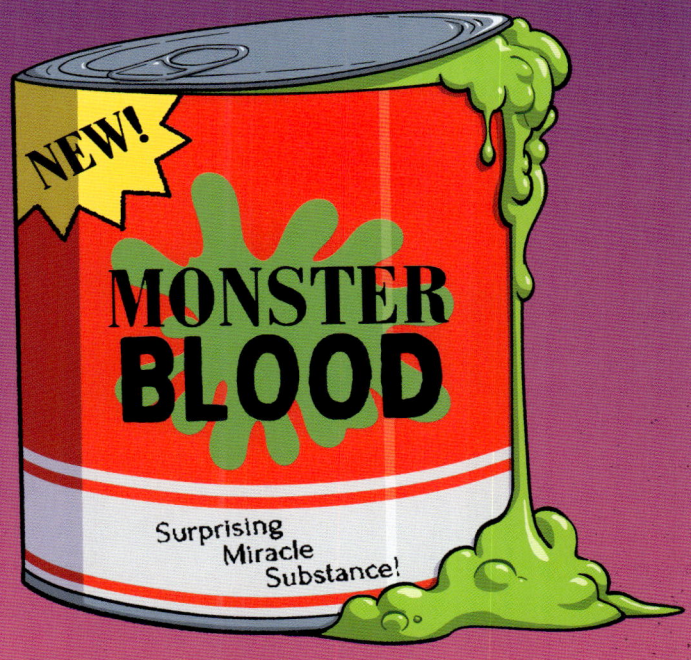

MONSTER BLOOD

ADAPTED BY MADDI GONZALEZ

WITH COLOR BY WES DZIOBA

graphix

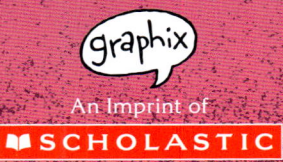

An Imprint of

SCHOLASTIC

Goosebumps book series created by Parachute Press
Text copyright © 1992 by Scholastic Inc.
Art copyright © 2025 by Maddi Gonzalez

All rights reserved. Published by Graphix, an imprint of Scholastic Inc., *Publishers since 1920.* SCHOLASTIC, GRAPHIX, GOOSEBUMPS, and associated logos are trademarks and/or registered trademarks of Scholastic Inc.

The publisher does not have any control over and does not assume any responsibility for author or third-party websites or their content.

No part of this publication may be reproduced, stored in a retrieval system, or transmitted in any form or by any means, electronic, mechanical, photocopying, recording, or otherwise, or used to train any artificial intelligence technologies, without written permission of the publisher. For information regarding permission, write to Scholastic Inc., Attention: Permissions Department, 557 Broadway, New York, NY 10012.

This book is a work of fiction. Names, characters, places, and incidents are either the product of the author's imagination or are used fictitiously, and any resemblance to actual persons, living or dead, business establishments, events, or locales is entirely coincidental.

ISBN 978-1-338-87943-8 (hardcover)
ISBN 978-1-338-87942-1 (paperback)

10 9 8 7 6 5 4 3 2 1   25 26 27 28 29

Printed in China 62
First edition, September 2025
Edited by Anna Bloom
Color by Wes Dzioba
Lettering by Jesse Post
Book design by Carina Taylor
Creative Director: Phil Falco
Publisher: David Saylor

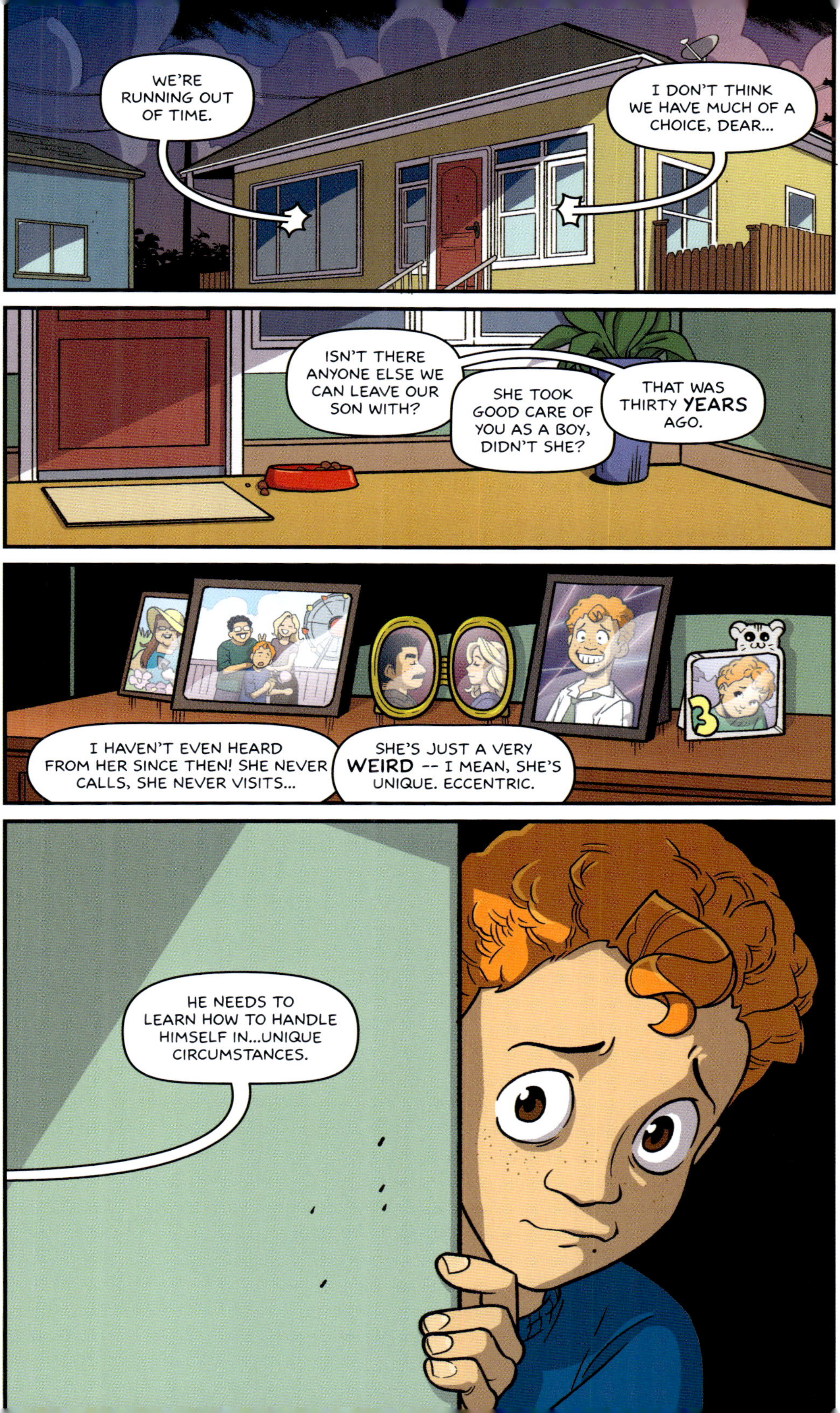

WE'RE RUNNING OUT OF TIME.
I DON'T THINK WE HAVE MUCH OF A CHOICE, DEAR...
ISN'T THERE ANYONE ELSE WE CAN LEAVE OUR SON WITH?
SHE TOOK GOOD CARE OF YOU AS A BOY, DIDN'T SHE?
THAT WAS THIRTY YEARS AGO.
I HAVEN'T EVEN HEARD FROM HER SINCE THEN! SHE NEVER CALLS, SHE NEVER VISITS...
SHE'S JUST A VERY WEIRD -- I MEAN, SHE'S UNIQUE. ECCENTRIC.
HE NEEDS TO LEARN HOW TO HANDLE HIMSELF IN...UNIQUE CIRCUMSTANCES.

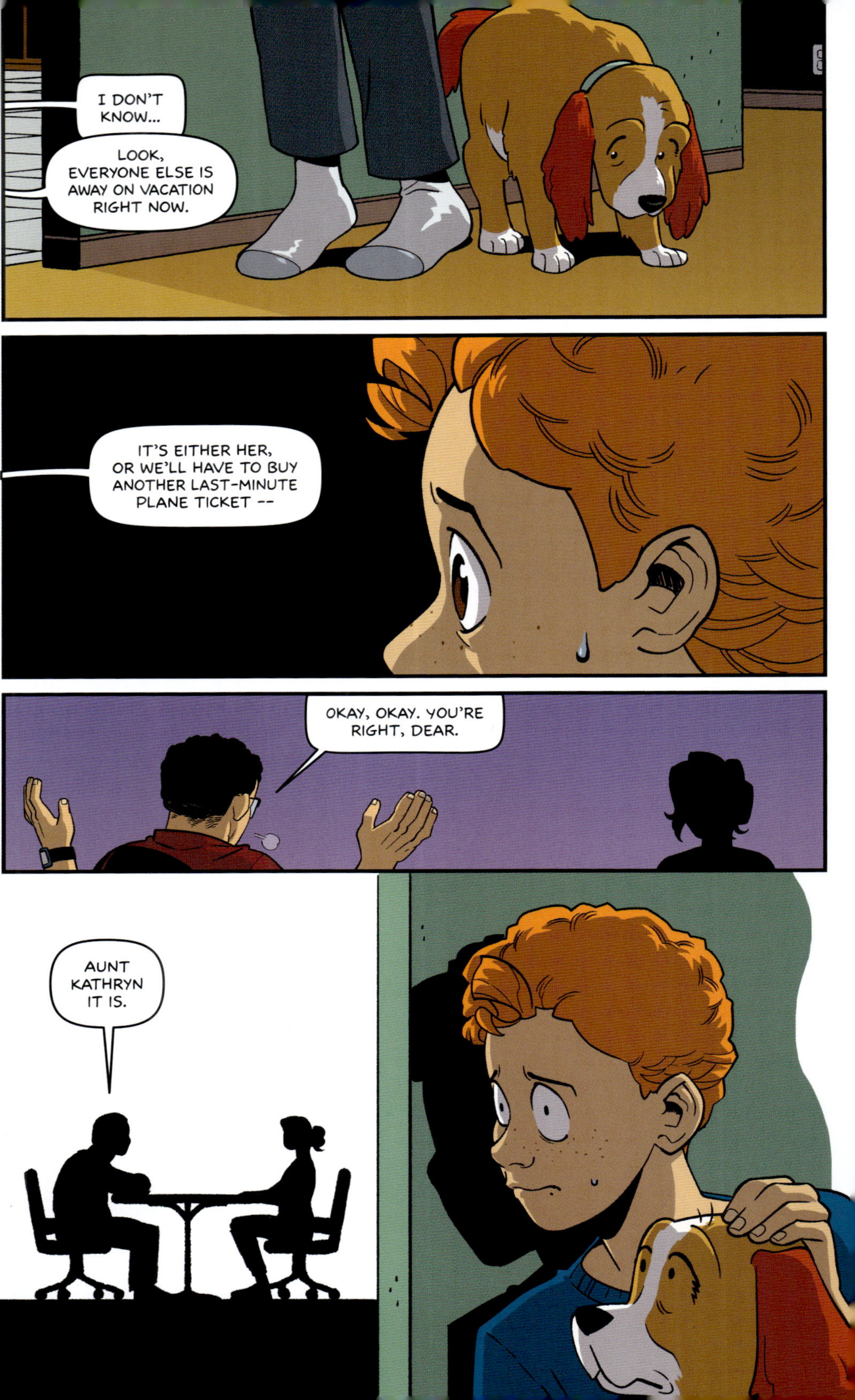
I DON'T KNOW...
LOOK, EVERYONE ELSE IS AWAY ON VACATION RIGHT NOW.
IT'S EITHER HER, OR WE'LL HAVE TO BUY ANOTHER LAST-MINUTE PLANE TICKET --
OKAY, OKAY. YOU'RE RIGHT, DEAR.
AUNT KATHRYN IT IS.

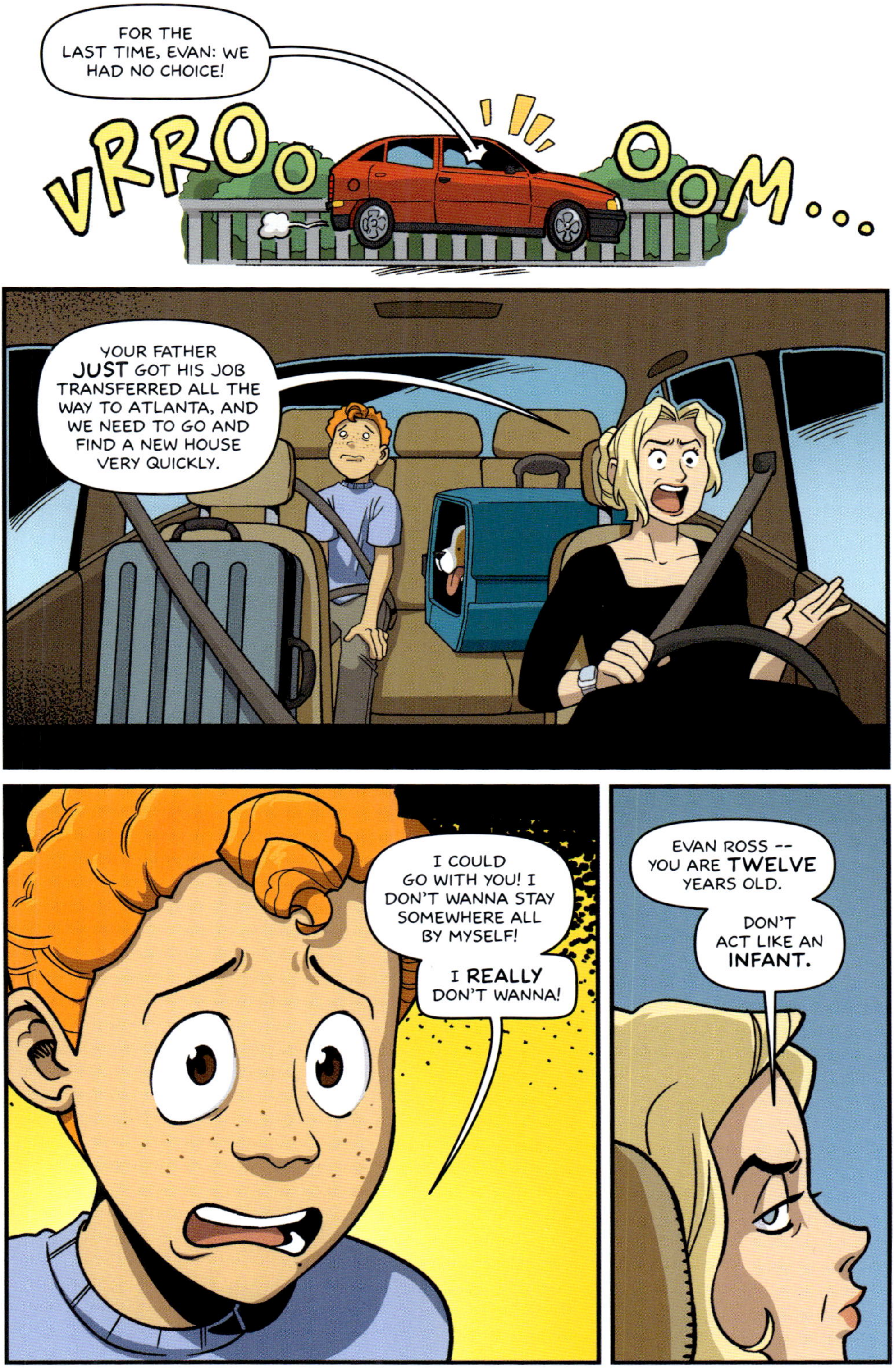
FOR THE LAST TIME, EVAN: WE HAD NO CHOICE!
VRROOOOOM...
YOUR FATHER **JUST** GOT HIS JOB TRANSFERRED ALL THE WAY TO ATLANTA, AND WE NEED TO GO AND FIND A NEW HOUSE VERY QUICKLY.
I COULD GO WITH YOU! I DON'T WANNA STAY SOMEWHERE ALL BY MYSELF!
I **REALLY** DON'T WANNA!
EVAN ROSS -- YOU ARE **TWELVE** YEARS OLD.
DON'T ACT LIKE AN **INFANT.**

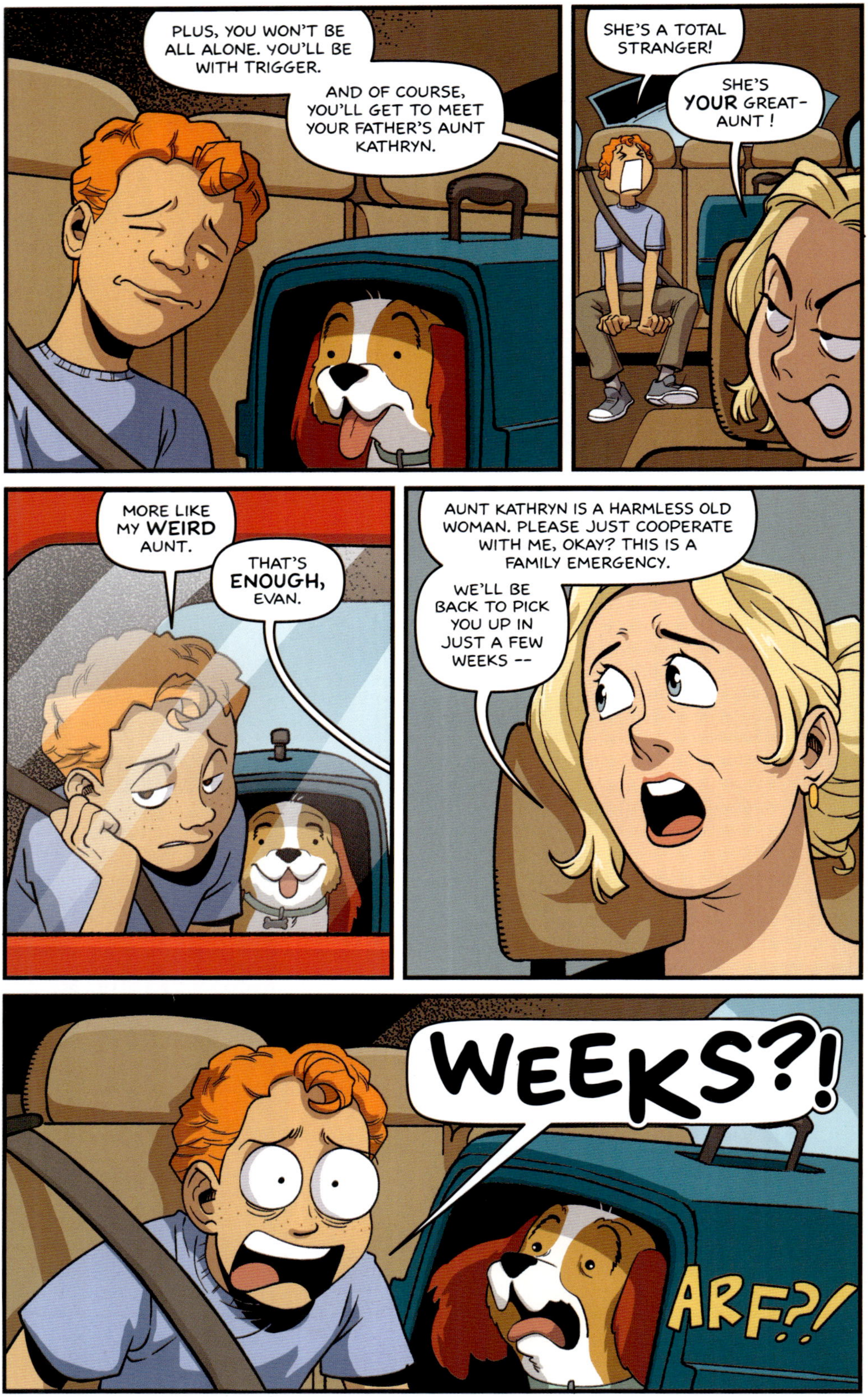

PLUS, YOU WON'T BE ALL ALONE. YOU'LL BE WITH TRIGGER.
AND OF COURSE, YOU'LL GET TO MEET YOUR FATHER'S AUNT KATHRYN.
SHE'S A TOTAL STRANGER!
SHE'S **YOUR** GREAT-AUNT !
MORE LIKE MY **WEIRD** AUNT.
THAT'S **ENOUGH,** EVAN.
AUNT KATHRYN IS A HARMLESS OLD WOMAN. PLEASE JUST COOPERATE WITH ME, OKAY? THIS IS A FAMILY EMERGENCY.
WE'LL BE BACK TO PICK YOU UP IN JUST A FEW WEEKS --
WEEKS?!
ARF?!

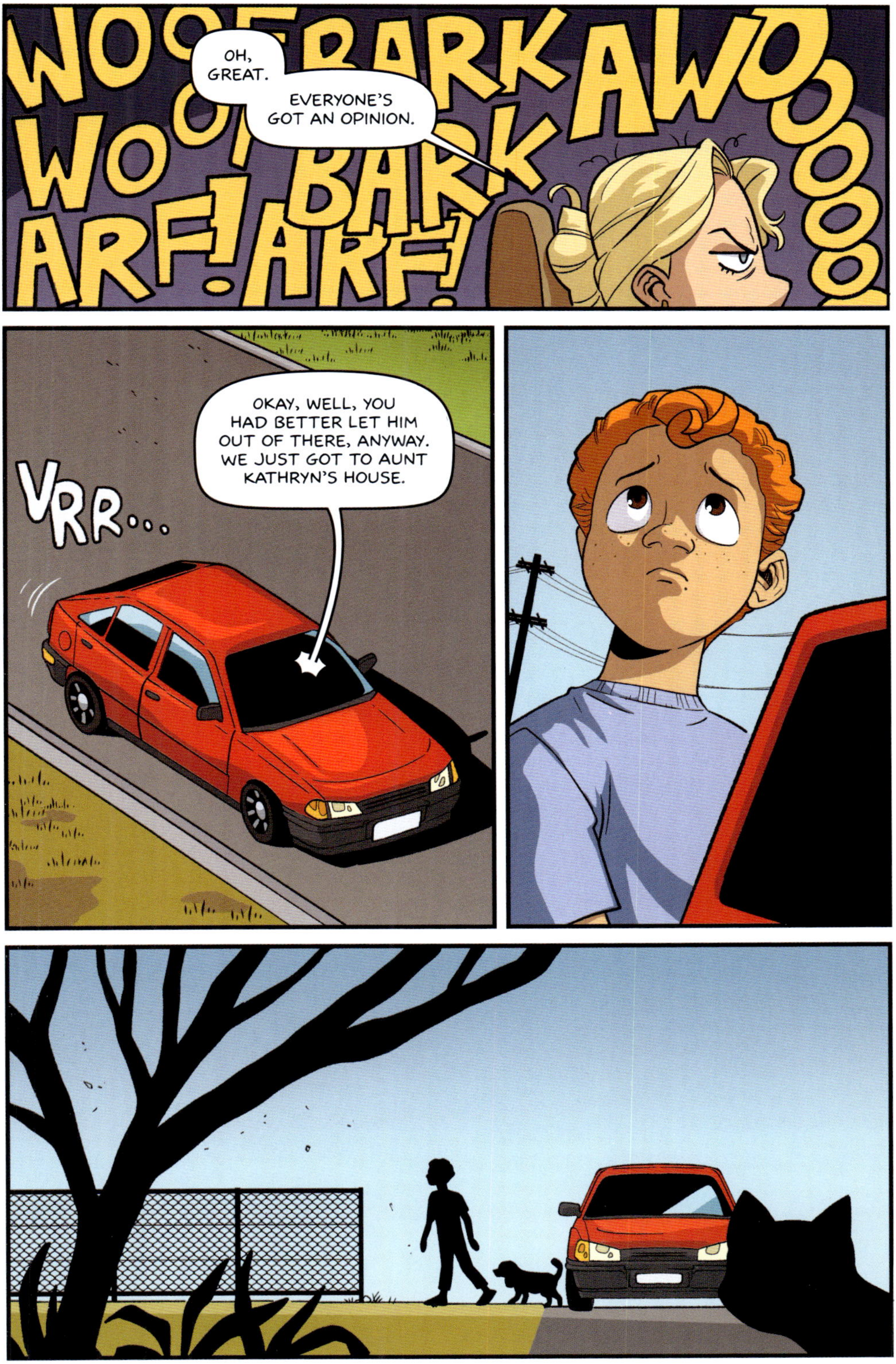

BARK
AWOOOOO
BARK
ARF! ARF!
OH, GREAT.
EVERYONE'S GOT AN OPINION.
VRR...
OKAY, WELL, YOU HAD BETTER LET HIM OUT OF THERE, ANYWAY. WE JUST GOT TO AUNT KATHRYN'S HOUSE.

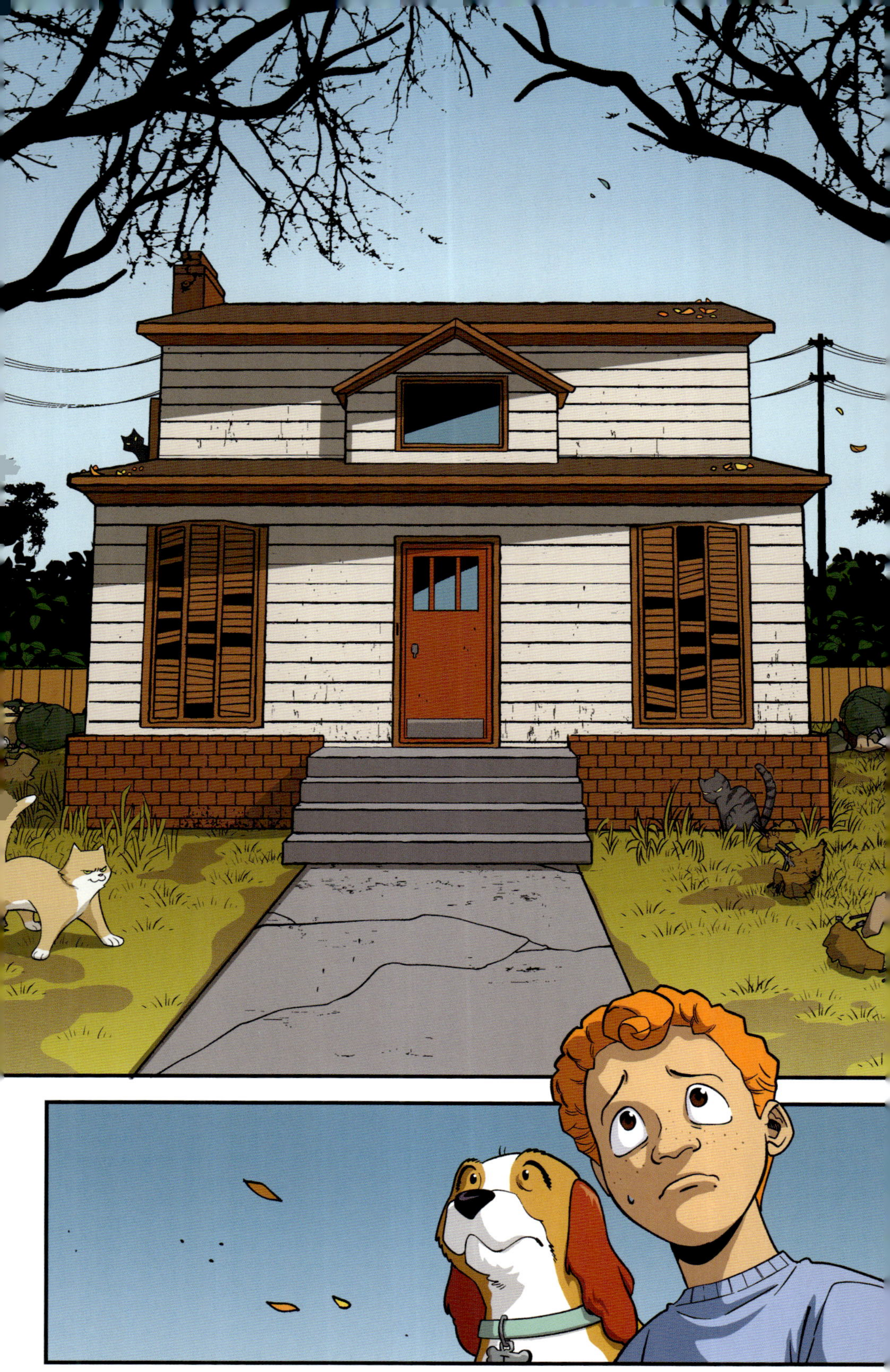

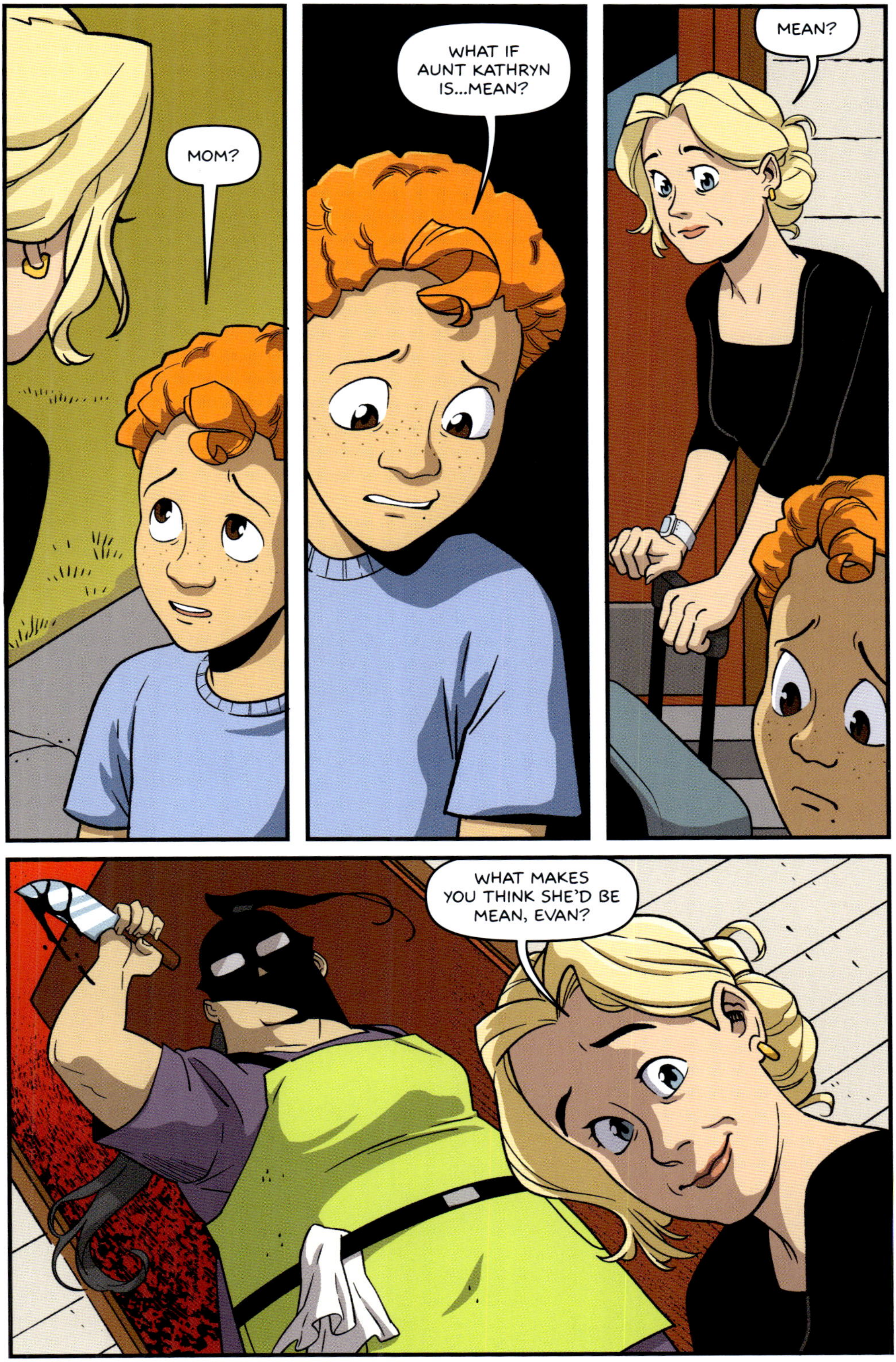
MOM?
WHAT IF AUNT KATHRYN IS...MEAN?
MEAN?
WHAT MAKES YOU THINK SHE'D BE MEAN, EVAN?

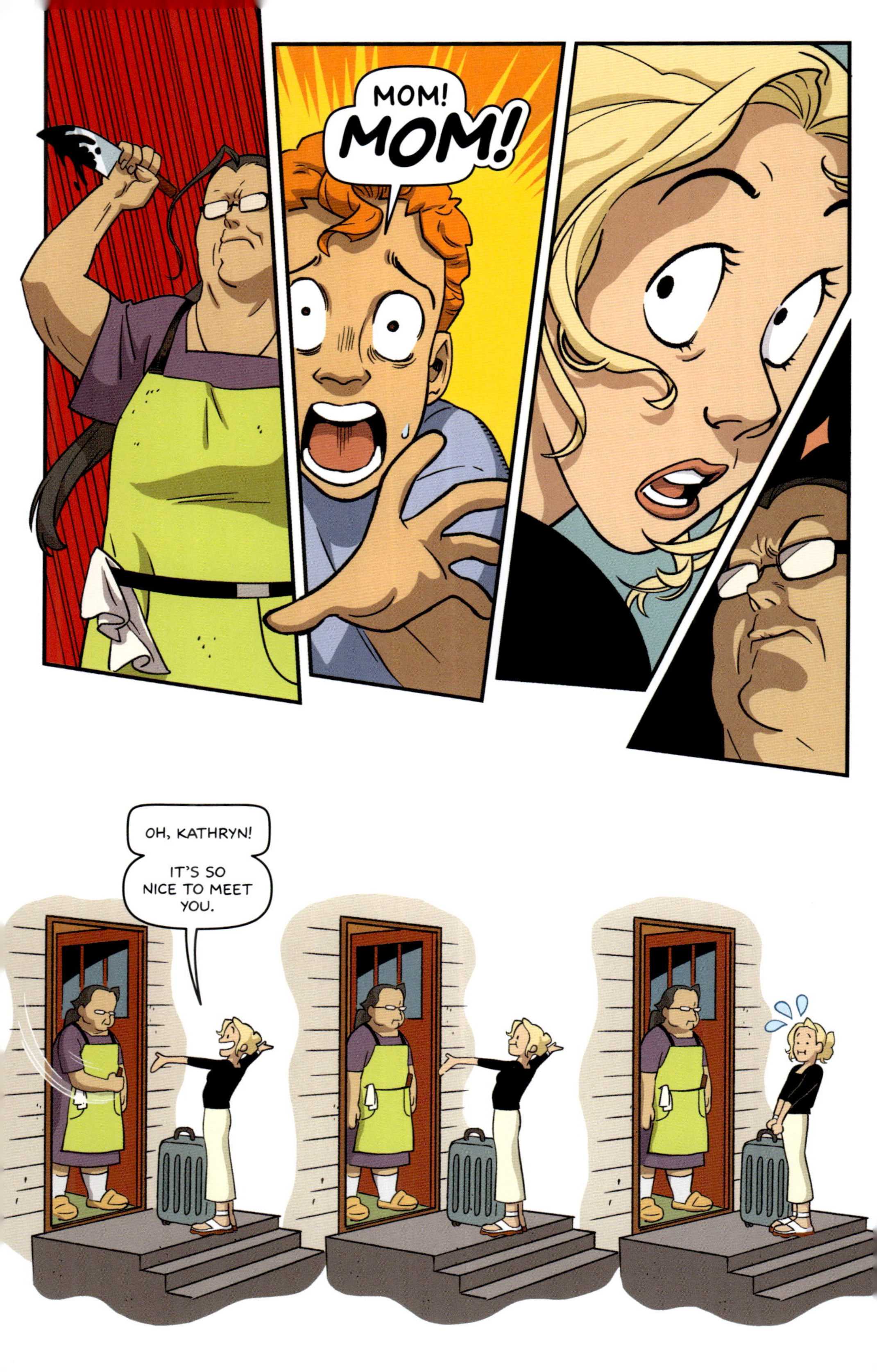
MOM!
MOM!
OH, KATHRYN!
IT'S SO NICE TO MEET YOU.

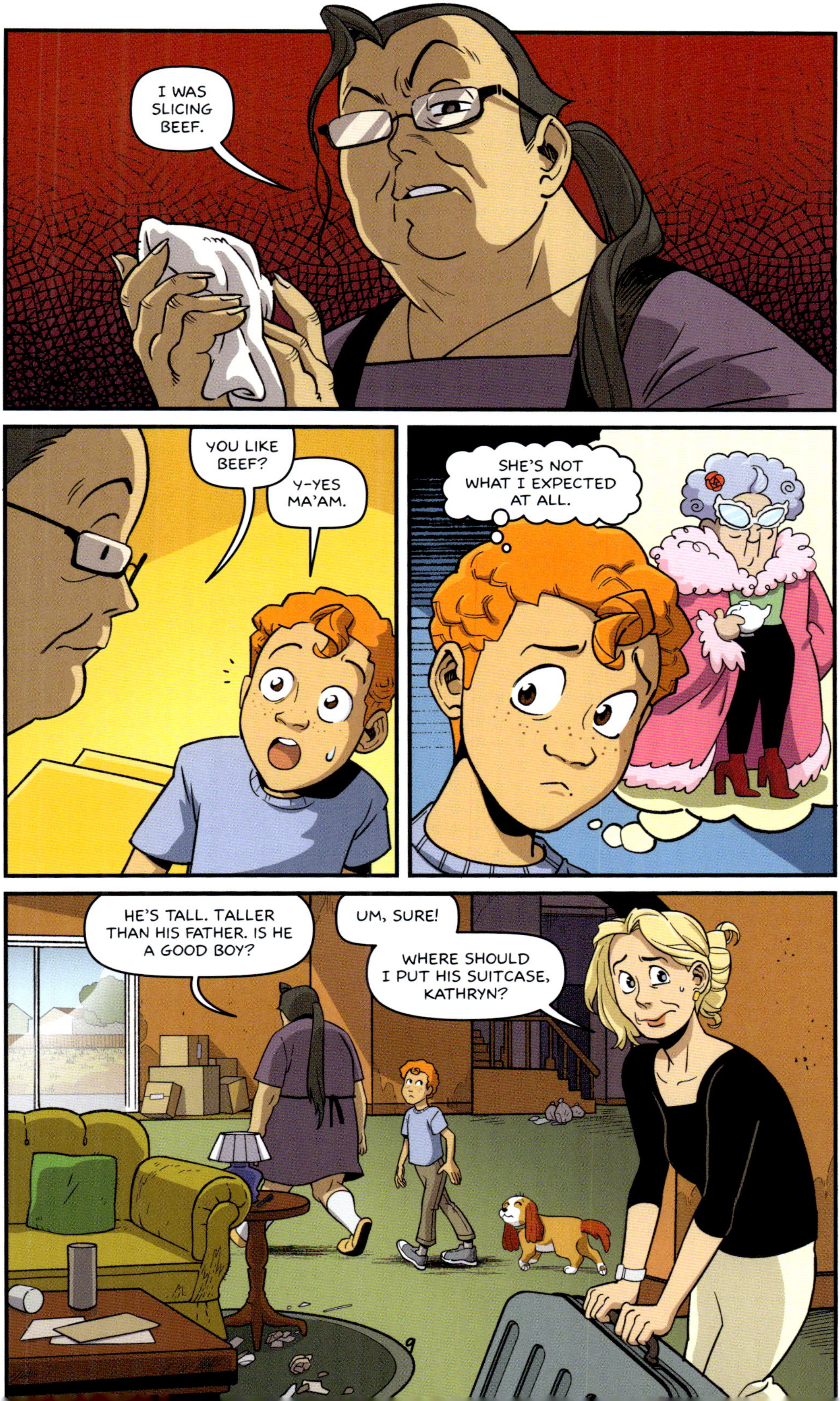
I WAS SLICING BEEF.
YOU LIKE BEEF?
Y-YES MA'AM.
SHE'S NOT WHAT I EXPECTED AT ALL.
HE'S TALL. TALLER THAN HIS FATHER. IS HE A GOOD BOY?
UM, SURE!
WHERE SHOULD I PUT HIS SUITCASE, KATHRYN?

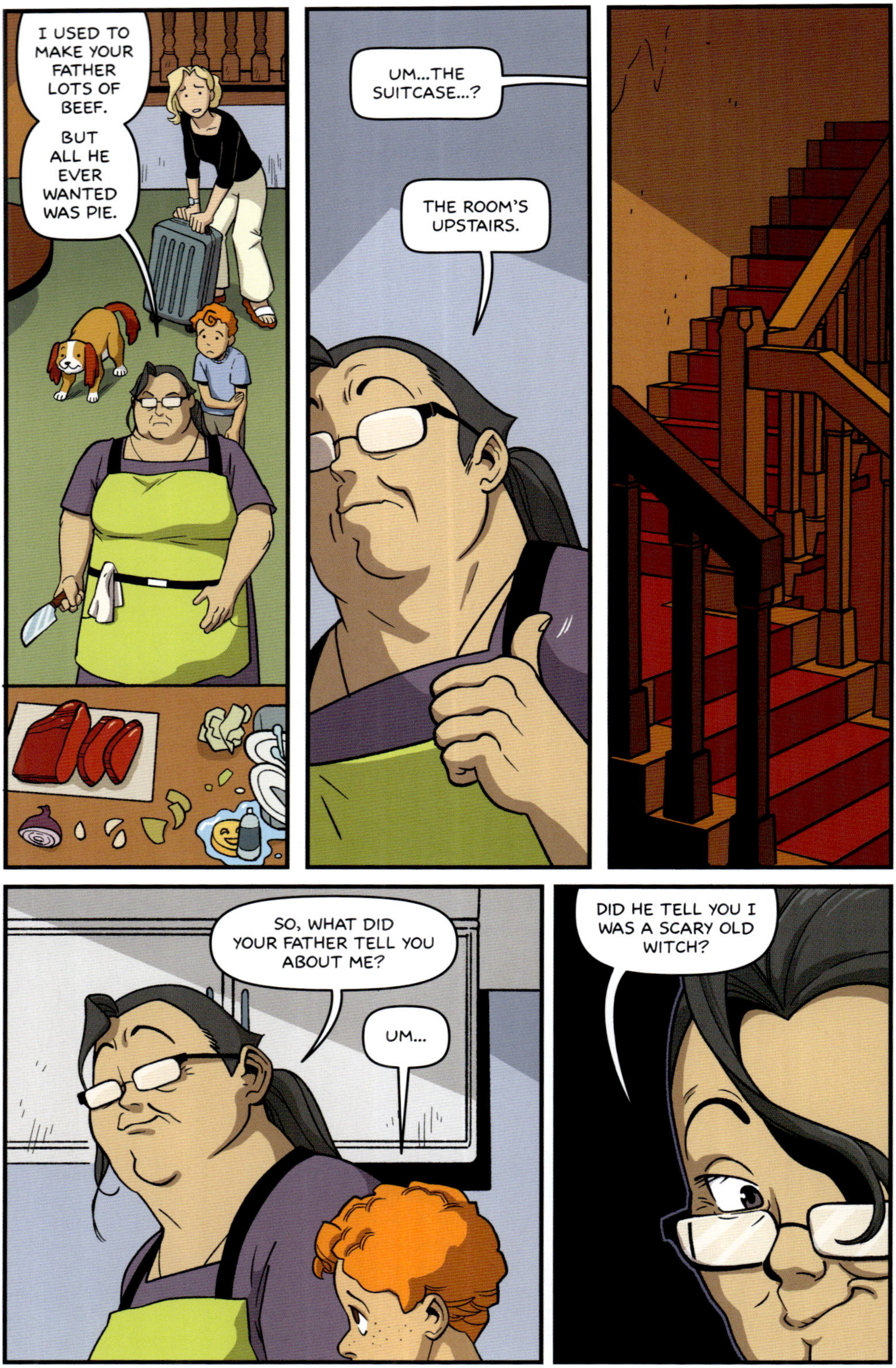
I USED TO MAKE YOUR FATHER LOTS OF BEEF.
BUT ALL HE EVER WANTED WAS PIE.
UM...THE SUITCASE...?
THE ROOM'S UPSTAIRS.
SO, WHAT DID YOUR FATHER TELL YOU ABOUT ME?
UM...
DID HE TELL YOU I WAS A SCARY OLD WITCH?

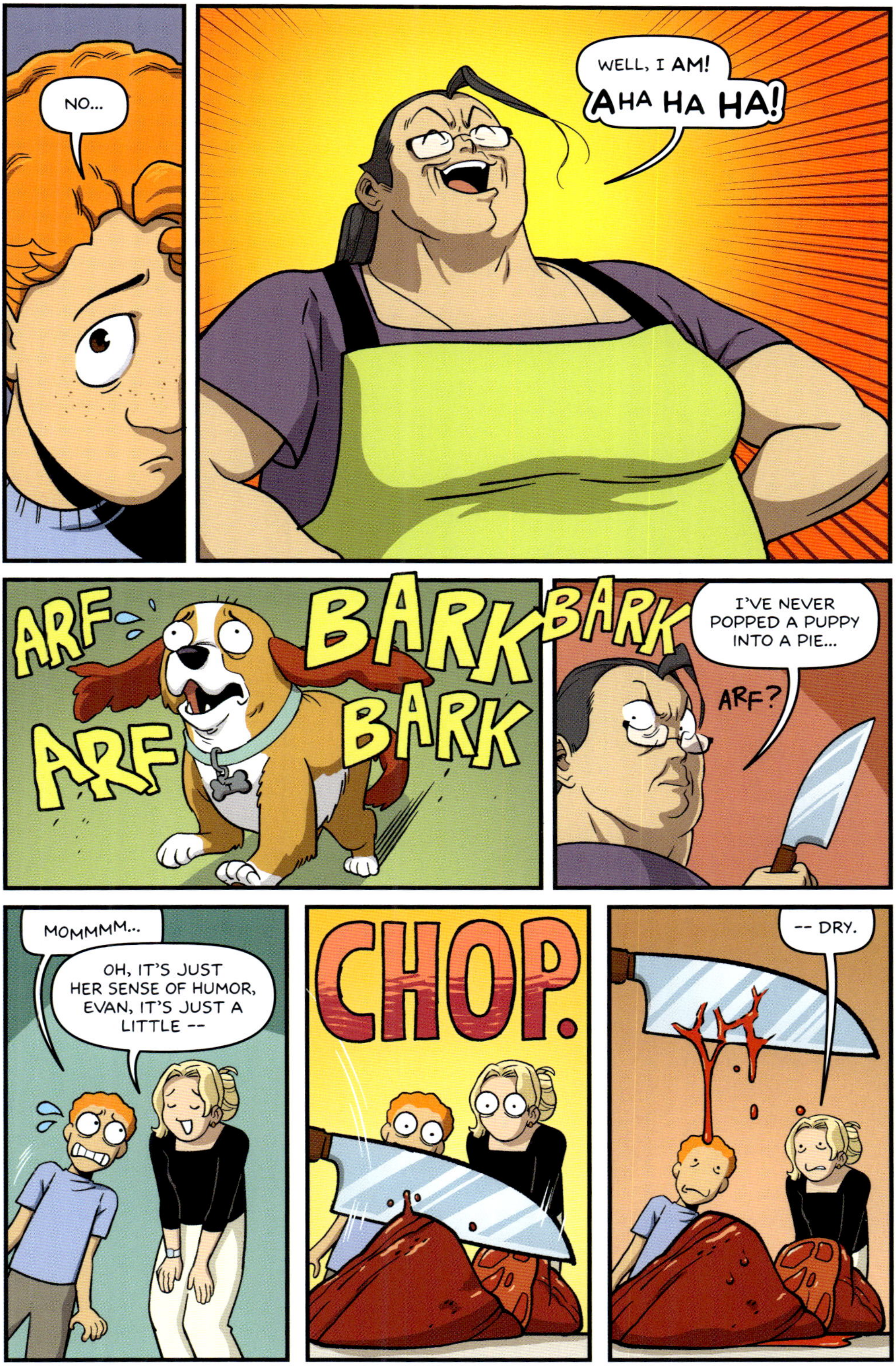
NO...
WELL, I AM!
AHA HA HA!
ARF
ARF
BARK
BARK
BARK
I'VE NEVER POPPED A PUPPY INTO A PIE...
ARF?
MOMMMM...
OH, IT'S JUST HER SENSE OF HUMOR, EVAN, IT'S JUST A LITTLE --
CHOP.
-- DRY.

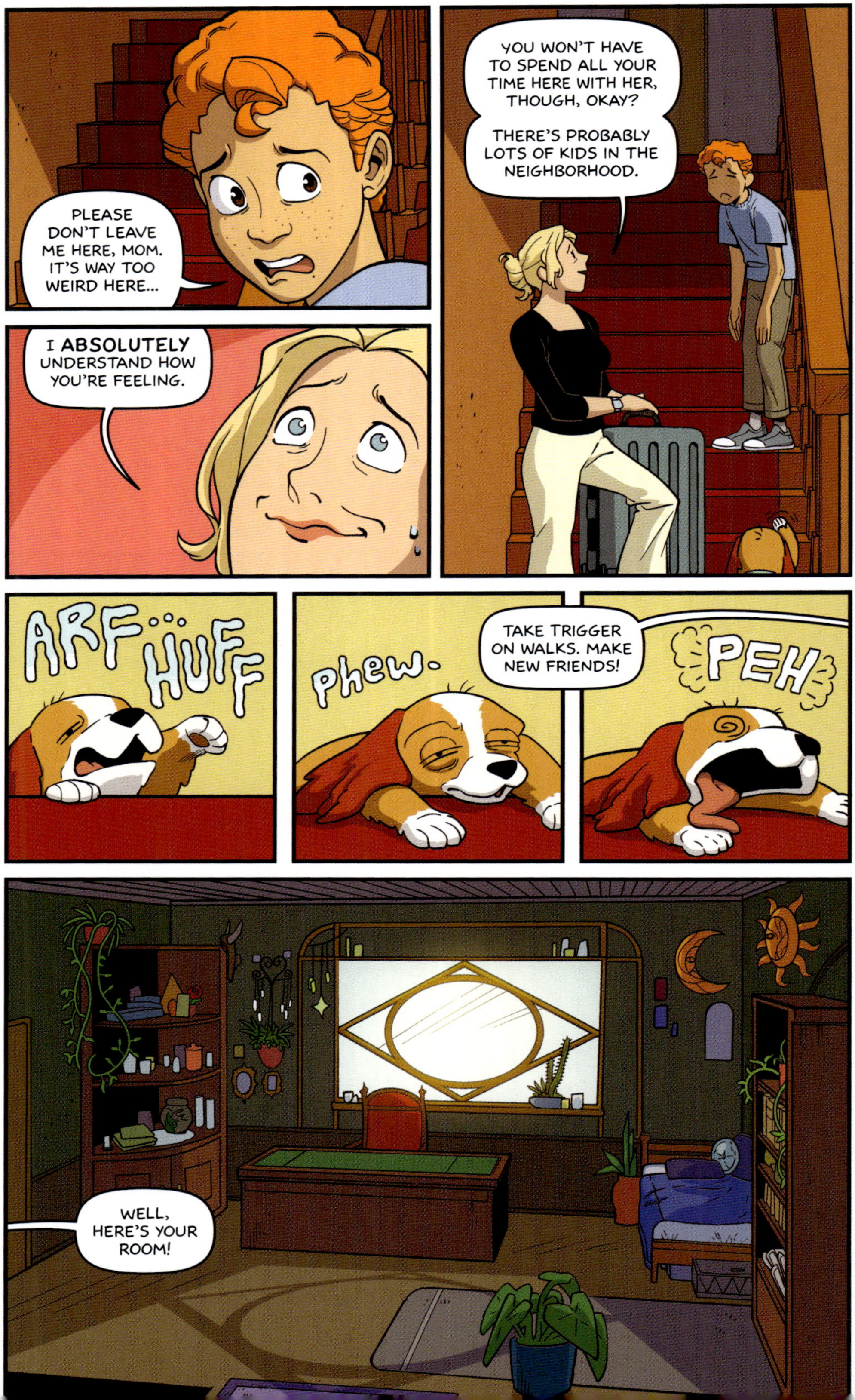
PLEASE DON'T LEAVE ME HERE, MOM. IT'S WAY TOO WEIRD HERE...
I **ABSOLUTELY** UNDERSTAND HOW YOU'RE FEELING.
YOU WON'T HAVE TO SPEND ALL YOUR TIME HERE WITH HER, THOUGH, OKAY?
THERE'S PROBABLY LOTS OF KIDS IN THE NEIGHBORHOOD.
ARF... HUFF
phew.
TAKE TRIGGER ON WALKS. MAKE NEW FRIENDS!
PEH
WELL, HERE'S YOUR ROOM!

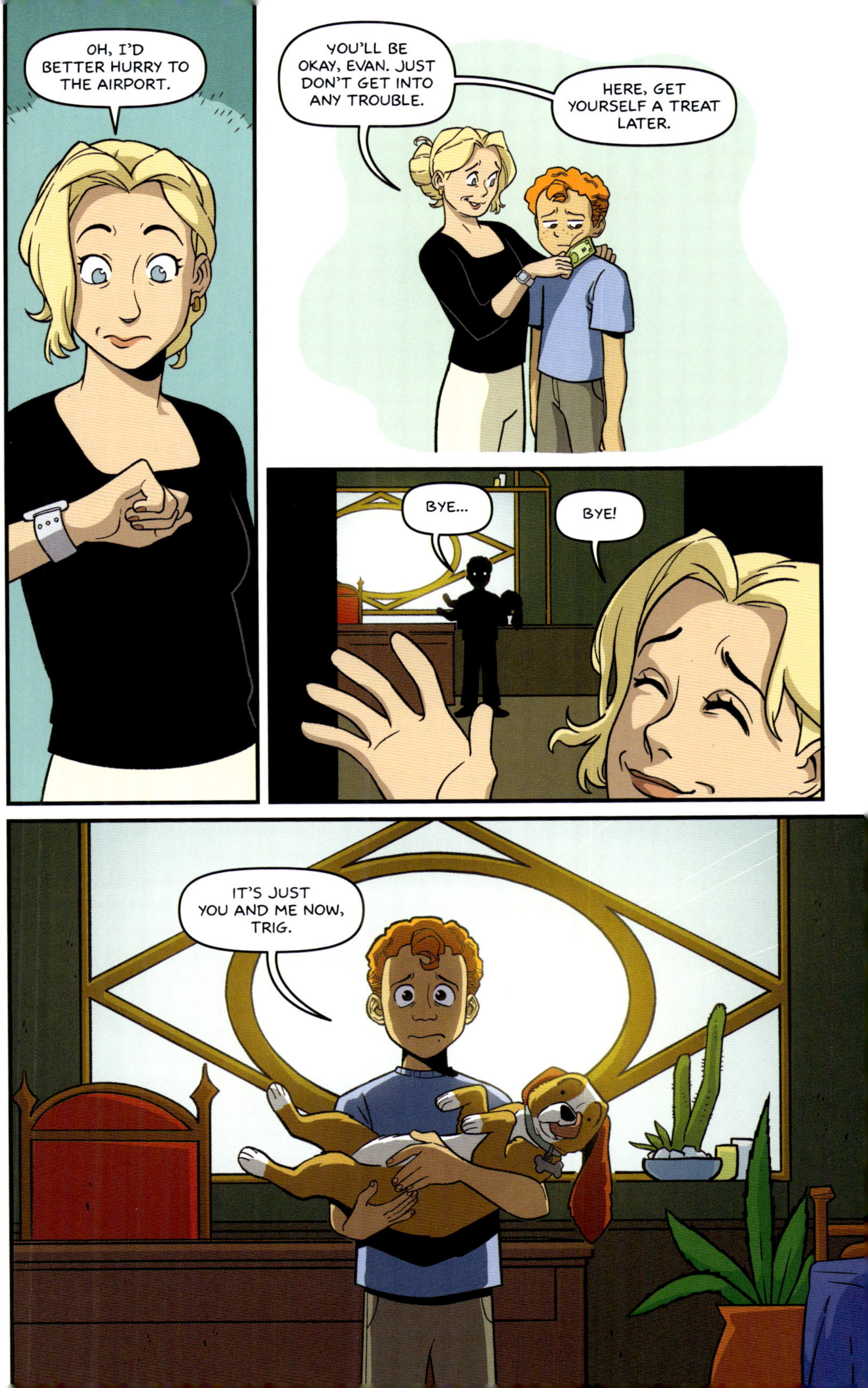
OH, I'D BETTER HURRY TO THE AIRPORT.
YOU'LL BE OKAY, EVAN. JUST DON'T GET INTO ANY TROUBLE.
HERE, GET YOURSELF A TREAT LATER.
BYE...
BYE!
IT'S JUST YOU AND ME NOW, TRIG.

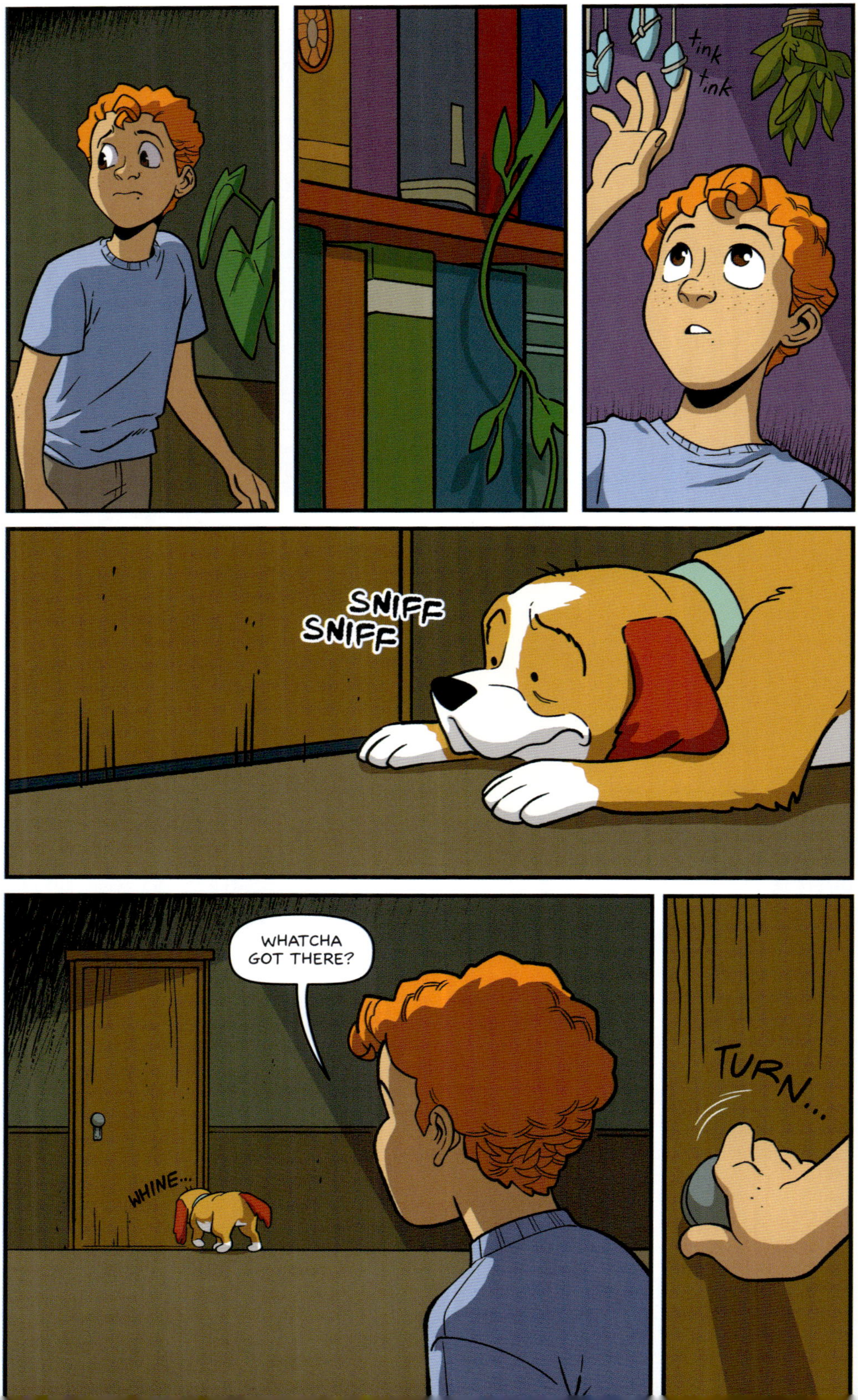
tink
tink
SNIFF
SNIFF
WHATCHA GOT THERE?
WHINE...
TURN...

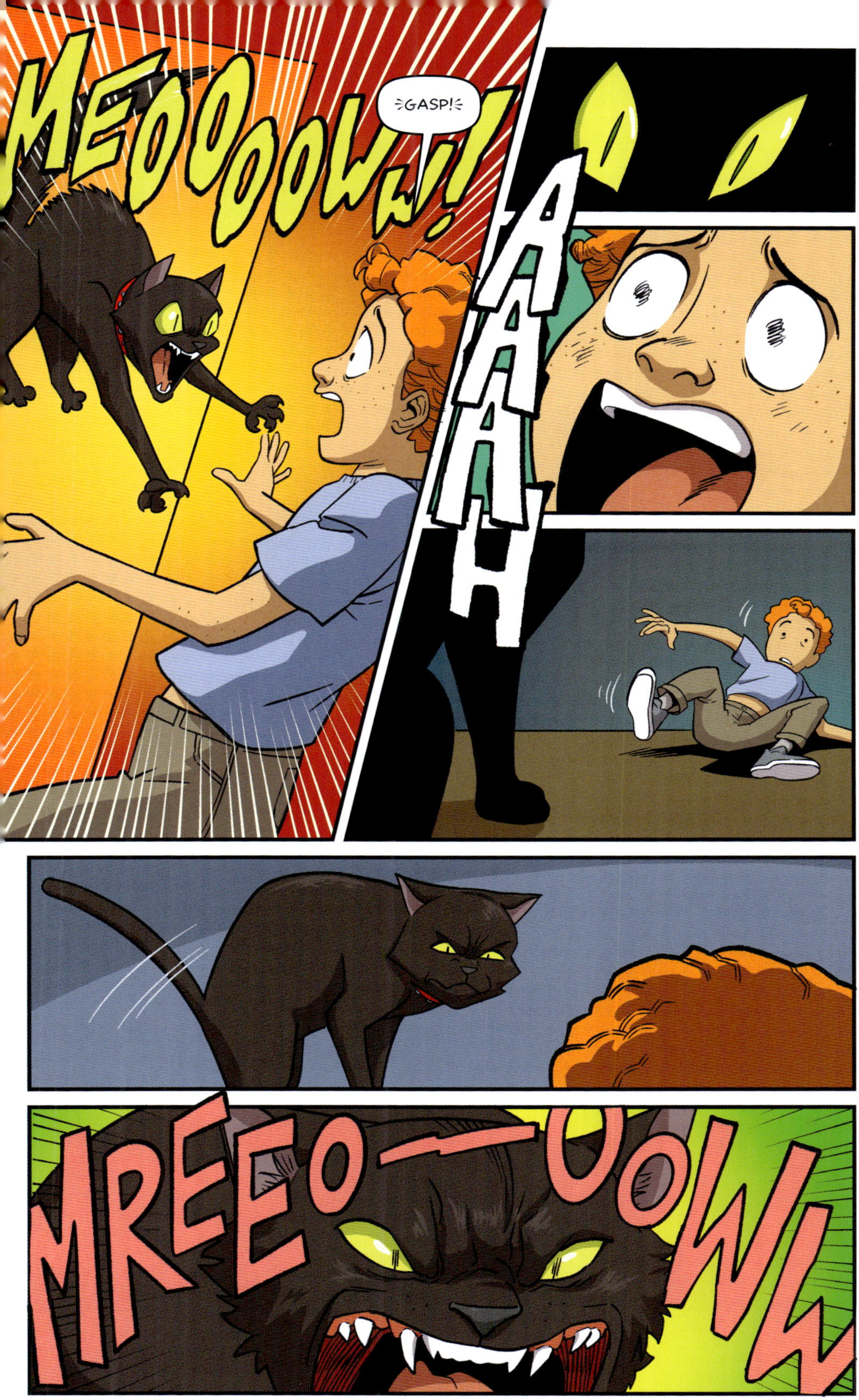
MEOOOOOWW!!
GASP!
AAAAAAH
MREEO—OOWW

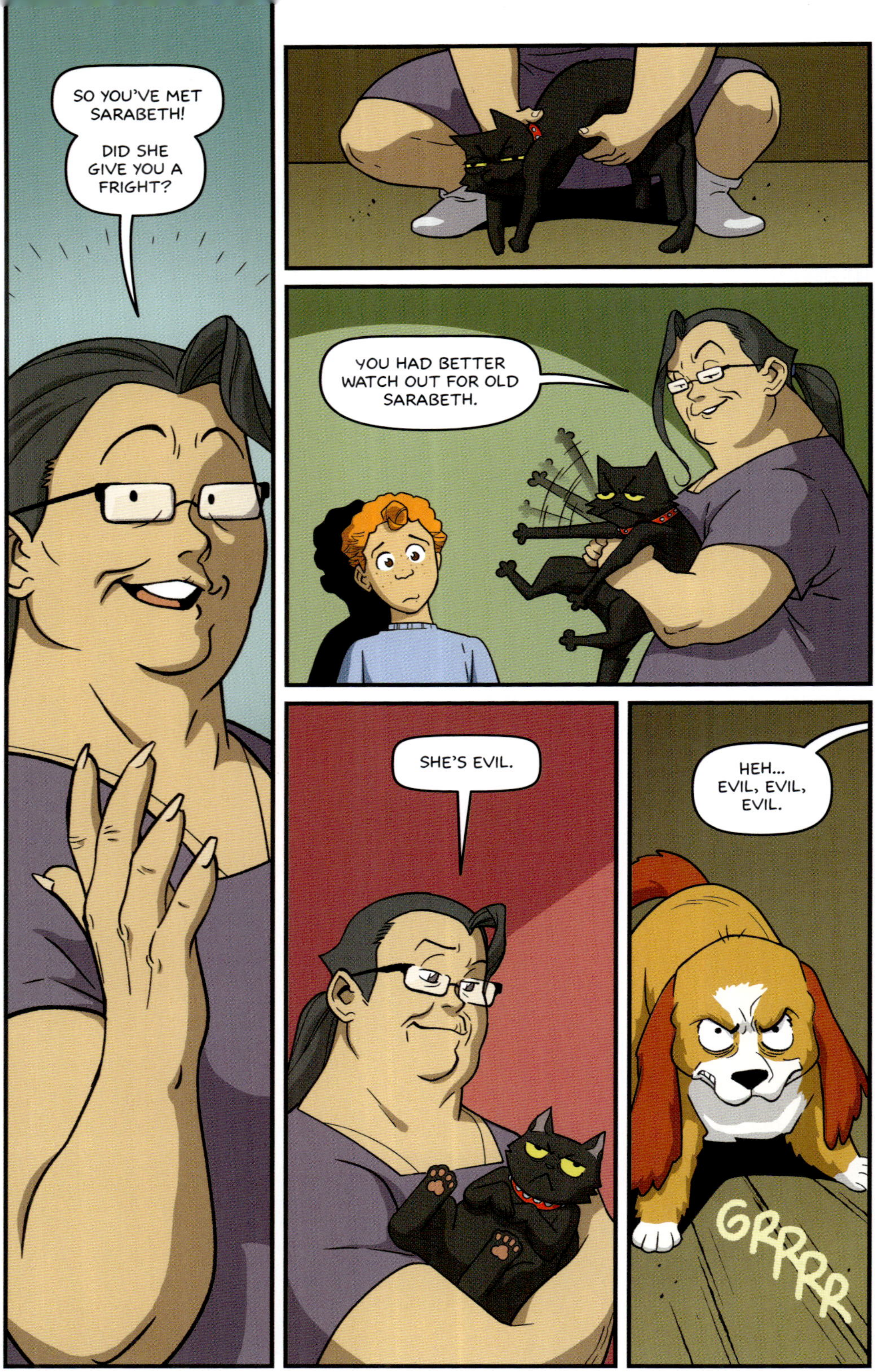
SO YOU'VE MET SARABETH!
DID SHE GIVE YOU A FRIGHT?
YOU HAD BETTER WATCH OUT FOR OLD SARABETH.
SHE'S EVIL.
HEH... EVIL, EVIL, EVIL.
GRRRR

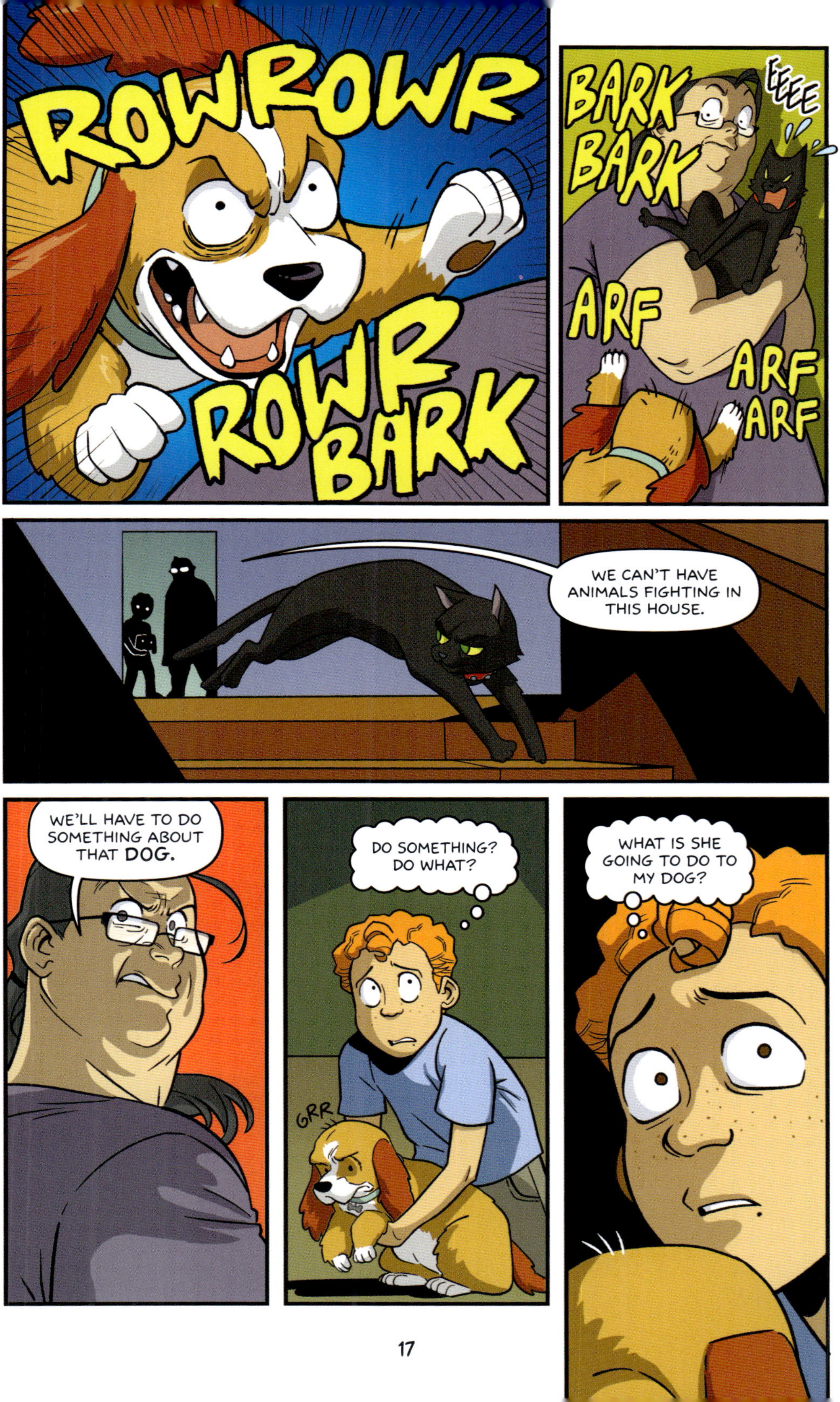
ROWROWR
ROWR
BARK
BARK
BARK
EEEE
ARF
ARF
ARF
WE CAN'T HAVE ANIMALS FIGHTING IN THIS HOUSE.
WE'LL HAVE TO DO SOMETHING ABOUT THAT **DOG.**
DO SOMETHING? DO WHAT?
GRR
WHAT IS SHE GOING TO DO TO MY DOG?

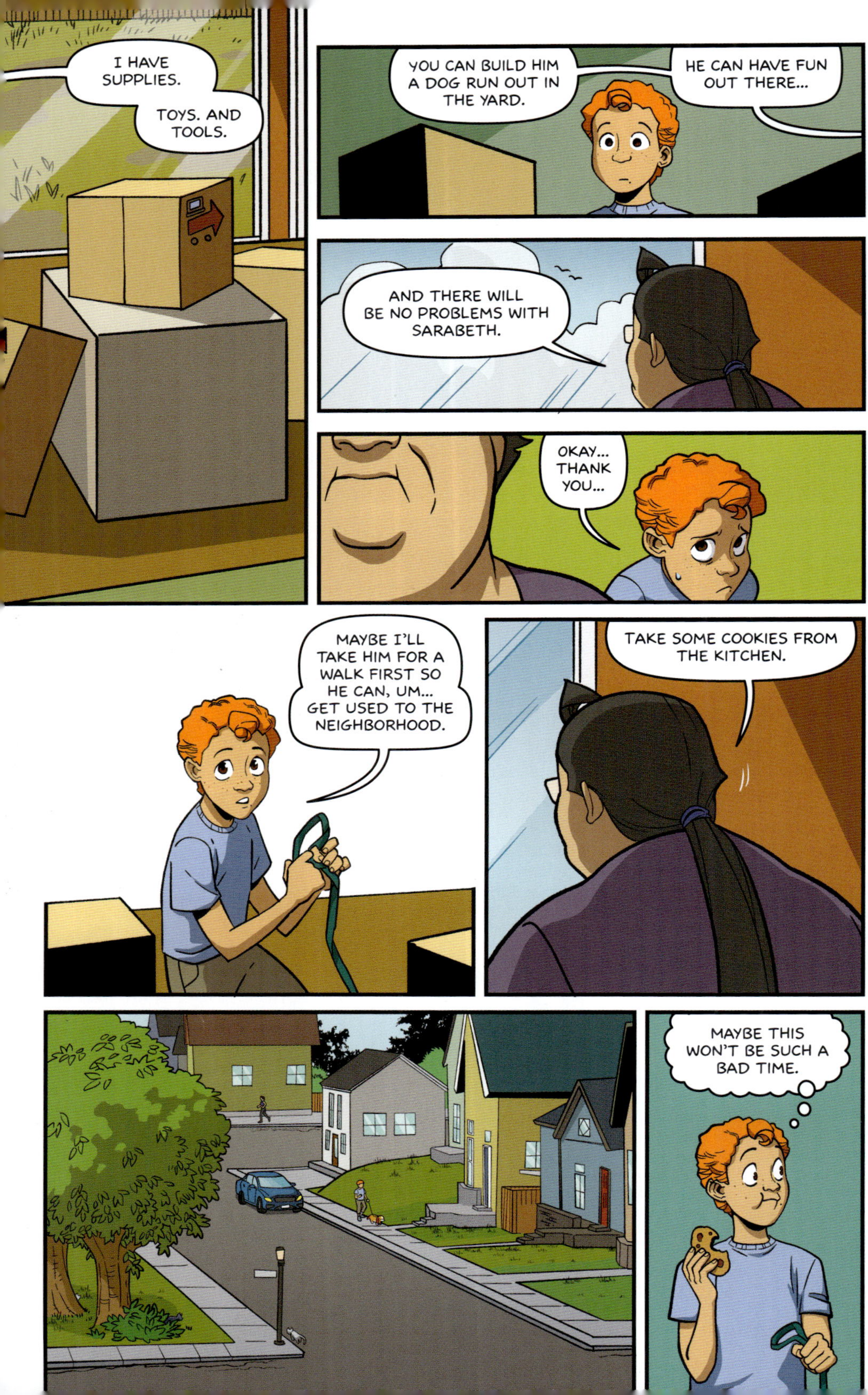
I HAVE SUPPLIES.
TOYS. AND TOOLS.
YOU CAN BUILD HIM A DOG RUN OUT IN THE YARD.
HE CAN HAVE FUN OUT THERE...
AND THERE WILL BE NO PROBLEMS WITH SARABETH.
OKAY... THANK YOU...
MAYBE I'LL TAKE HIM FOR A WALK FIRST SO HE CAN, UM... GET USED TO THE NEIGHBORHOOD.
TAKE SOME COOKIES FROM THE KITCHEN.
MAYBE THIS WON'T BE SUCH A BAD TIME.

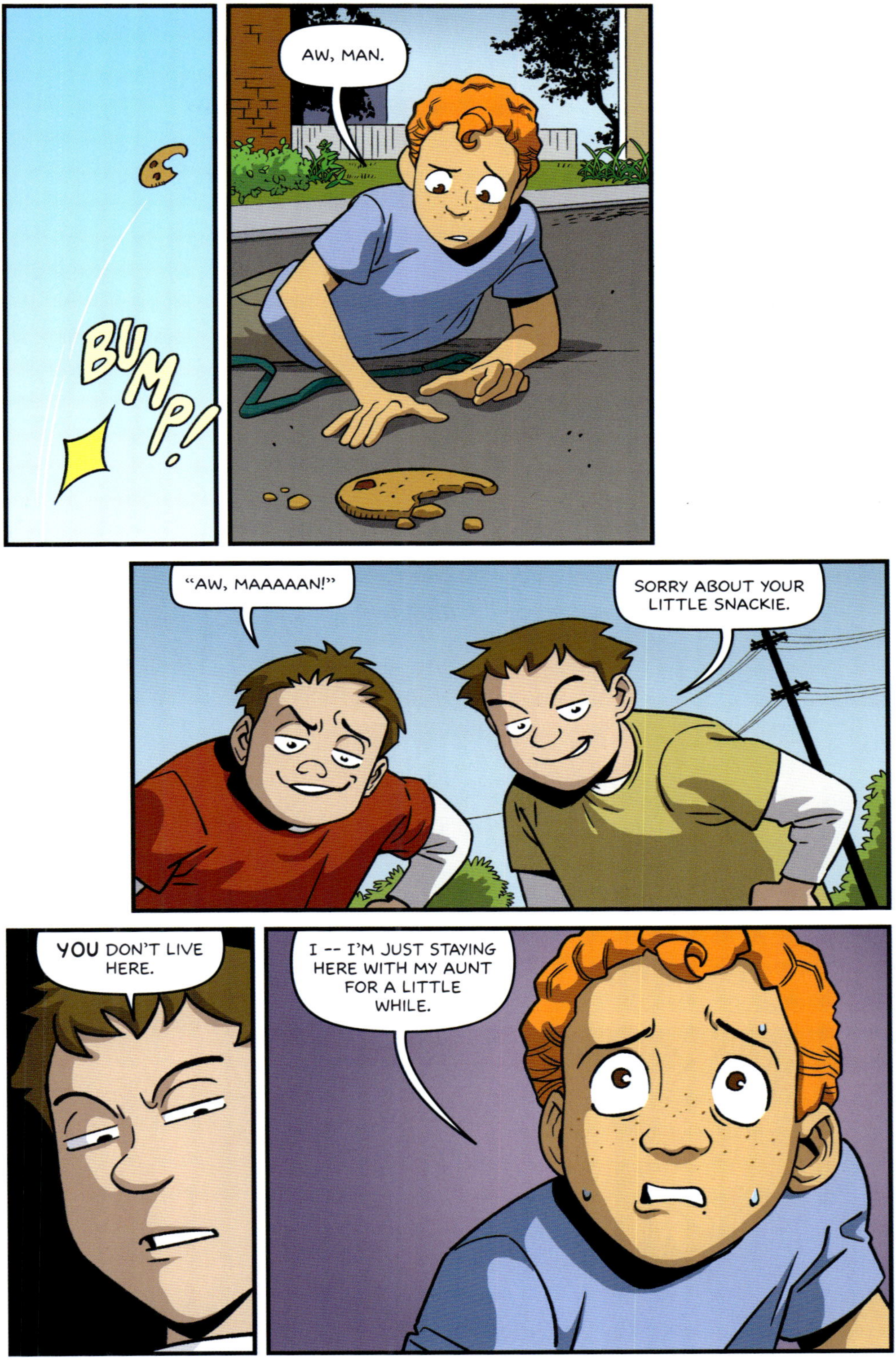
BUMP!
AW, MAN.
"AW, MAAAAAN!"
SORRY ABOUT YOUR LITTLE SNACKIE.
YOU DON'T LIVE HERE.
I -- I'M JUST STAYING HERE WITH MY AUNT FOR A LITTLE WHILE.

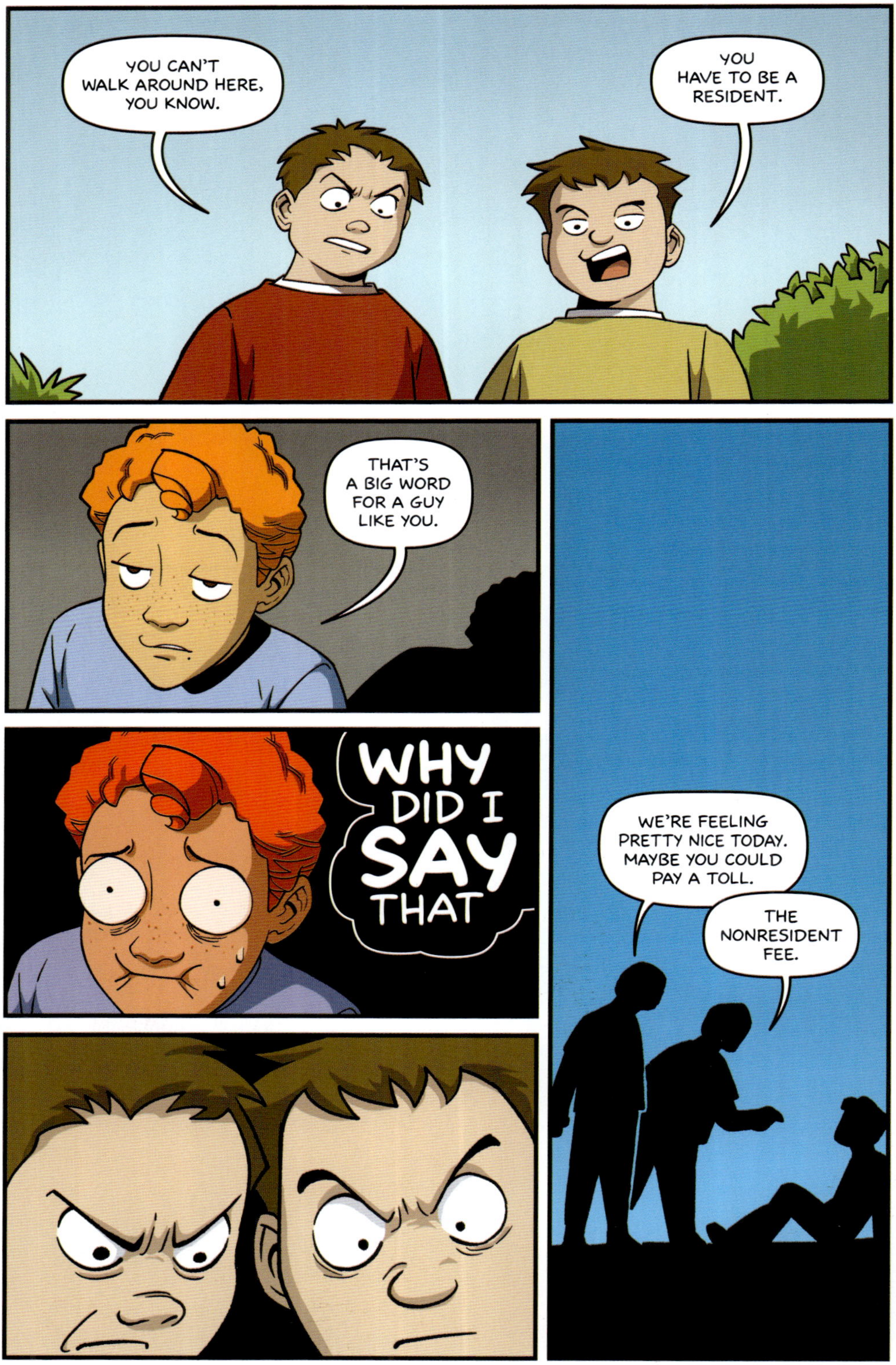
YOU CAN'T WALK AROUND HERE, YOU KNOW.
YOU HAVE TO BE A RESIDENT.
THAT'S A BIG WORD FOR A GUY LIKE YOU.
WHY DID I SAY THAT
WE'RE FEELING PRETTY NICE TODAY. MAYBE YOU COULD PAY A TOLL.
THE NONRESIDENT FEE.

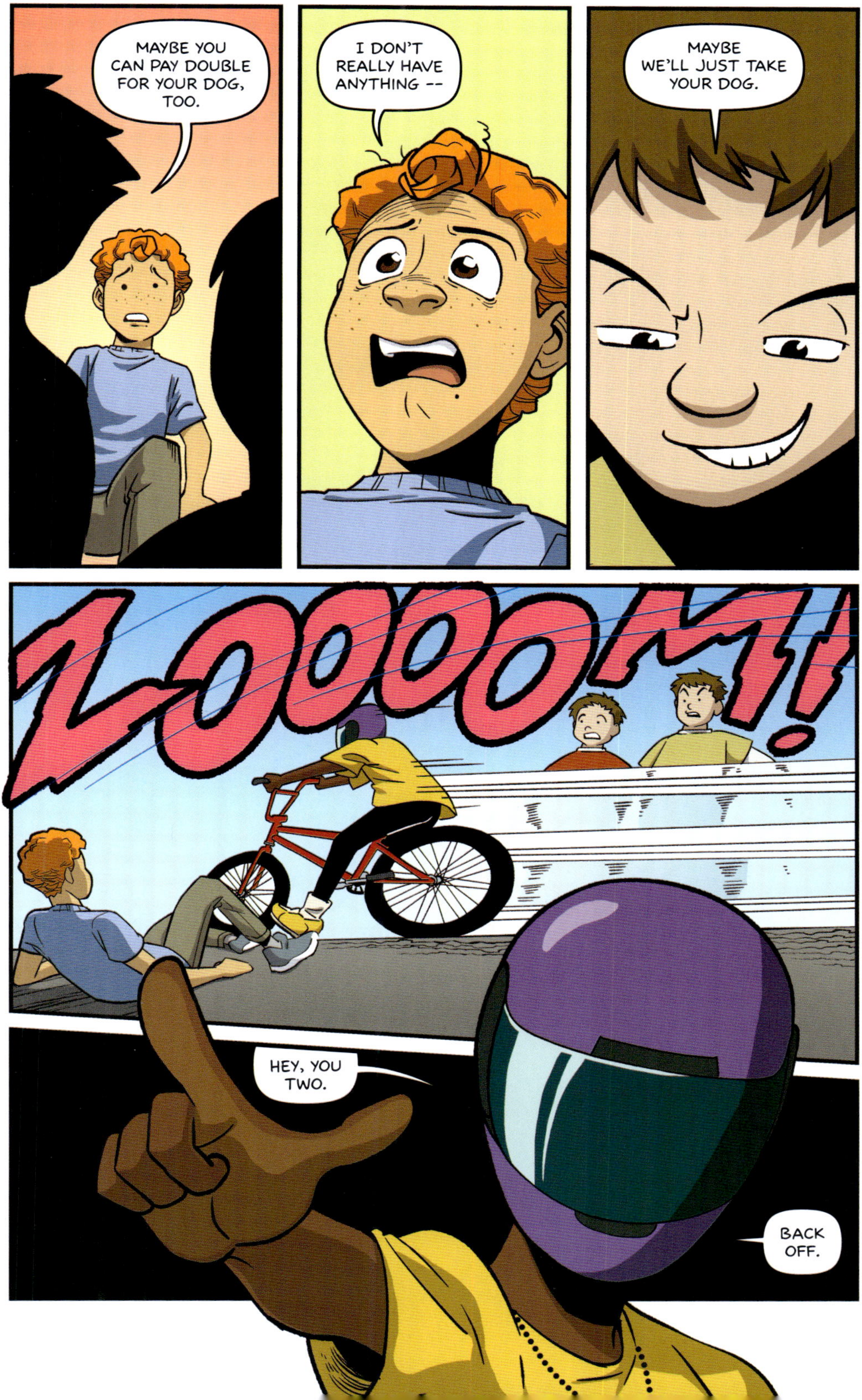
MAYBE YOU CAN PAY DOUBLE FOR YOUR DOG, TOO.
I DON'T REALLY HAVE ANYTHING --
MAYBE WE'LL JUST TAKE YOUR DOG.
ZOOOOM!!
HEY, YOU TWO.
BACK OFF.

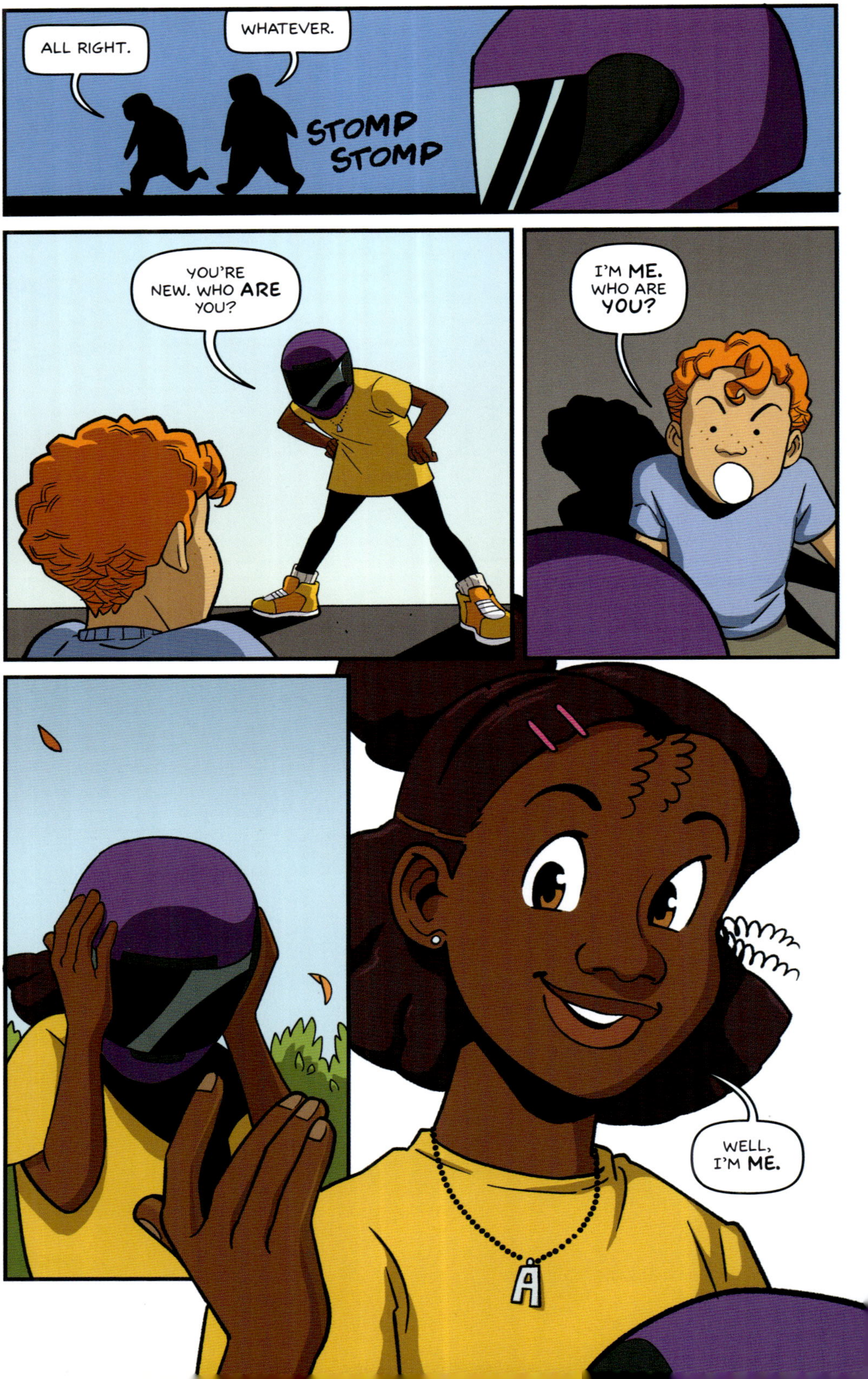
ALL RIGHT.
WHATEVER.
STOMP STOMP
YOU'RE NEW. WHO **ARE** YOU?
I'M **ME.** WHO ARE **YOU?**
WELL, I'M **ME.**

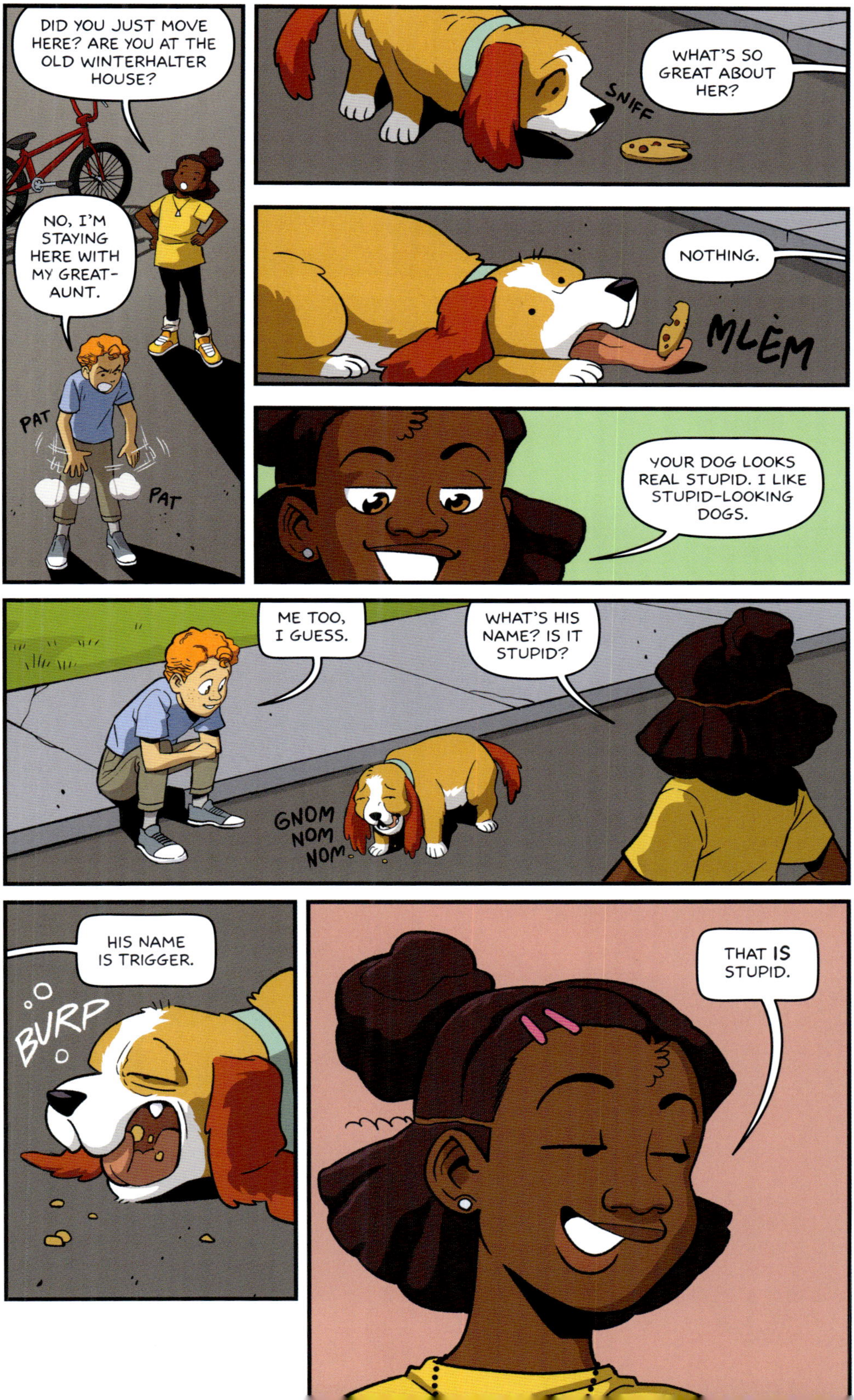
DID YOU JUST MOVE HERE? ARE YOU AT THE OLD WINTERHALTER HOUSE?
NO, I'M STAYING HERE WITH MY GREAT-AUNT.
PAT
PAT
WHAT'S SO GREAT ABOUT HER?
SNIFF
NOTHING.
MLEM
YOUR DOG LOOKS REAL STUPID. I LIKE STUPID-LOOKING DOGS.
ME TOO, I GUESS.
WHAT'S HIS NAME? IS IT STUPID?
GNOM NOM NOM
HIS NAME IS TRIGGER.
BURP
THAT IS STUPID.

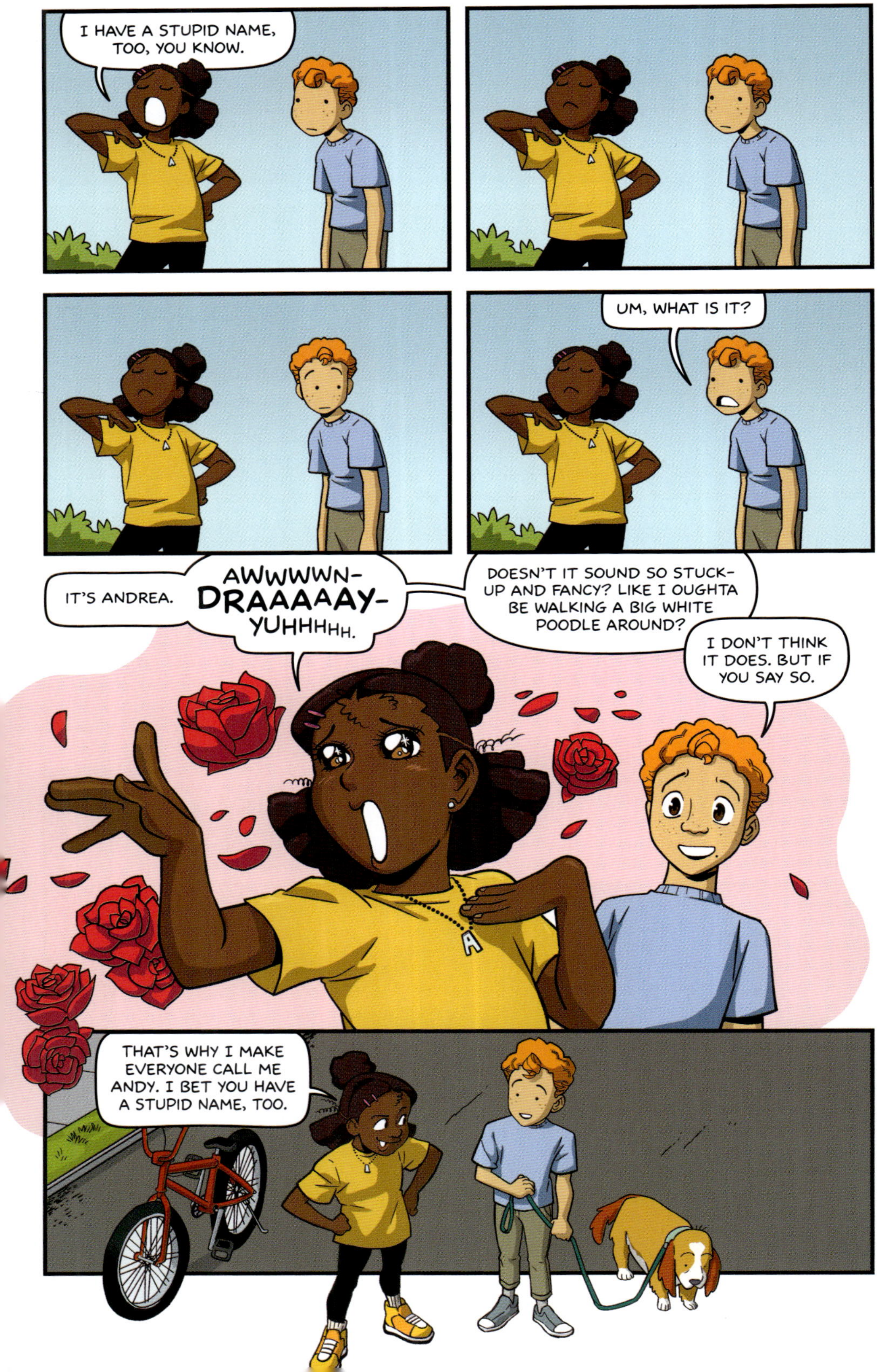

I HAVE A STUPID NAME, TOO, YOU KNOW.
UM, WHAT IS IT?
IT'S ANDREA.
AWWWWN-DRAAAAAY-YUHHHHH.
DOESN'T IT SOUND SO STUCK-UP AND FANCY? LIKE I OUGHTA BE WALKING A BIG WHITE POODLE AROUND?
I DON'T THINK IT DOES. BUT IF YOU SAY SO.
THAT'S WHY I MAKE EVERYONE CALL ME ANDY. I BET YOU HAVE A STUPID NAME, TOO.

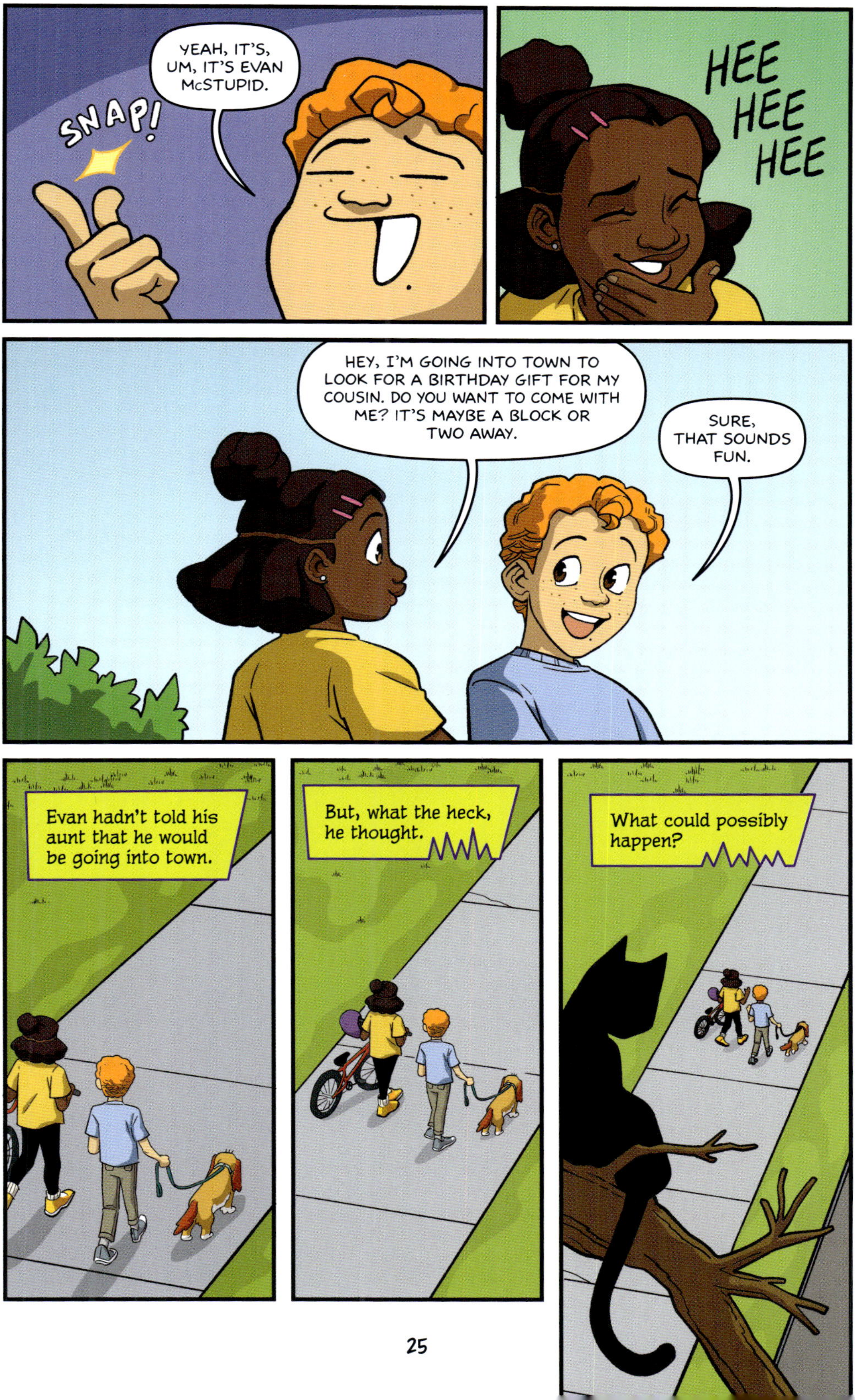
YEAH, IT'S, UM, IT'S EVAN McSTUPID.
SNAP!
HEE HEE HEE
HEY, I'M GOING INTO TOWN TO LOOK FOR A BIRTHDAY GIFT FOR MY COUSIN. DO YOU WANT TO COME WITH ME? IT'S MAYBE A BLOCK OR TWO AWAY.
SURE, THAT SOUNDS FUN.
Evan hadn't told his aunt that he would be going into town.
But, what the heck, he thought.
What could possibly happen?

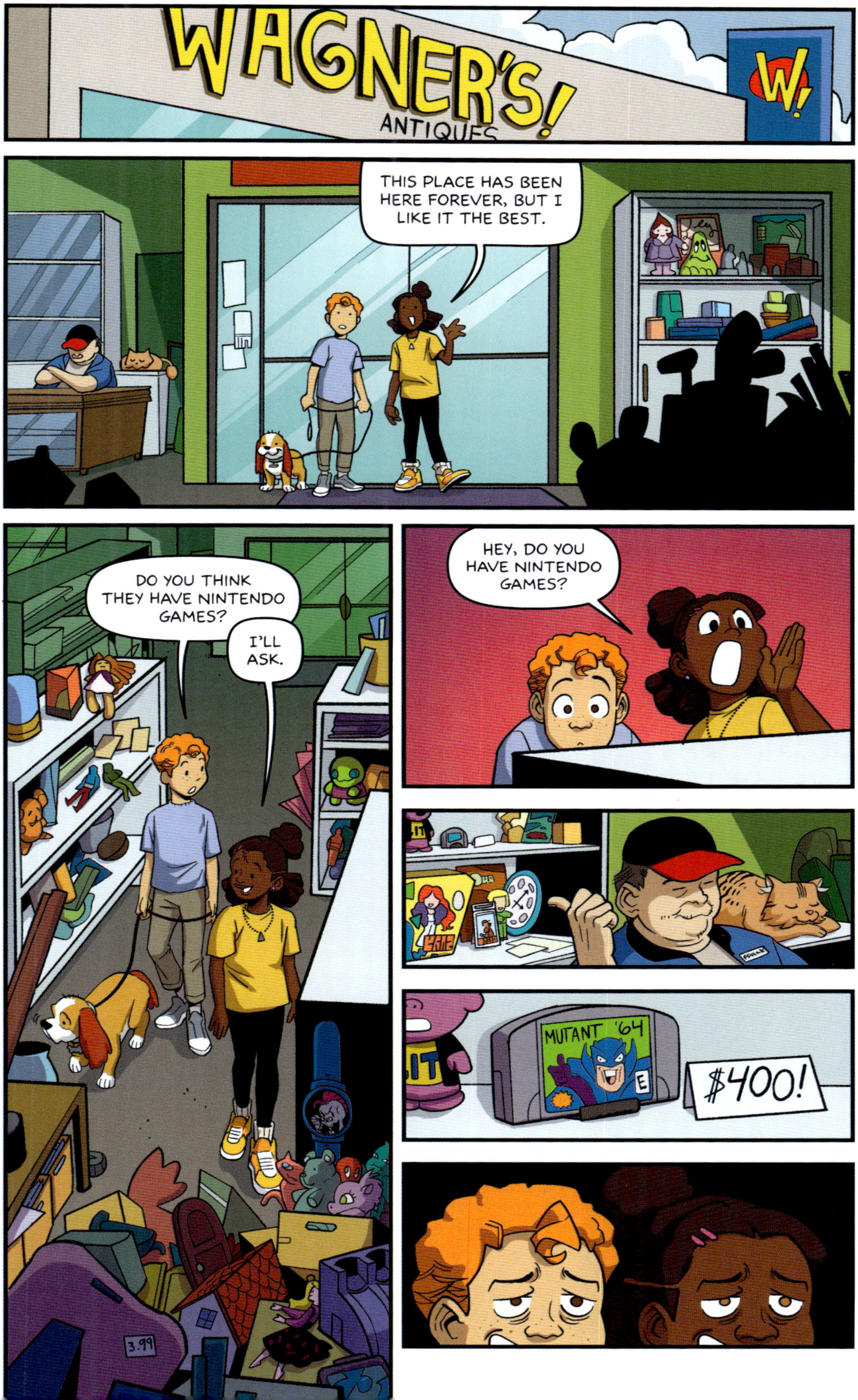
WAGNER'S!
ANTIQUES
W!
THIS PLACE HAS BEEN HERE FOREVER, BUT I LIKE IT THE BEST.
DO YOU THINK THEY HAVE NINTENDO GAMES?
I'LL ASK.
3.99
HEY, DO YOU HAVE NINTENDO GAMES?
MUTANT '64
E
$400!

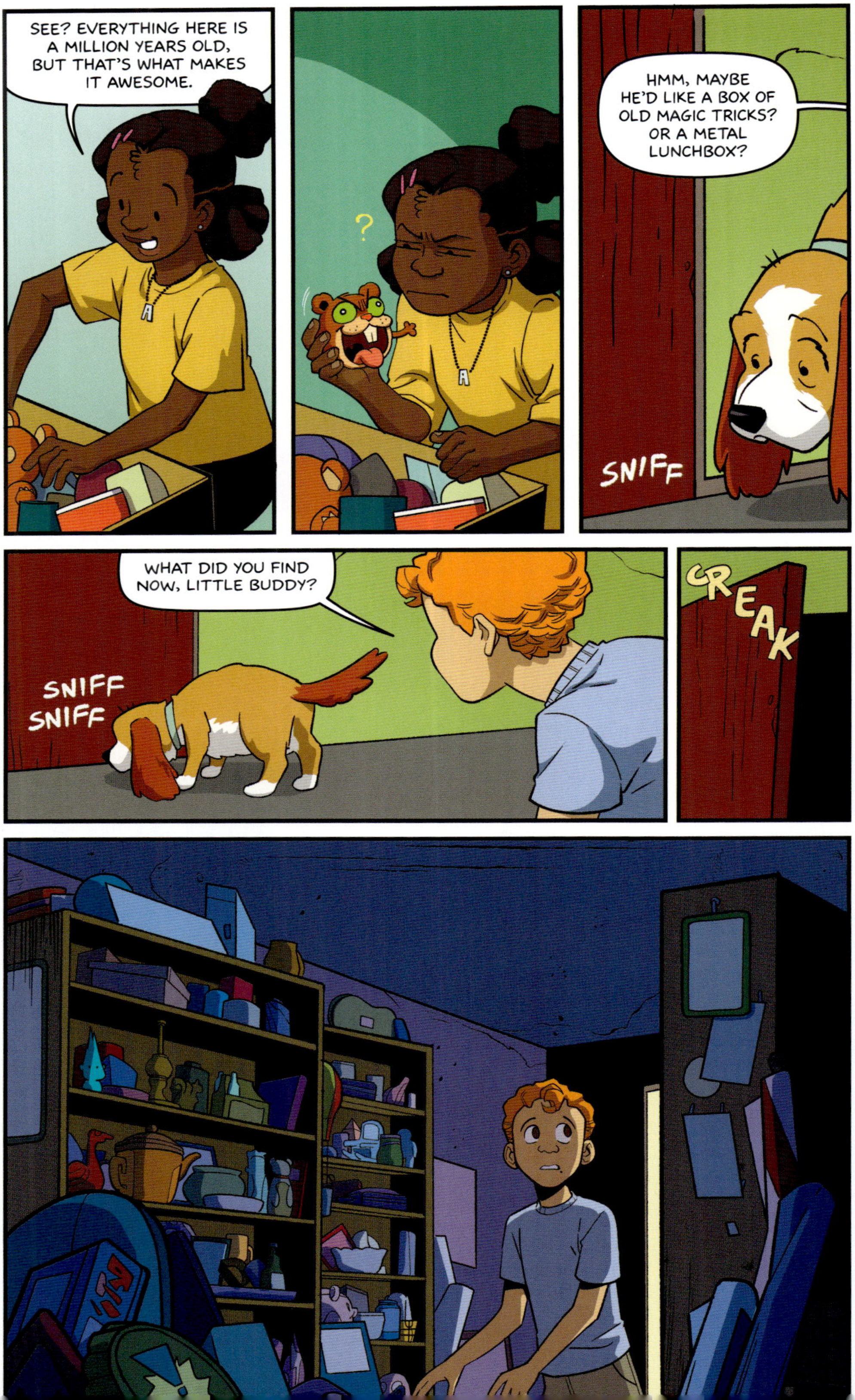
SEE? EVERYTHING HERE IS A MILLION YEARS OLD, BUT THAT'S WHAT MAKES IT AWESOME.
?
HMM, MAYBE HE'D LIKE A BOX OF OLD MAGIC TRICKS? OR A METAL LUNCHBOX?
SNIFF
WHAT DID YOU FIND NOW, LITTLE BUDDY?
SNIFF SNIFF
CREAK

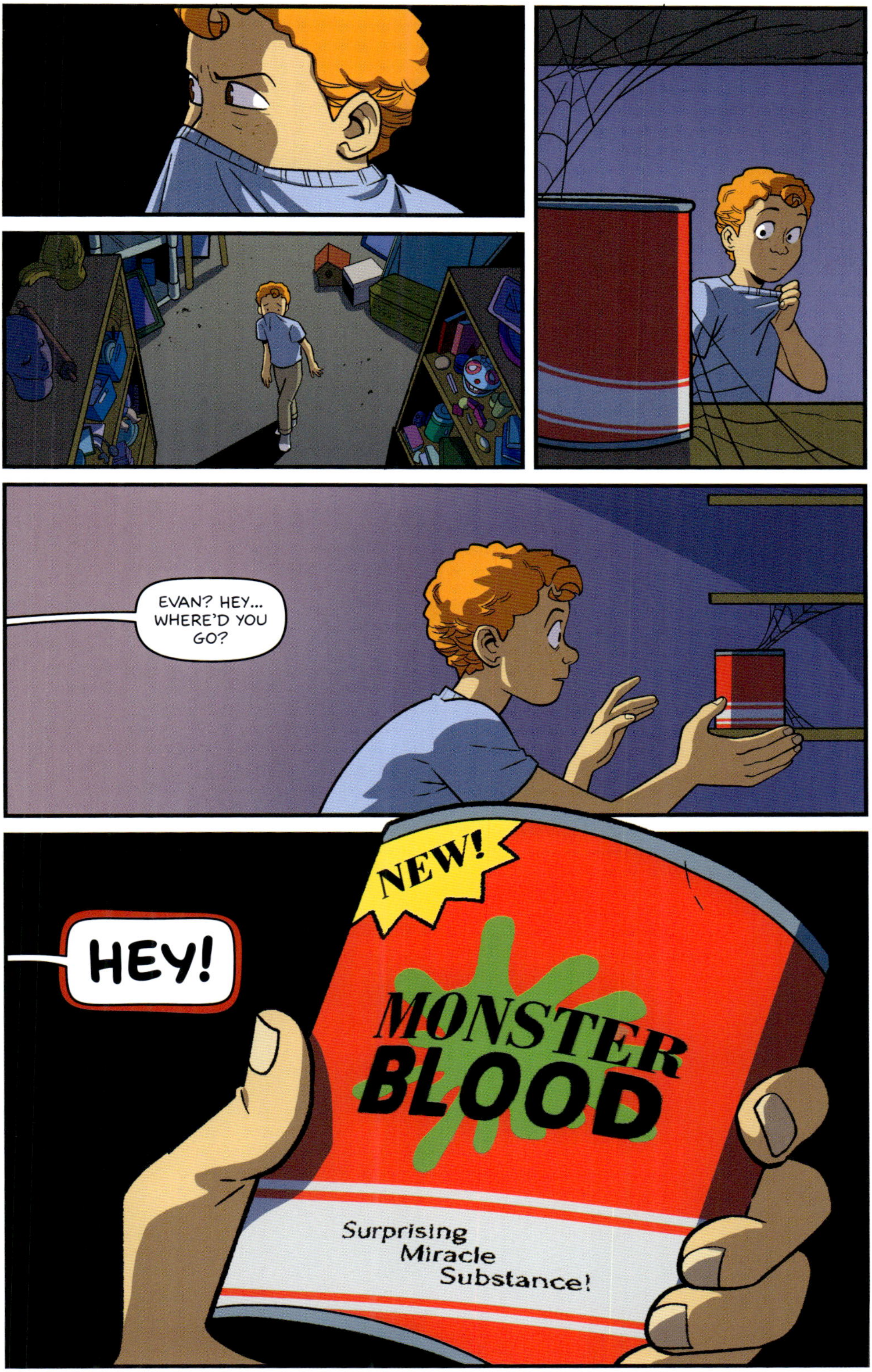
EVAN? HEY... WHERE'D YOU GO?
HEY!
NEW!
MONSTER BLOOD
Surprising Miracle Substance!

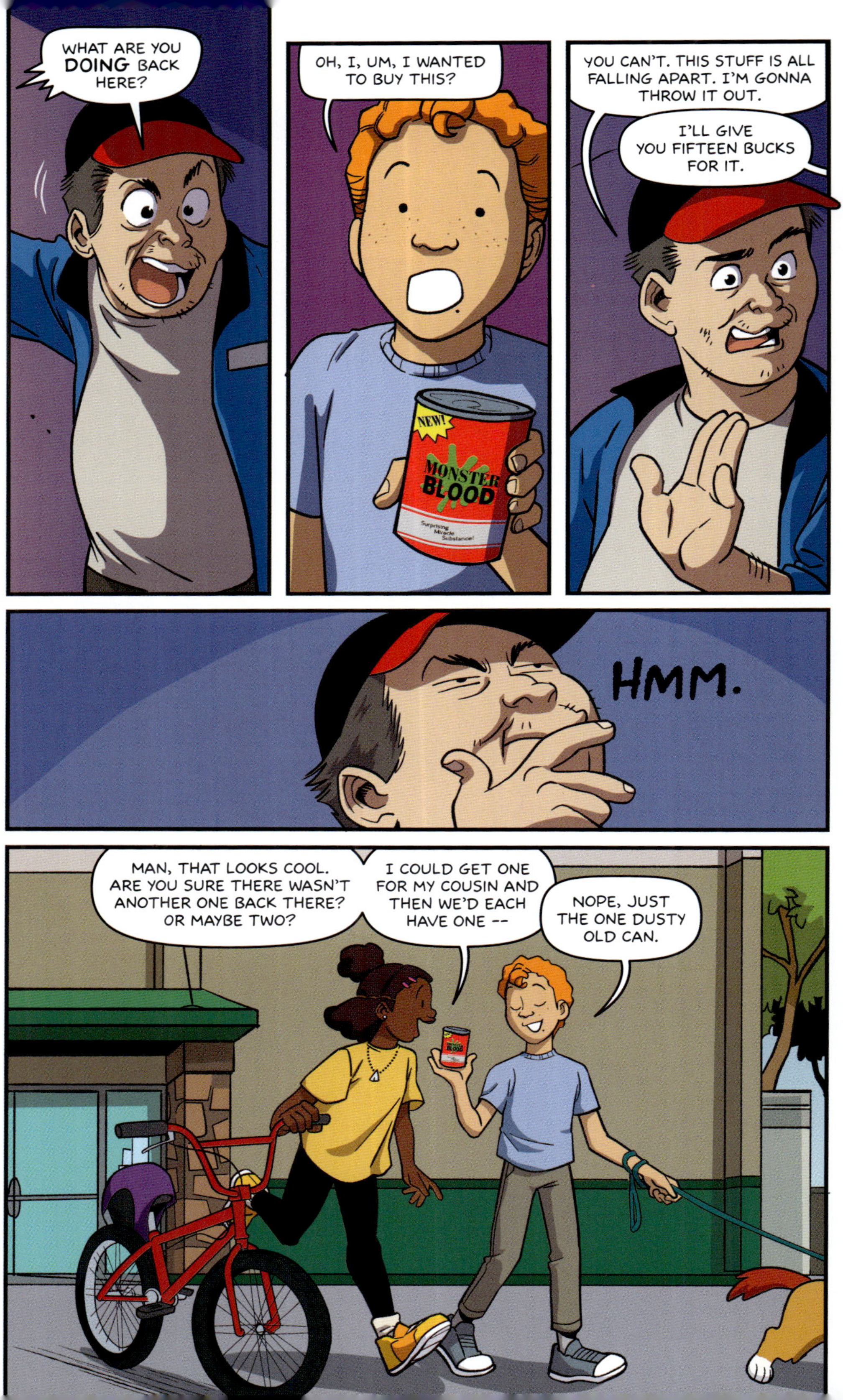
WHAT ARE YOU DOING BACK HERE?
OH, I, UM, I WANTED TO BUY THIS?
NEW!
MONSTER BLOOD
Surprising Miracle Substance!
YOU CAN'T. THIS STUFF IS ALL FALLING APART. I'M GONNA THROW IT OUT.
I'LL GIVE YOU FIFTEEN BUCKS FOR IT.
HMM.
MAN, THAT LOOKS COOL. ARE YOU SURE THERE WASN'T ANOTHER ONE BACK THERE? OR MAYBE TWO?
I COULD GET ONE FOR MY COUSIN AND THEN WE'D EACH HAVE ONE --
NOPE, JUST THE ONE DUSTY OLD CAN.

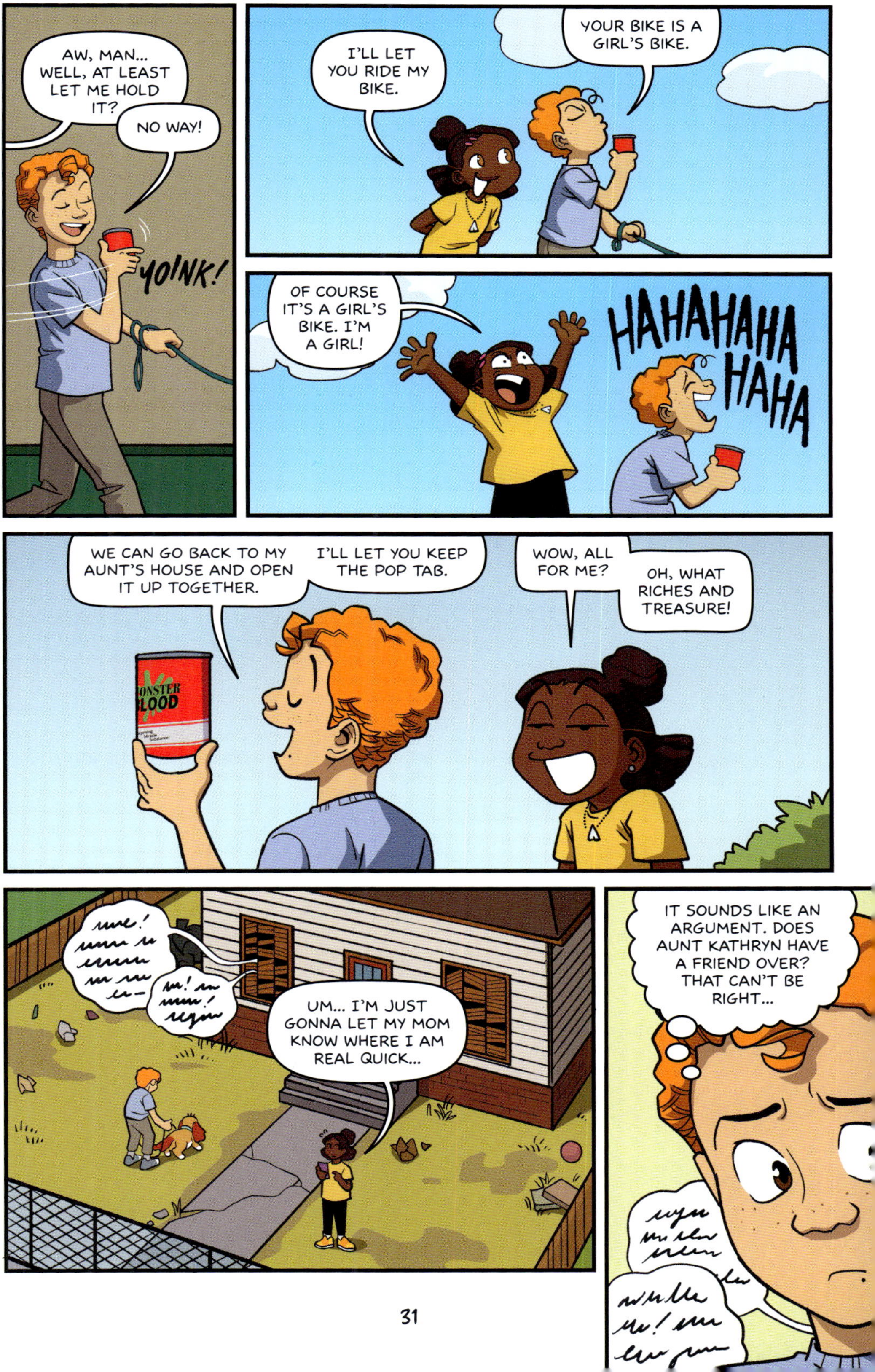
AW, MAN... WELL, AT LEAST LET ME HOLD IT?
NO WAY!
YOINK!
I'LL LET YOU RIDE MY BIKE.
YOUR BIKE IS A GIRL'S BIKE.
OF COURSE IT'S A GIRL'S BIKE. I'M A GIRL!
HAHAHAHA HAHA
WE CAN GO BACK TO MY AUNT'S HOUSE AND OPEN IT UP TOGETHER.
I'LL LET YOU KEEP THE POP TAB.
WOW, ALL FOR ME?
OH, WHAT RICHES AND TREASURE!
UM... I'M JUST GONNA LET MY MOM KNOW WHERE I AM REAL QUICK...
IT SOUNDS LIKE AN ARGUMENT. DOES AUNT KATHRYN HAVE A FRIEND OVER? THAT CAN'T BE RIGHT...

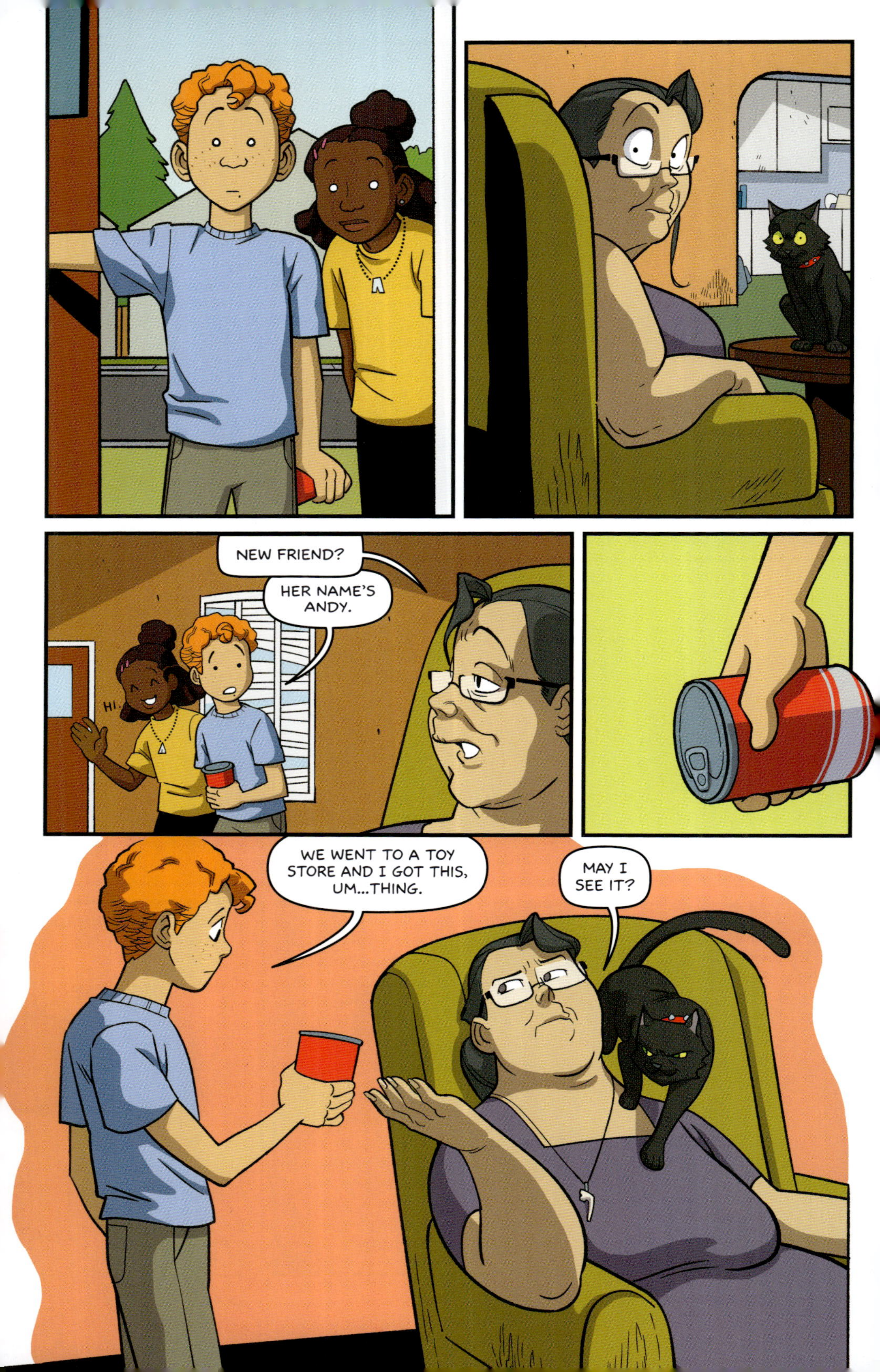
NEW FRIEND?
HER NAME'S ANDY.
HI.
WE WENT TO A TOY STORE AND I GOT THIS, UM...THING.
MAY I SEE IT?

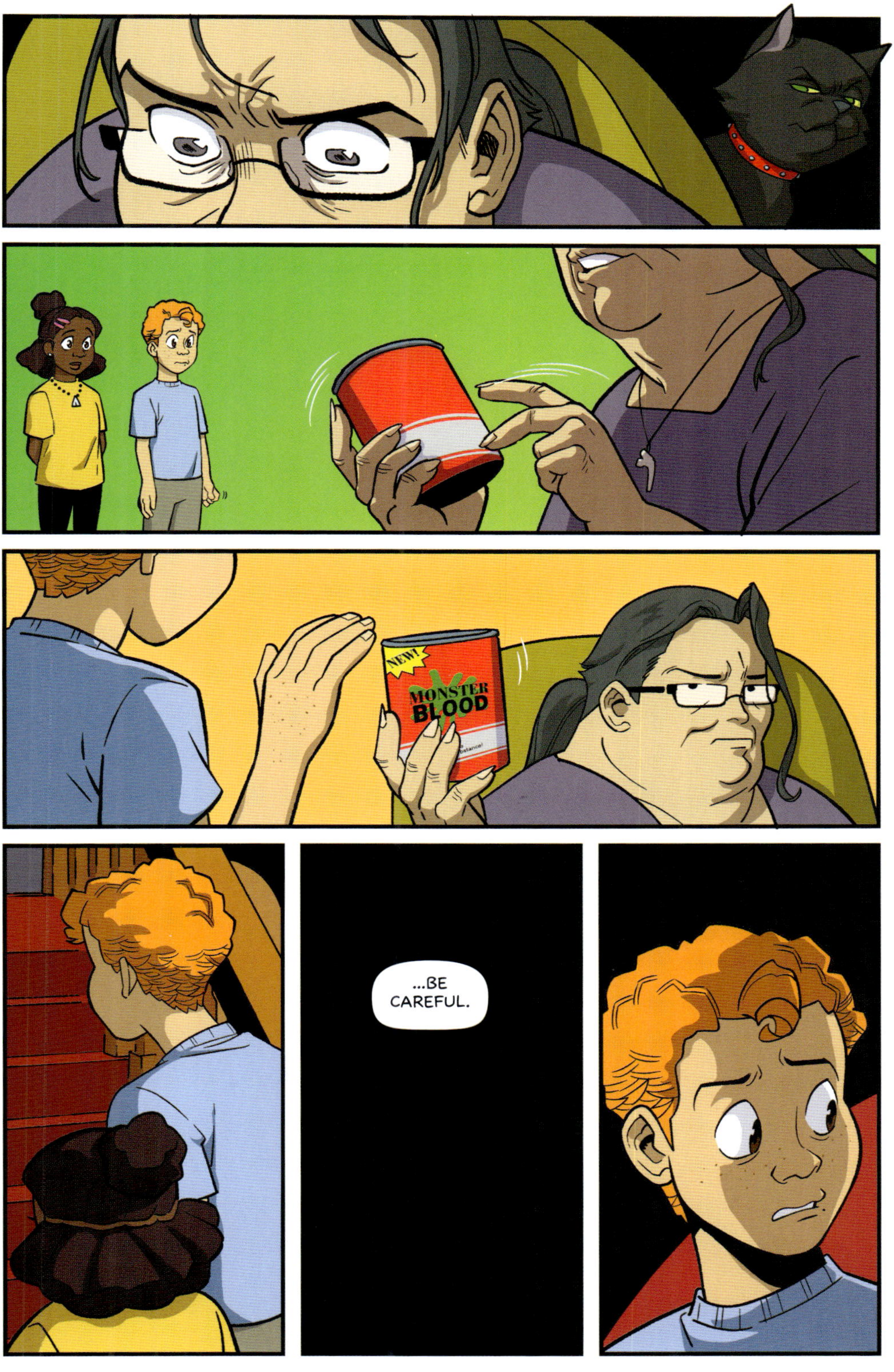
NEW!
MONSTER BLOOD
...BE CAREFUL.

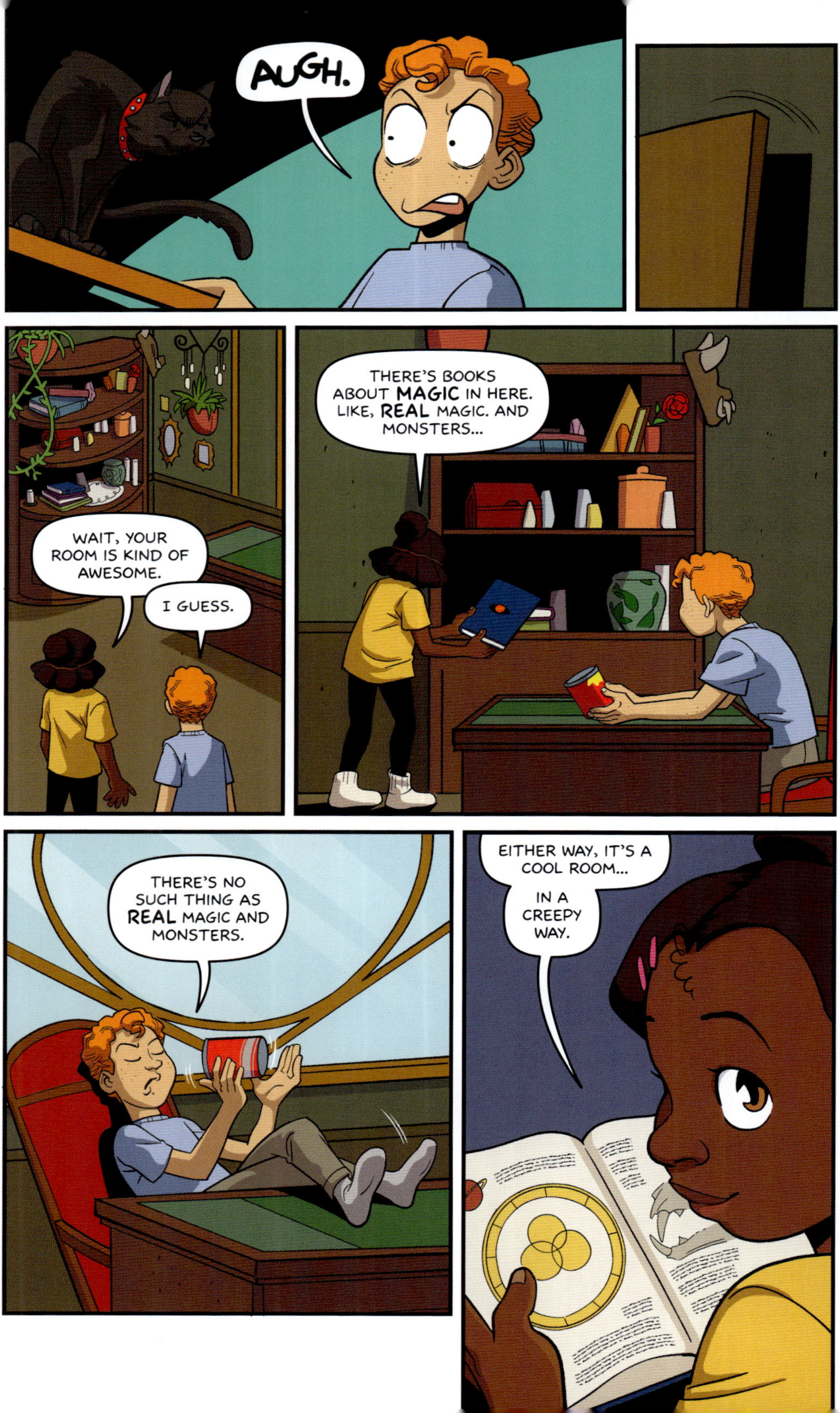
AUGH.
WAIT, YOUR ROOM IS KIND OF AWESOME.
I GUESS.
THERE'S BOOKS ABOUT MAGIC IN HERE. LIKE, REAL MAGIC. AND MONSTERS...
THERE'S NO SUCH THING AS REAL MAGIC AND MONSTERS.
EITHER WAY, IT'S A COOL ROOM...
IN A CREEPY WAY.

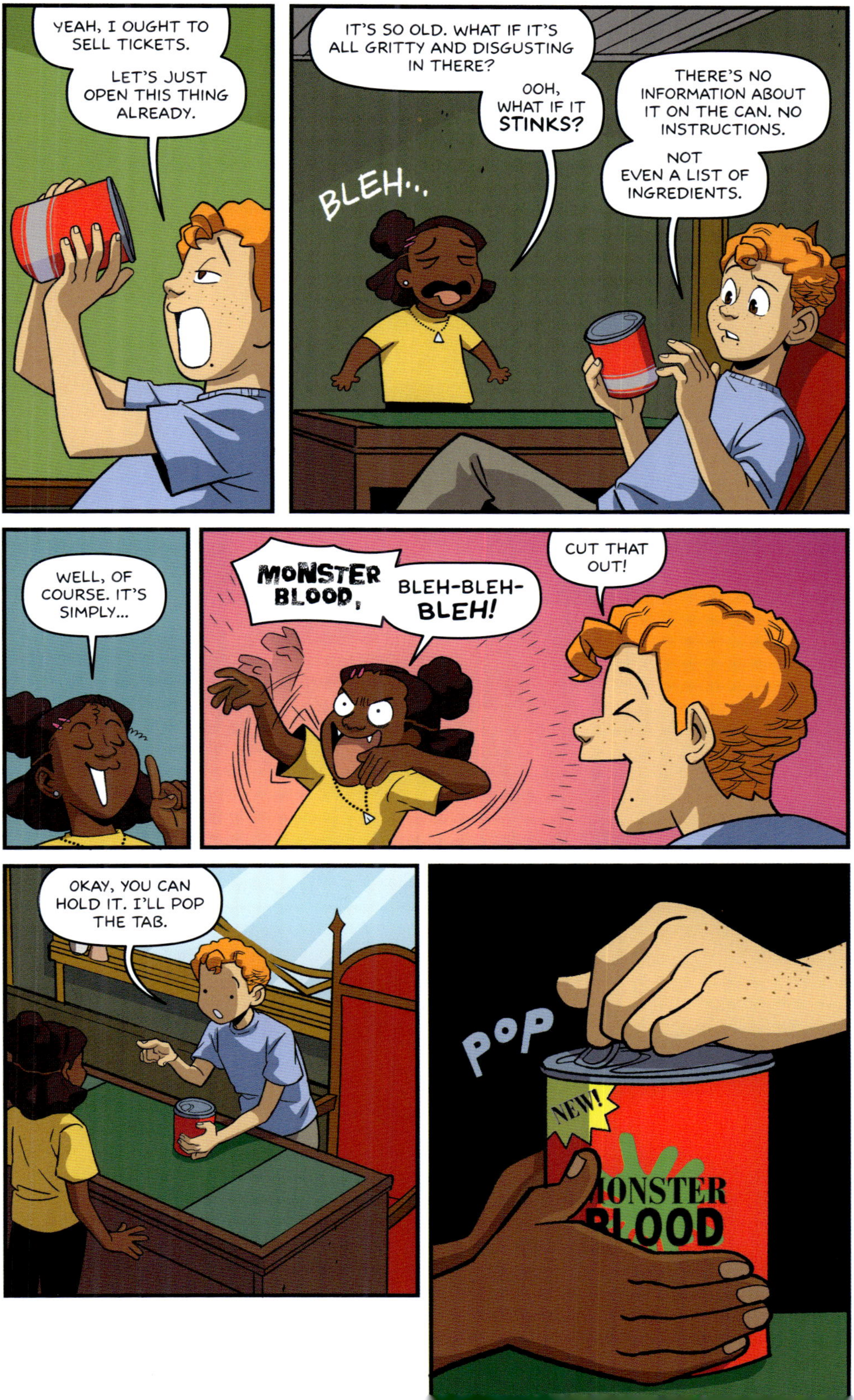
YEAH, I OUGHT TO SELL TICKETS.
LET'S JUST OPEN THIS THING ALREADY.
IT'S SO OLD. WHAT IF IT'S ALL GRITTY AND DISGUSTING IN THERE?
OOH, WHAT IF IT STINKS?
BLEH...
THERE'S NO INFORMATION ABOUT IT ON THE CAN. NO INSTRUCTIONS.
NOT EVEN A LIST OF INGREDIENTS.
WELL, OF COURSE. IT'S SIMPLY...
MONSTER BLOOD,
BLEH-BLEH-BLEH!
CUT THAT OUT!
OKAY, YOU CAN HOLD IT. I'LL POP THE TAB.
POP
NEW!
MONSTER BLOOD

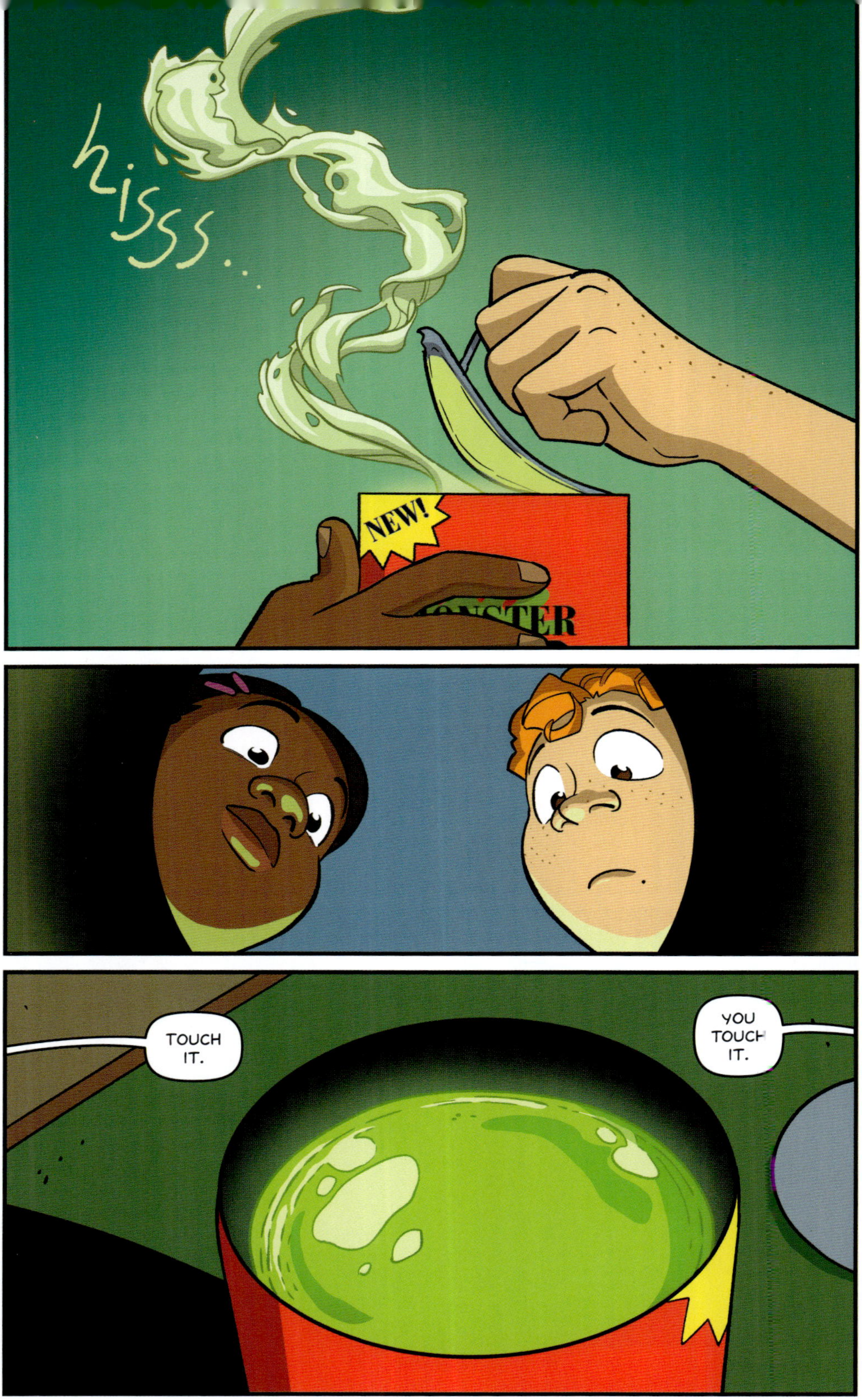
hisss...
NEW!
TOUCH IT.
YOU TOUCH IT.

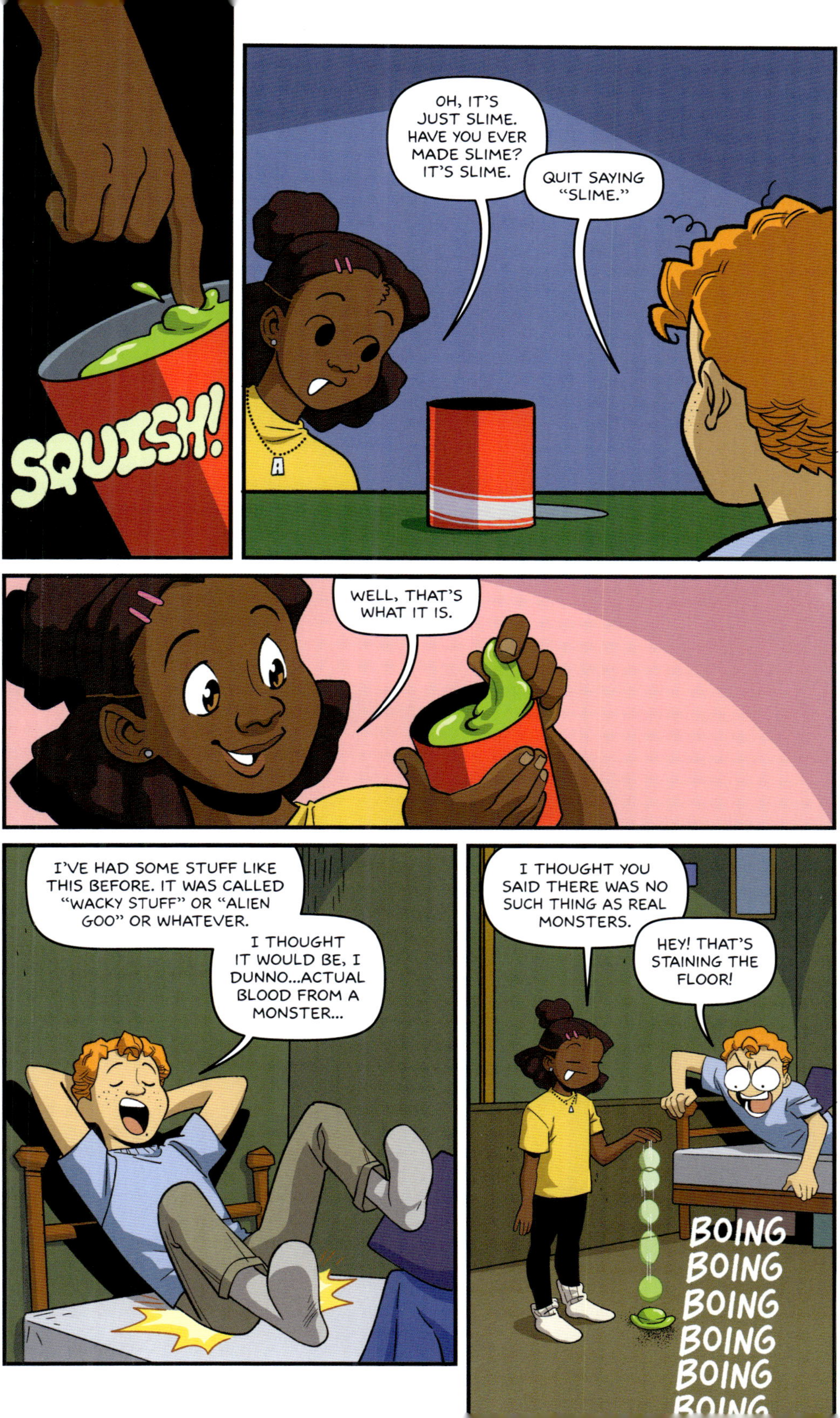
SQUISH!
OH, IT'S JUST SLIME. HAVE YOU EVER MADE SLIME? IT'S SLIME.
QUIT SAYING "SLIME."
WELL, THAT'S WHAT IT IS.
I'VE HAD SOME STUFF LIKE THIS BEFORE. IT WAS CALLED "WACKY STUFF" OR "ALIEN GOO" OR WHATEVER.
I THOUGHT IT WOULD BE, I DUNNO...ACTUAL BLOOD FROM A MONSTER...
I THOUGHT YOU SAID THERE WAS NO SUCH THING AS REAL MONSTERS.
HEY! THAT'S STAINING THE FLOOR!
BOING
BOING
BOING
BOING
BOING

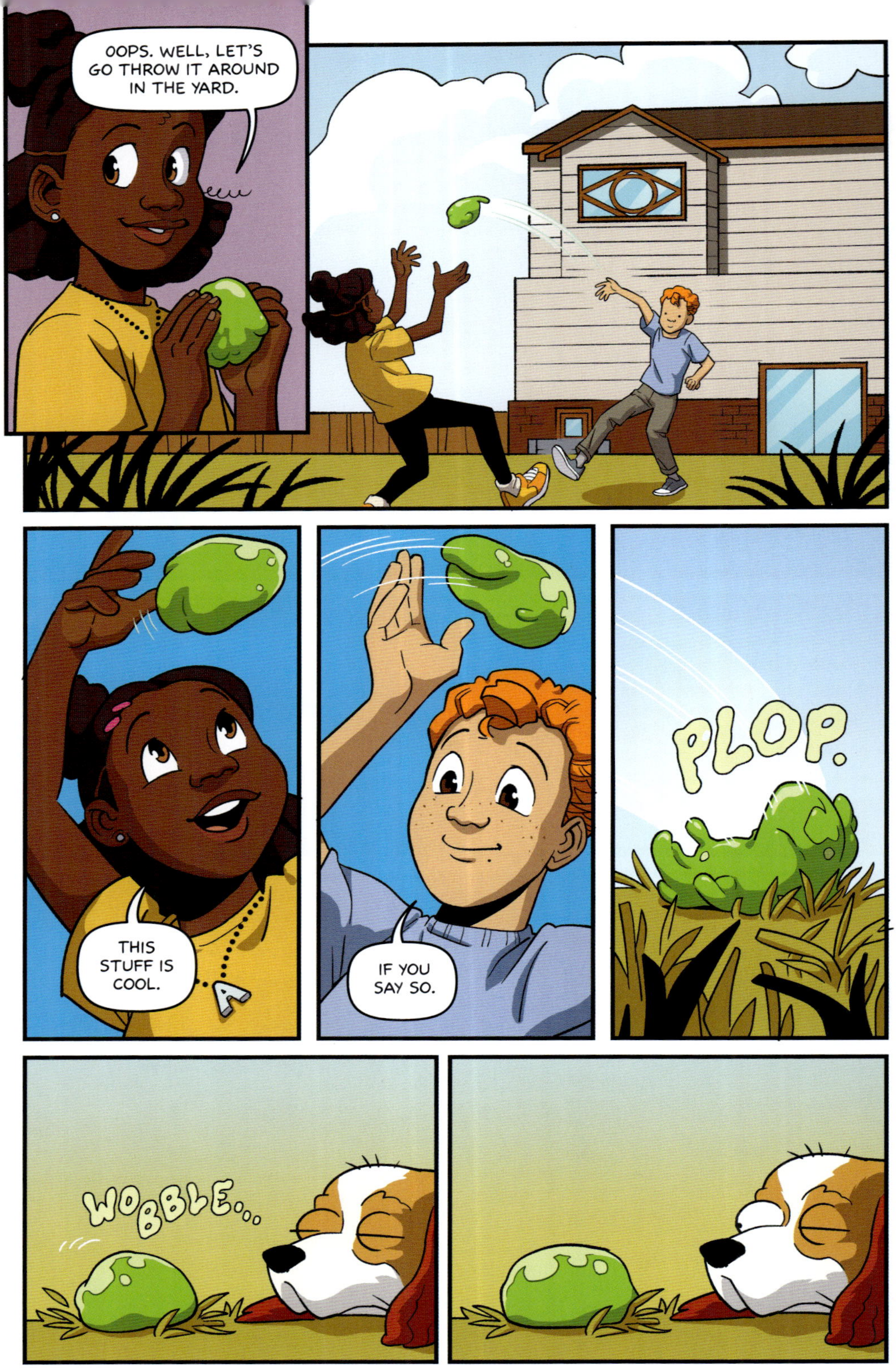
OOPS. WELL, LET'S GO THROW IT AROUND IN THE YARD.
THIS STUFF IS COOL.
IF YOU SAY SO.
PLOP.
WOBBLE...

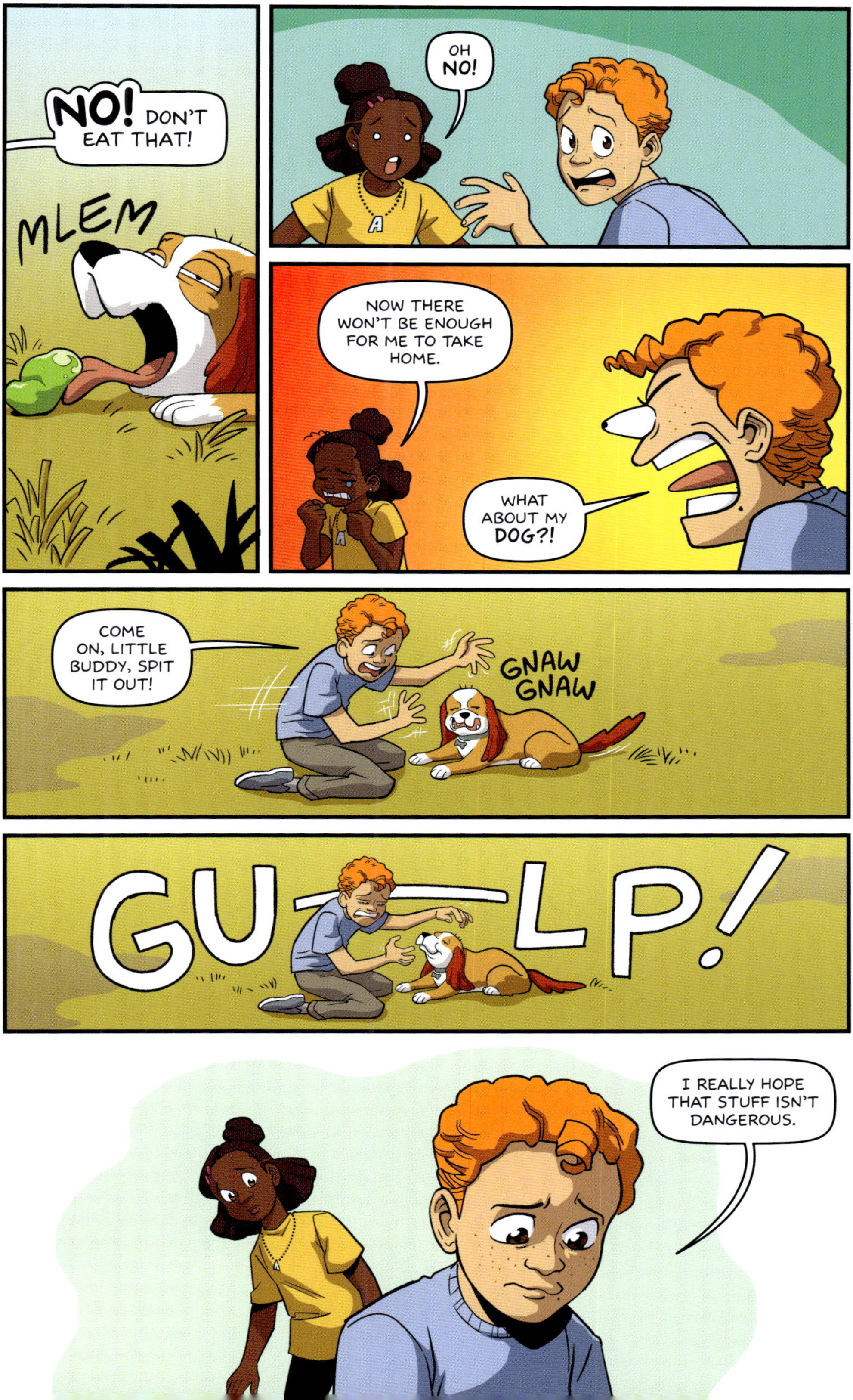
NO! DON'T EAT THAT!
MLEM
OH NO!
NOW THERE WON'T BE ENOUGH FOR ME TO TAKE HOME.
WHAT ABOUT MY DOG?!
COME ON, LITTLE BUDDY, SPIT IT OUT!
GNAW GNAW
GULP!
I REALLY HOPE THAT STUFF ISN'T DANGEROUS.

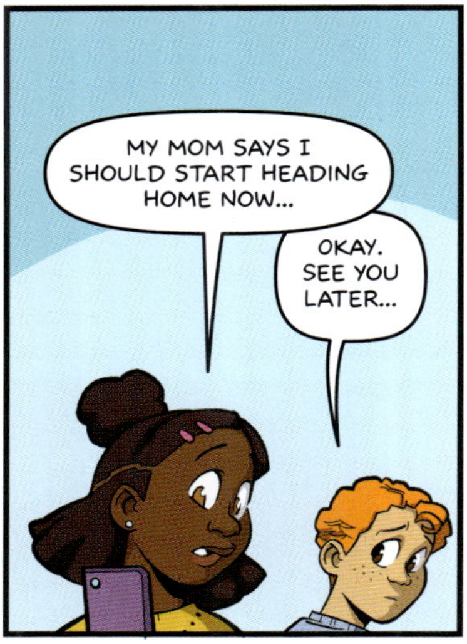
MY MOM SAYS I SHOULD START HEADING HOME NOW...
OKAY. SEE YOU LATER...

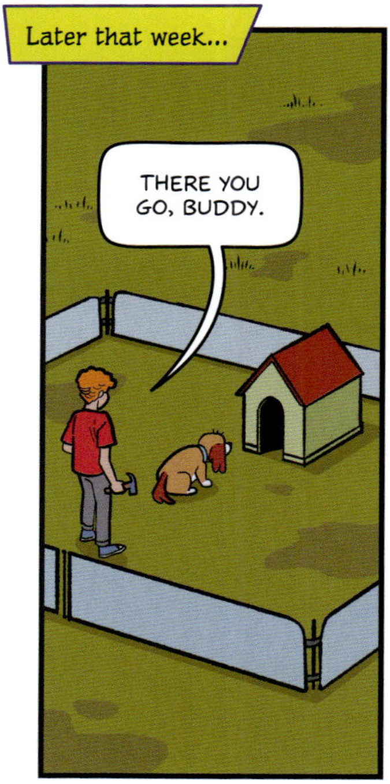
Later that week...
THERE YOU GO, BUDDY.

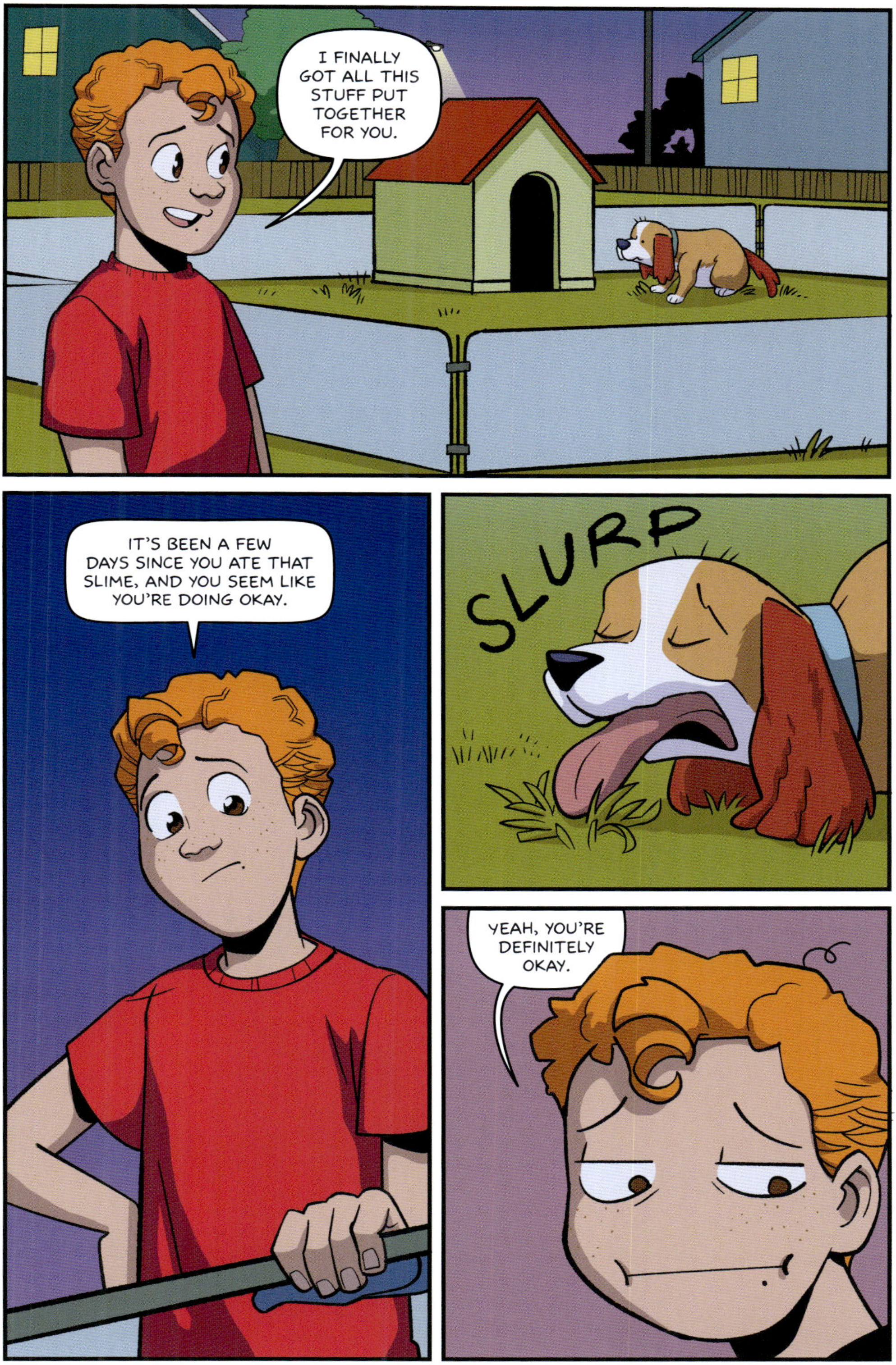
I FINALLY GOT ALL THIS STUFF PUT TOGETHER FOR YOU.
IT'S BEEN A FEW DAYS SINCE YOU ATE THAT SLIME, AND YOU SEEM LIKE YOU'RE DOING OKAY.
SLURP
YEAH, YOU'RE DEFINITELY OKAY.

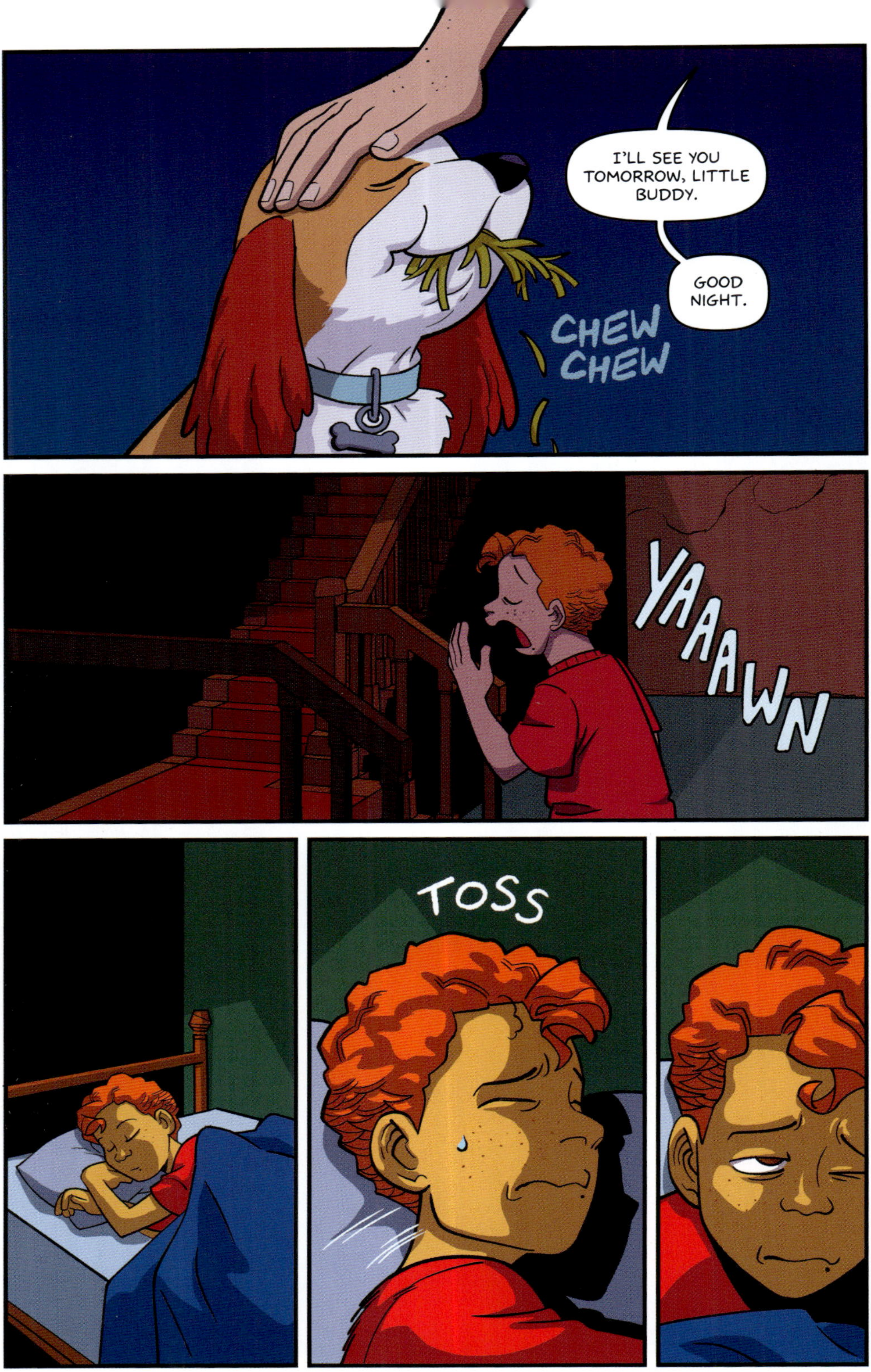
I'LL SEE YOU TOMORROW, LITTLE BUDDY.
GOOD NIGHT.
CHEW CHEW
YAAAWN
TOSS

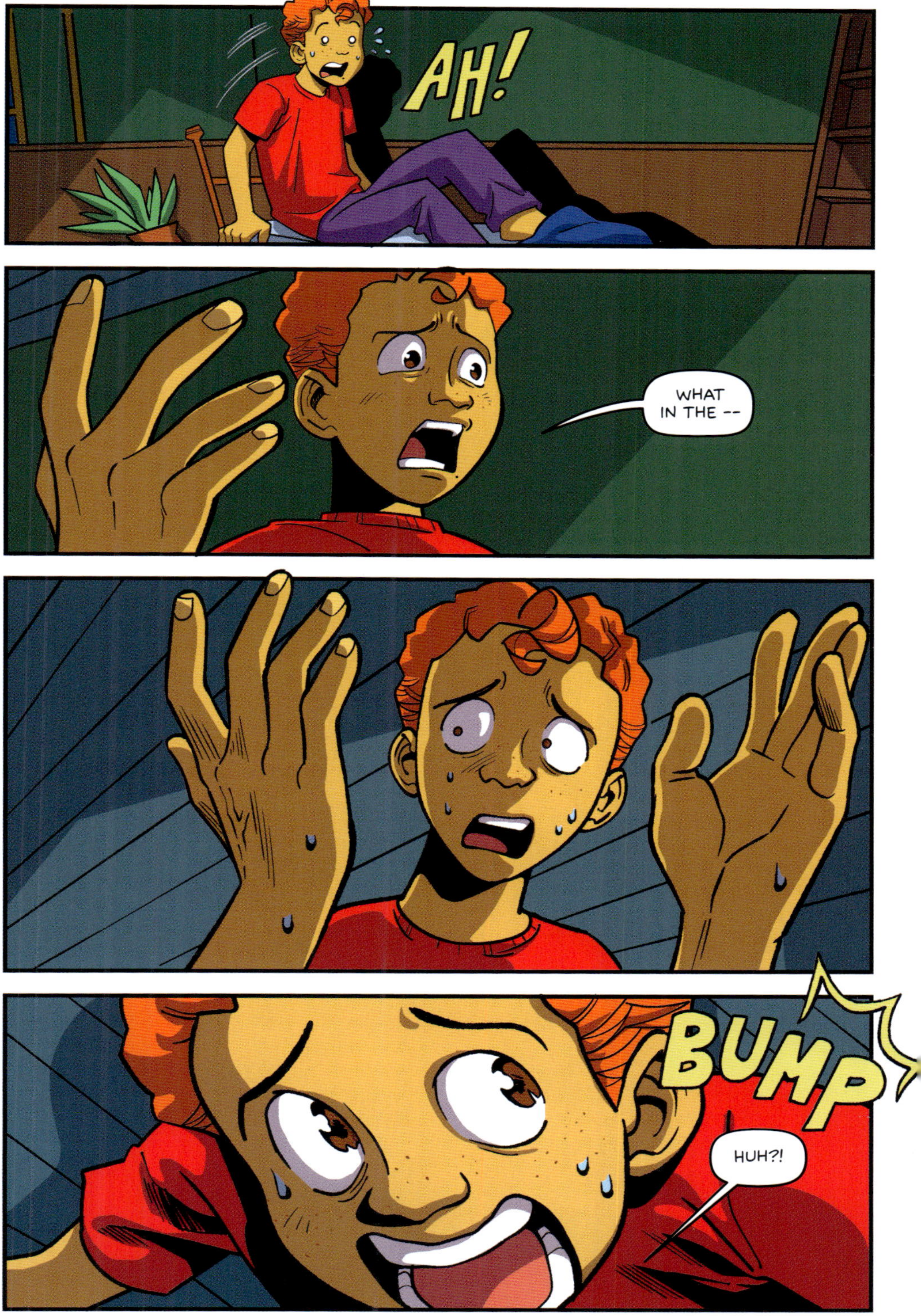
AH!
WHAT IN THE --
BUMP
HUH?!

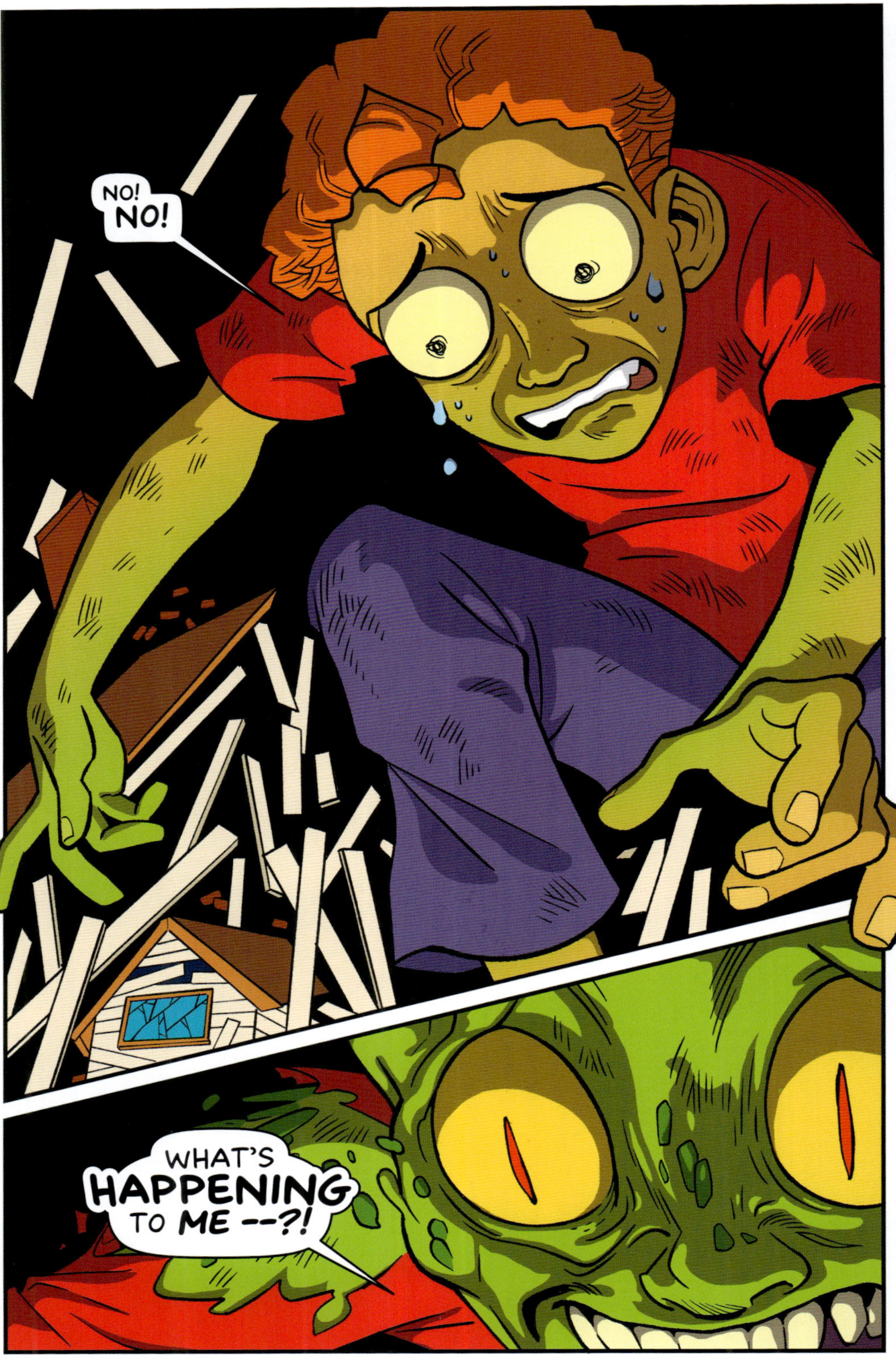
NO! NO!
WHAT'S HAPPENING TO ME --?!

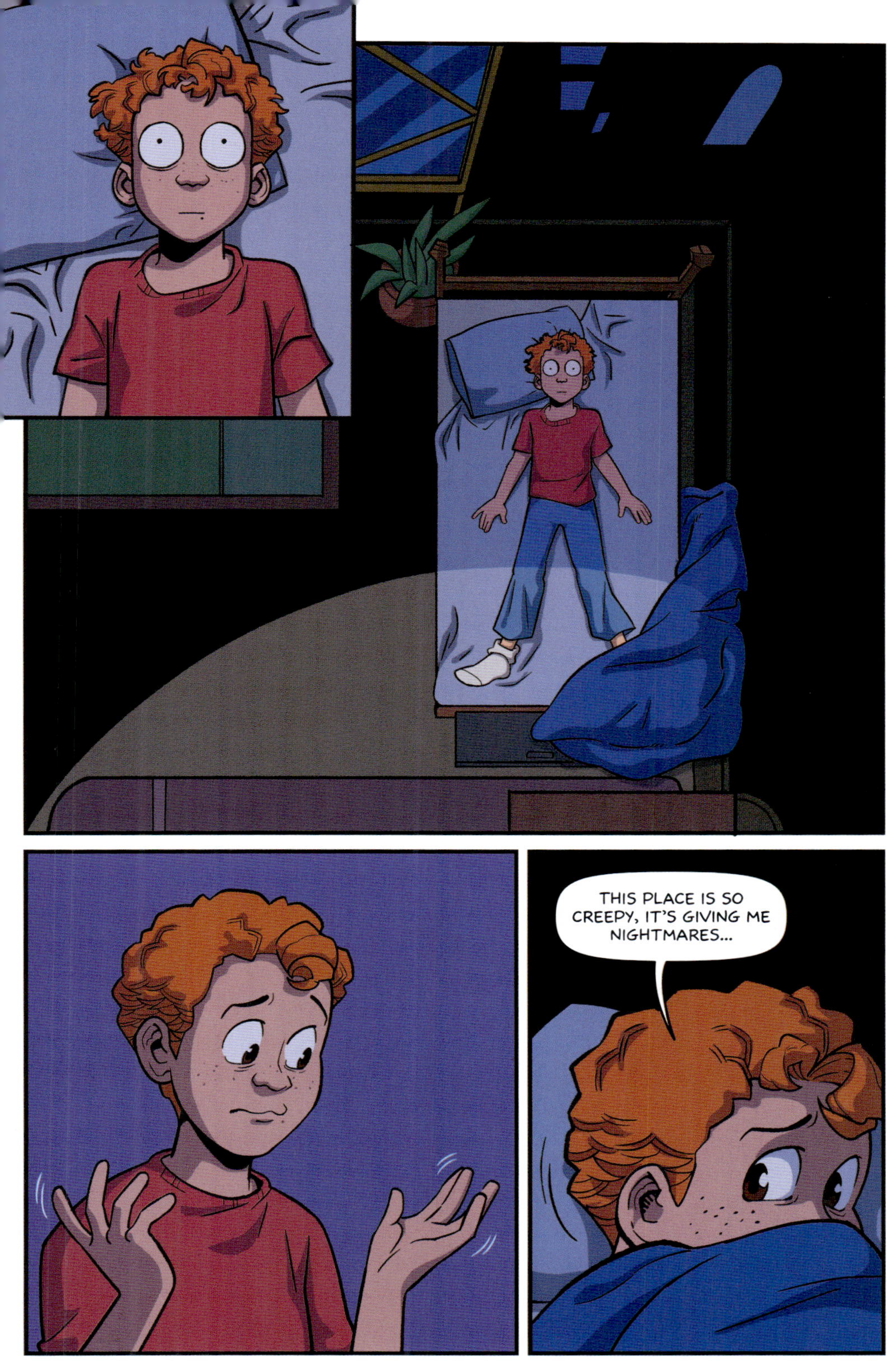
THIS PLACE IS SO CREEPY, IT'S GIVING ME NIGHTMARES...

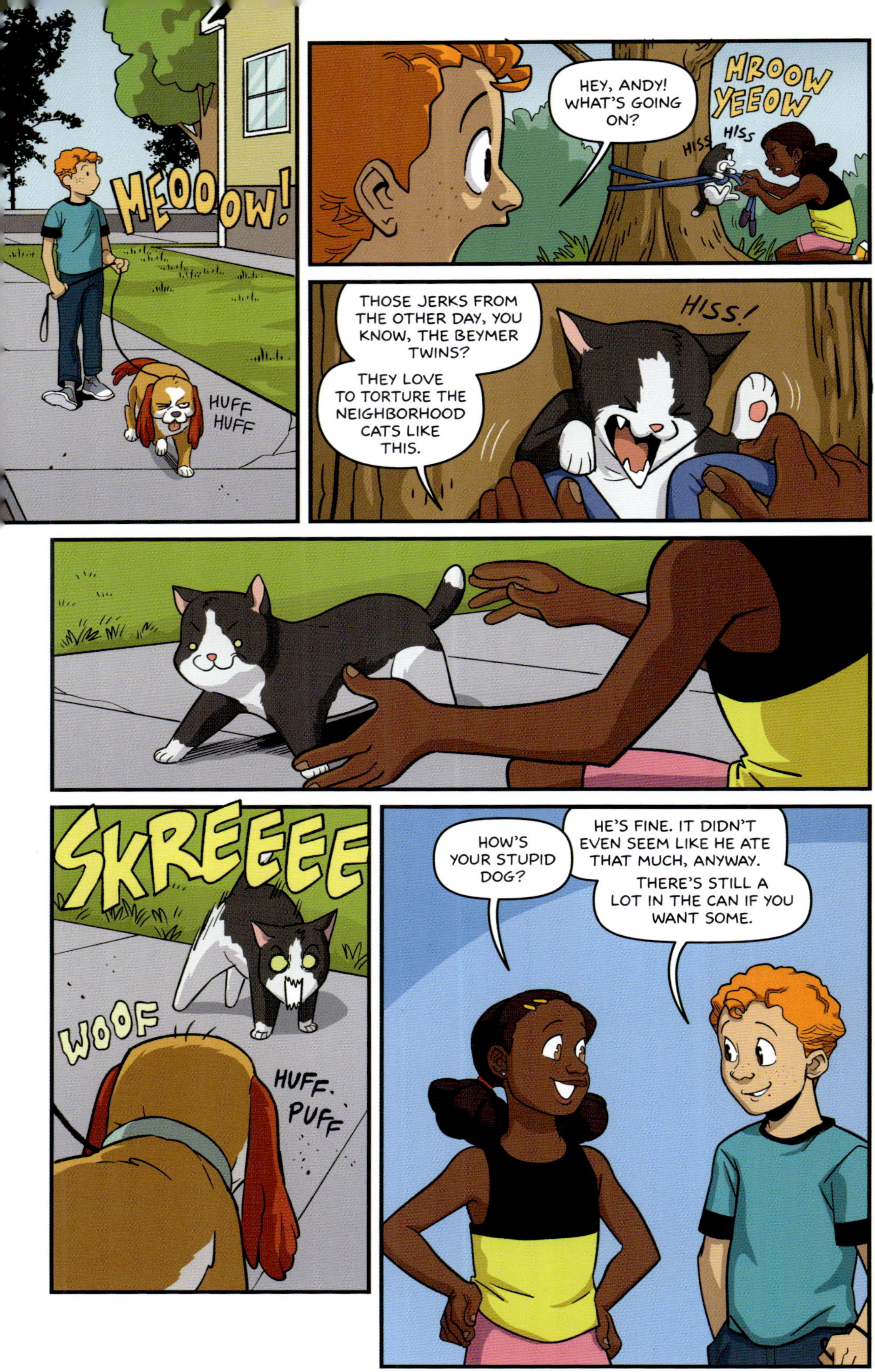
MEOOOOW!
HUFF HUFF
HEY, ANDY! WHAT'S GOING ON?
MROOW YEEOW
HISS HISS
THOSE JERKS FROM THE OTHER DAY, YOU KNOW, THE BEYMER TWINS?
THEY LOVE TO TORTURE THE NEIGHBORHOOD CATS LIKE THIS.
HISS!
SKREEEE
WOOF
HUFF. PUFF
HOW'S YOUR STUPID DOG?
HE'S FINE. IT DIDN'T EVEN SEEM LIKE HE ATE THAT MUCH, ANYWAY.
THERE'S STILL A LOT IN THE CAN IF YOU WANT SOME.

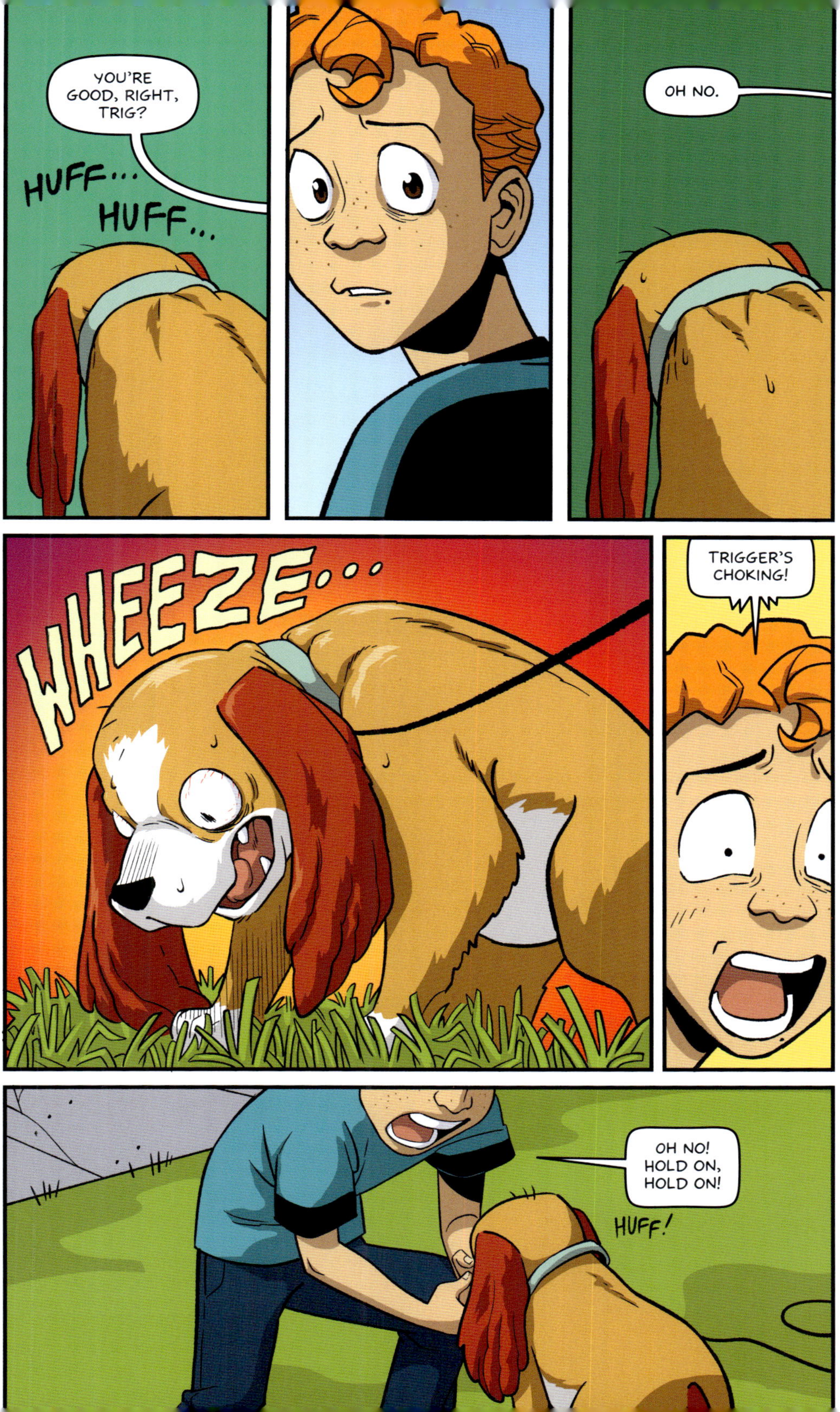
YOU'RE GOOD, RIGHT, TRIG?
HUFF... HUFF...
OH NO.
WHEEZE...
TRIGGER'S CHOKING!
OH NO! HOLD ON, HOLD ON!
HUFF!

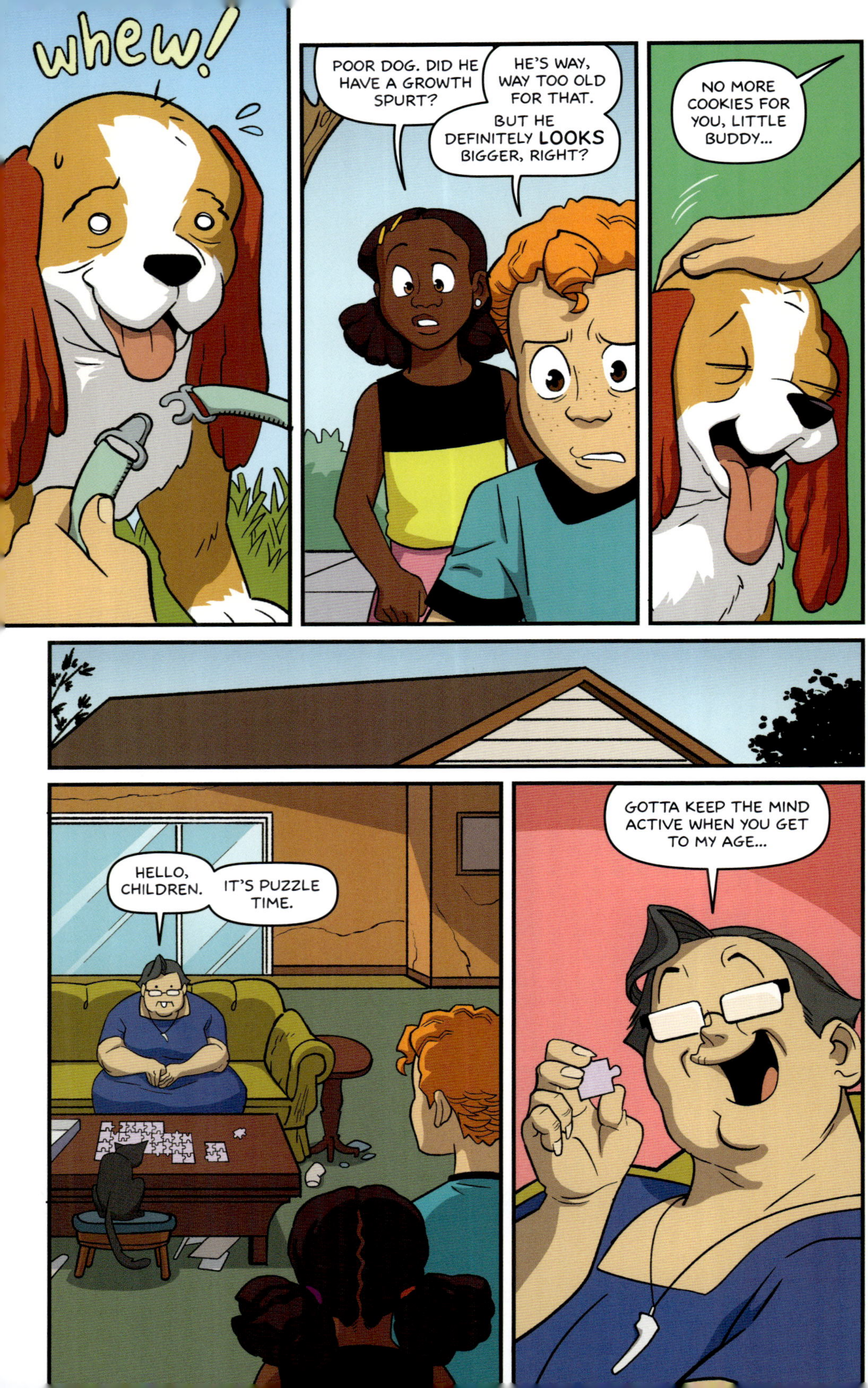
whew!
POOR DOG. DID HE HAVE A GROWTH SPURT?
HE'S WAY, WAY TOO OLD FOR THAT.
BUT HE DEFINITELY LOOKS BIGGER, RIGHT?
NO MORE COOKIES FOR YOU, LITTLE BUDDY...
HELLO, CHILDREN.
IT'S PUZZLE TIME.
GOTTA KEEP THE MIND ACTIVE WHEN YOU GET TO MY AGE...

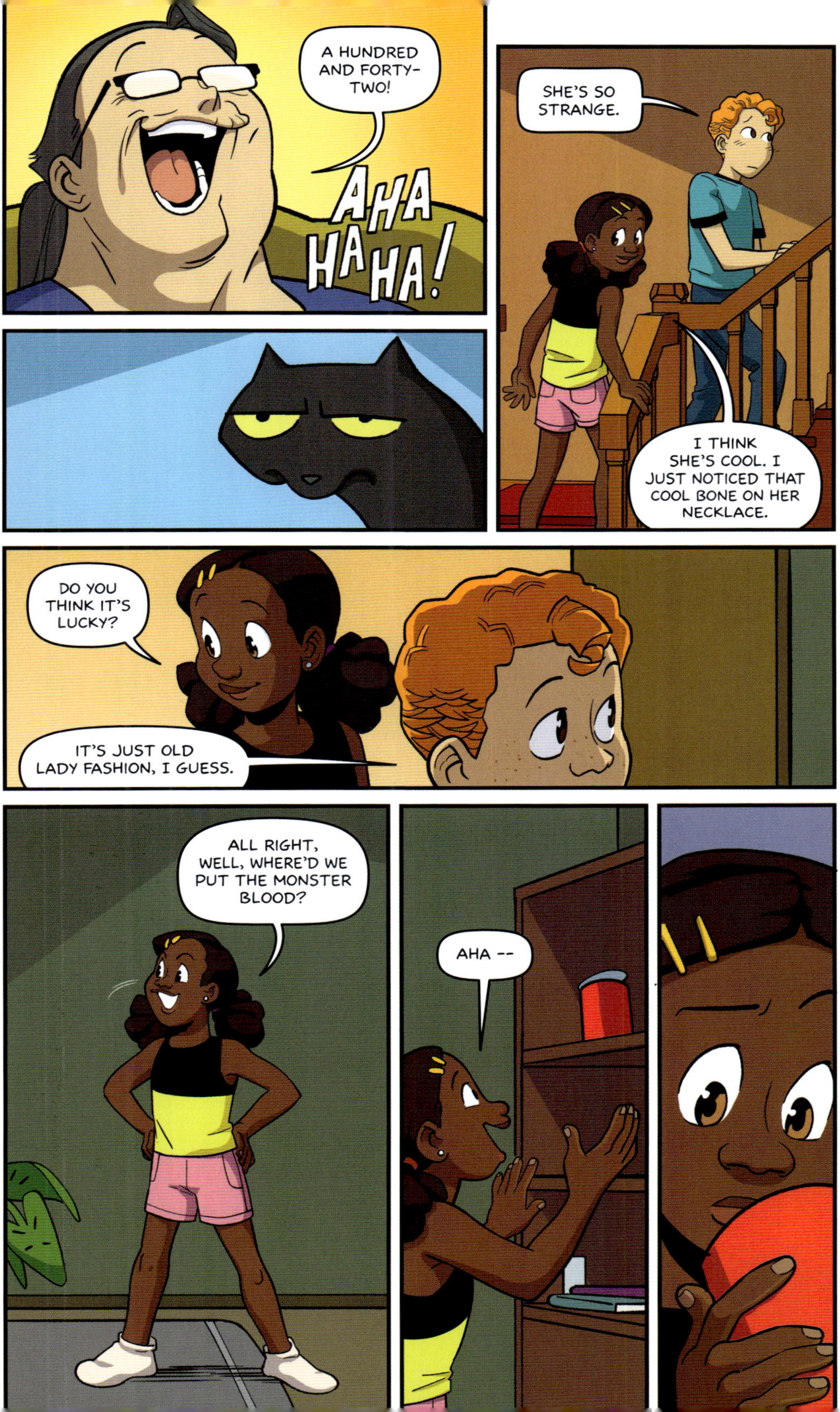
A HUNDRED AND FORTY-TWO!
AHAHAHA!
SHE'S SO STRANGE.
I THINK SHE'S COOL. I JUST NOTICED THAT COOL BONE ON HER NECKLACE.
DO YOU THINK IT'S LUCKY?
IT'S JUST OLD LADY FASHION, I GUESS.
ALL RIGHT, WELL, WHERE'D WE PUT THE MONSTER BLOOD?
AHA --

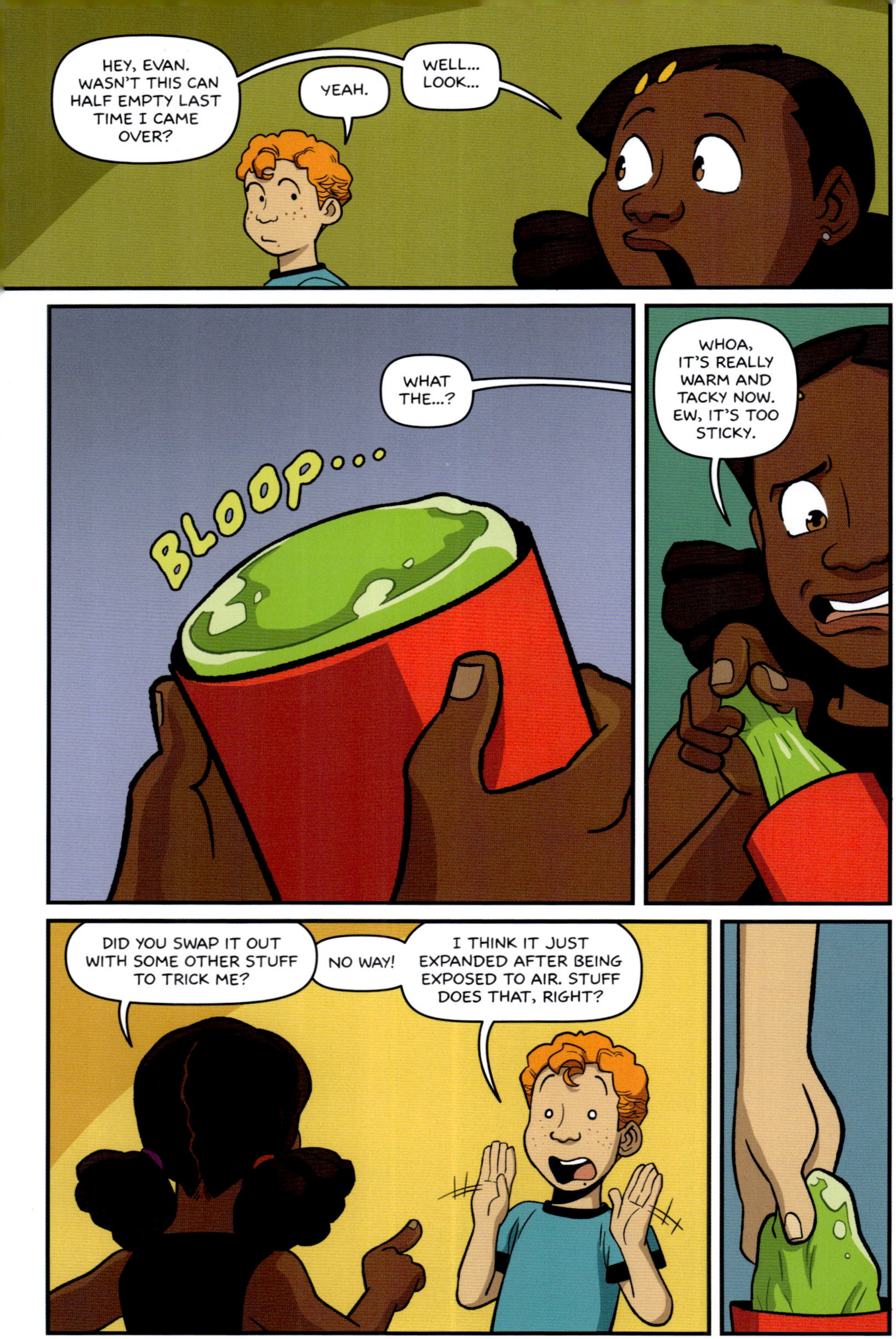
HEY, EVAN. WASN'T THIS CAN HALF EMPTY LAST TIME I CAME OVER?
YEAH.
WELL... LOOK...
WHAT THE...?
BLOOP...
WHOA, IT'S REALLY WARM AND TACKY NOW. EW, IT'S TOO STICKY.
DID YOU SWAP IT OUT WITH SOME OTHER STUFF TO TRICK ME?
NO WAY!
I THINK IT JUST EXPANDED AFTER BEING EXPOSED TO AIR. STUFF DOES THAT, RIGHT?

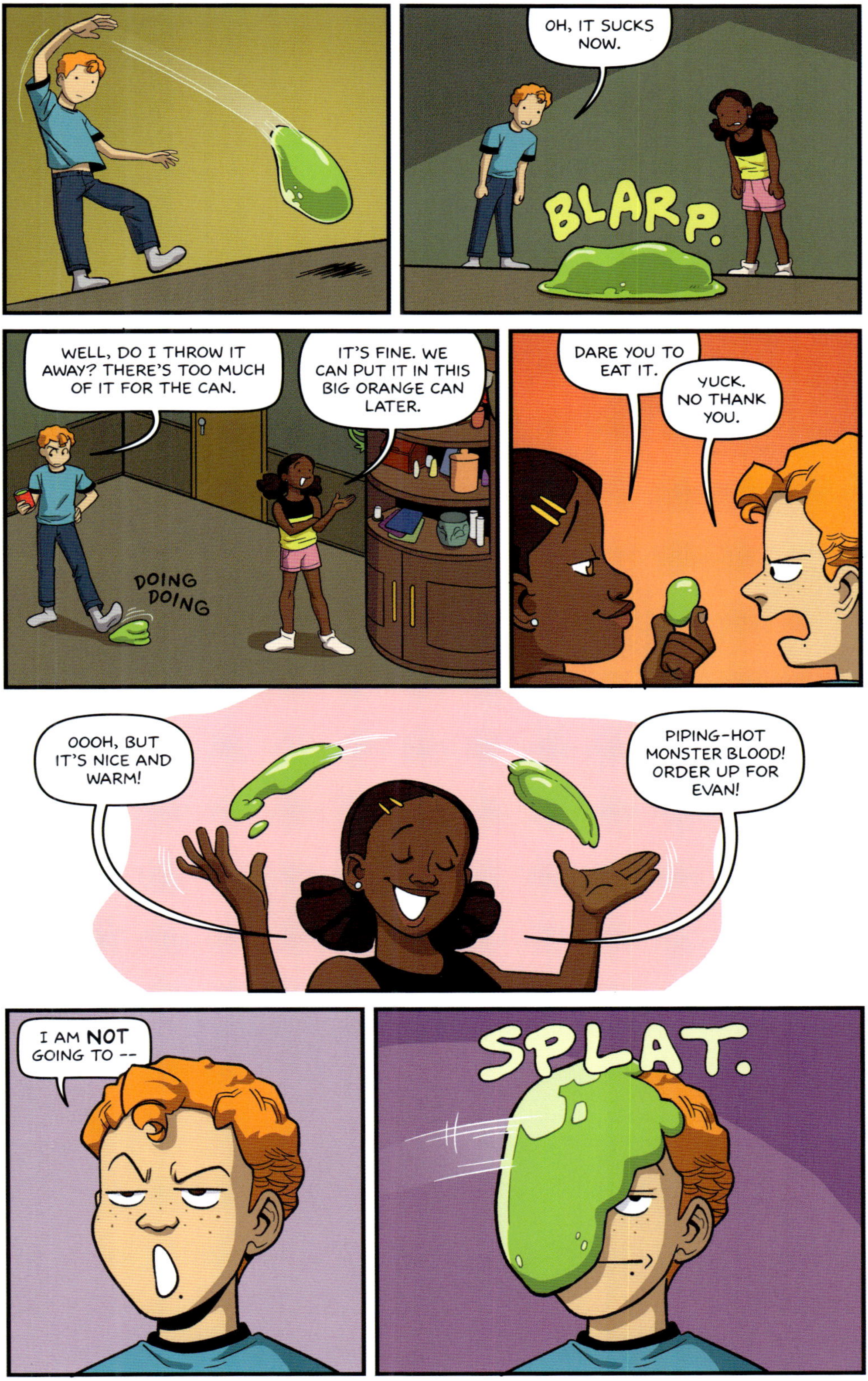
OH, IT SUCKS NOW.
BLARP.
WELL, DO I THROW IT AWAY? THERE'S TOO MUCH OF IT FOR THE CAN.
IT'S FINE. WE CAN PUT IT IN THIS BIG ORANGE CAN LATER.
DOING DOING
DARE YOU TO EAT IT.
YUCK. NO THANK YOU.
OOOH, BUT IT'S NICE AND WARM!
PIPING-HOT MONSTER BLOOD! ORDER UP FOR EVAN!
I AM **NOT** GOING TO --
SPLAT.

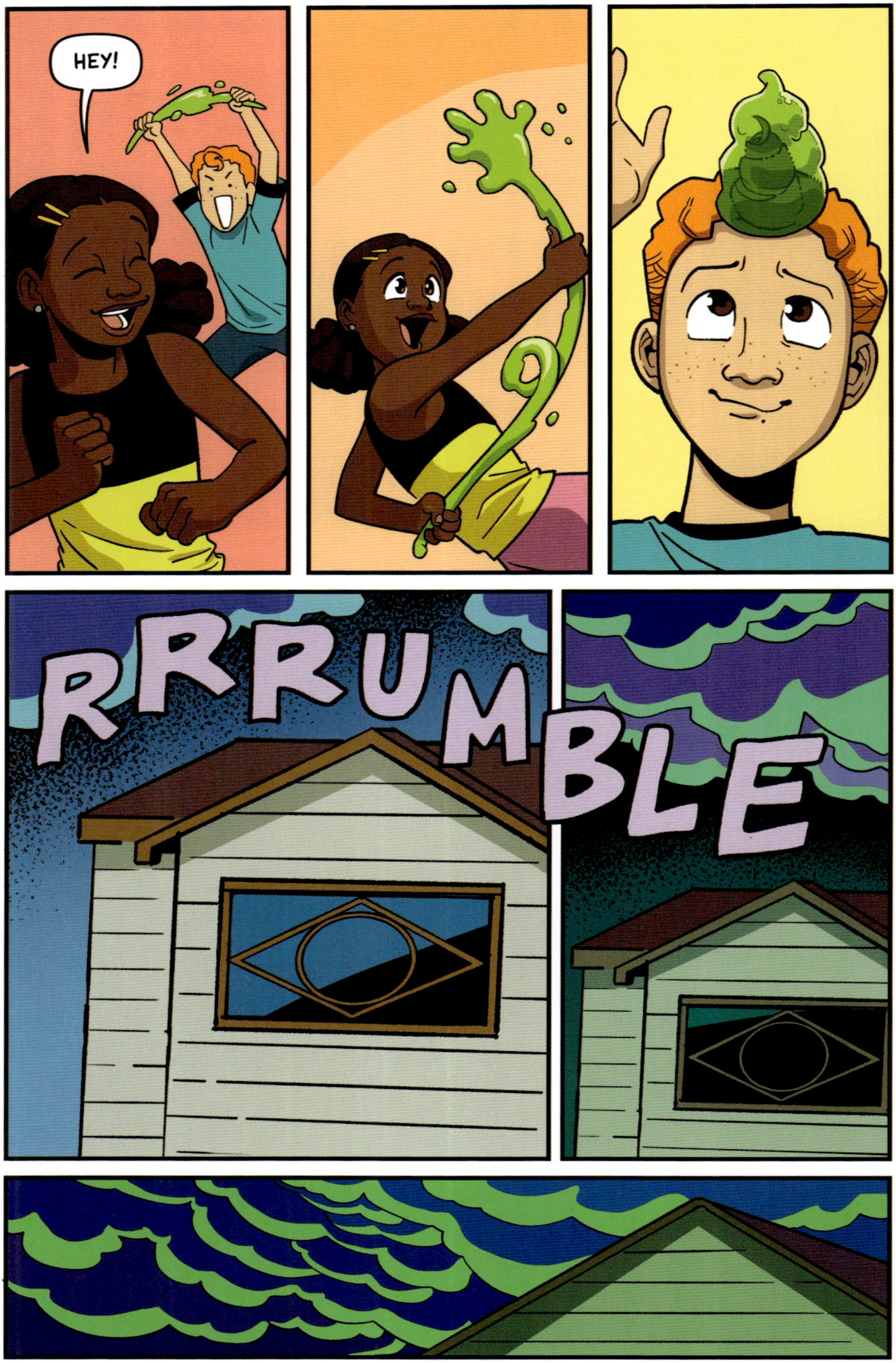
HEY!
RRRUMBLE

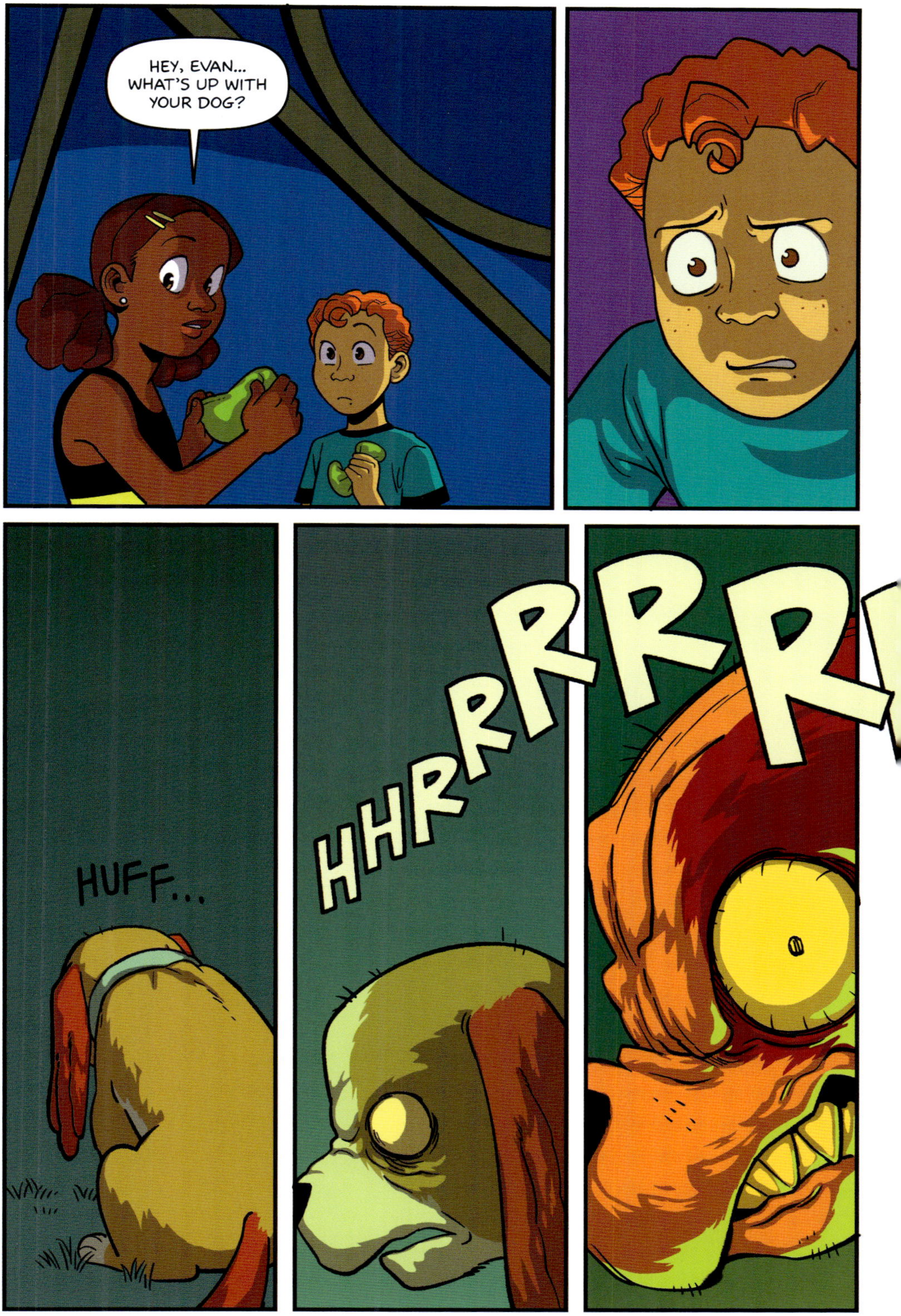
HEY, EVAN... WHAT'S UP WITH YOUR DOG?
HUFF...
HHRRRRR

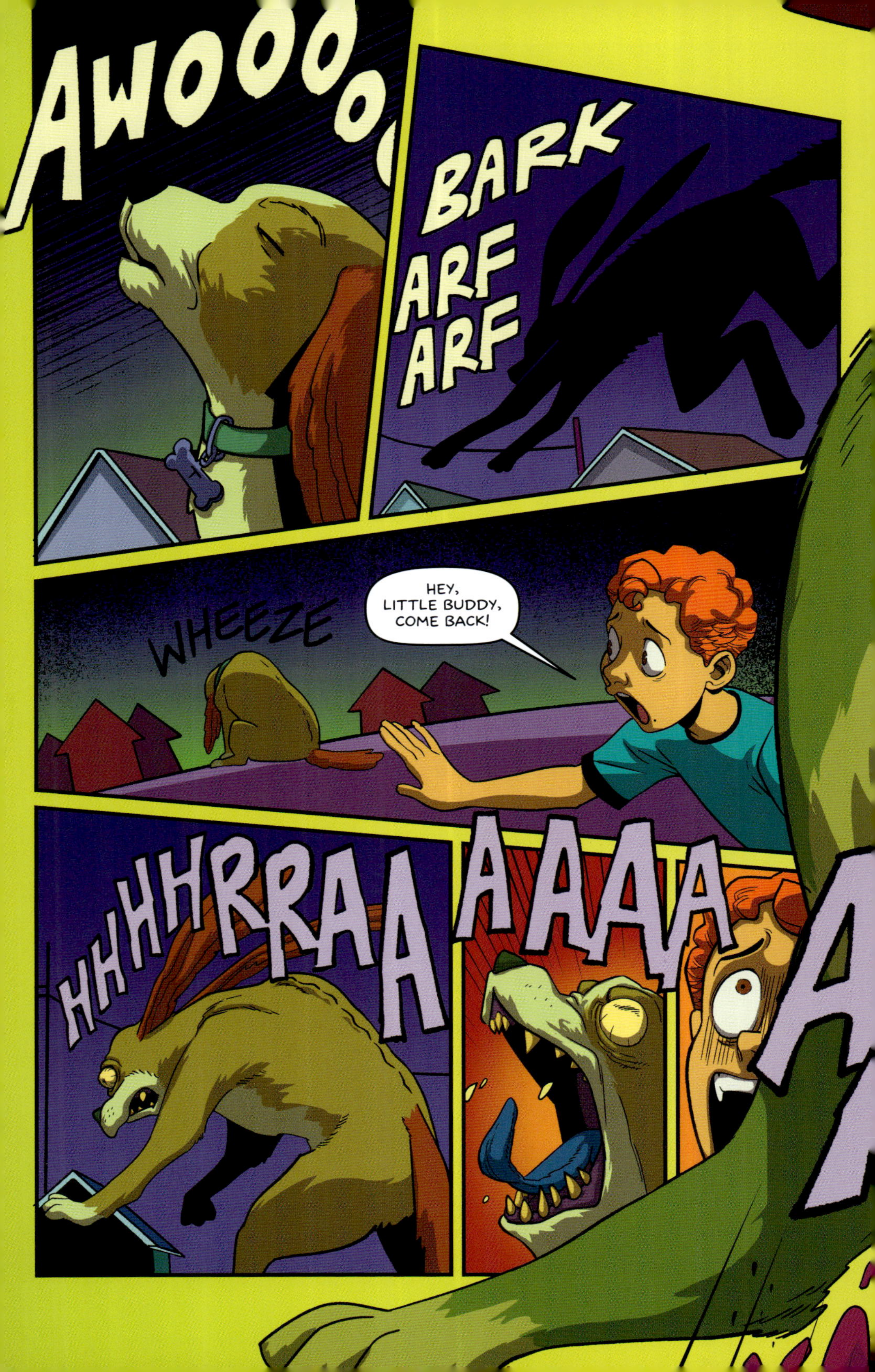
AWOOO
BARK
ARF
ARF
WHEEZE
HEY, LITTLE BUDDY, COME BACK!
HHHHRRAAAAAAA

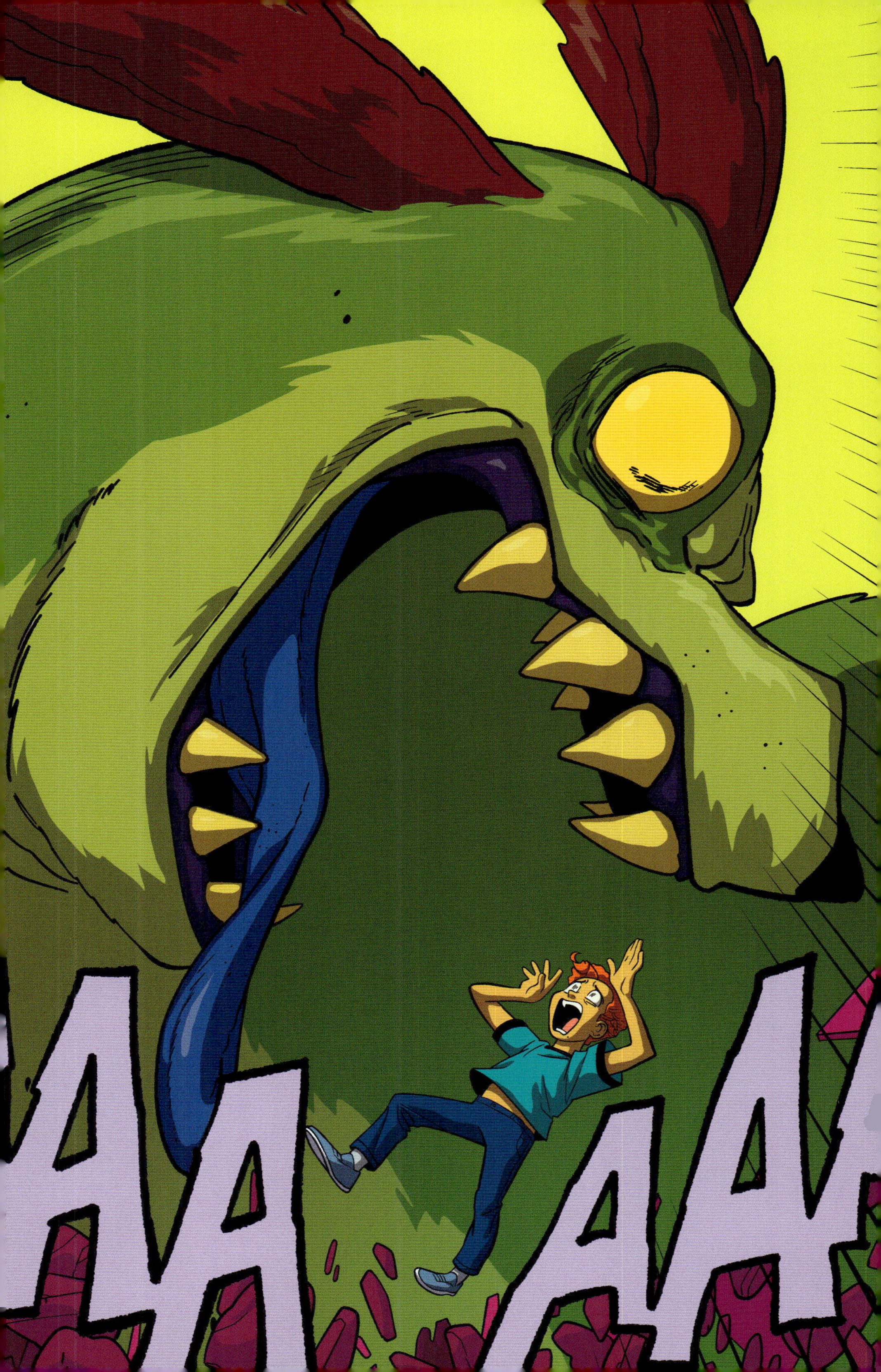
AAAAA

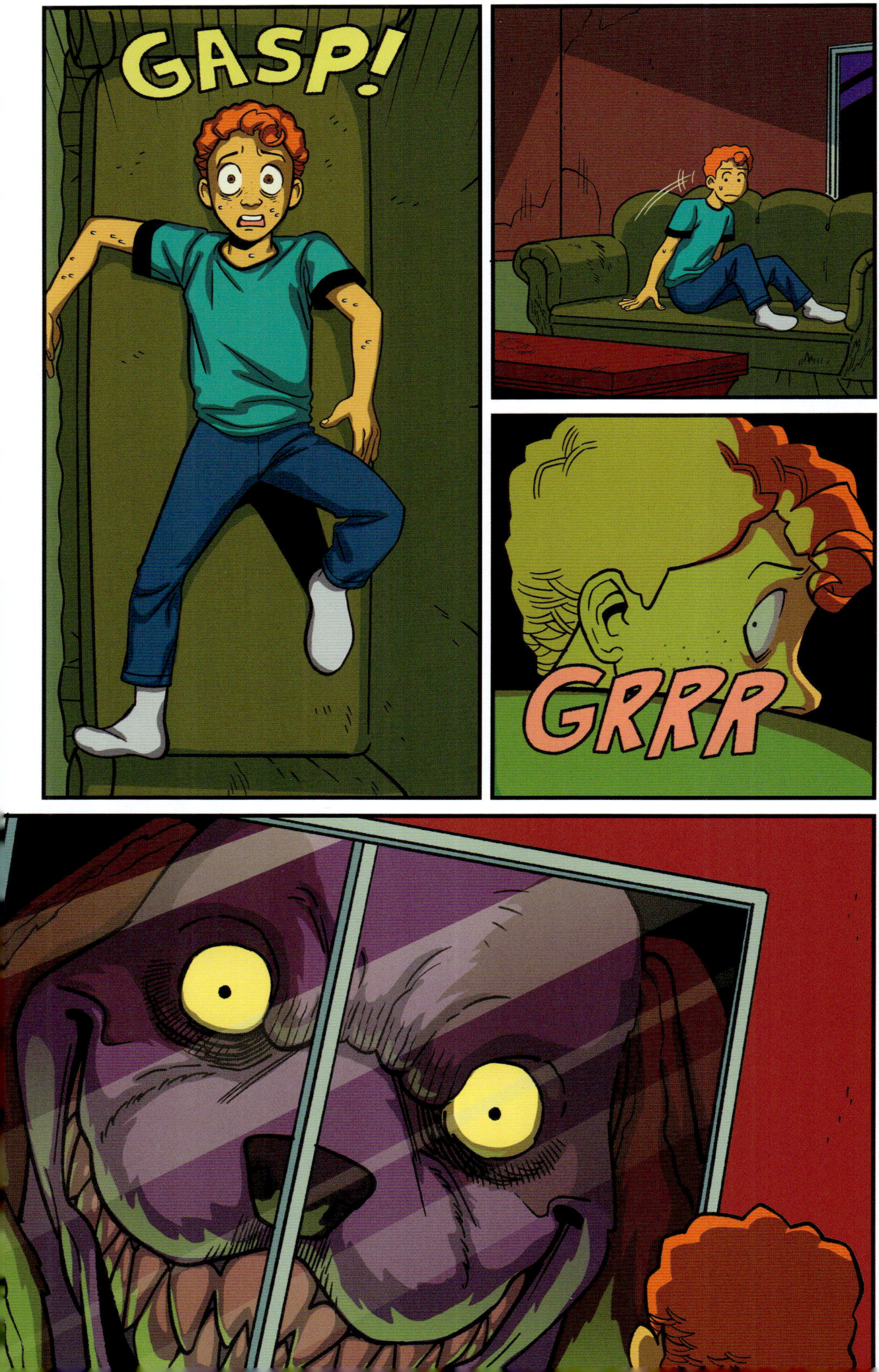
GASP!
GRRR

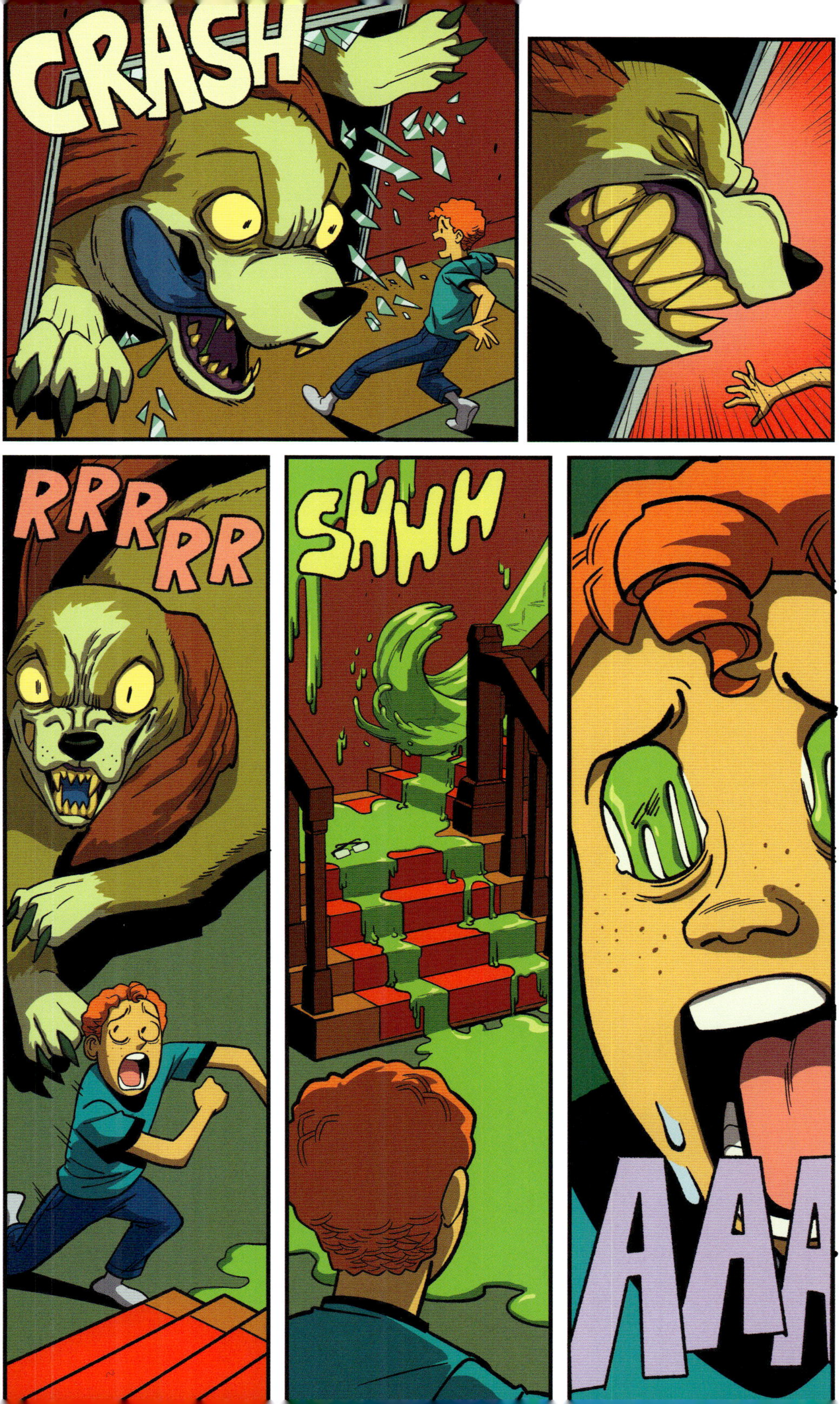
CRASH
RRRRRR
SHHH
AAA

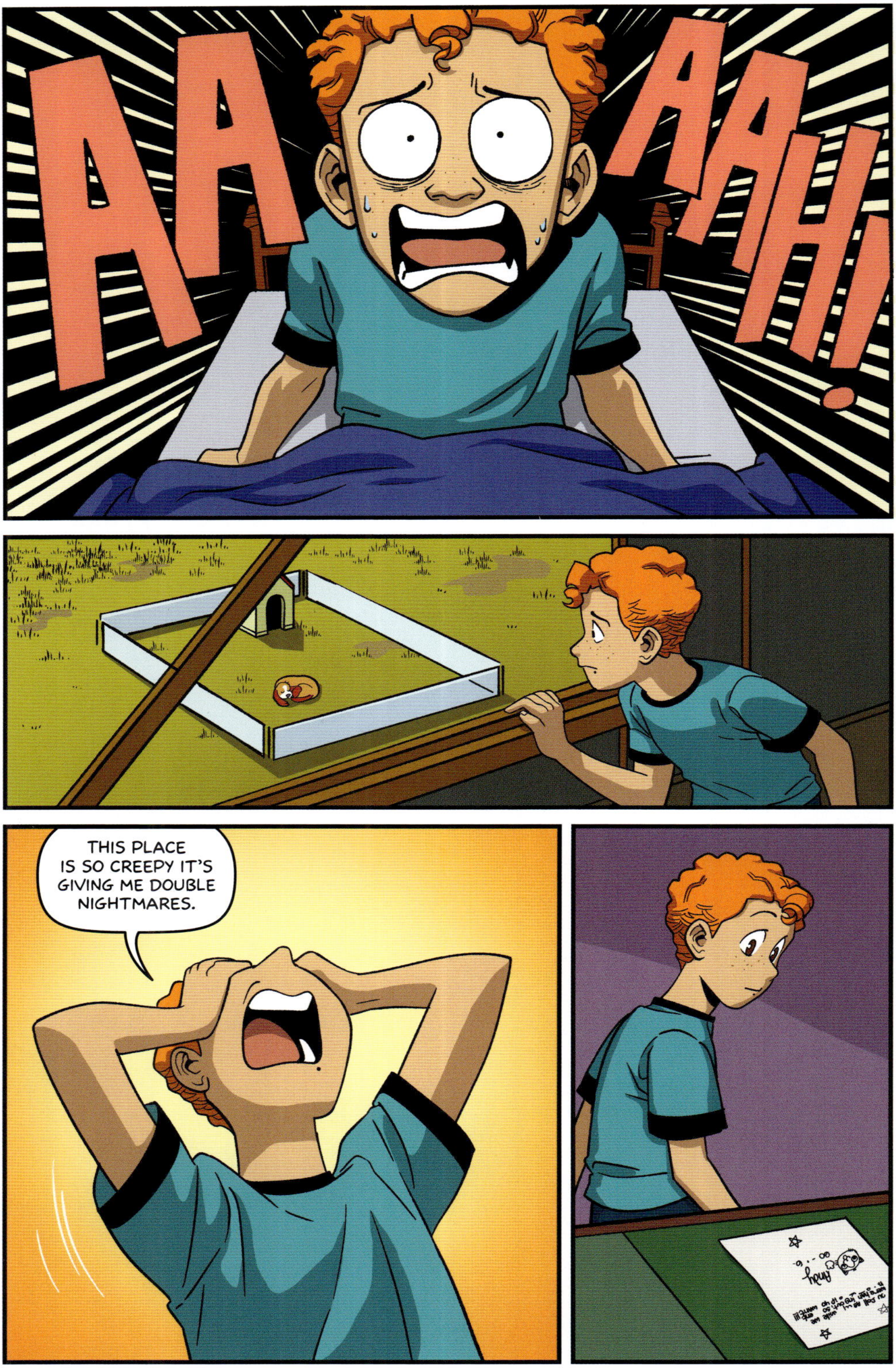
AAAAAH!
THIS PLACE IS SO CREEPY IT'S GIVING ME DOUBLE NIGHTMARES.

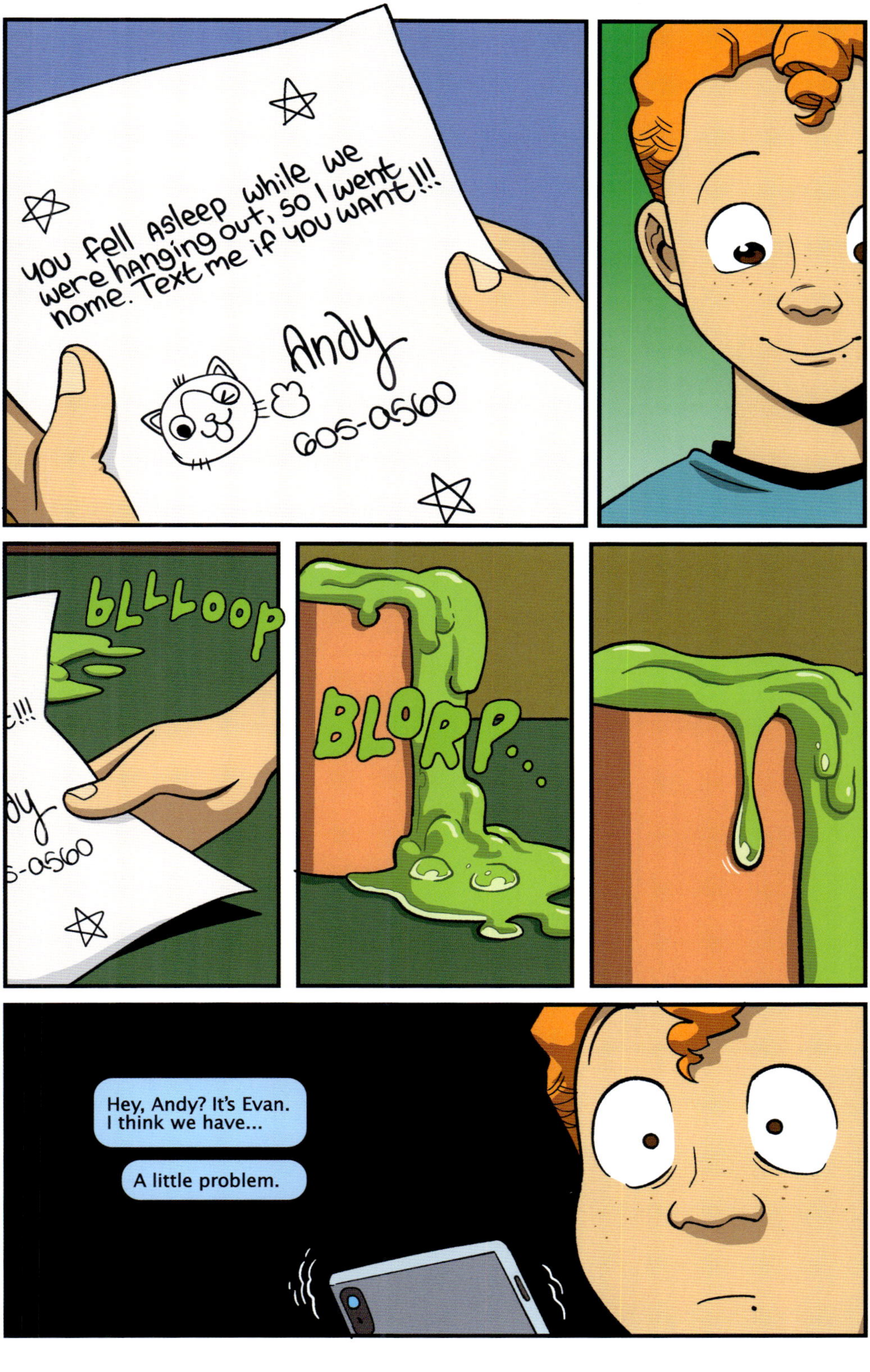
you fell Asleep while we were hanging out, so I went home. Text me if you WANT!!!
Andy
605-0560
bLLLoop
BLORP...
Hey, Andy? It's Evan. I think we have...
A little problem.

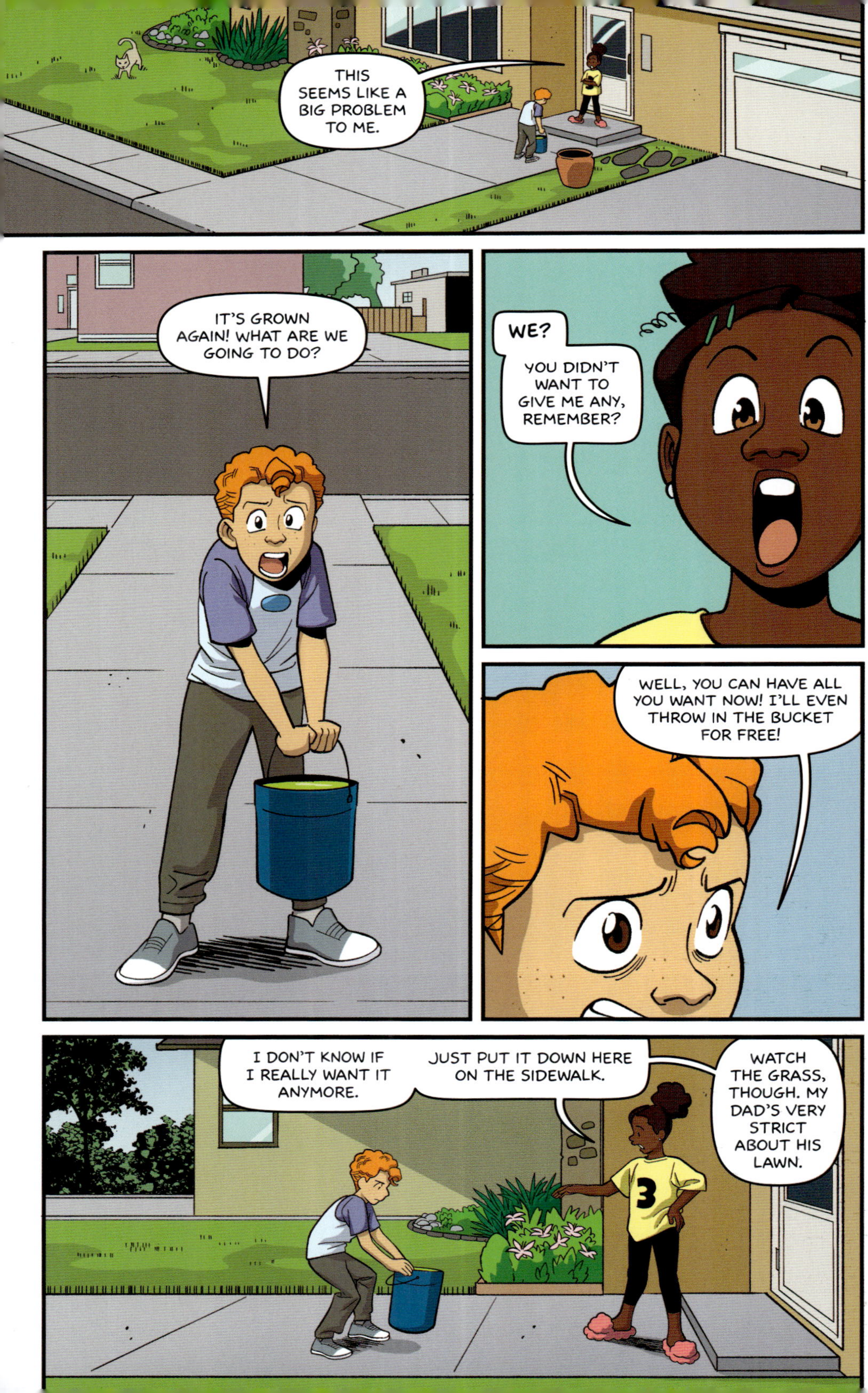
THIS SEEMS LIKE A BIG PROBLEM TO ME.
IT'S GROWN AGAIN! WHAT ARE WE GOING TO DO?
WE?
YOU DIDN'T WANT TO GIVE ME ANY, REMEMBER?
WELL, YOU CAN HAVE ALL YOU WANT NOW! I'LL EVEN THROW IN THE BUCKET FOR FREE!
I DON'T KNOW IF I REALLY WANT IT ANYMORE.
JUST PUT IT DOWN HERE ON THE SIDEWALK.
WATCH THE GRASS, THOUGH. MY DAD'S VERY STRICT ABOUT HIS LAWN.
3

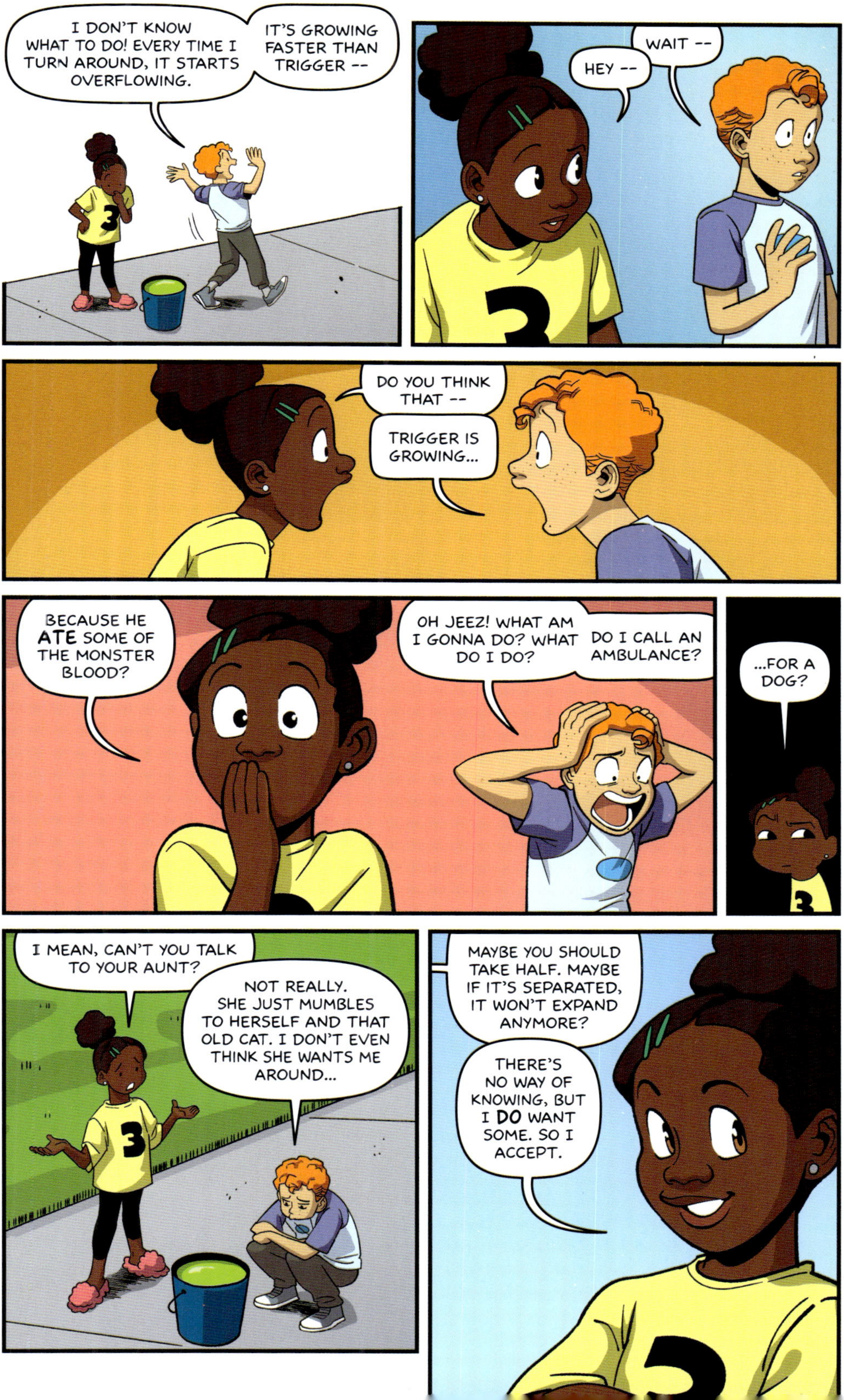
I DON'T KNOW WHAT TO DO! EVERY TIME I TURN AROUND, IT STARTS OVERFLOWING.
IT'S GROWING FASTER THAN TRIGGER --
HEY --
WAIT --
DO YOU THINK THAT --
TRIGGER IS GROWING...
BECAUSE HE ATE SOME OF THE MONSTER BLOOD?
OH JEEZ! WHAT AM I GONNA DO? WHAT DO I DO?
DO I CALL AN AMBULANCE?
...FOR A DOG?
I MEAN, CAN'T YOU TALK TO YOUR AUNT?
NOT REALLY. SHE JUST MUMBLES TO HERSELF AND THAT OLD CAT. I DON'T EVEN THINK SHE WANTS ME AROUND...
MAYBE YOU SHOULD TAKE HALF. MAYBE IF IT'S SEPARATED, IT WON'T EXPAND ANYMORE?
THERE'S NO WAY OF KNOWING, BUT I DO WANT SOME. SO I ACCEPT.

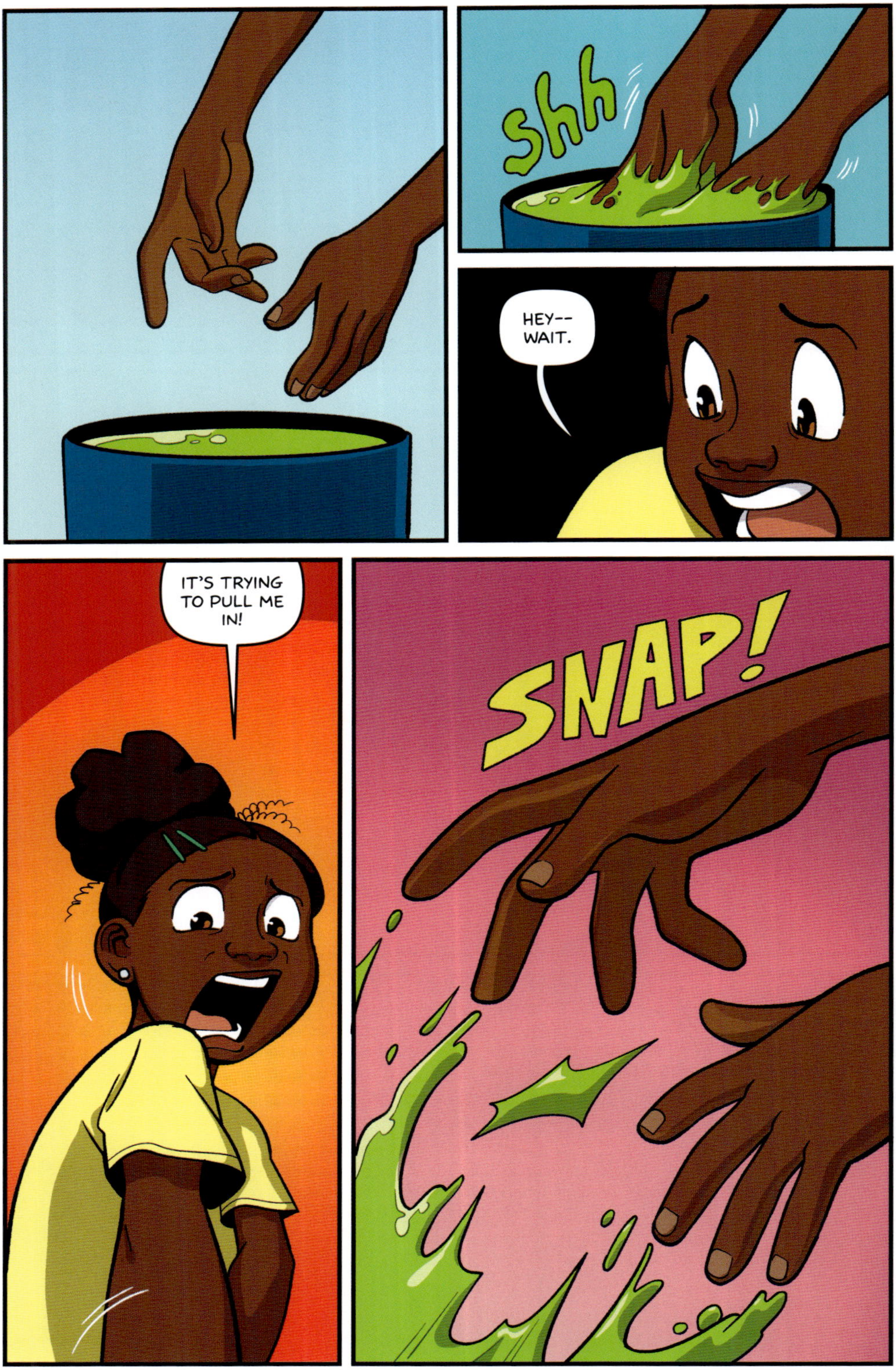
Shh
HEY-- WAIT.
IT'S TRYING TO PULL ME IN!
SNAP!

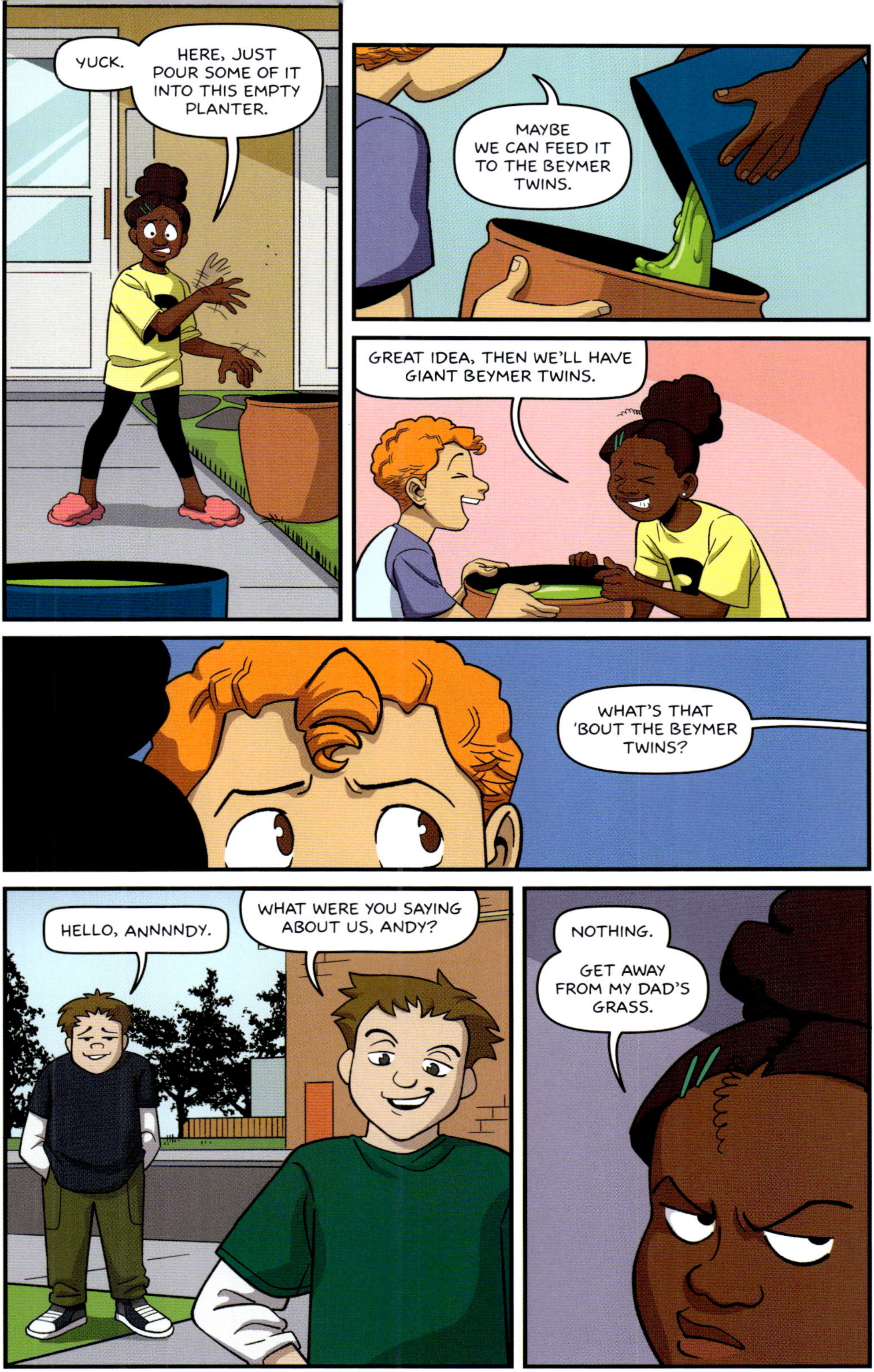
YUCK.
HERE, JUST POUR SOME OF IT INTO THIS EMPTY PLANTER.
MAYBE WE CAN FEED IT TO THE BEYMER TWINS.
GREAT IDEA, THEN WE'LL HAVE GIANT BEYMER TWINS.
WHAT'S THAT 'BOUT THE BEYMER TWINS?
HELLO, ANNNNDY.
WHAT WERE YOU SAYING ABOUT US, ANDY?
NOTHING.
GET AWAY FROM MY DAD'S GRASS.

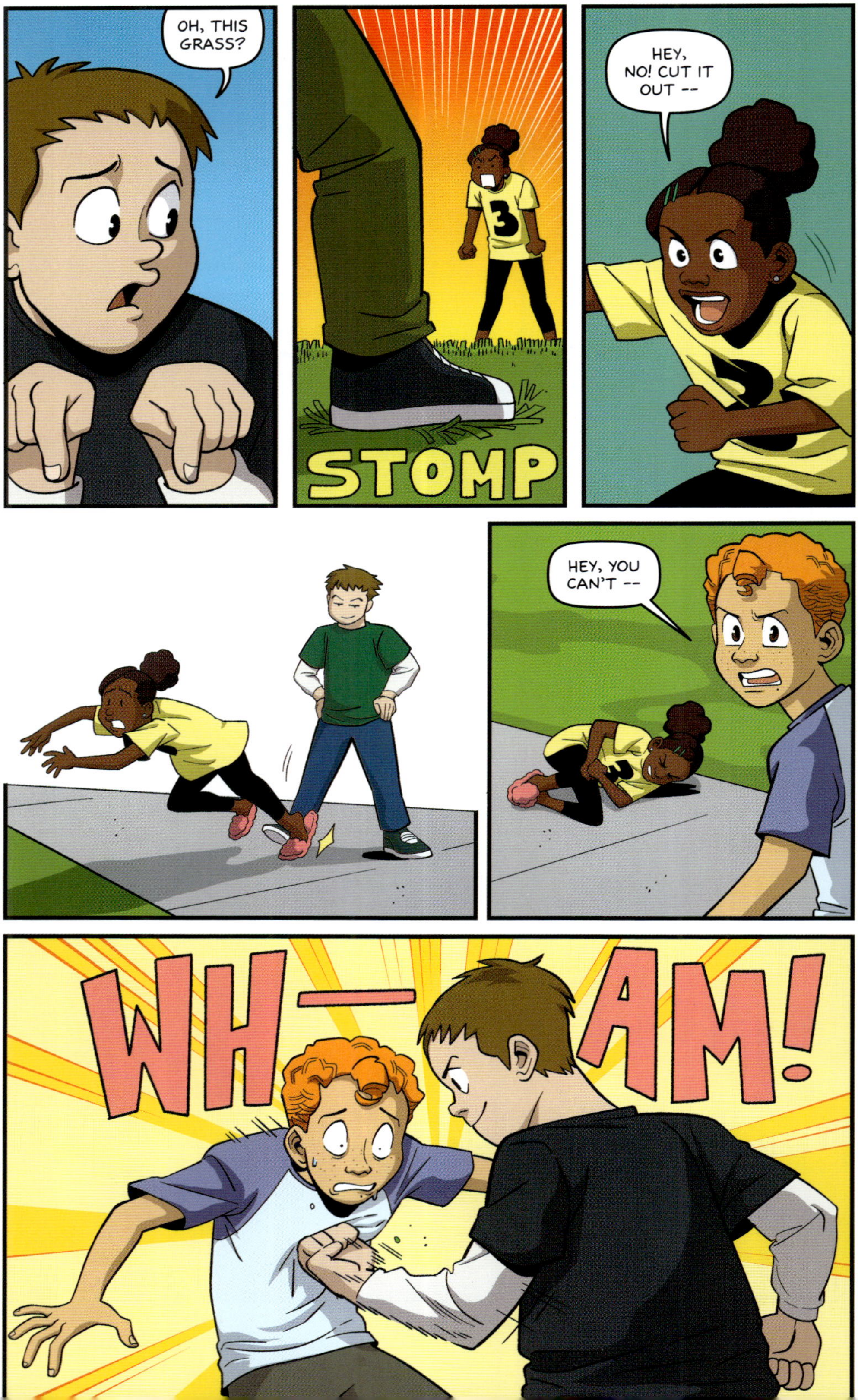
OH, THIS GRASS?
STOMP
HEY, NO! CUT IT OUT --
HEY, YOU CAN'T --
WH—AM!

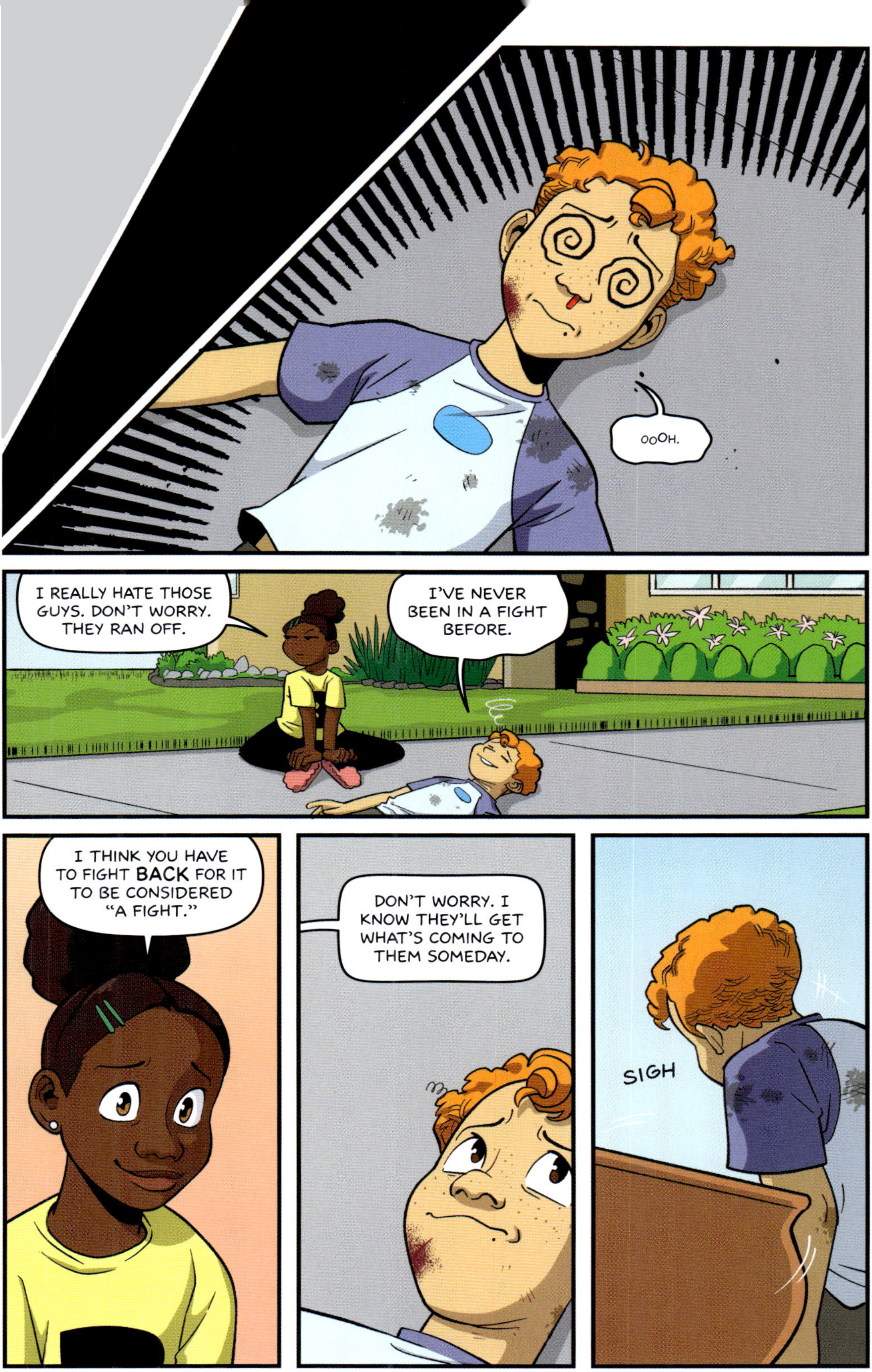
OOOH.
I REALLY HATE THOSE GUYS. DON'T WORRY. THEY RAN OFF.
I'VE NEVER BEEN IN A FIGHT BEFORE.
I THINK YOU HAVE TO FIGHT BACK FOR IT TO BE CONSIDERED "A FIGHT."
DON'T WORRY. I KNOW THEY'LL GET WHAT'S COMING TO THEM SOMEDAY.
SIGH

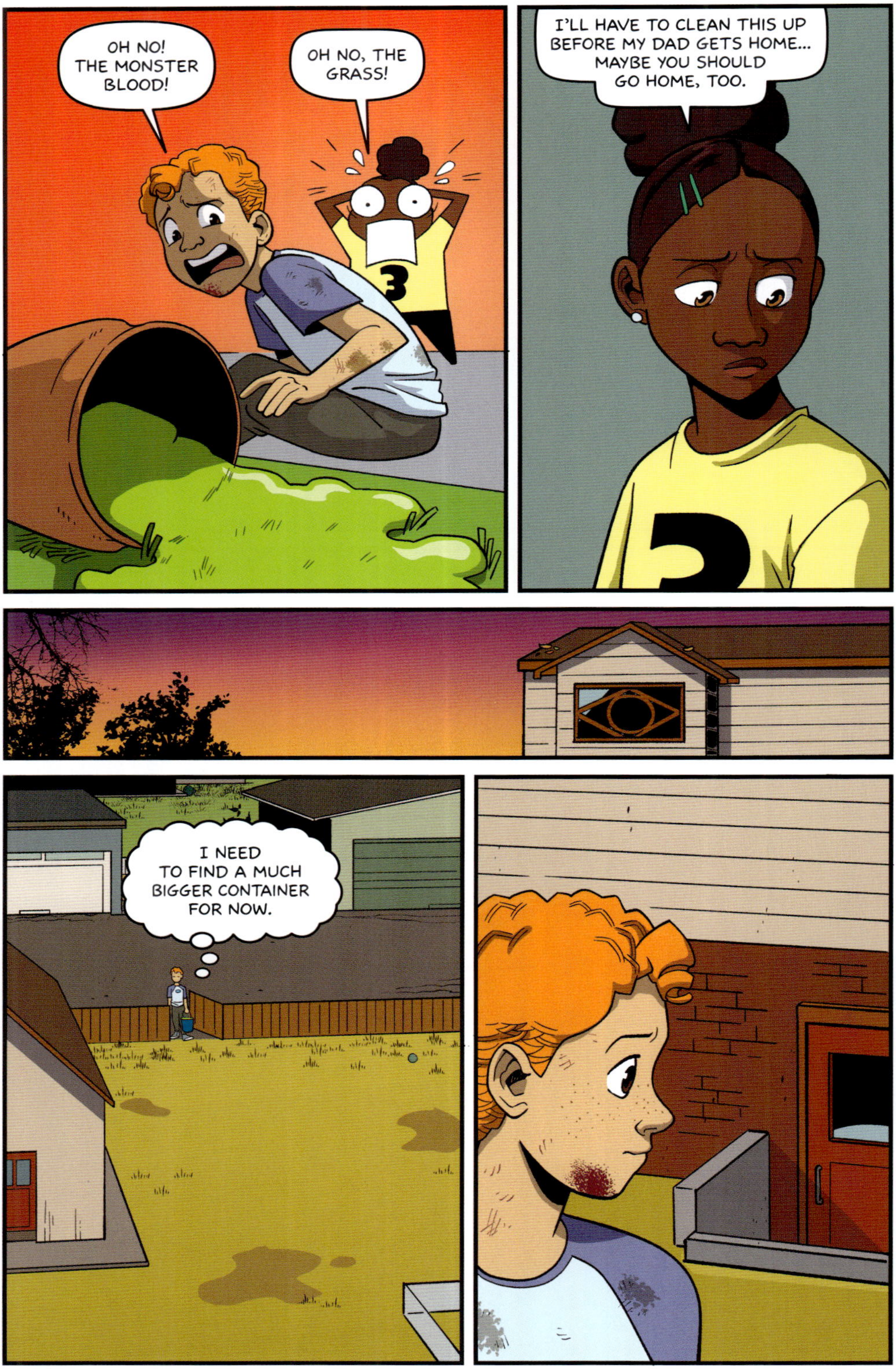
OH NO! THE MONSTER BLOOD!
OH NO, THE GRASS!
I'LL HAVE TO CLEAN THIS UP BEFORE MY DAD GETS HOME... MAYBE YOU SHOULD GO HOME, TOO.
I NEED TO FIND A MUCH BIGGER CONTAINER FOR NOW.

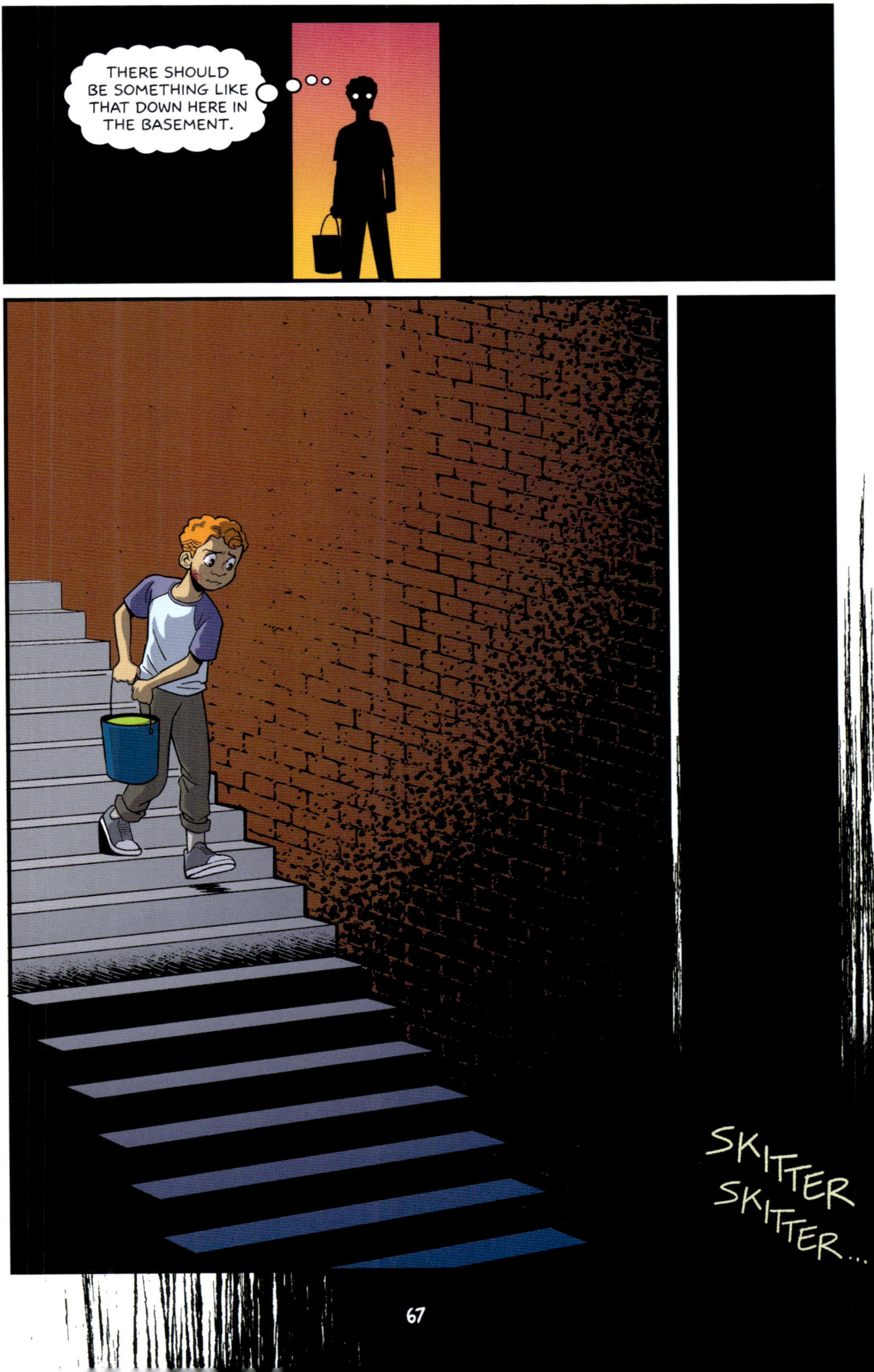
THERE SHOULD BE SOMETHING LIKE THAT DOWN HERE IN THE BASEMENT.
SKITTER SKITTER...

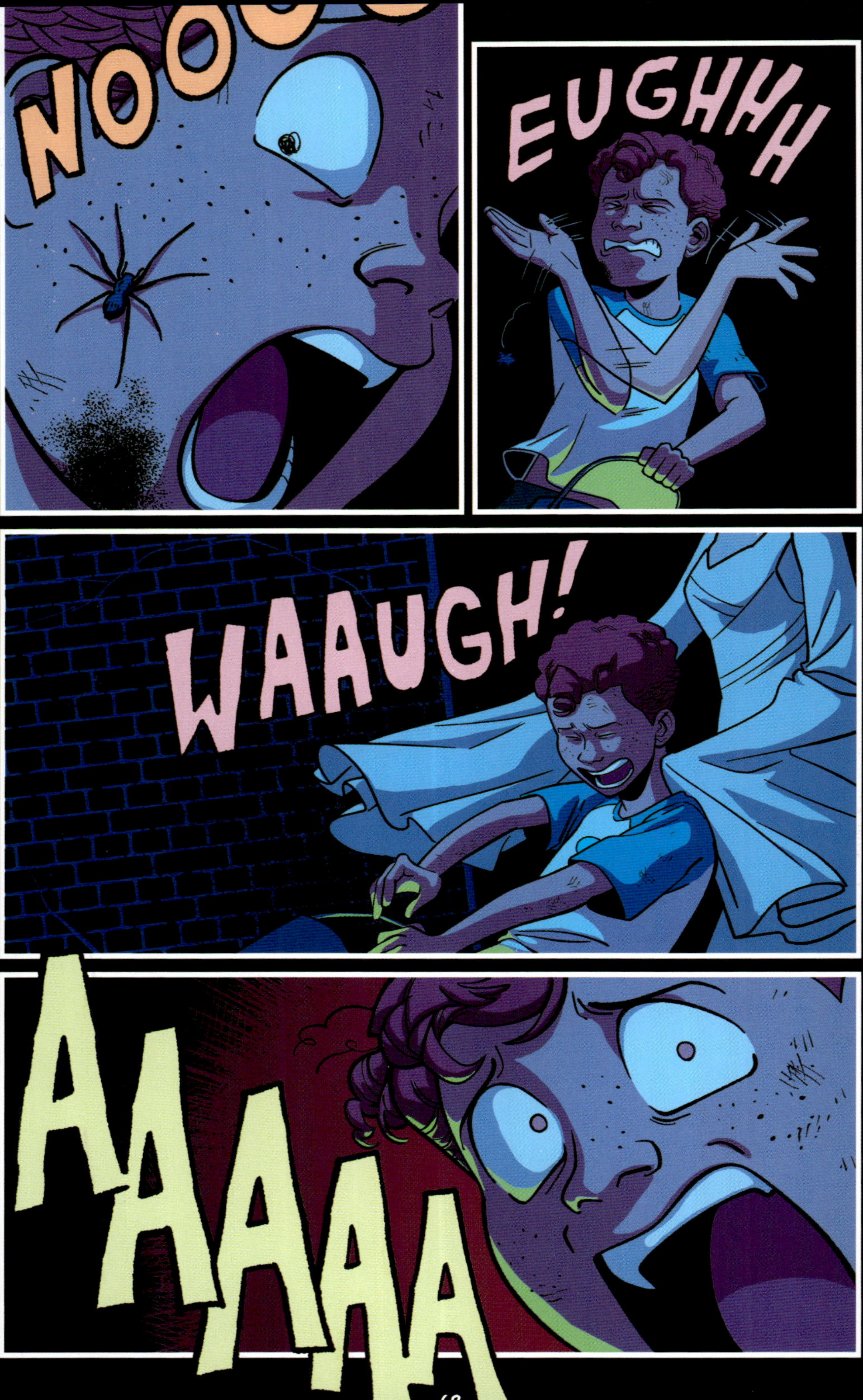
NOOO
EUGHHH
WAAUGH!
AAAAAA

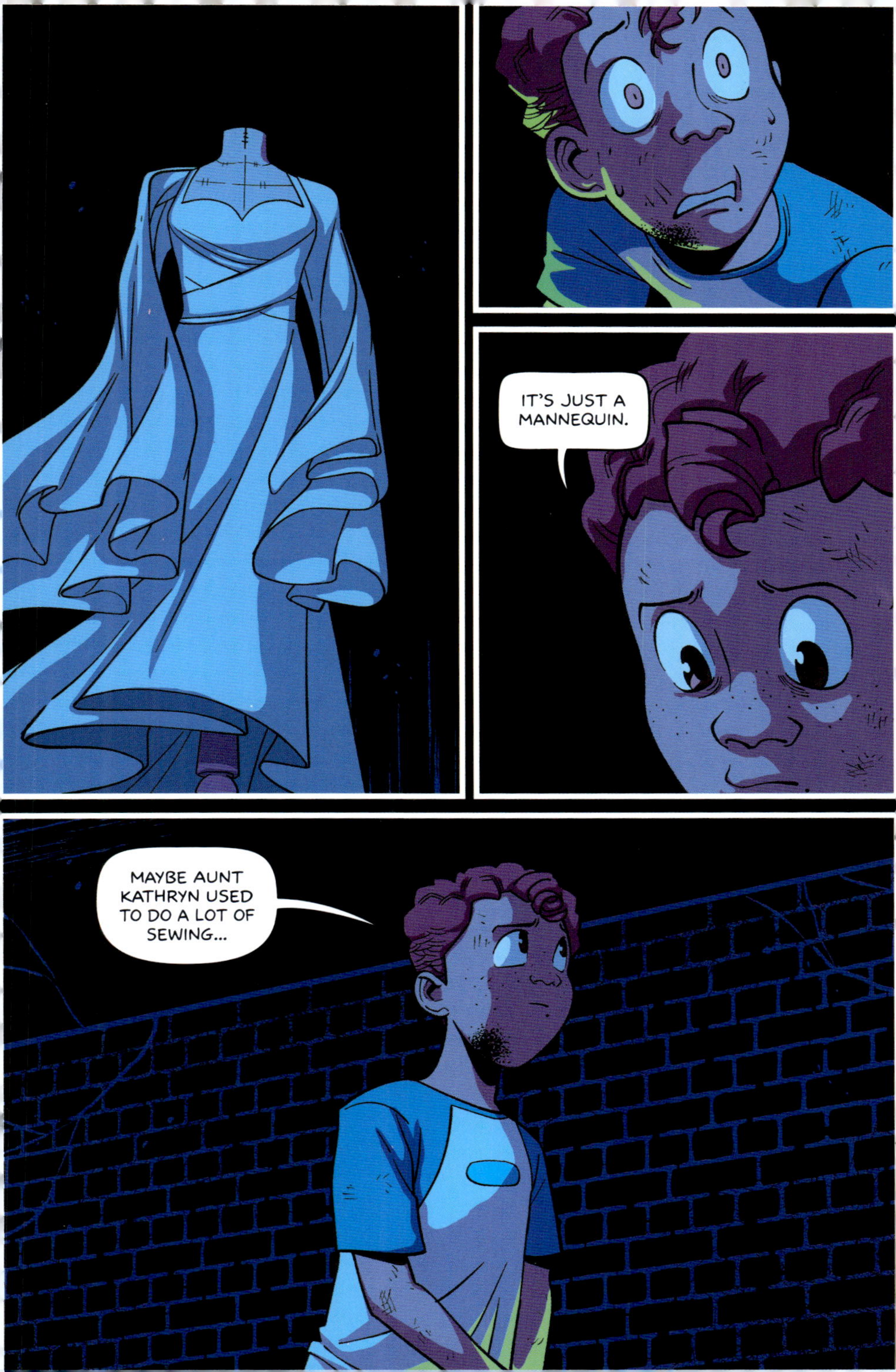
IT'S JUST A MANNEQUIN.
MAYBE AUNT KATHRYN USED TO DO A LOT OF SEWING...

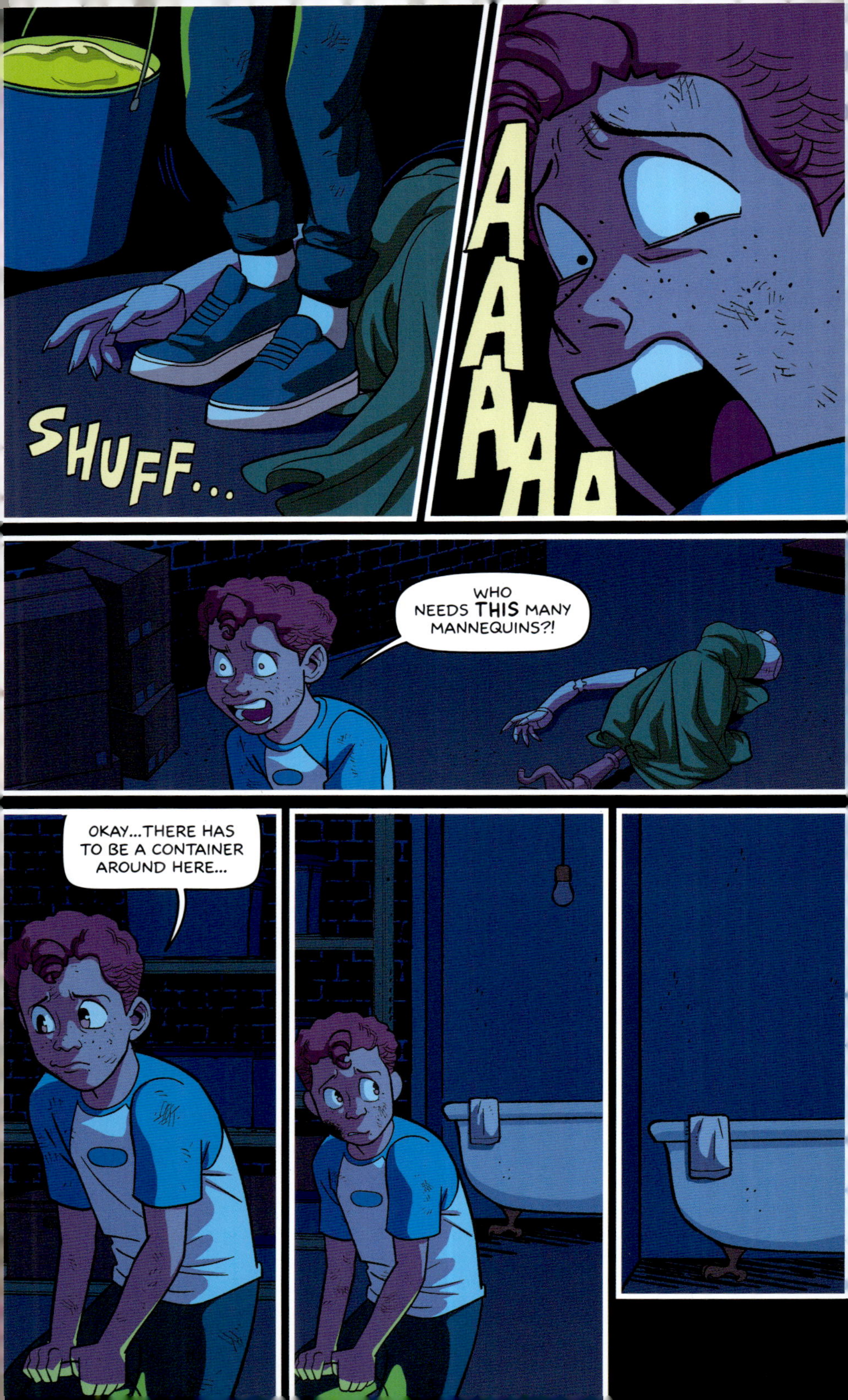
SHUFF...
AAAAA
WHO NEEDS THIS MANY MANNEQUINS?!
OKAY...THERE HAS TO BE A CONTAINER AROUND HERE...

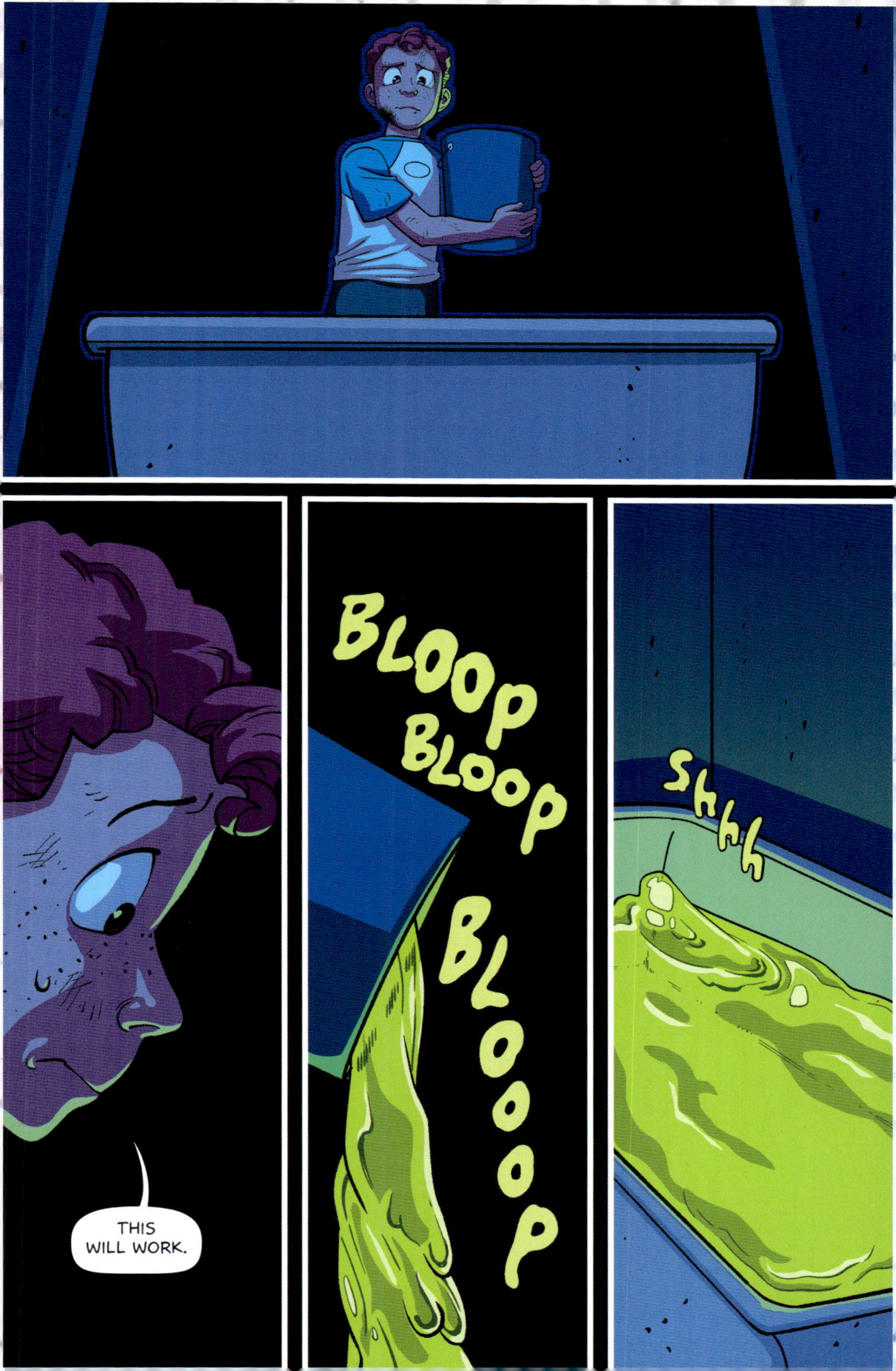
THIS WILL WORK.
BLOOP
BLOOP
BLOOOOP
Shhh

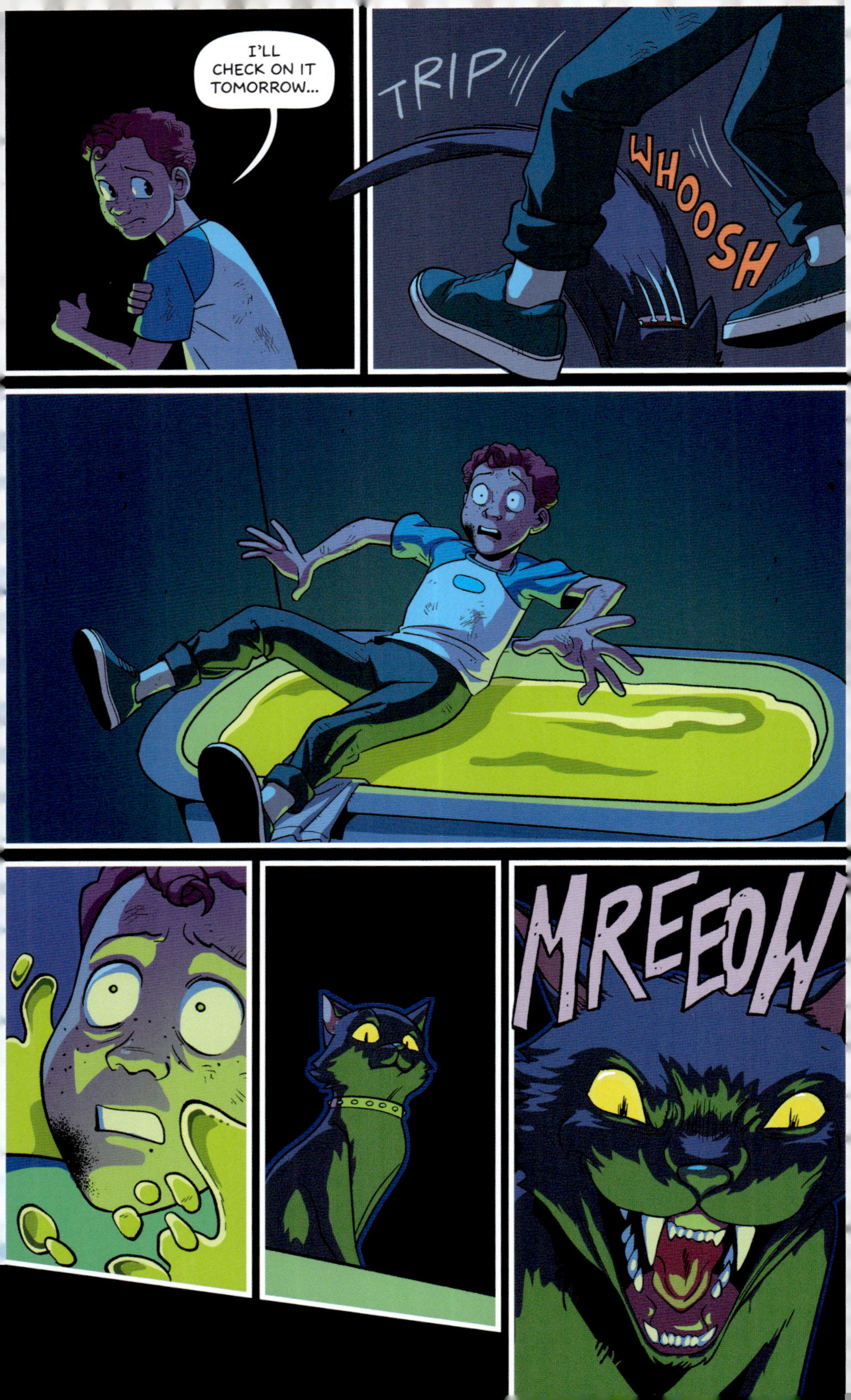
I'LL CHECK ON IT TOMORROW...
TRIP
WHOOSH
MREEOW

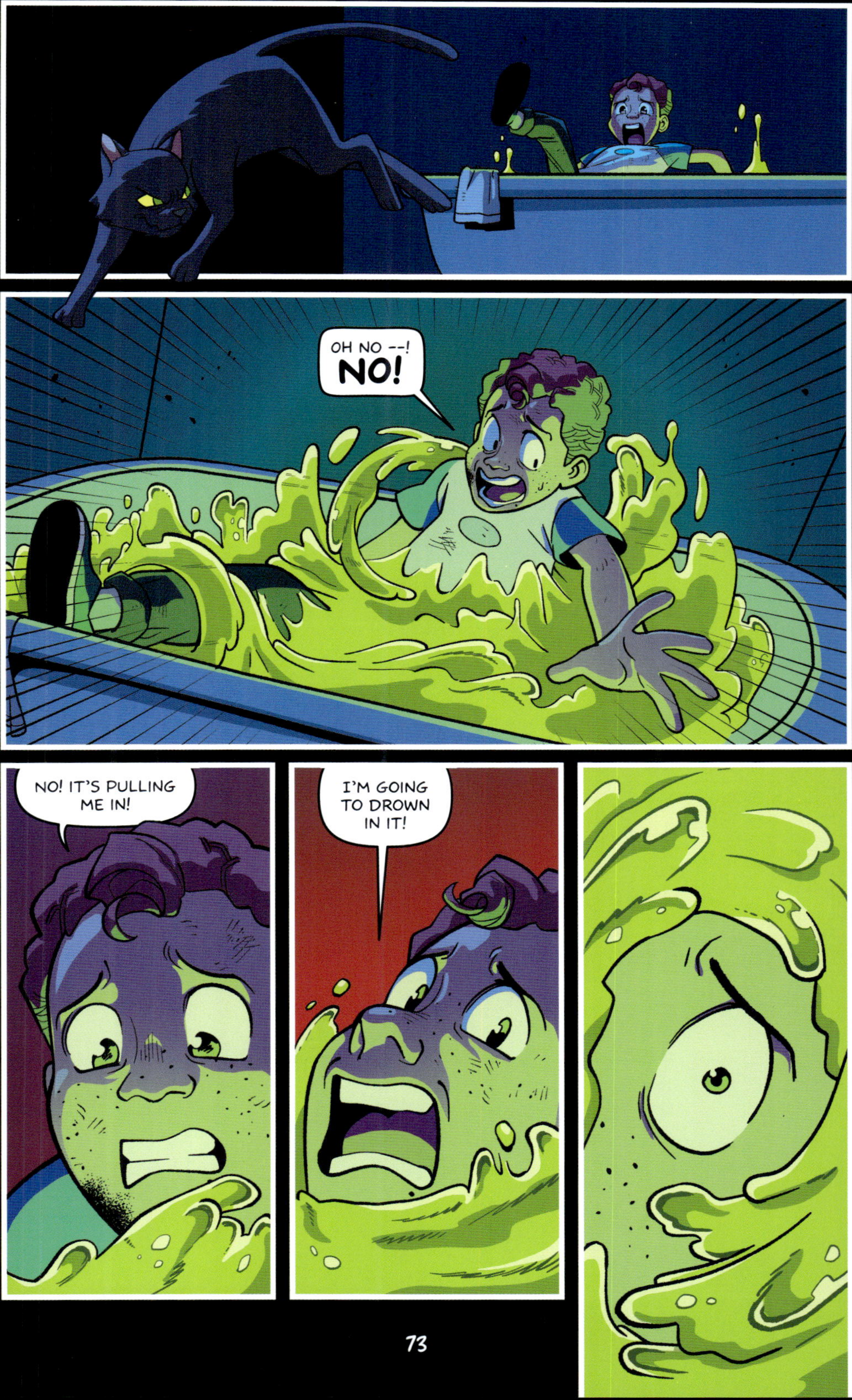
OH NO --!
NO!
NO! IT'S PULLING ME IN!
I'M GOING TO DROWN IN IT!

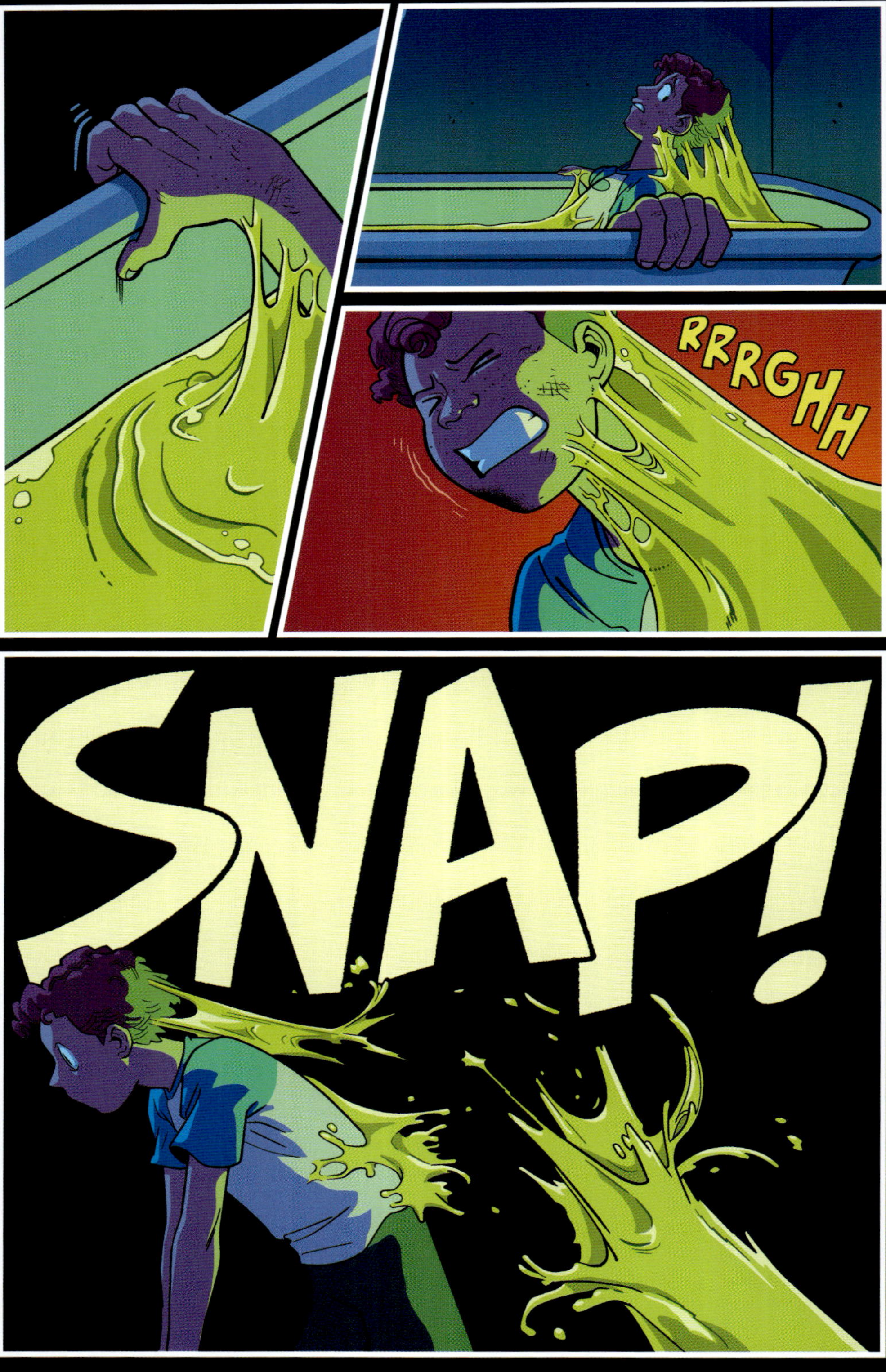
RRRGHH
SNAP!

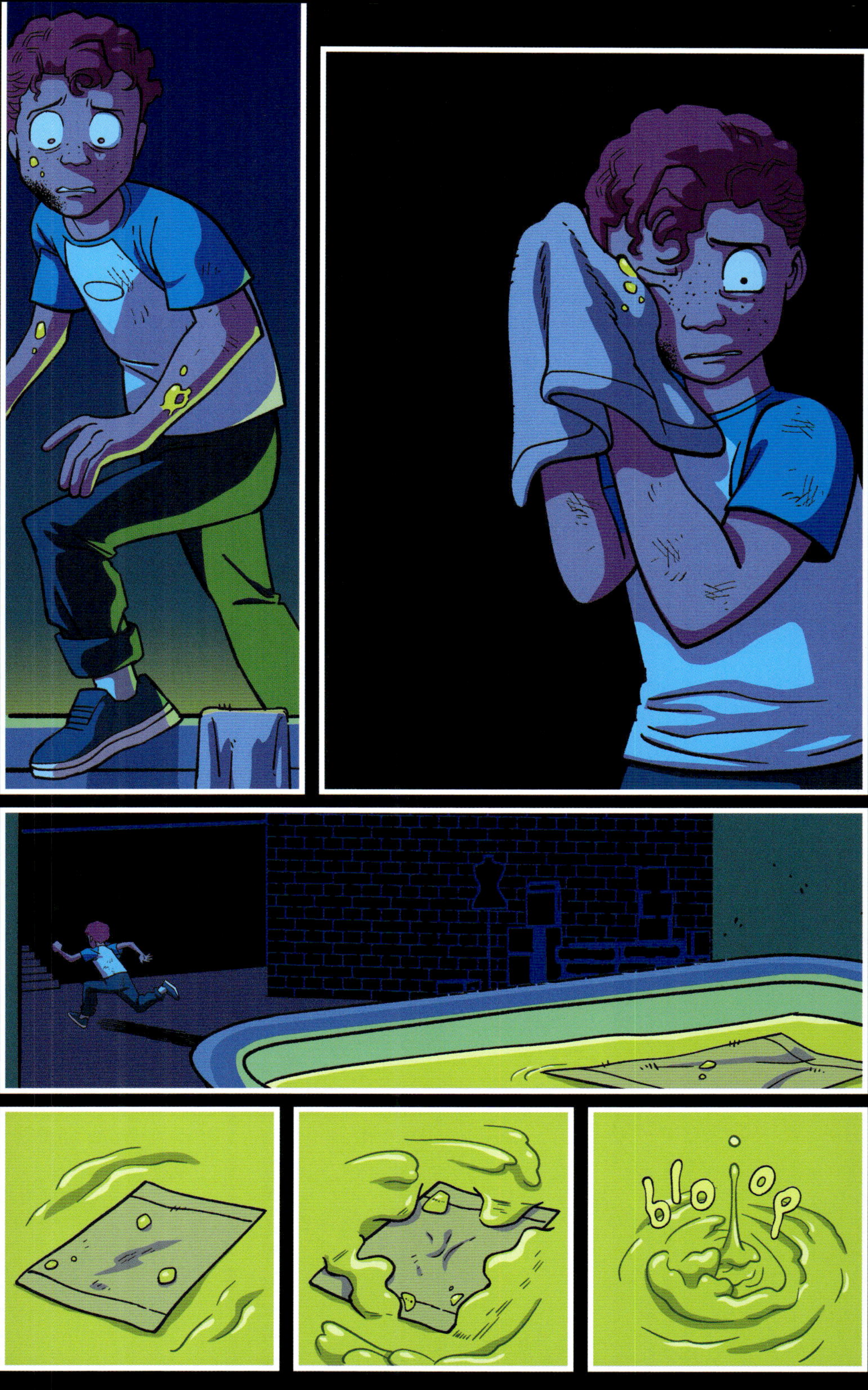
bloop

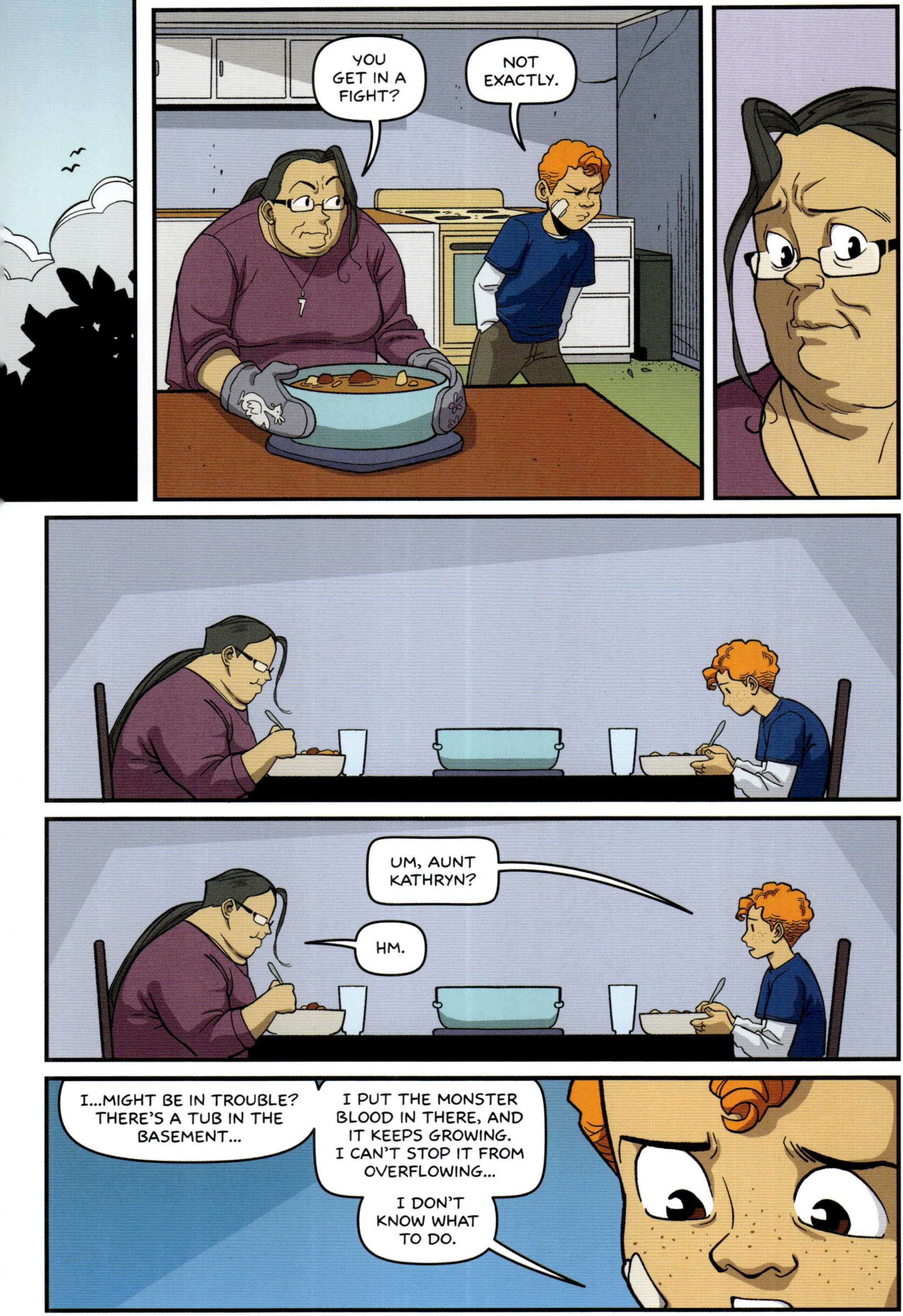
YOU GET IN A FIGHT?
NOT EXACTLY.
UM, AUNT KATHRYN?
HM.
I...MIGHT BE IN TROUBLE? THERE'S A TUB IN THE BASEMENT...
I PUT THE MONSTER BLOOD IN THERE, AND IT KEEPS GROWING. I CAN'T STOP IT FROM OVERFLOWING...
I DON'T KNOW WHAT TO DO.

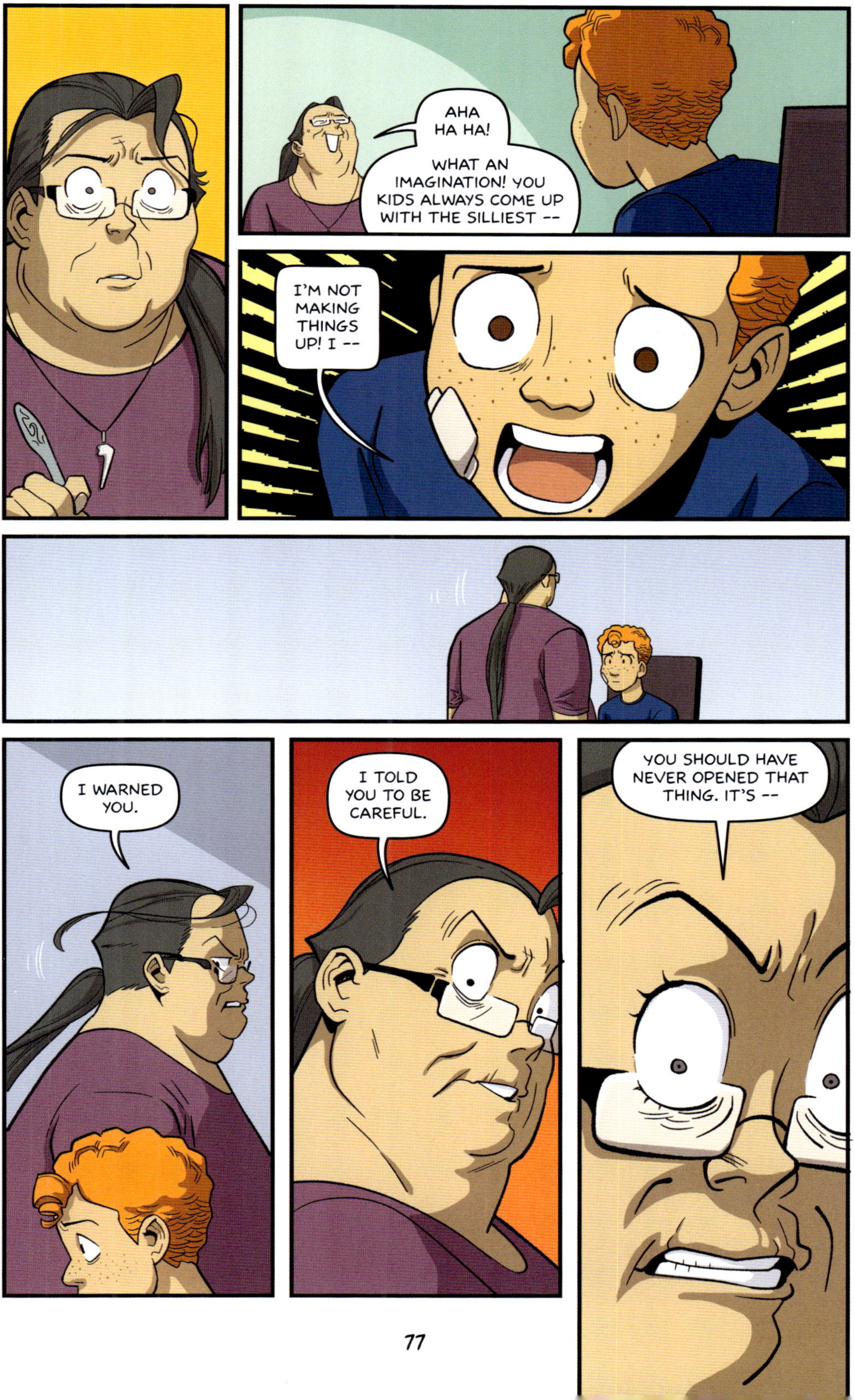
AHA HA HA!
WHAT AN IMAGINATION! YOU KIDS ALWAYS COME UP WITH THE SILLIEST --
I'M NOT MAKING THINGS UP! I --
I WARNED YOU.
I TOLD YOU TO BE CAREFUL.
YOU SHOULD HAVE NEVER OPENED THAT THING. IT'S --

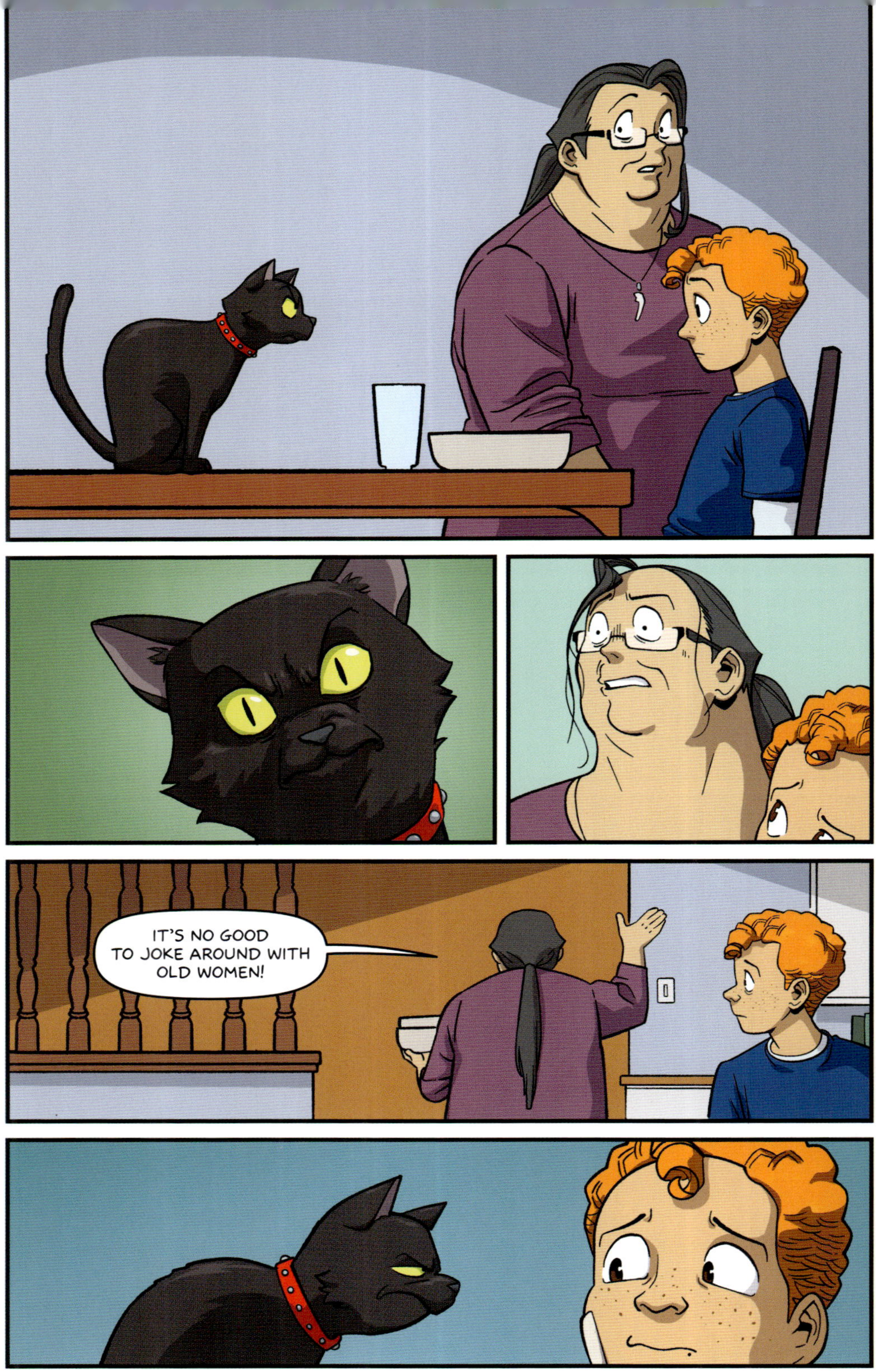
IT'S NO GOOD
TO JOKE AROUND WITH
OLD WOMEN!

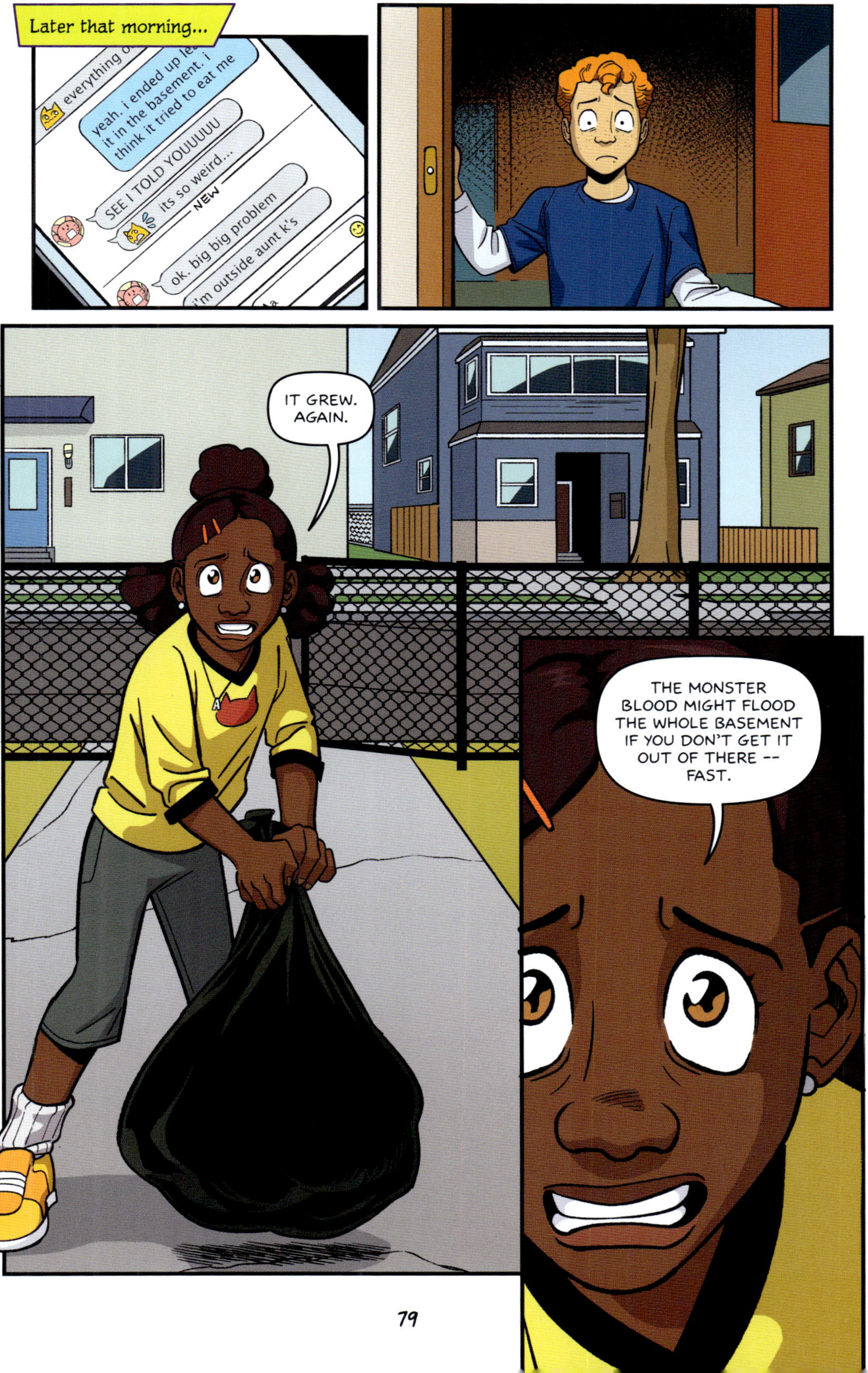
Later that morning...
yeah. i ended up le
it in the basement. i
think it tried to eat me
SEE I TOLD YOUUUUU
its so weird...
NEW
ok. big big problem
i'm outside aunt k's
IT GREW. AGAIN.
THE MONSTER BLOOD MIGHT FLOOD THE WHOLE BASEMENT IF YOU DON'T GET IT OUT OF THERE -- FAST.

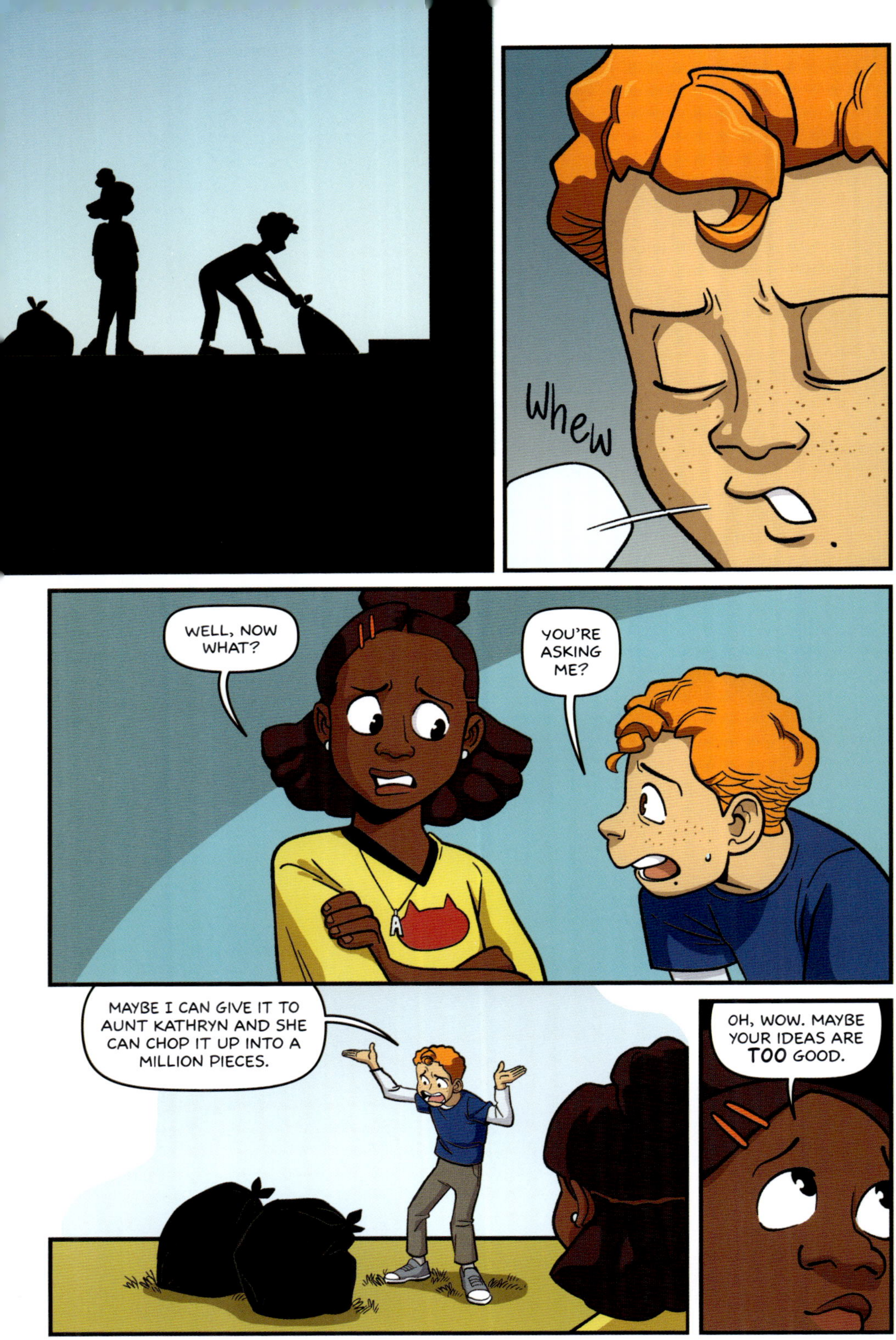
Whew
WELL, NOW WHAT?
YOU'RE ASKING ME?
MAYBE I CAN GIVE IT TO AUNT KATHRYN AND SHE CAN CHOP IT UP INTO A MILLION PIECES.
OH, WOW. MAYBE YOUR IDEAS ARE **TOO** GOOD.

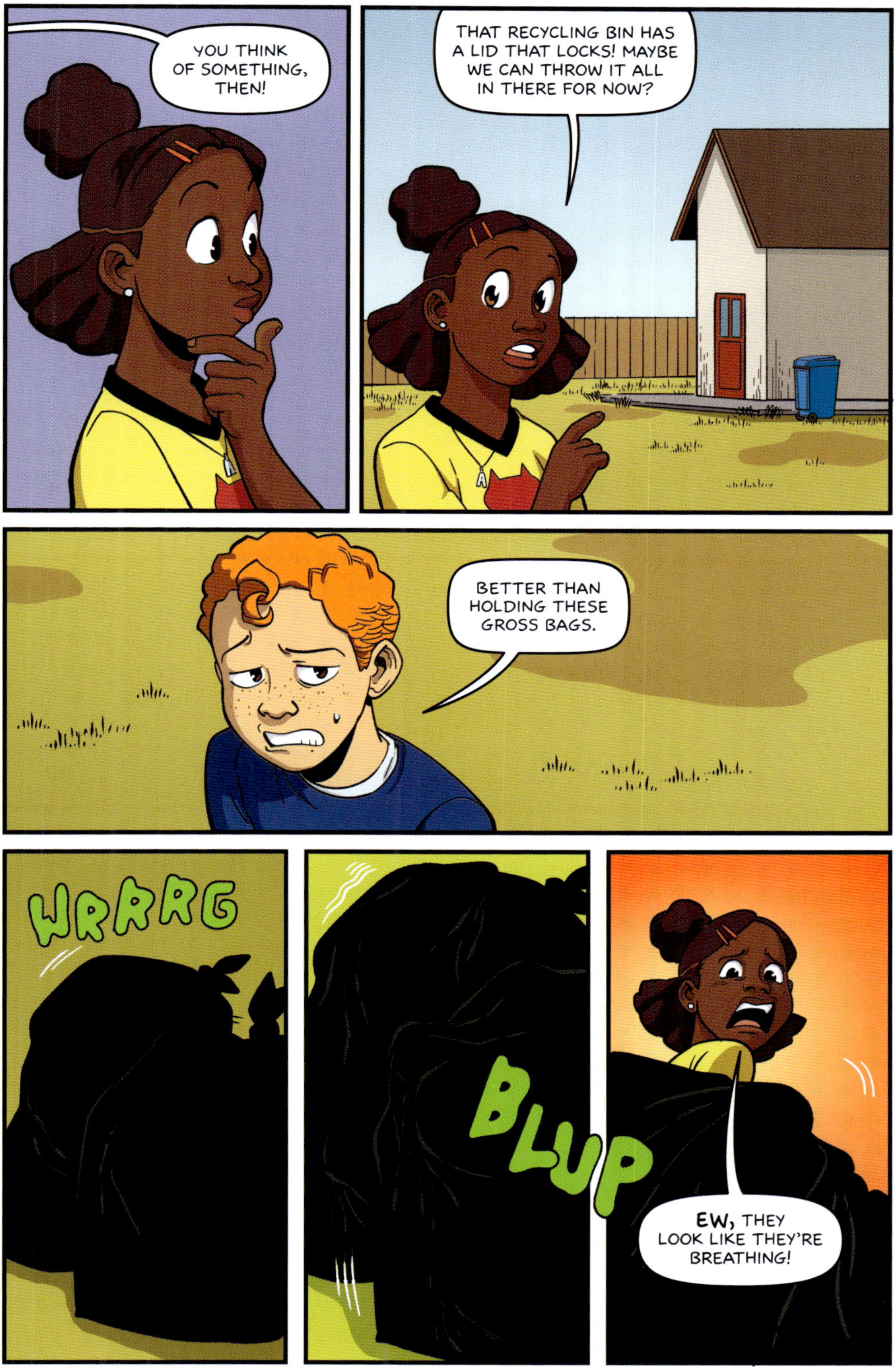
YOU THINK OF SOMETHING, THEN!
THAT RECYCLING BIN HAS A LID THAT LOCKS! MAYBE WE CAN THROW IT ALL IN THERE FOR NOW?
BETTER THAN HOLDING THESE GROSS BAGS.
WRRRG
BLUP
EW, THEY LOOK LIKE THEY'RE BREATHING!

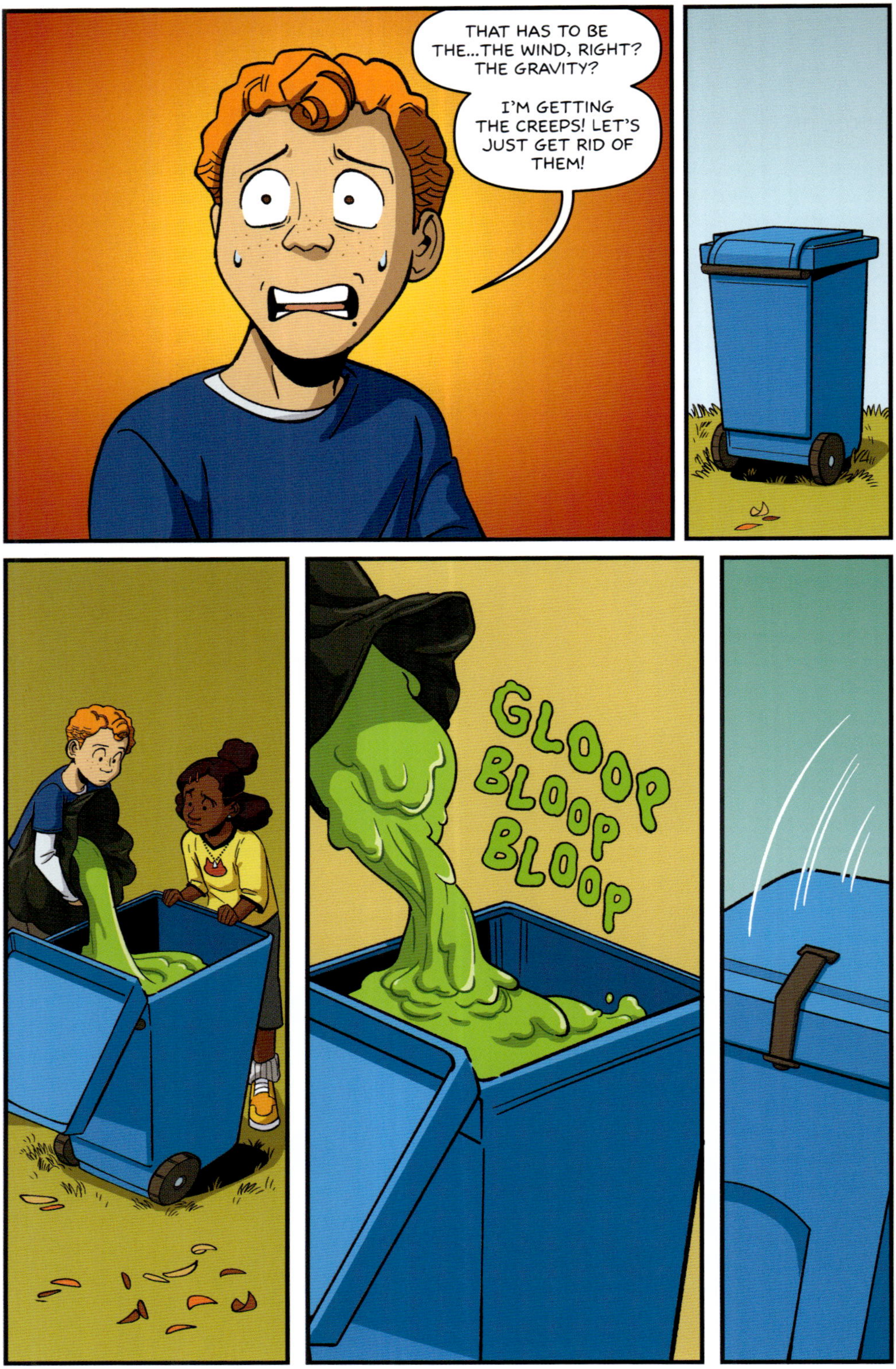
THAT HAS TO BE THE...THE WIND, RIGHT? THE GRAVITY?
I'M GETTING THE CREEPS! LET'S JUST GET RID OF THEM!
GLOOP BLOOP BLOOP

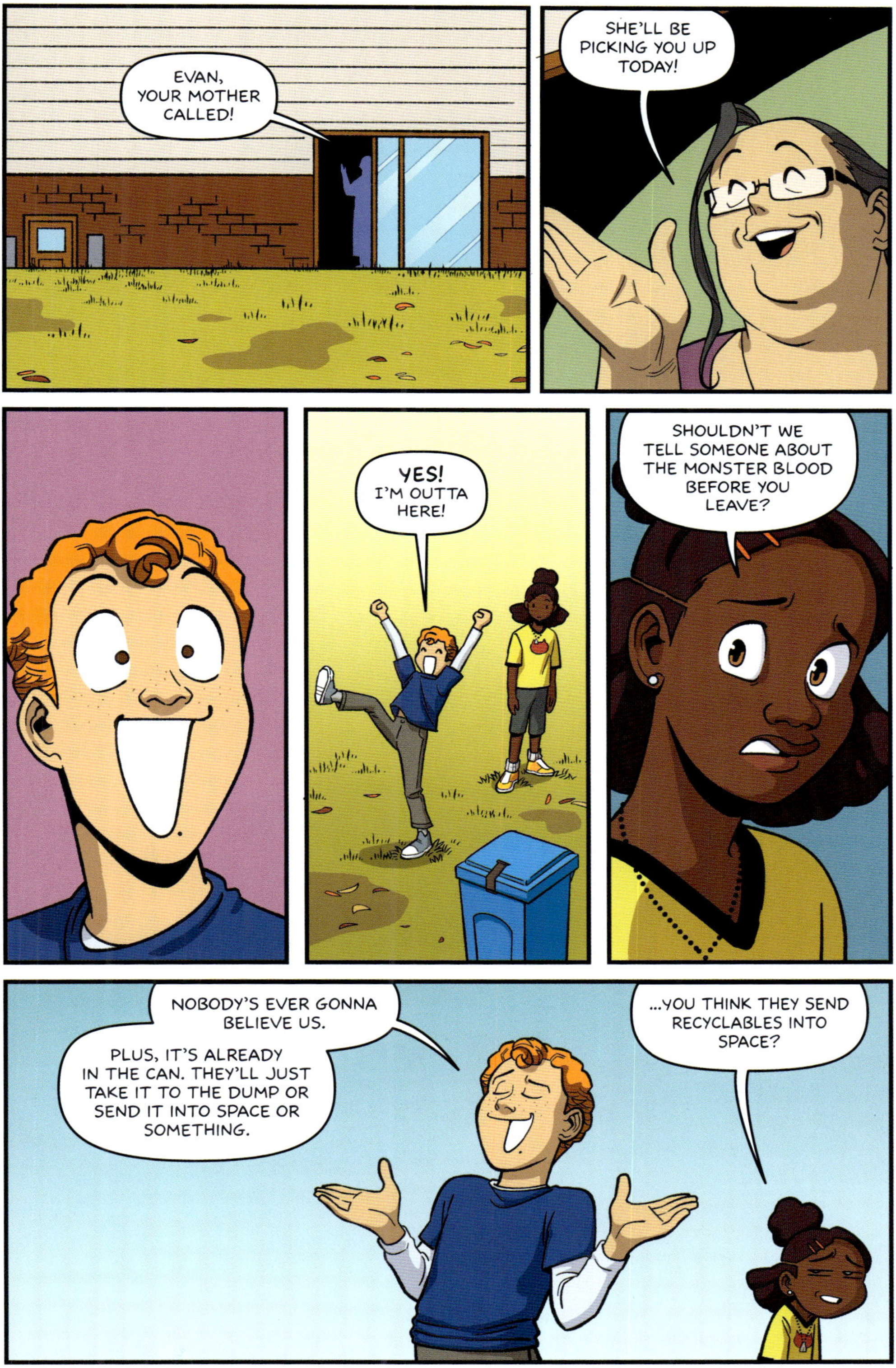
EVAN, YOUR MOTHER CALLED!
SHE'LL BE PICKING YOU UP TODAY!
YES! I'M OUTTA HERE!
SHOULDN'T WE TELL SOMEONE ABOUT THE MONSTER BLOOD BEFORE YOU LEAVE?
NOBODY'S EVER GONNA BELIEVE US.
PLUS, IT'S ALREADY IN THE CAN. THEY'LL JUST TAKE IT TO THE DUMP OR SEND IT INTO SPACE OR SOMETHING.
...YOU THINK THEY SEND RECYCLABLES INTO SPACE?

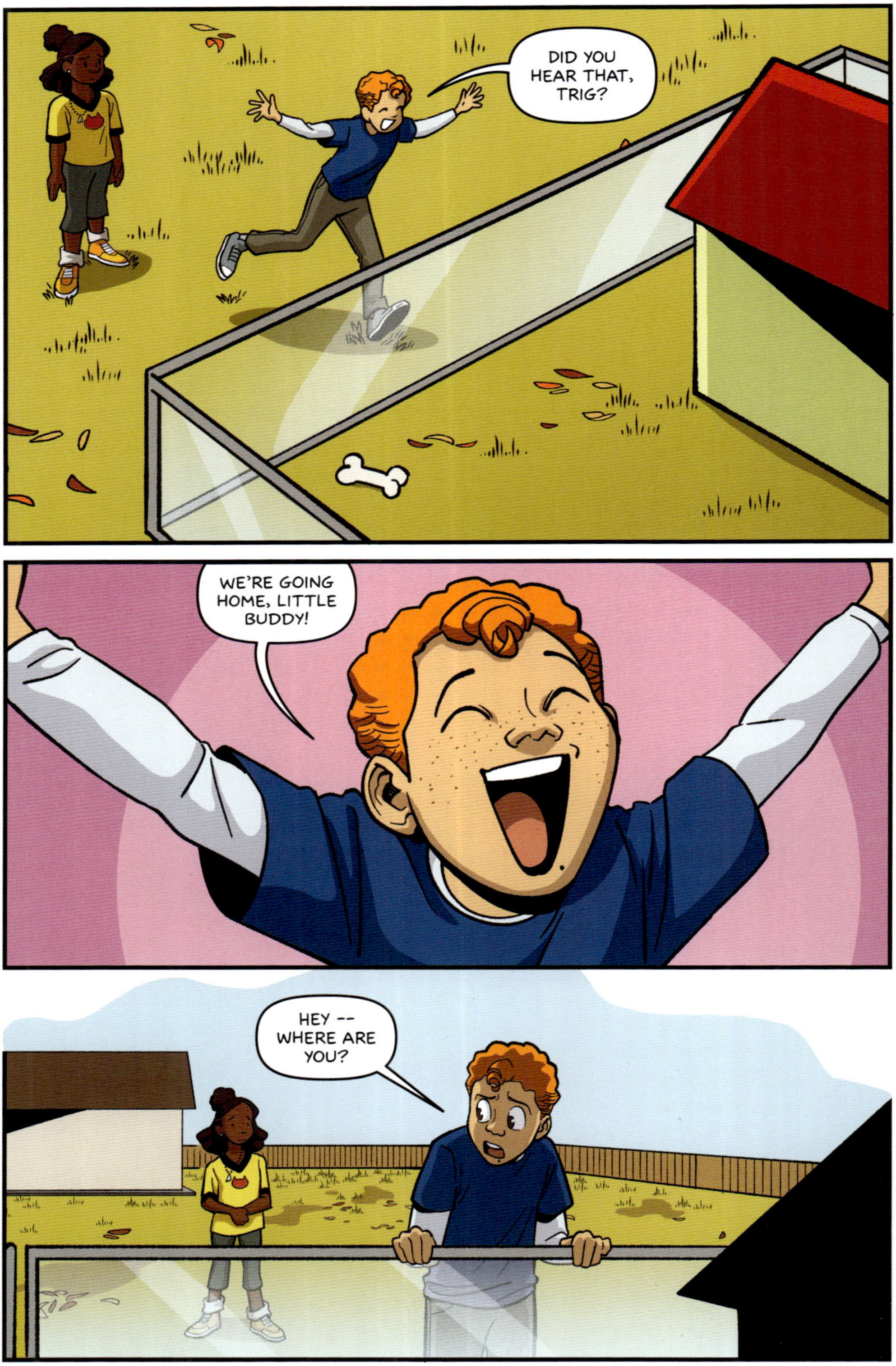
DID YOU HEAR THAT, TRIG?
WE'RE GOING HOME, LITTLE BUDDY!
HEY -- WHERE ARE YOU?

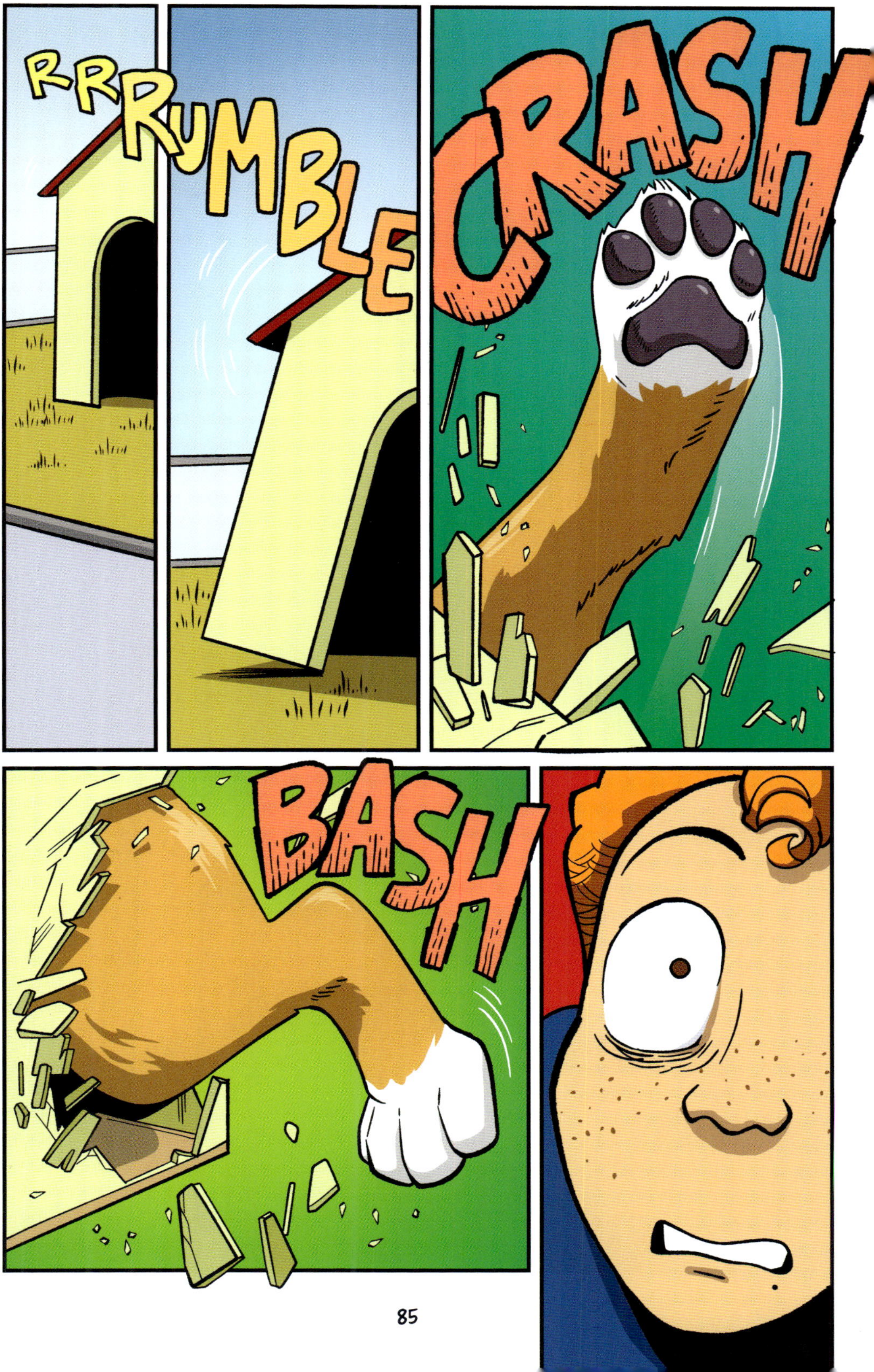
RRRUMBLE
CRASH
BASH

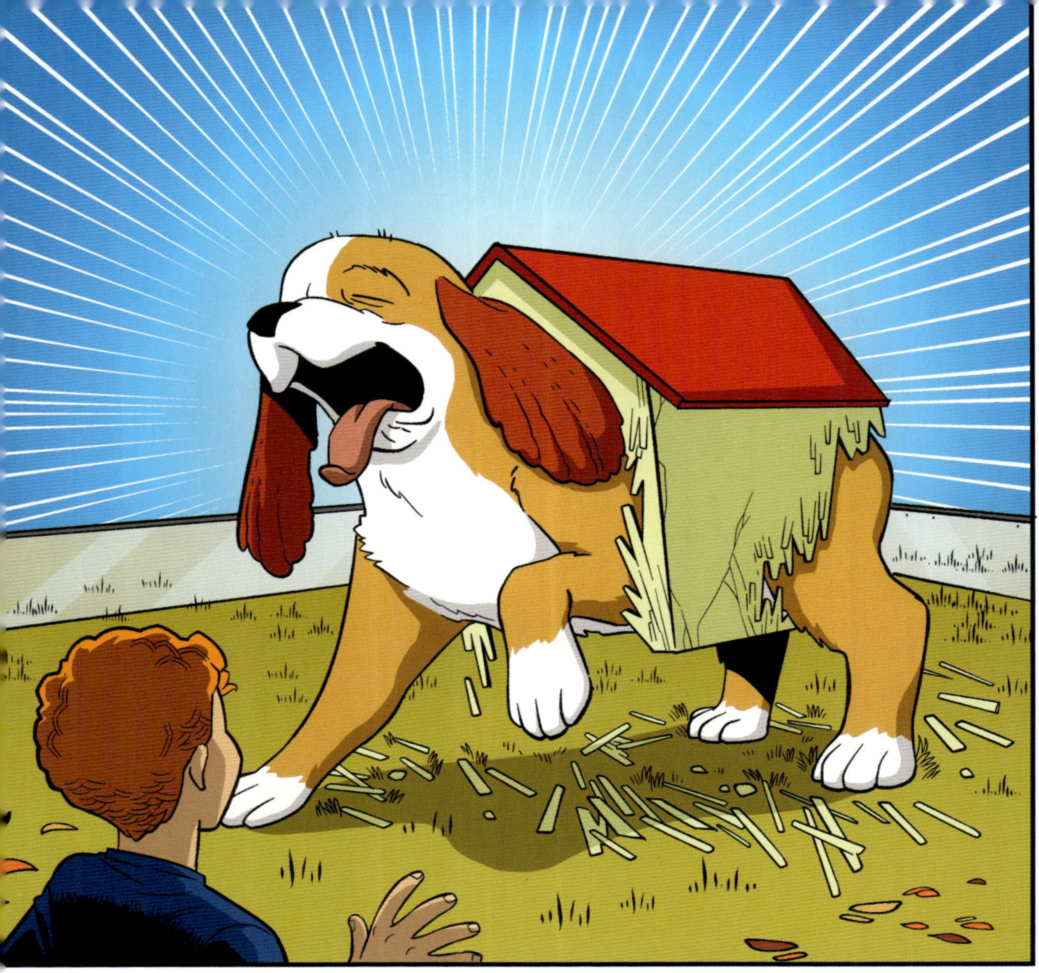

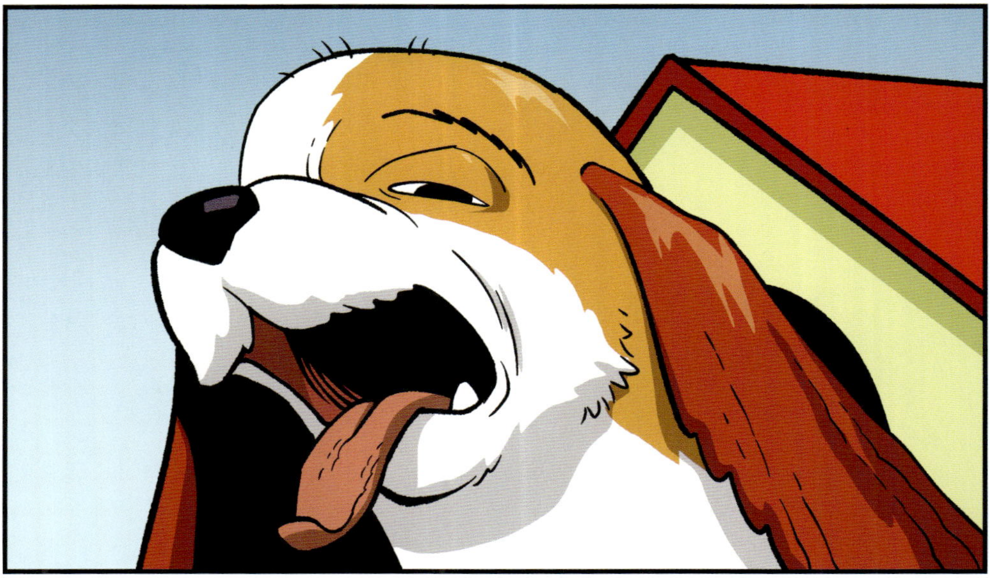

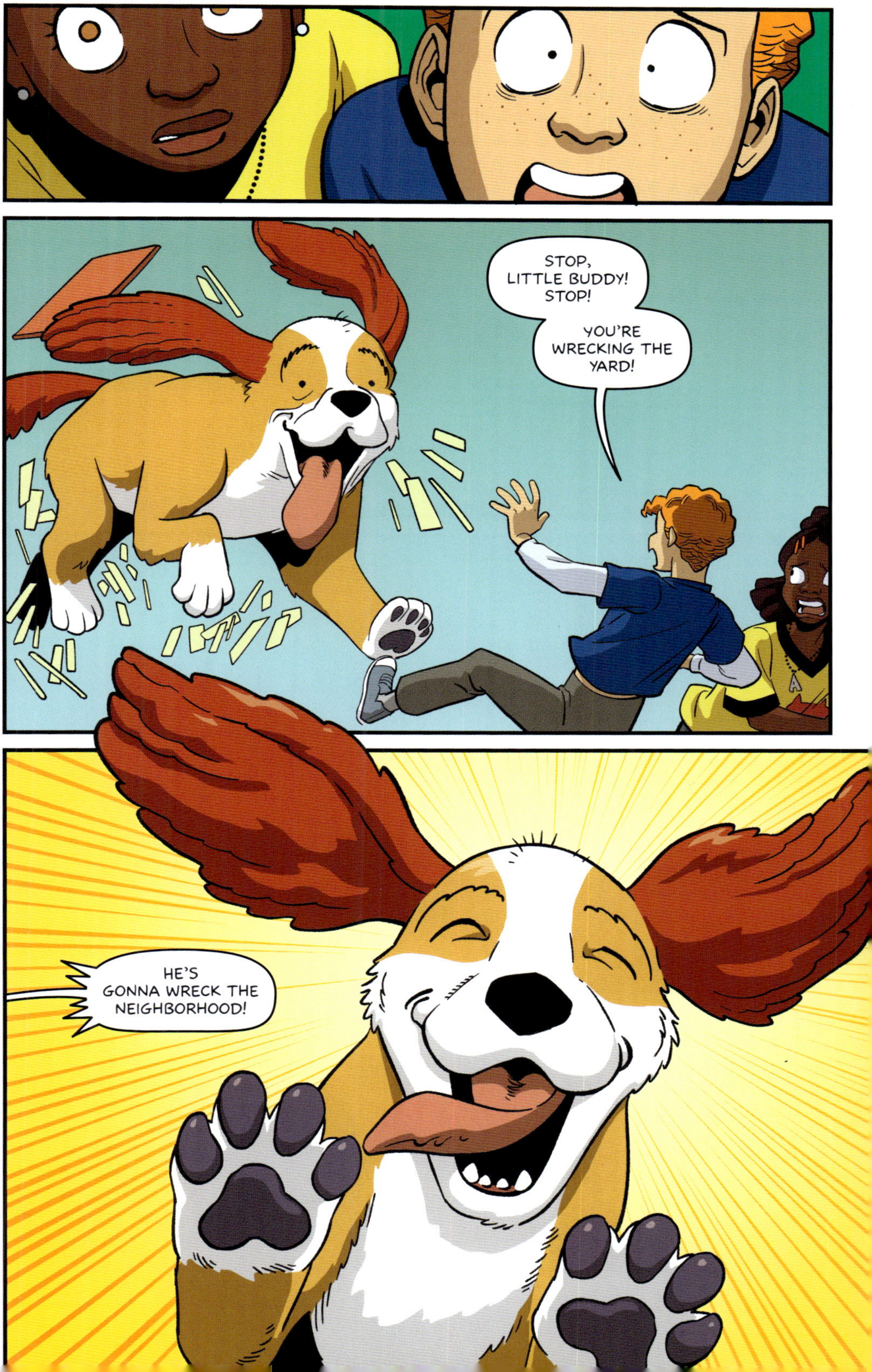
STOP, LITTLE BUDDY! STOP!
YOU'RE WRECKING THE YARD!
HE'S GONNA WRECK THE NEIGHBORHOOD!

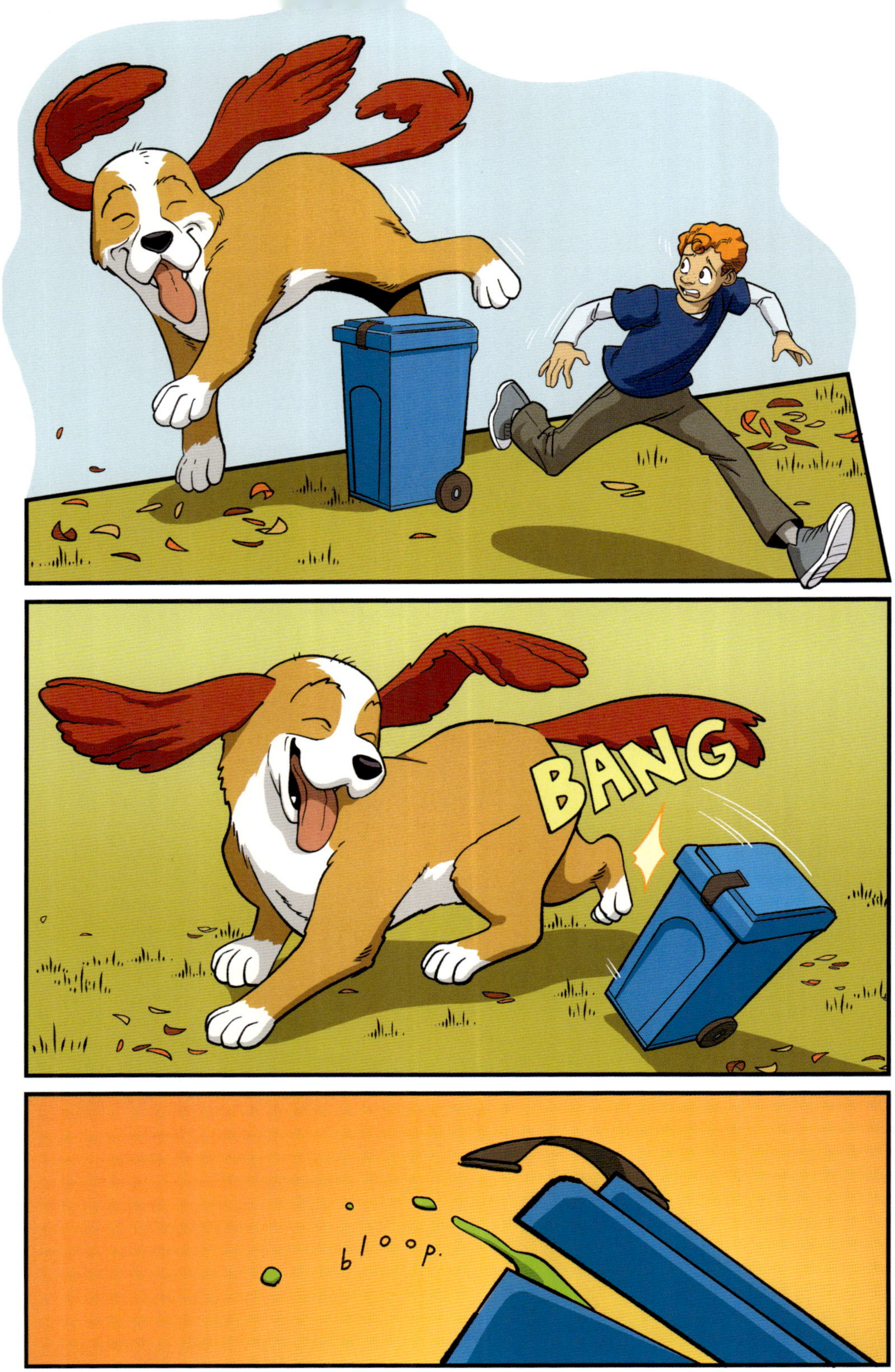
BANG
bloop.

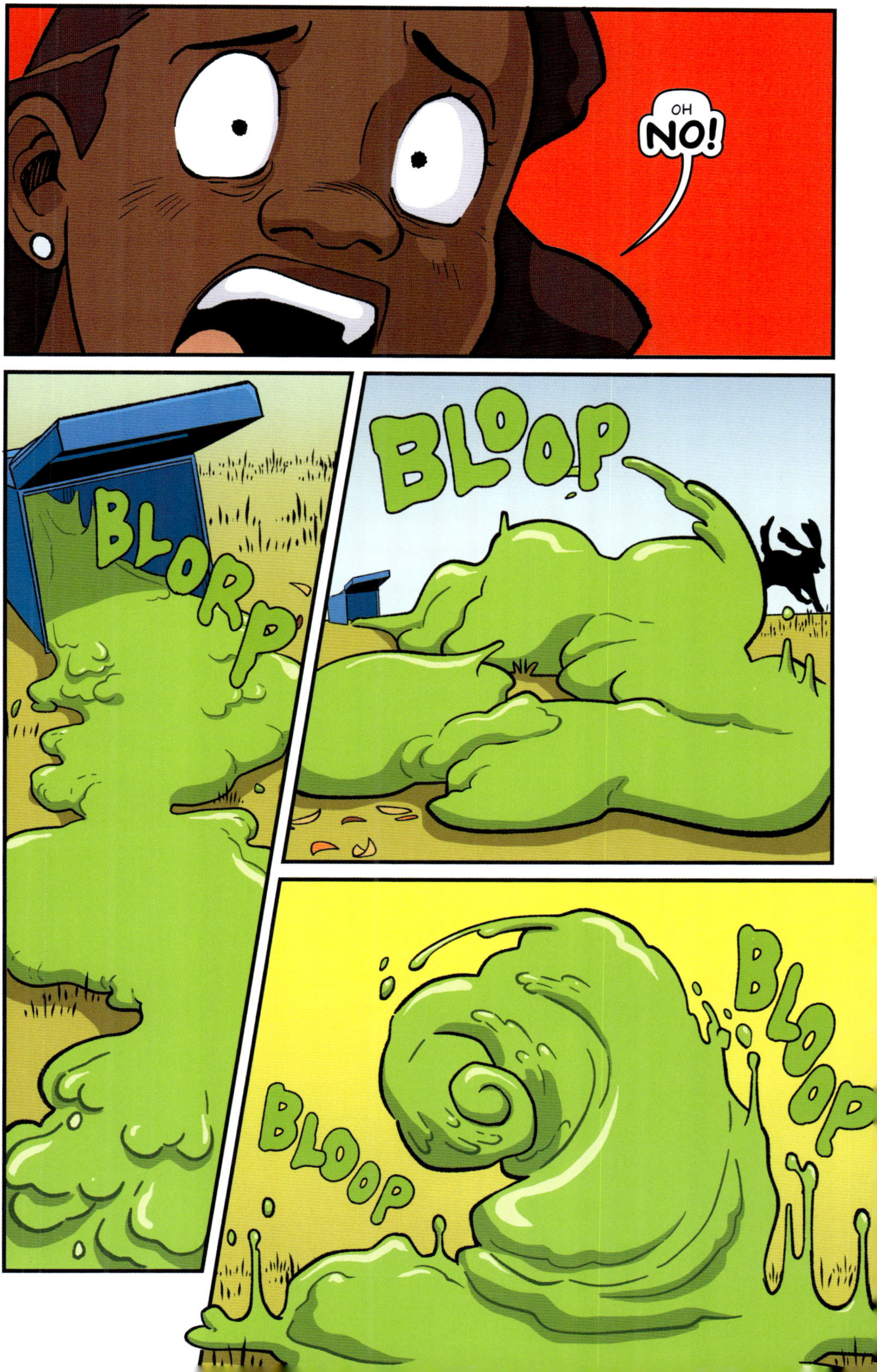
OH NO!
BLORP
BLOOP
BLOOP
BLOOP

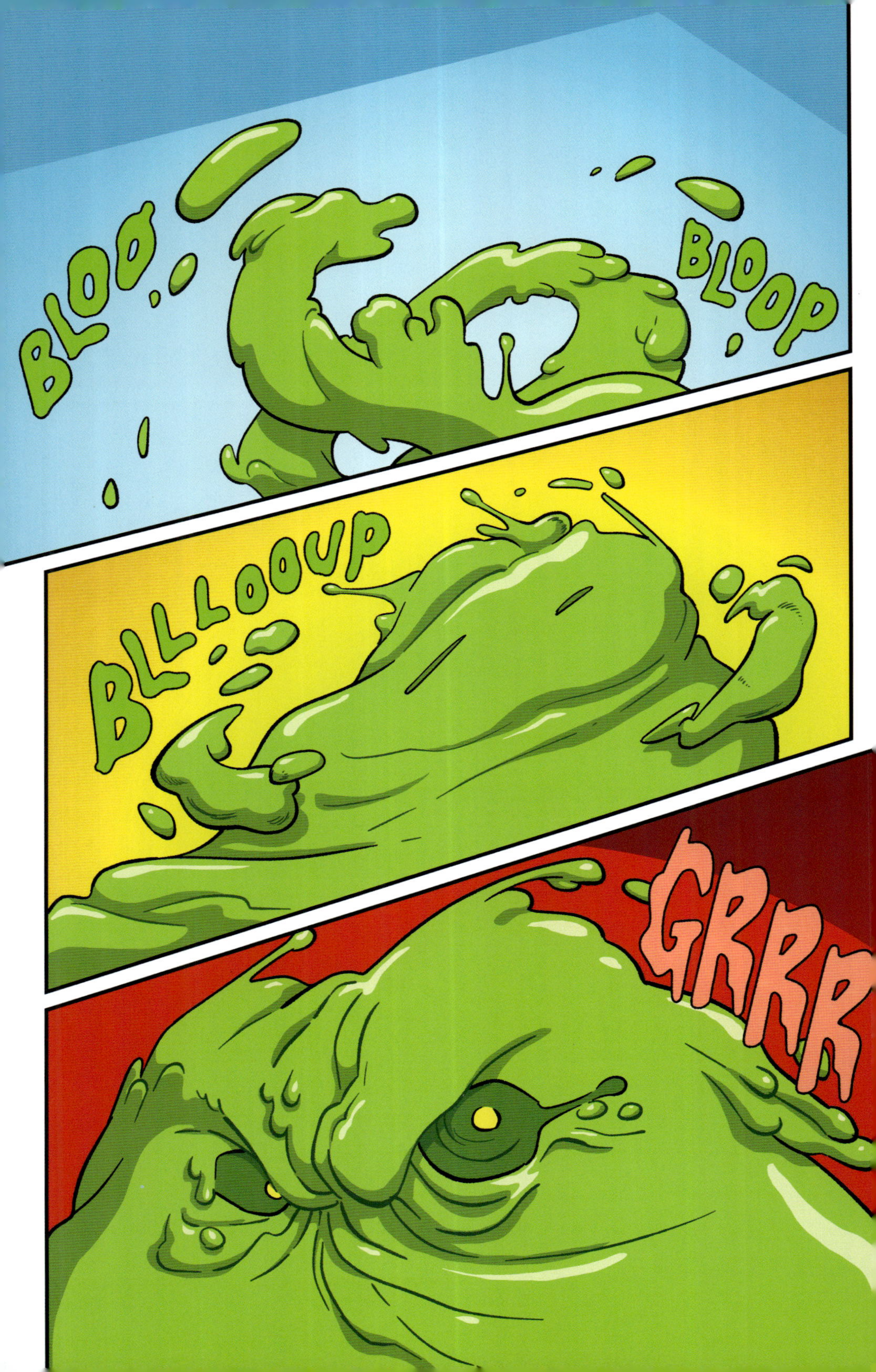
BLOO
BLOOP
BLLLOOUP
GRRR

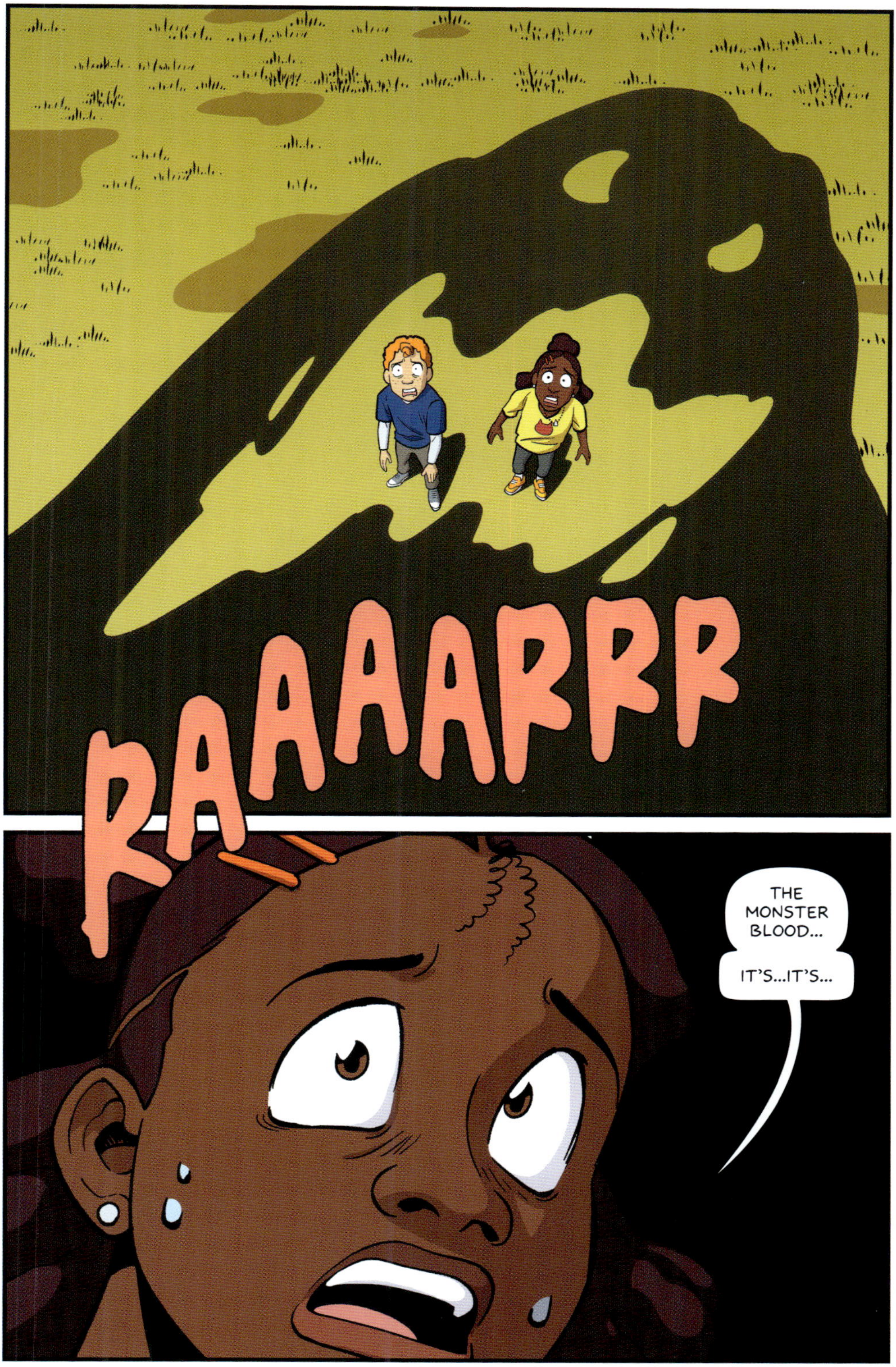
RAAAARRR
THE MONSTER BLOOD...
IT'S...IT'S...

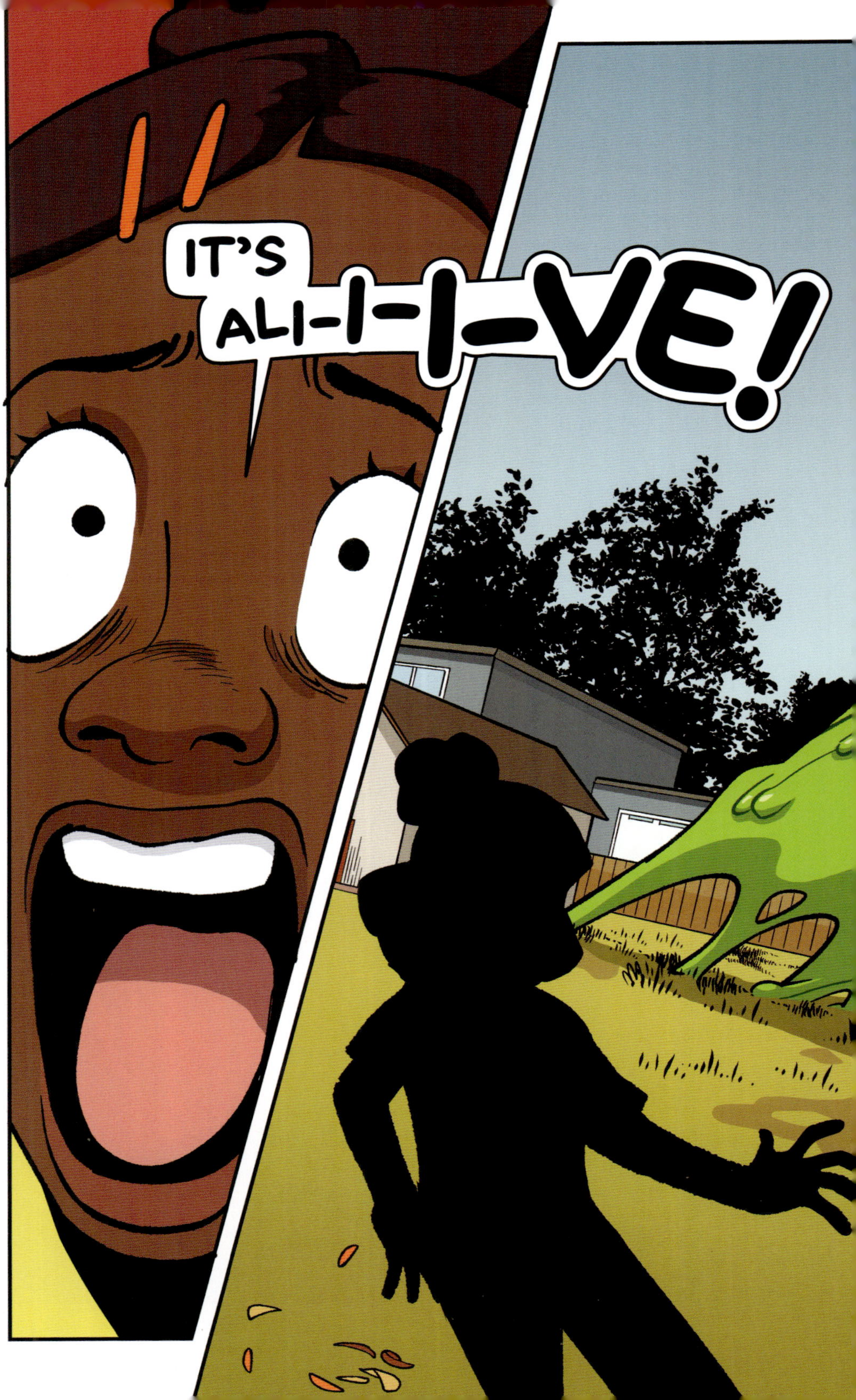
IT'S ALI-I-I-VE!

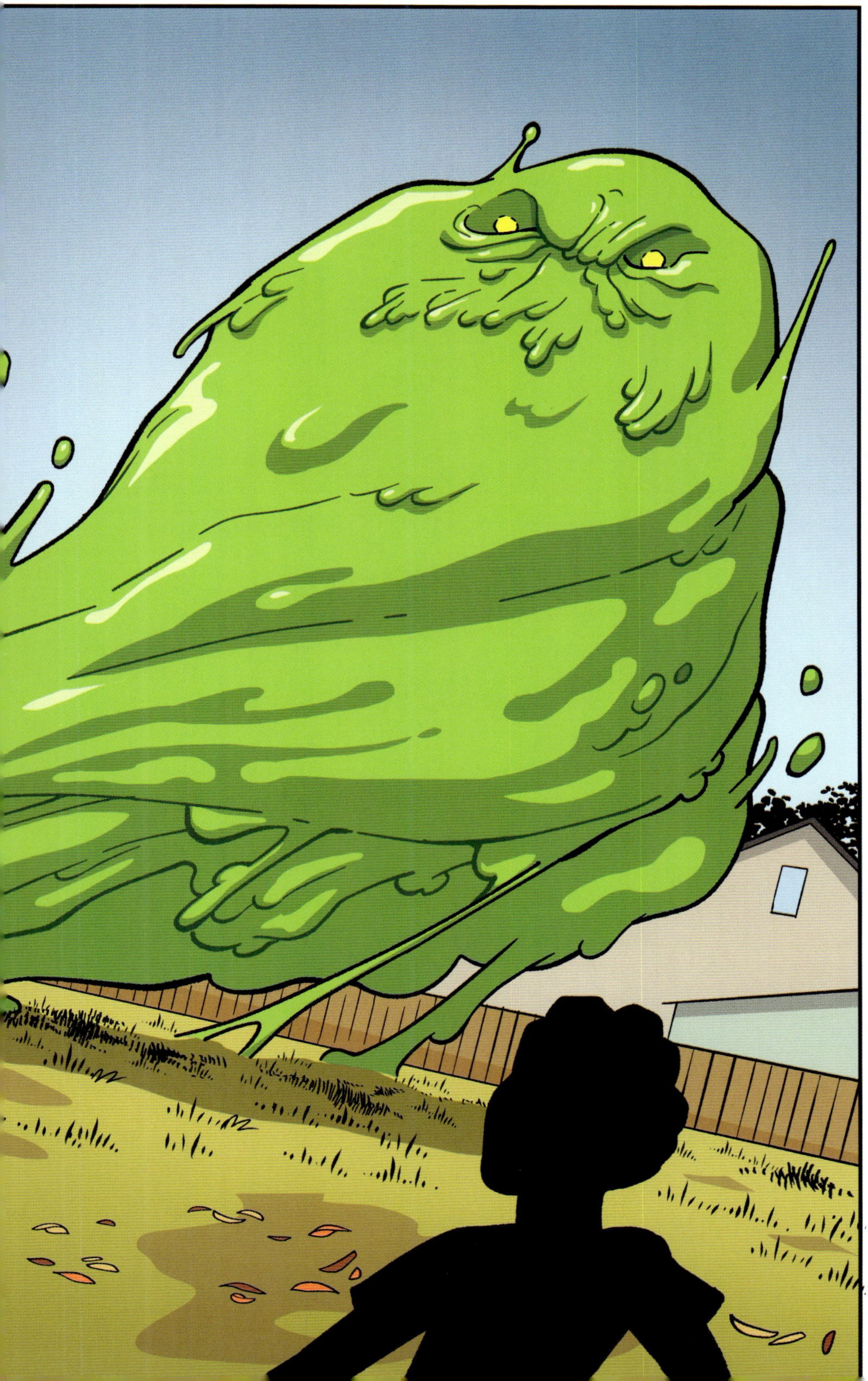

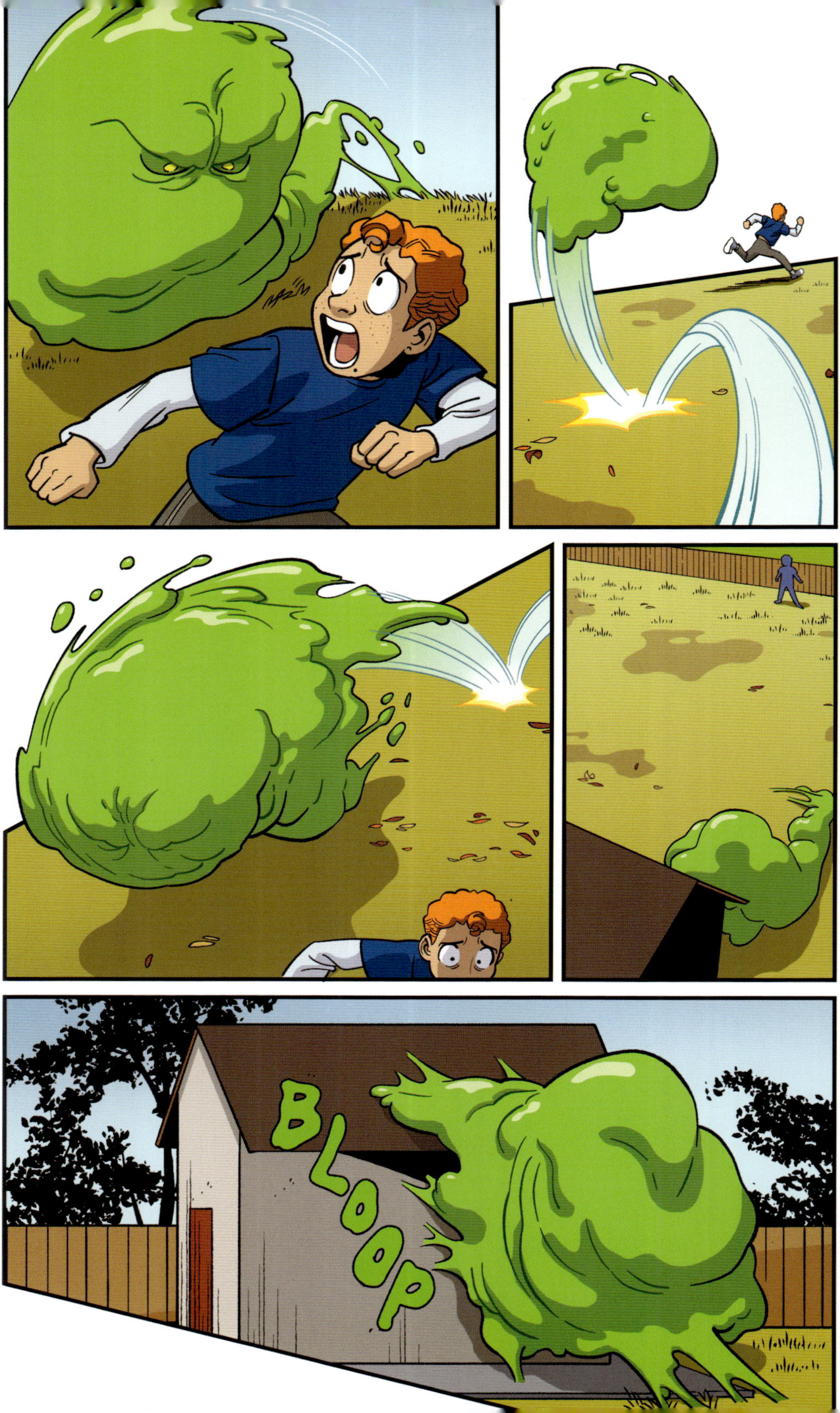
BLOOP

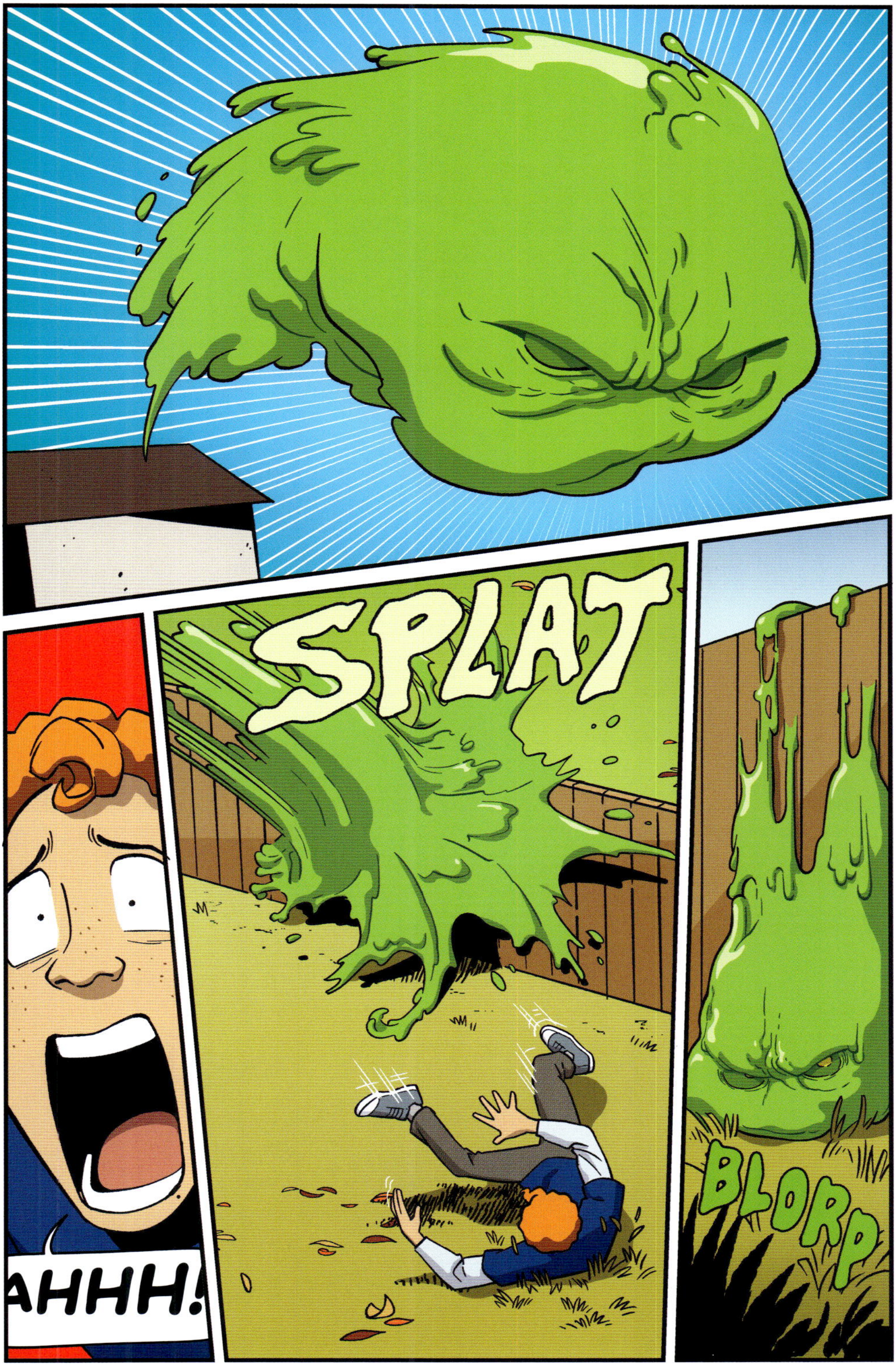
SPLAT
AHHH!
BLORP

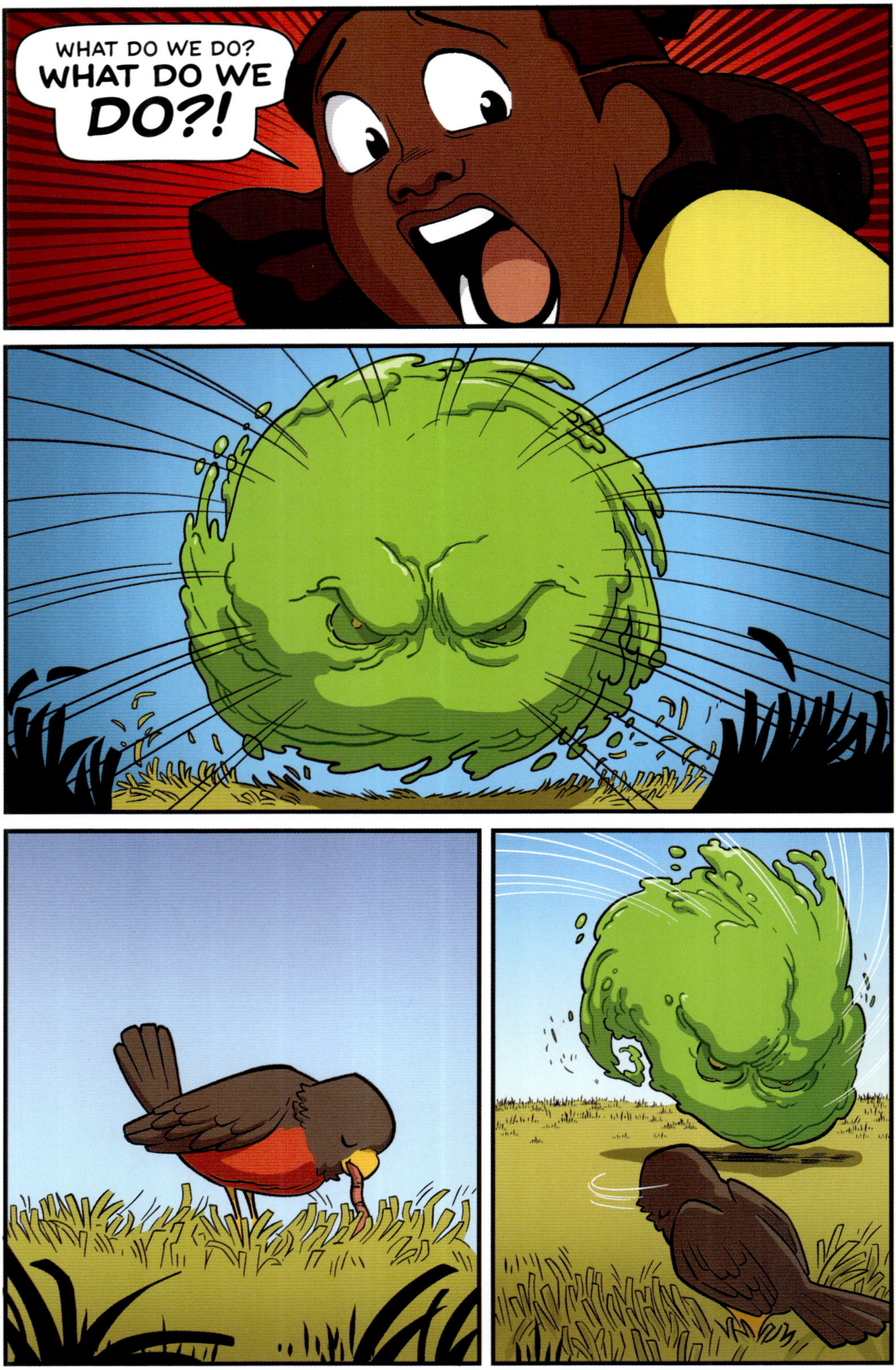
WHAT DO WE DO? WHAT DO WE DO?!

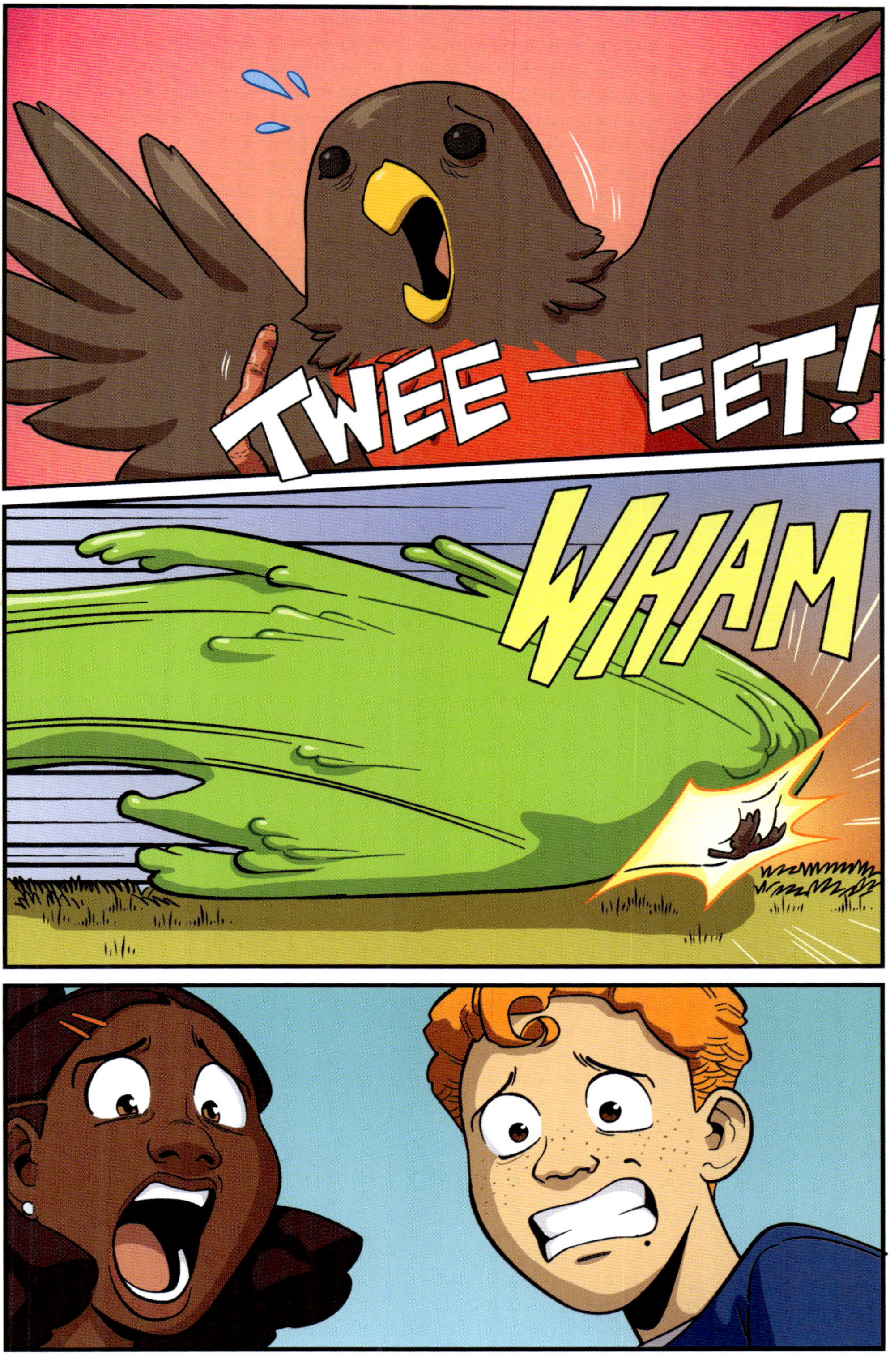
TWEE—EET!
WHAM

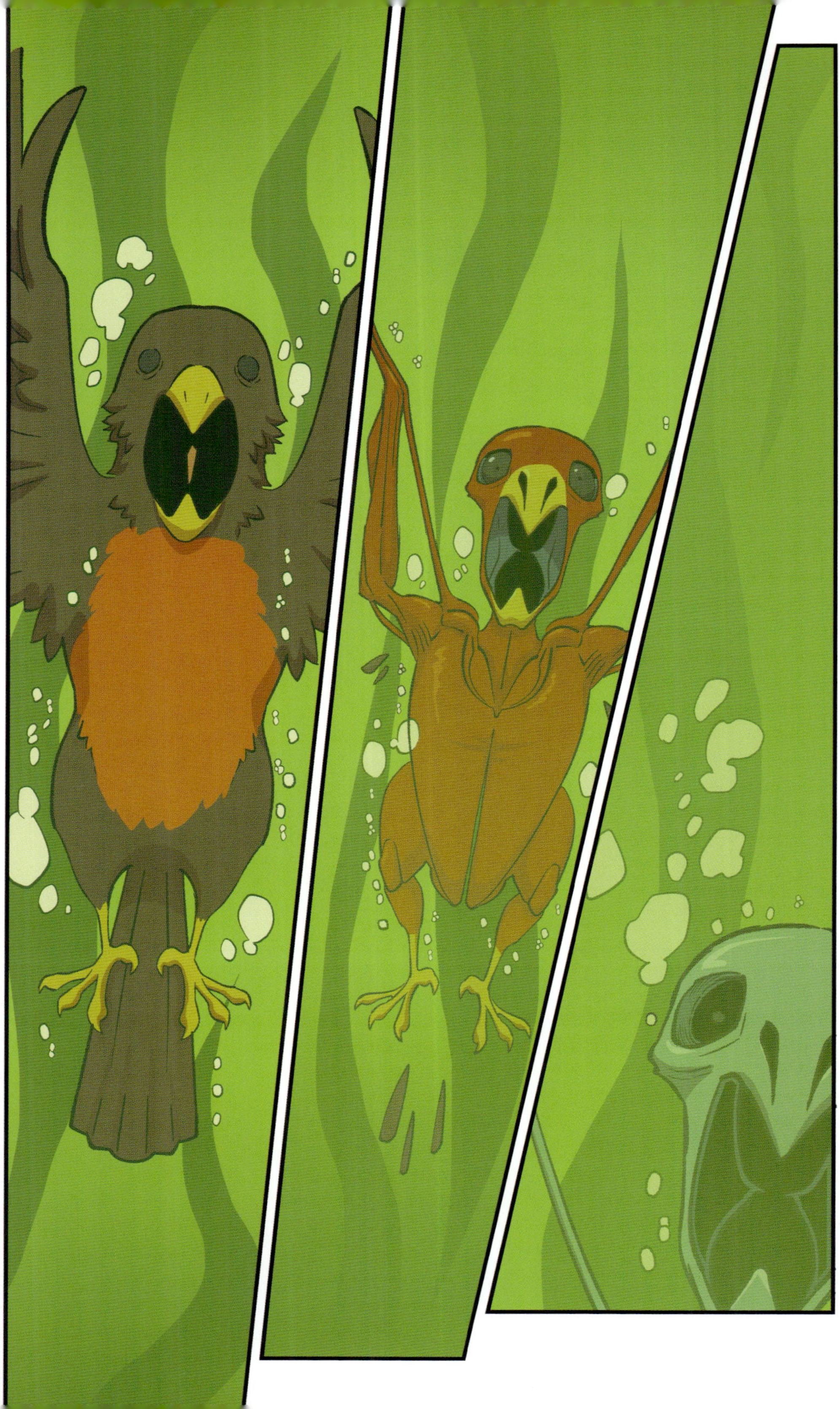

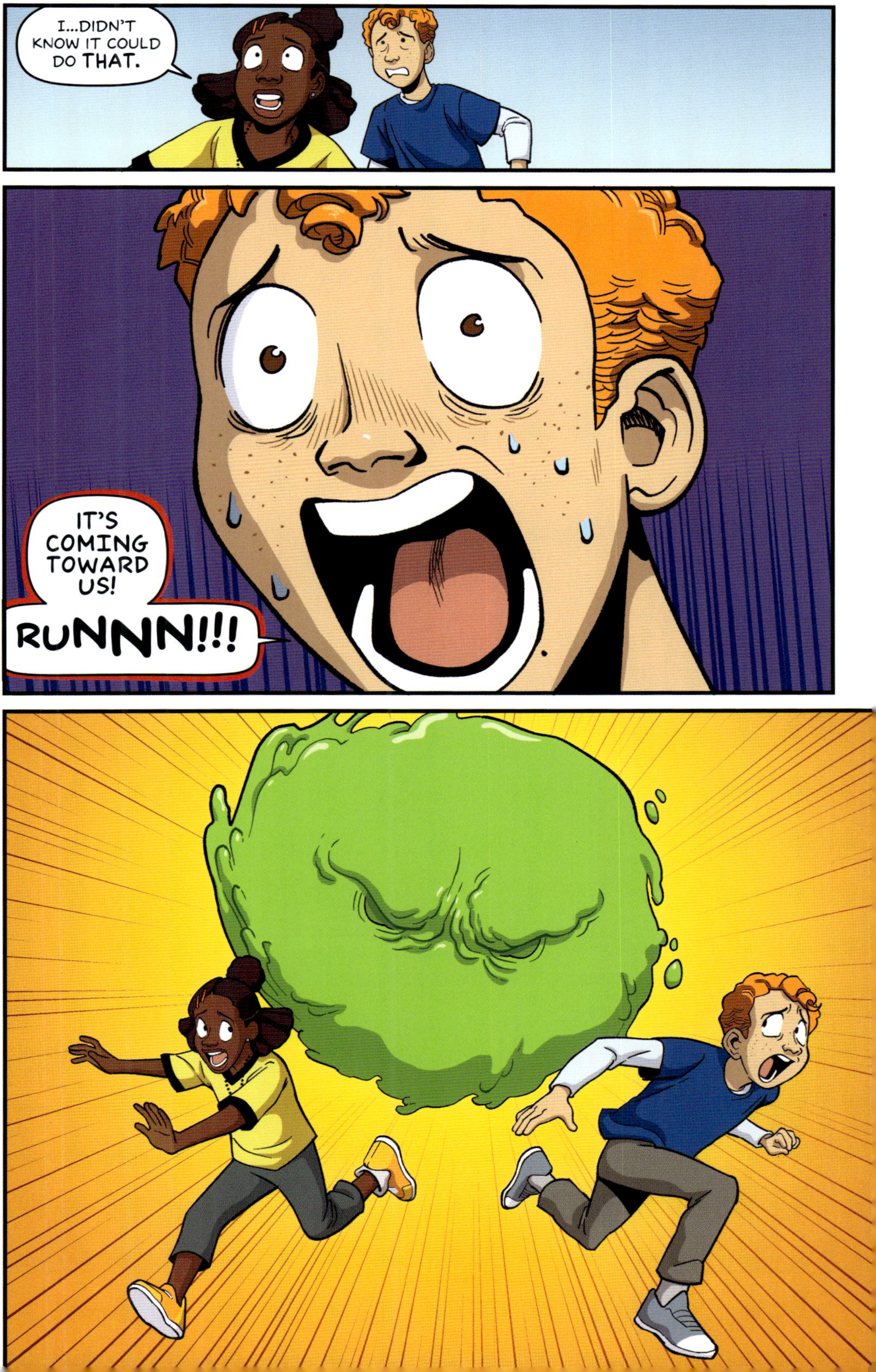
I...DIDN'T KNOW IT COULD DO THAT.
IT'S COMING TOWARD US!
RUNNN!!!

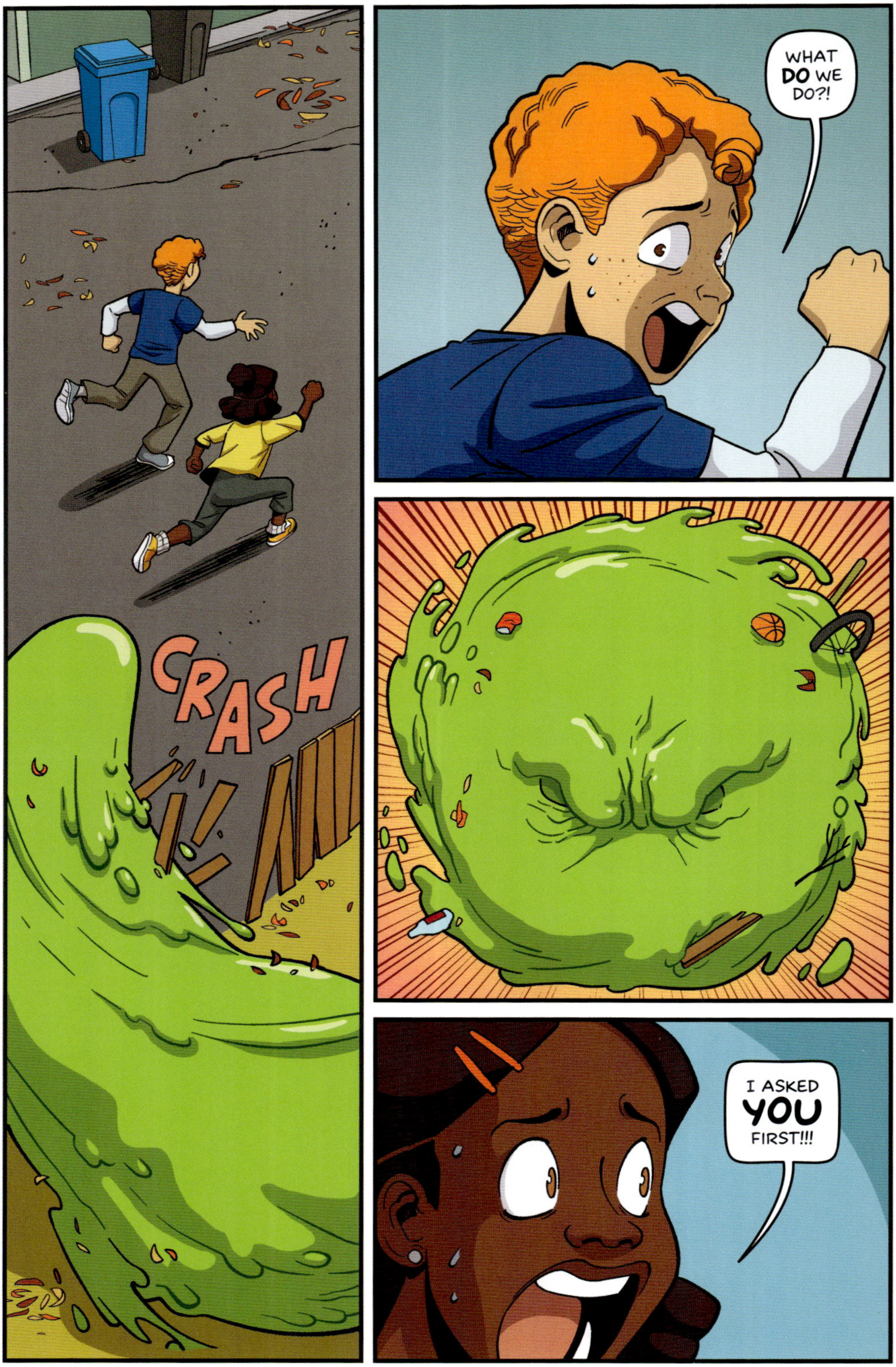
CRASH
WHAT DO WE DO?!
I ASKED YOU FIRST!!!

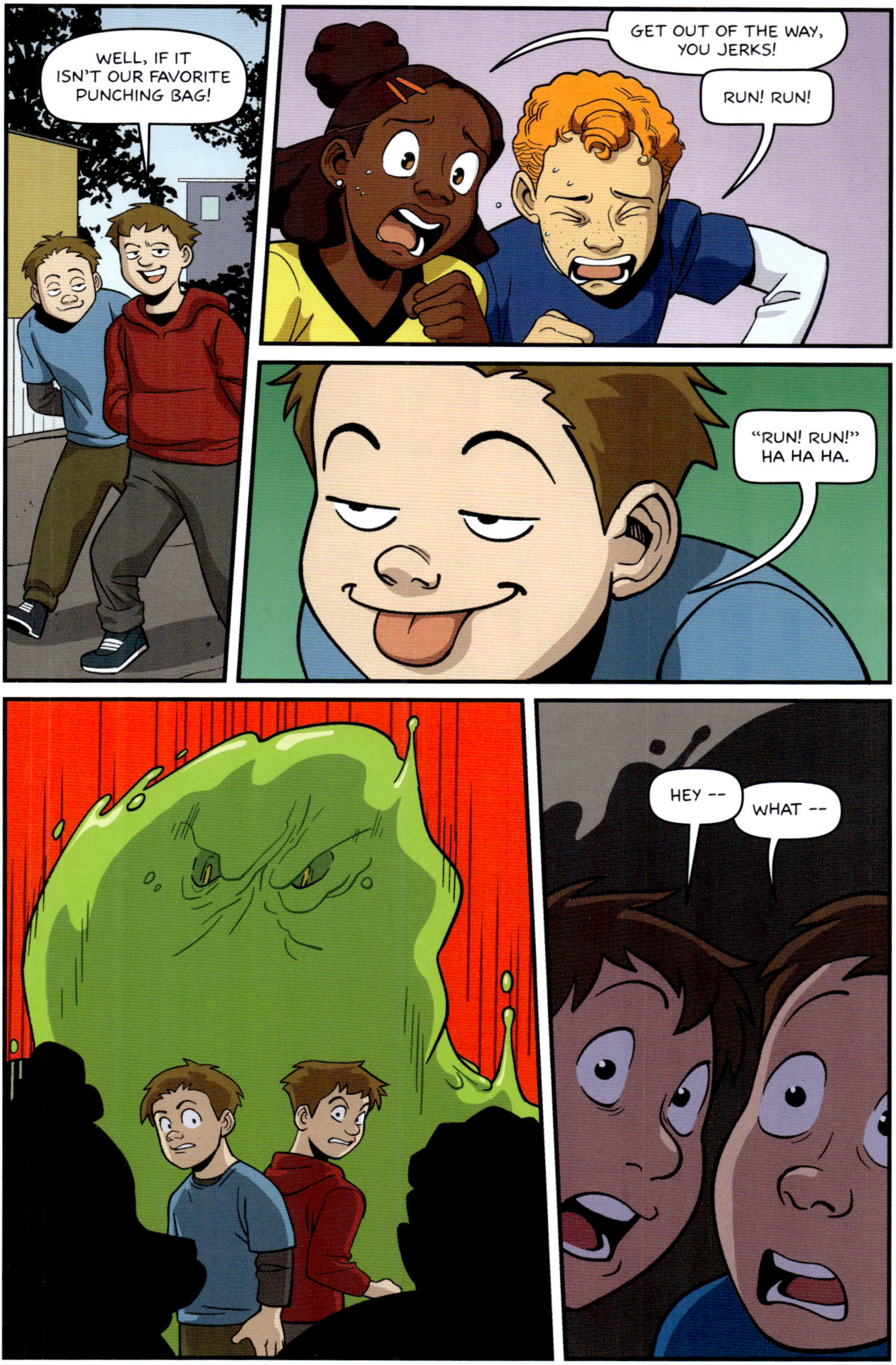
WELL, IF IT ISN'T OUR FAVORITE PUNCHING BAG!
GET OUT OF THE WAY, YOU JERKS!
RUN! RUN!
"RUN! RUN!" HA HA HA.
HEY --
WHAT --

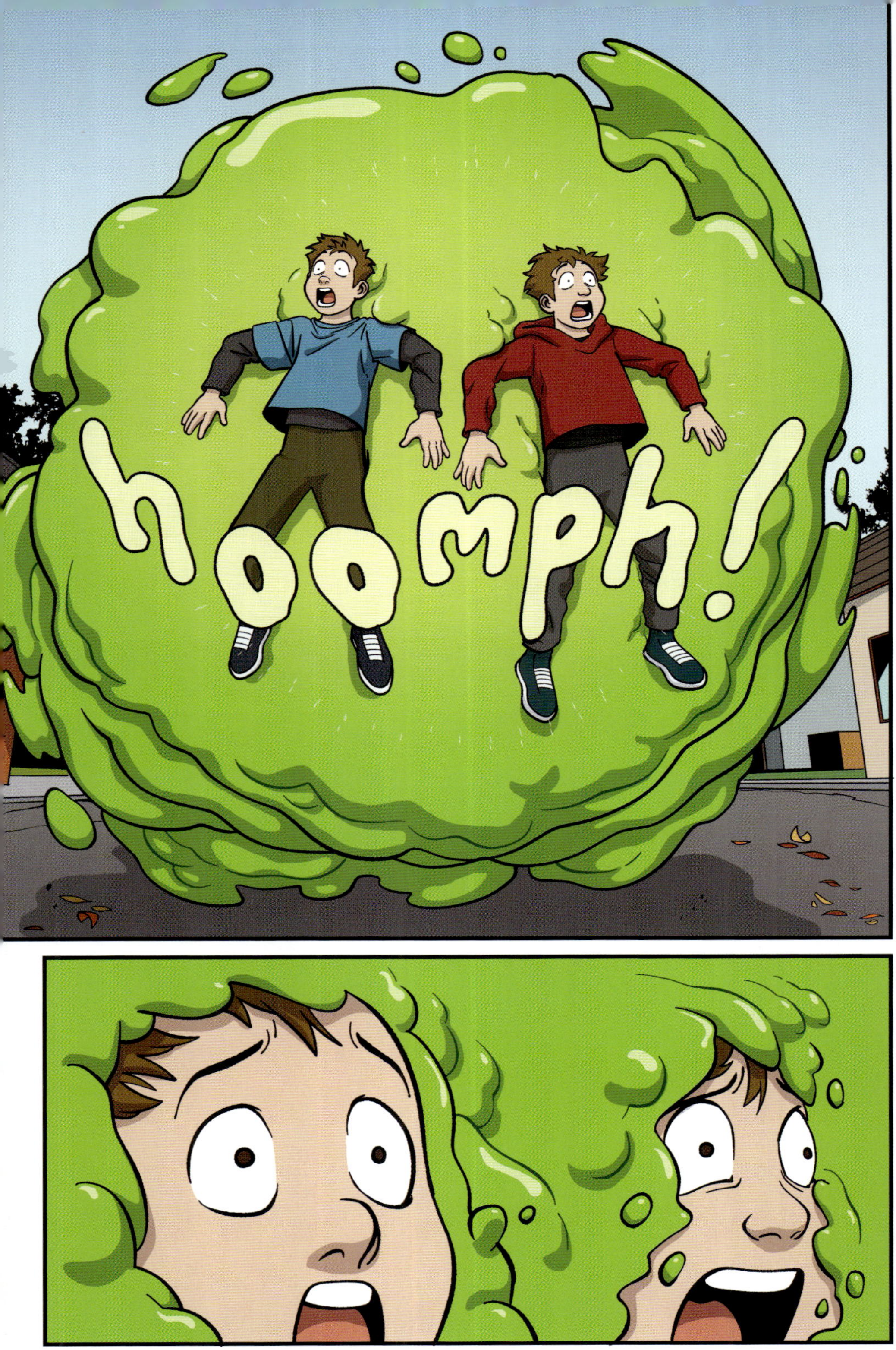
hoomph!

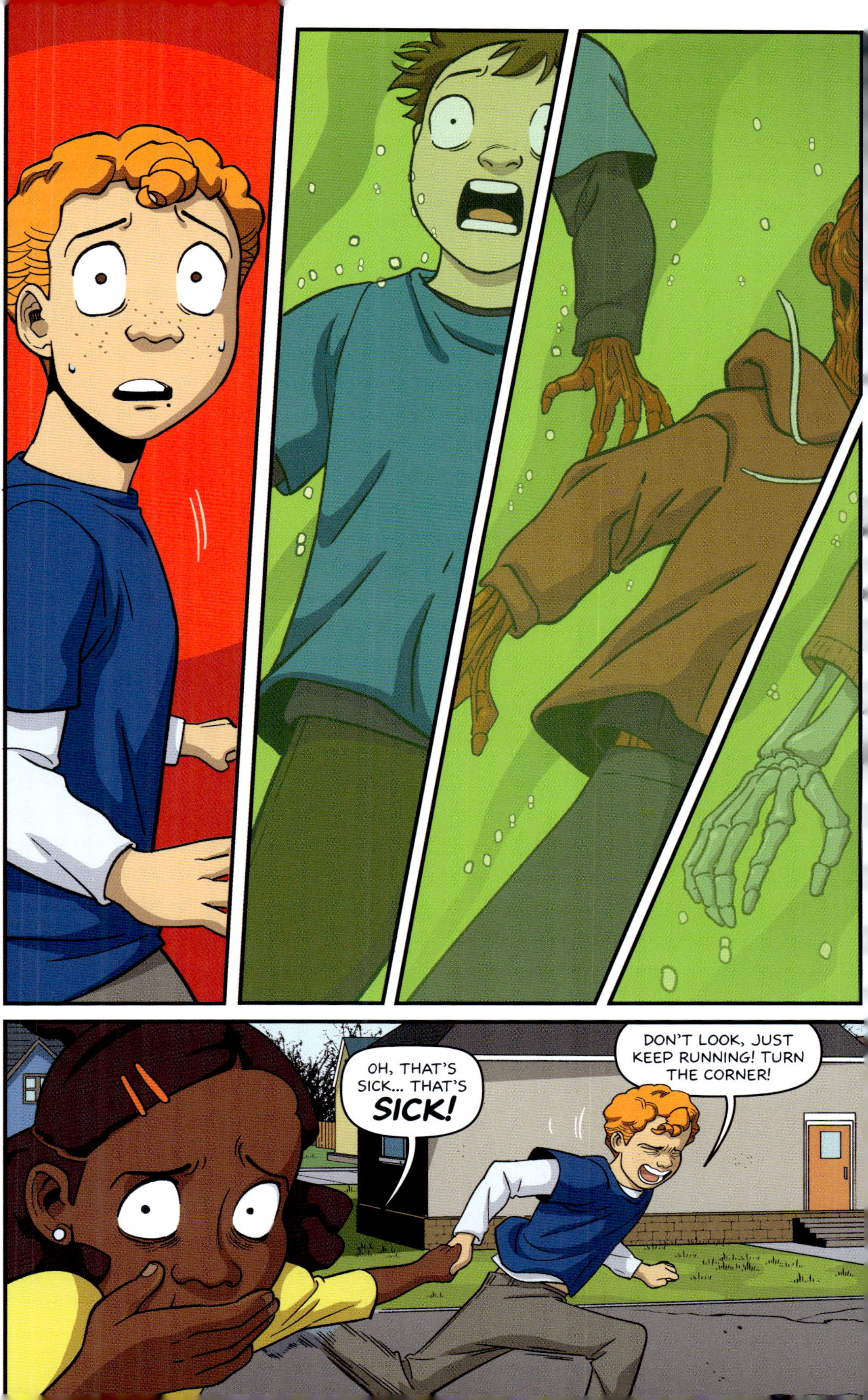
OH, THAT'S SICK... THAT'S SICK!
DON'T LOOK, JUST KEEP RUNNING! TURN THE CORNER!

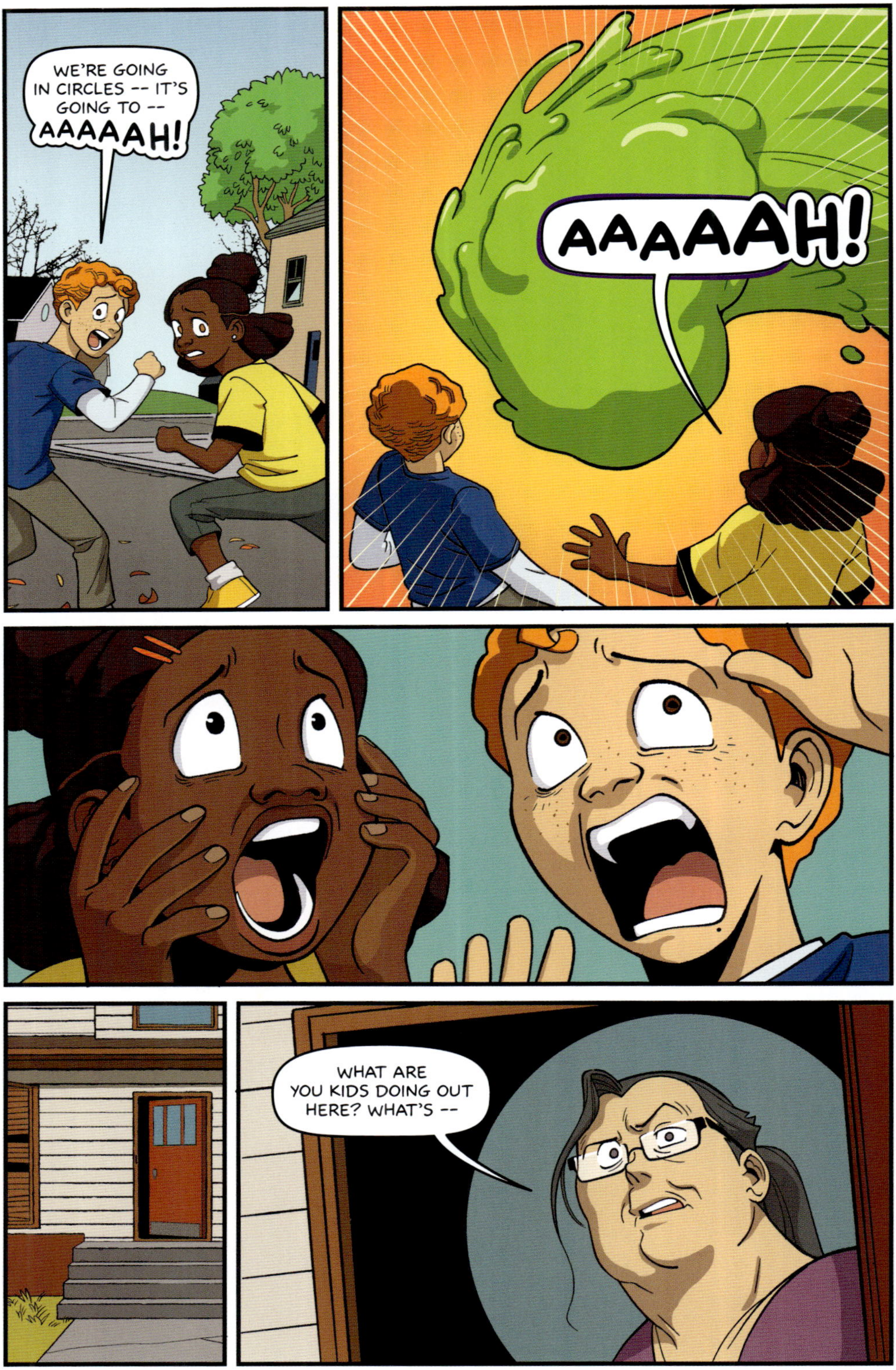
WE'RE GOING IN CIRCLES -- IT'S GOING TO -- AAAAAH!
AAAAAH!
WHAT ARE YOU KIDS DOING OUT HERE? WHAT'S --

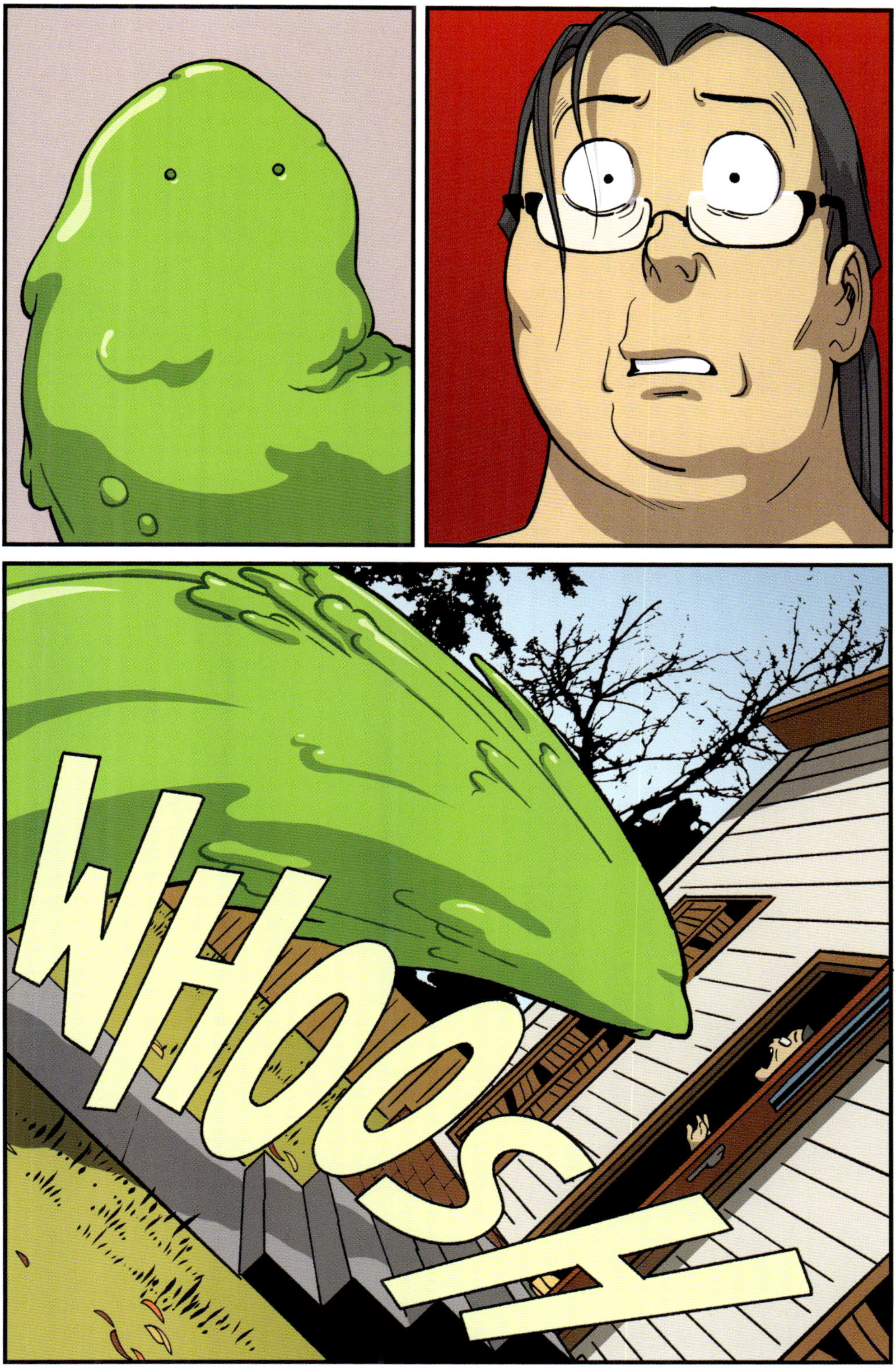
WHOOSH

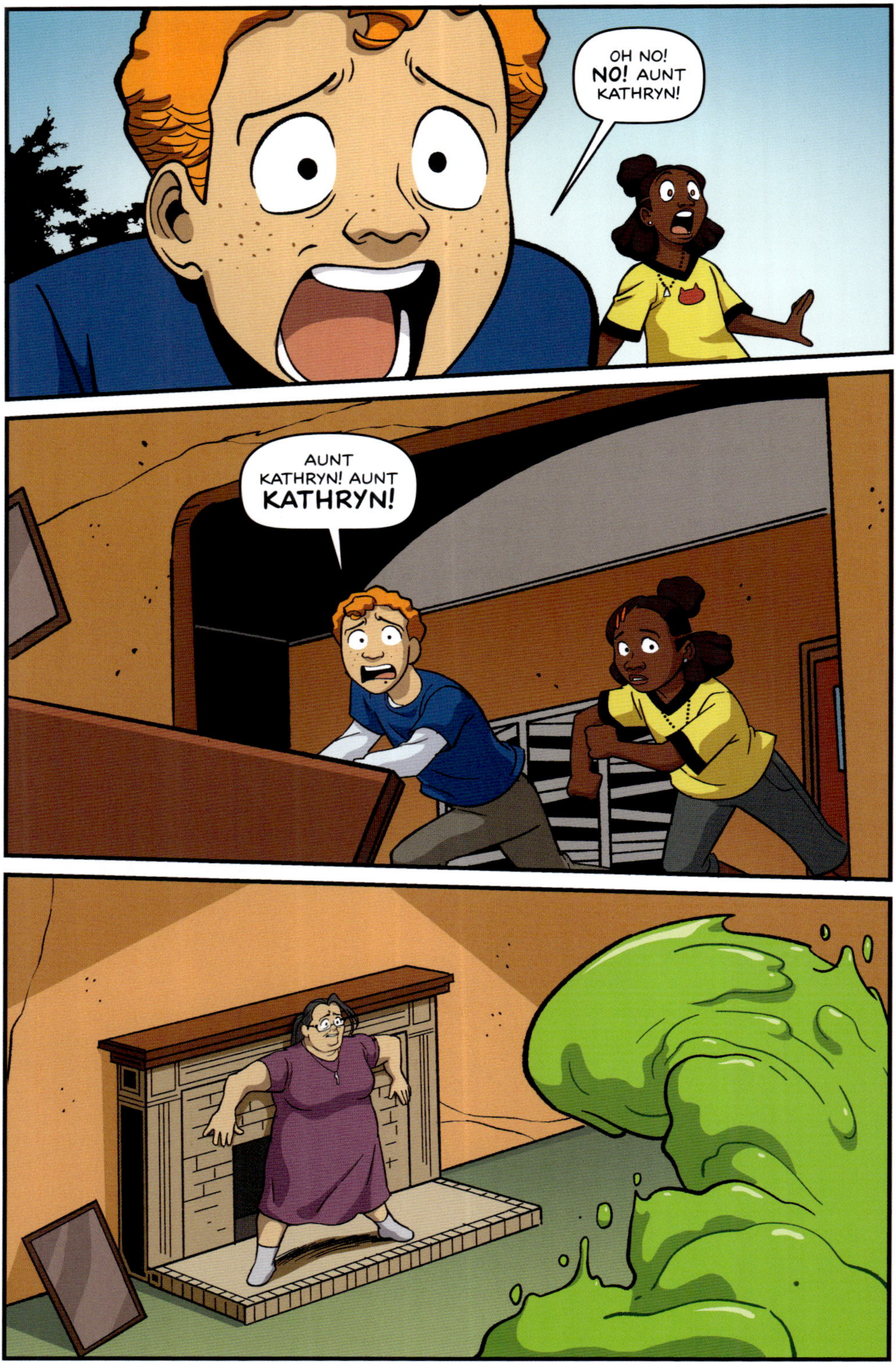
OH NO! NO! AUNT KATHRYN!
AUNT KATHRYN! AUNT KATHRYN!

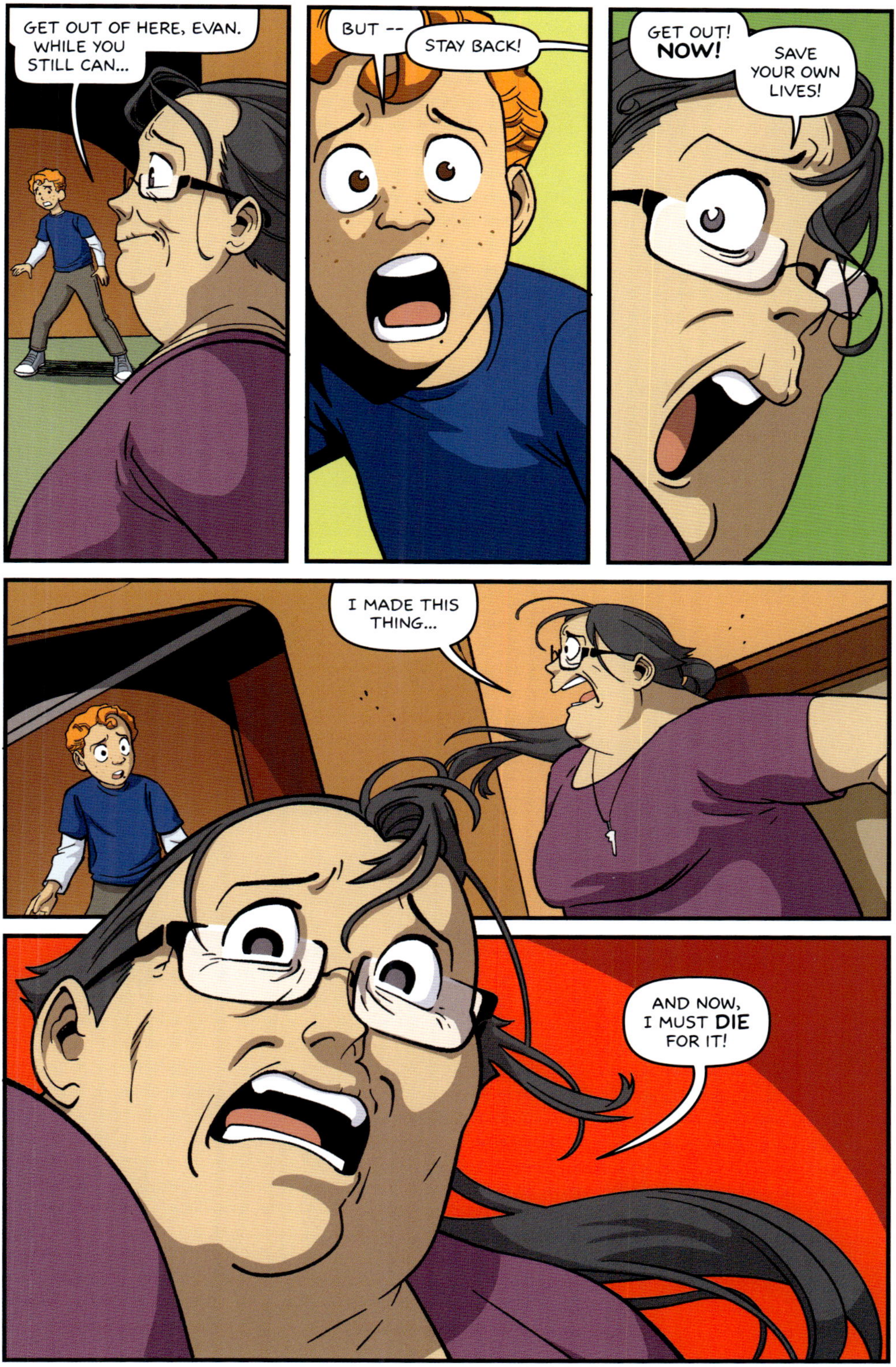
GET OUT OF HERE, EVAN. WHILE YOU STILL CAN...
BUT --
STAY BACK!
GET OUT! **NOW!**
SAVE YOUR OWN LIVES!
I MADE THIS THING...
AND NOW, I MUST **DIE** FOR IT!

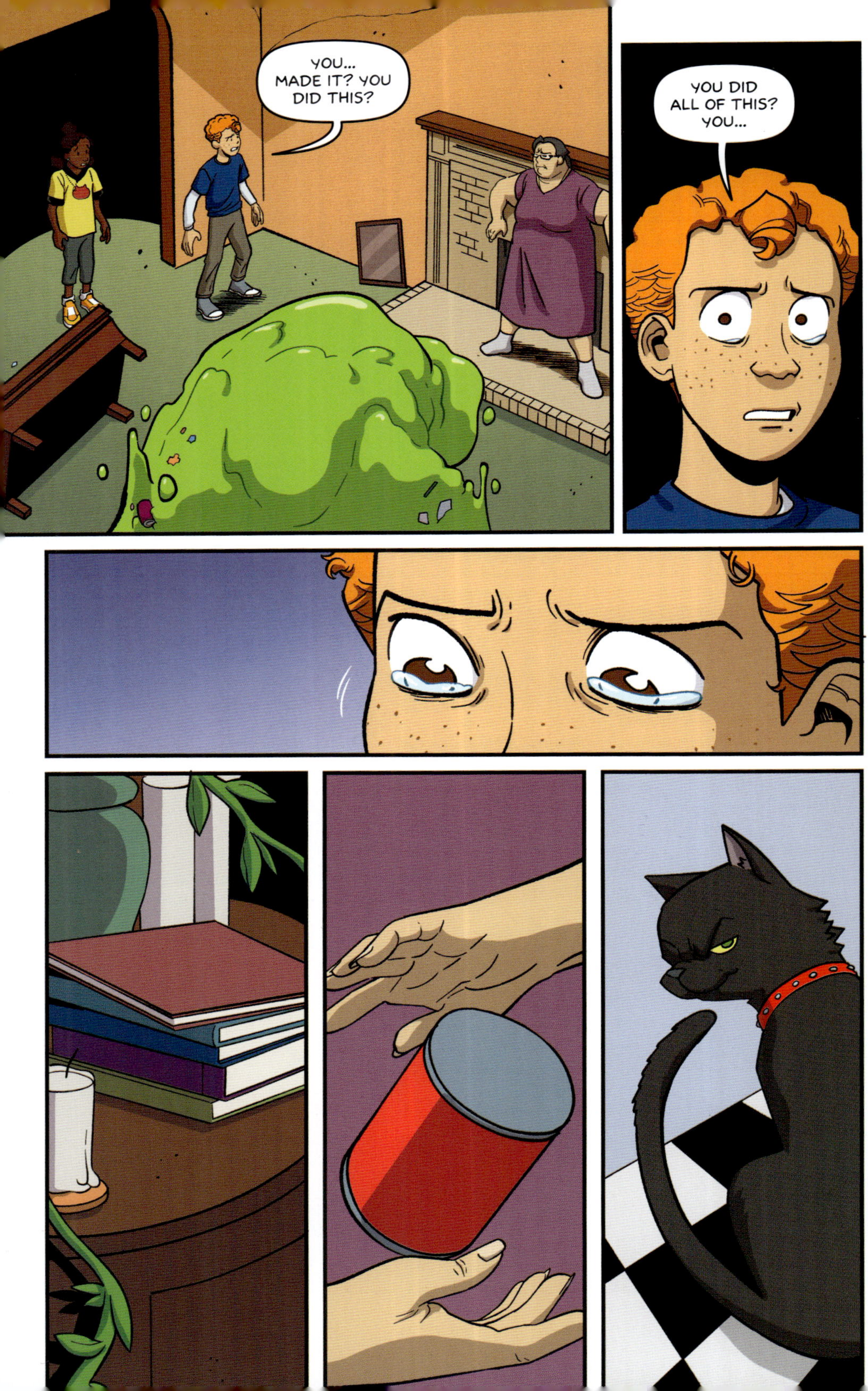
YOU... MADE IT? YOU DID THIS?
YOU DID ALL OF THIS? YOU...

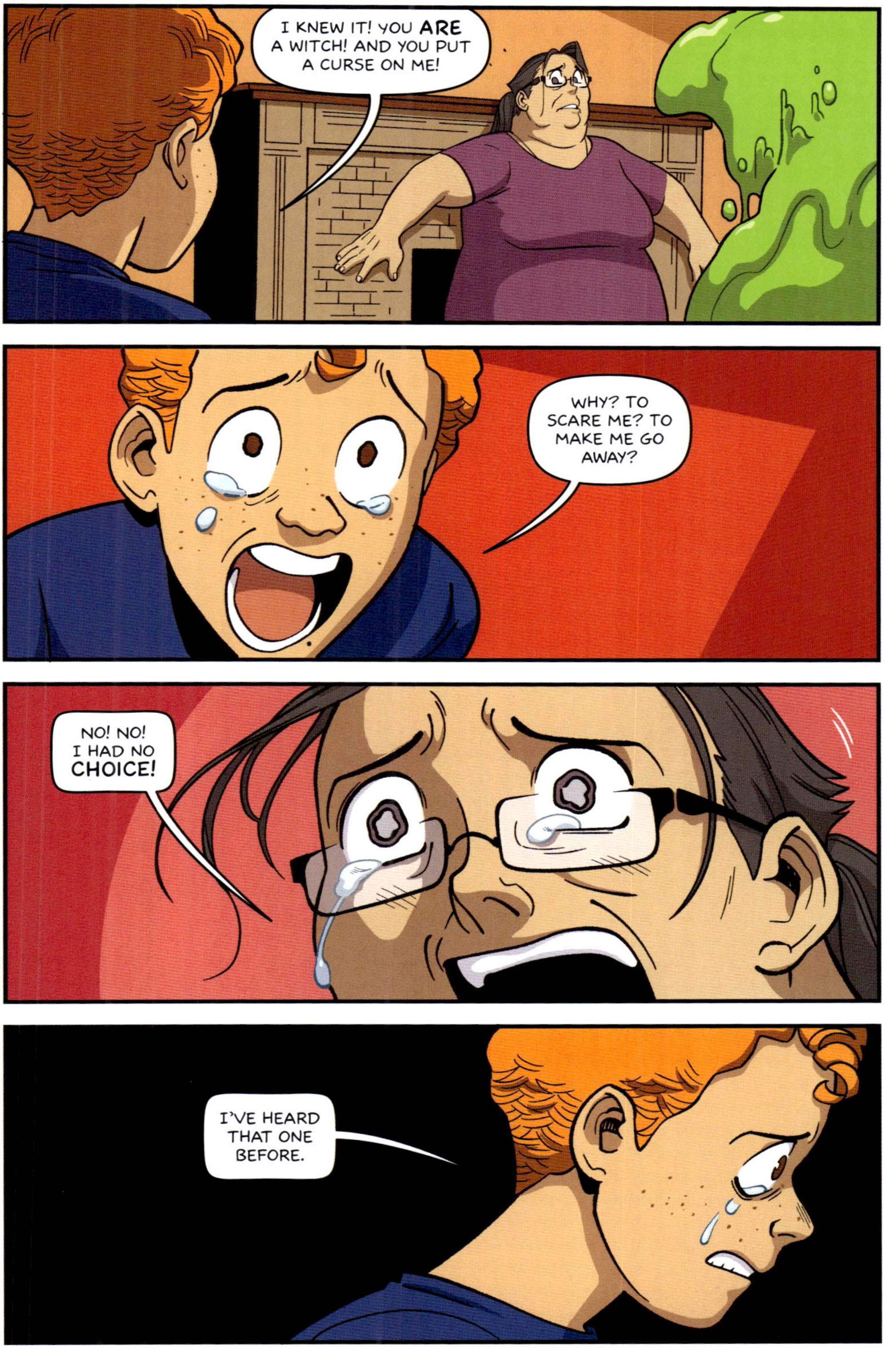
I KNEW IT! YOU **ARE** A WITCH! AND YOU PUT A CURSE ON ME!
WHY? TO SCARE ME? TO MAKE ME GO AWAY?
NO! NO! I HAD NO **CHOICE!**
I'VE HEARD THAT ONE BEFORE.

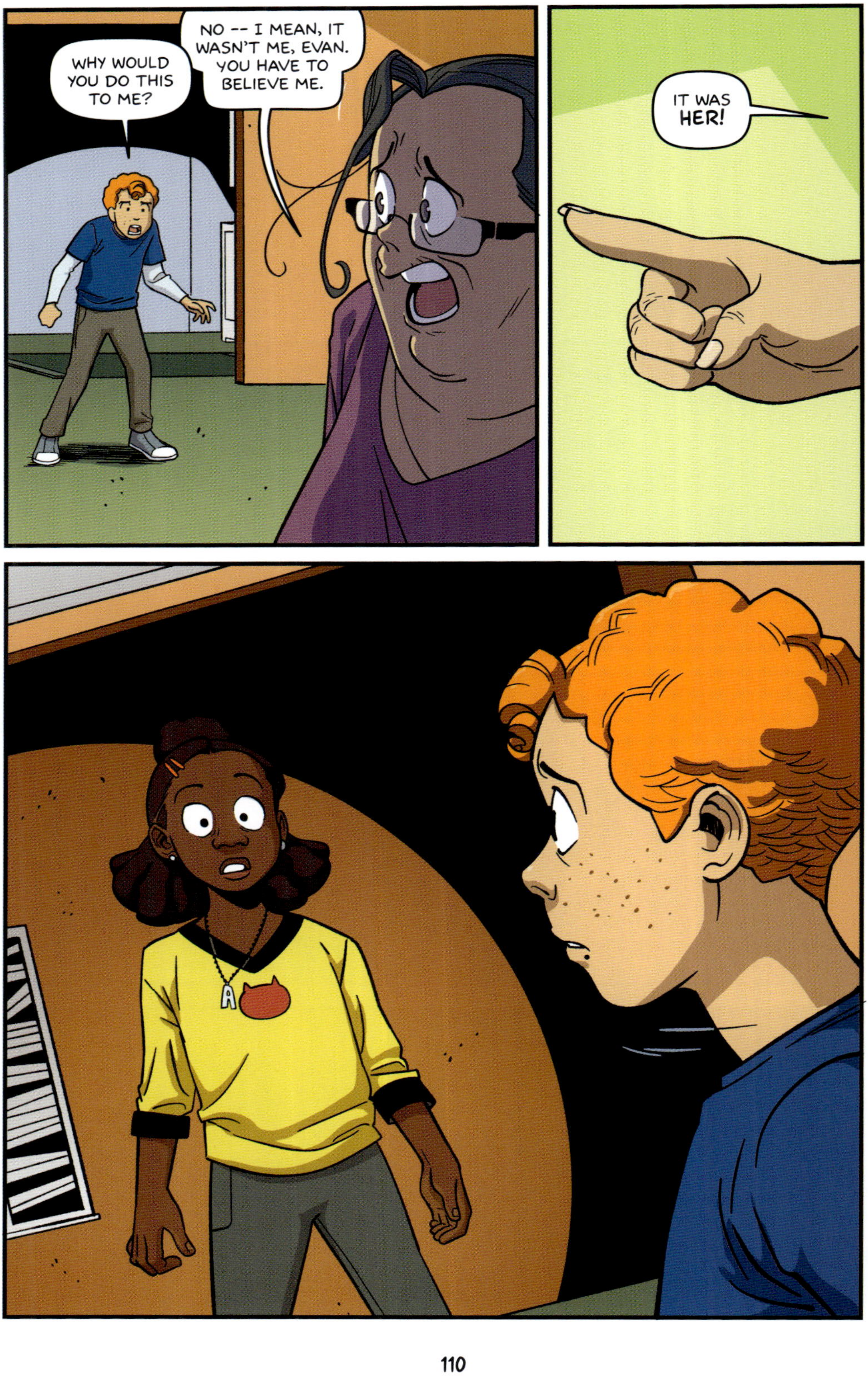

WHY WOULD YOU DO THIS TO ME?
NO -- I MEAN, IT WASN'T ME, EVAN. YOU HAVE TO BELIEVE ME.
IT WAS **HER!**

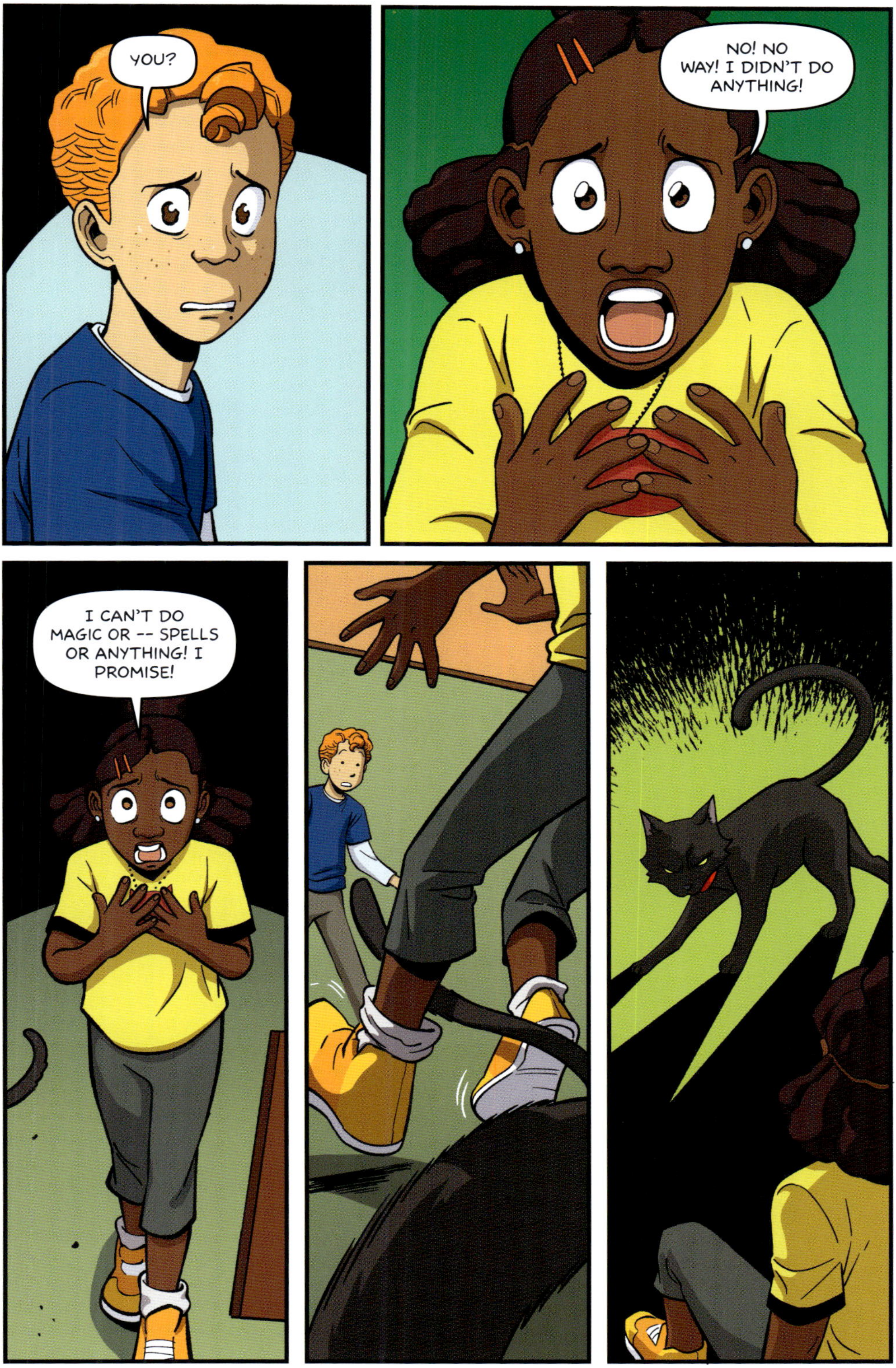
YOU?
NO! NO WAY! I DIDN'T DO ANYTHING!
I CAN'T DO MAGIC OR -- SPELLS OR ANYTHING! I PROMISE!

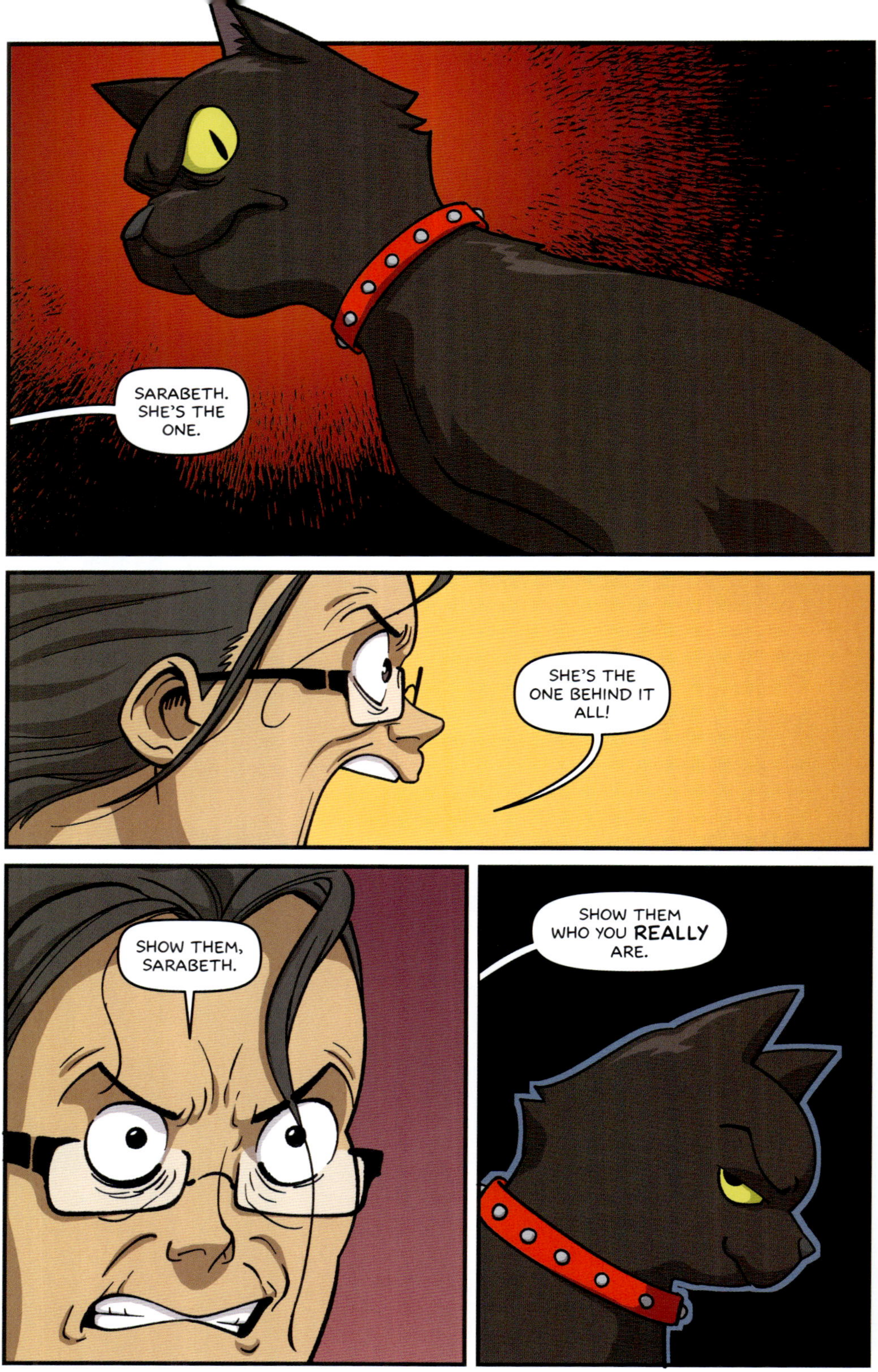
SARABETH. SHE'S THE ONE.
SHE'S THE ONE BEHIND IT ALL!
SHOW THEM, SARABETH.
SHOW THEM WHO YOU **REALLY** ARE.

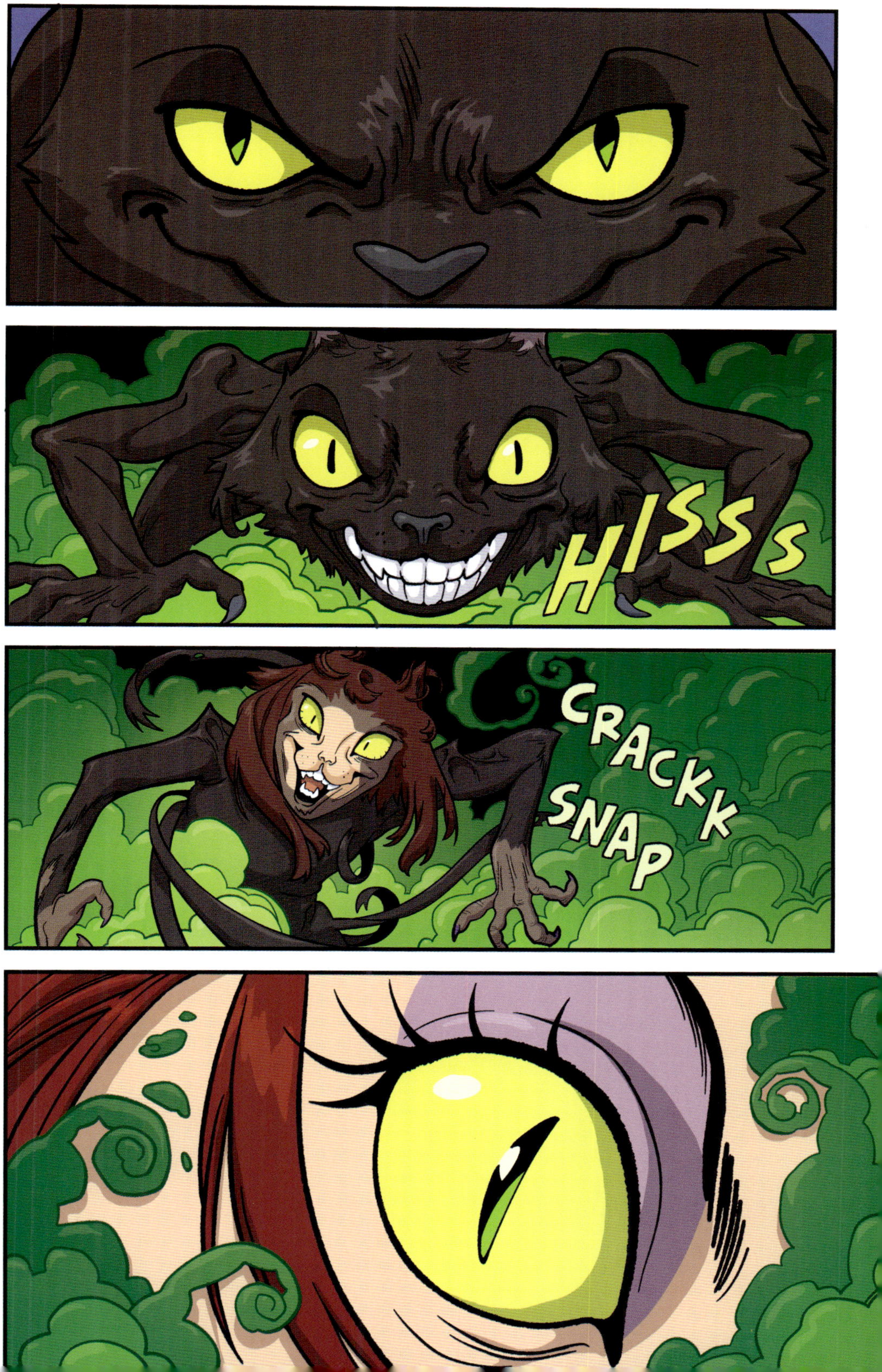
HISSs
CRACKK
SNAP

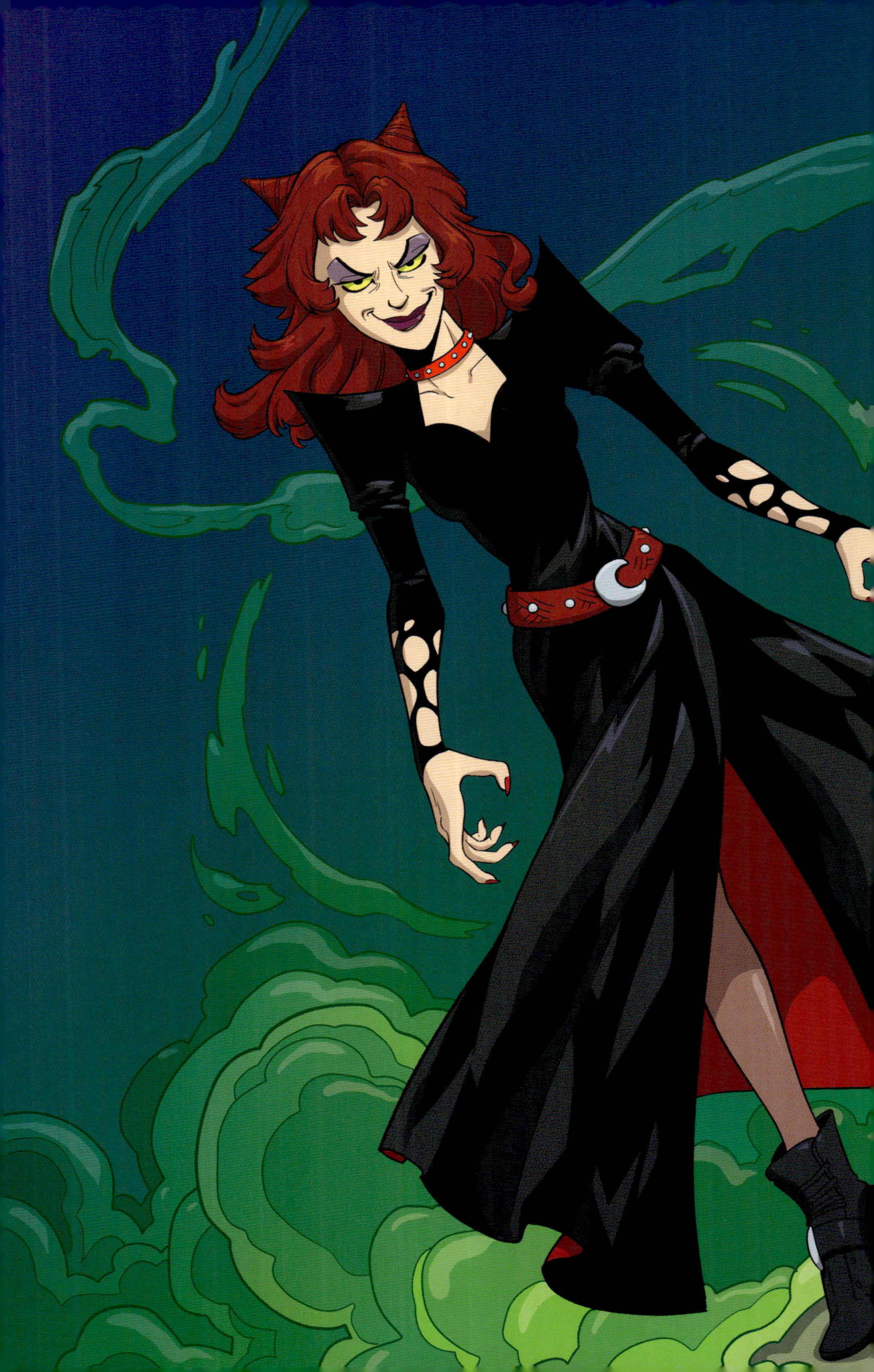

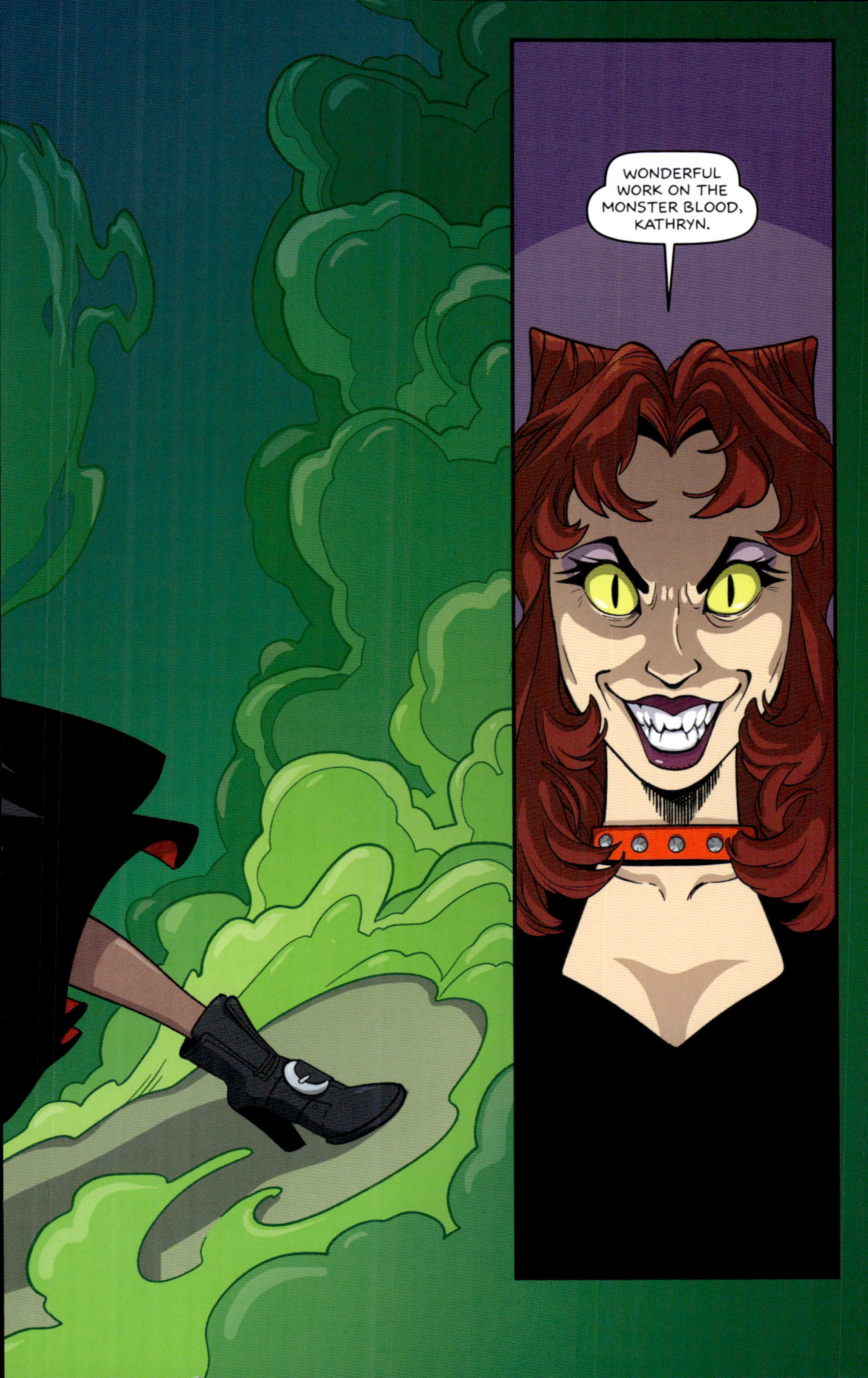
WONDERFUL WORK ON THE MONSTER BLOOD, KATHRYN.

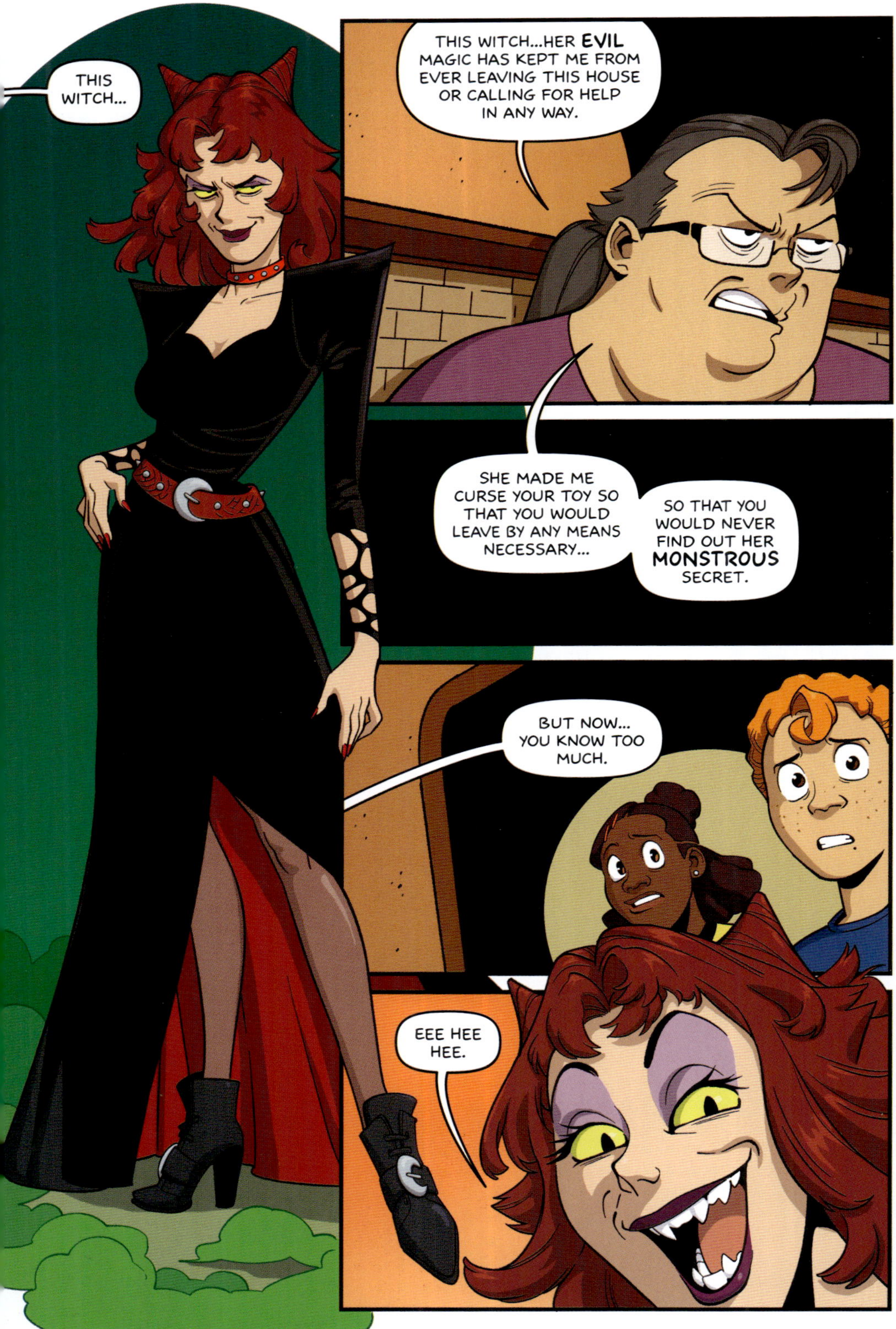
THIS WITCH...
THIS WITCH...HER **EVIL** MAGIC HAS KEPT ME FROM EVER LEAVING THIS HOUSE OR CALLING FOR HELP IN ANY WAY.
SHE MADE ME CURSE YOUR TOY SO THAT YOU WOULD LEAVE BY ANY MEANS NECESSARY...
SO THAT YOU WOULD NEVER FIND OUT HER **MONSTROUS** SECRET.
BUT NOW... YOU KNOW TOO MUCH.
EEE HEE HEE.

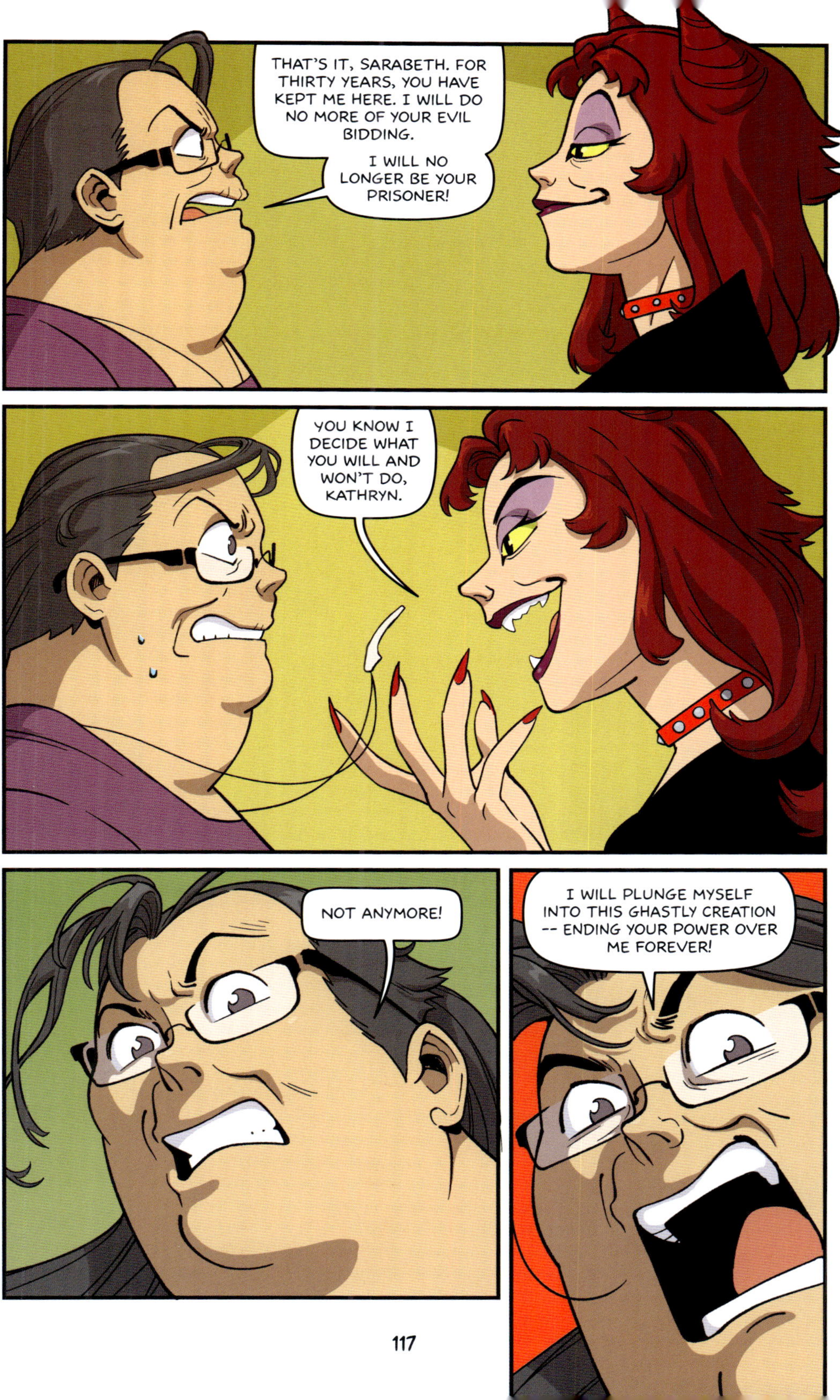
THAT'S IT, SARABETH. FOR THIRTY YEARS, YOU HAVE KEPT ME HERE. I WILL DO NO MORE OF YOUR EVIL BIDDING.
I WILL NO LONGER BE YOUR PRISONER!
YOU KNOW I DECIDE WHAT YOU WILL AND WON'T DO, KATHRYN.
NOT ANYMORE!
I WILL PLUNGE MYSELF INTO THIS GHASTLY CREATION -- ENDING YOUR POWER OVER ME FOREVER!

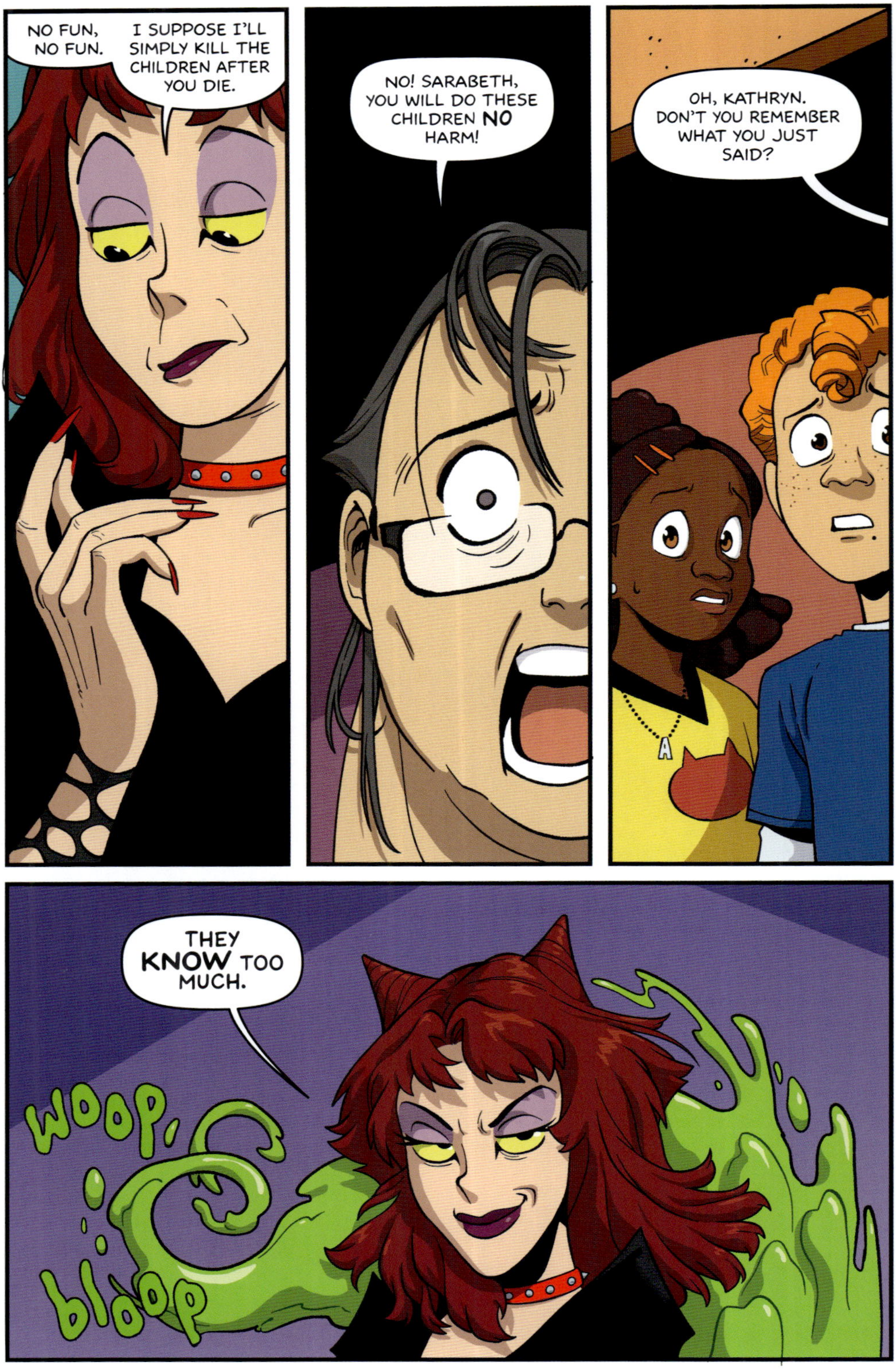
NO FUN, NO FUN.
I SUPPOSE I'LL SIMPLY KILL THE CHILDREN AFTER YOU DIE.
NO! SARABETH, YOU WILL DO THESE CHILDREN **NO** HARM!
OH, KATHRYN. DON'T YOU REMEMBER WHAT YOU JUST SAID?
THEY **KNOW** TOO MUCH.
WOOP,
BLOOP

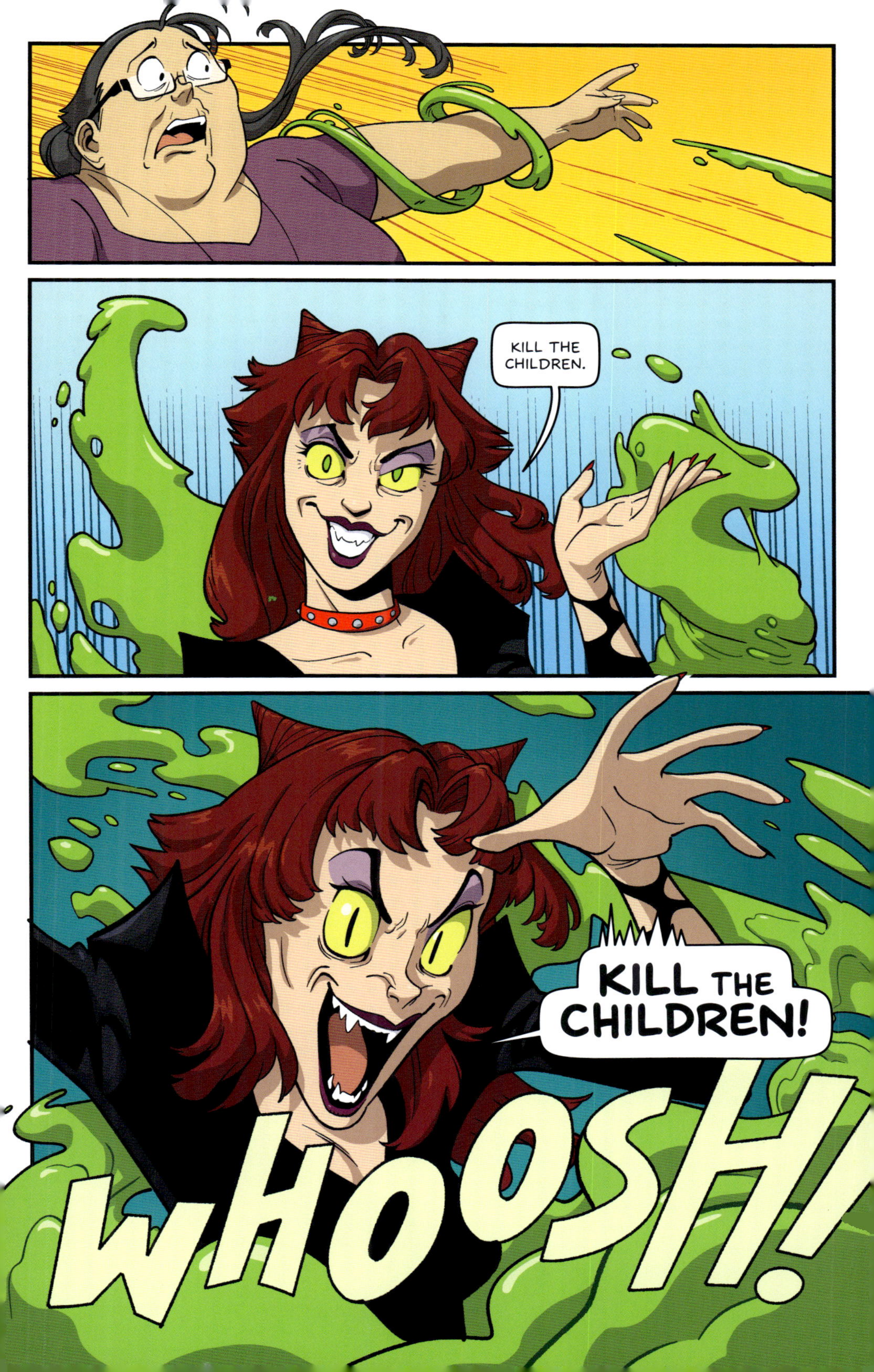
KILL THE CHILDREN.
KILL THE CHILDREN!
WHOOSH!

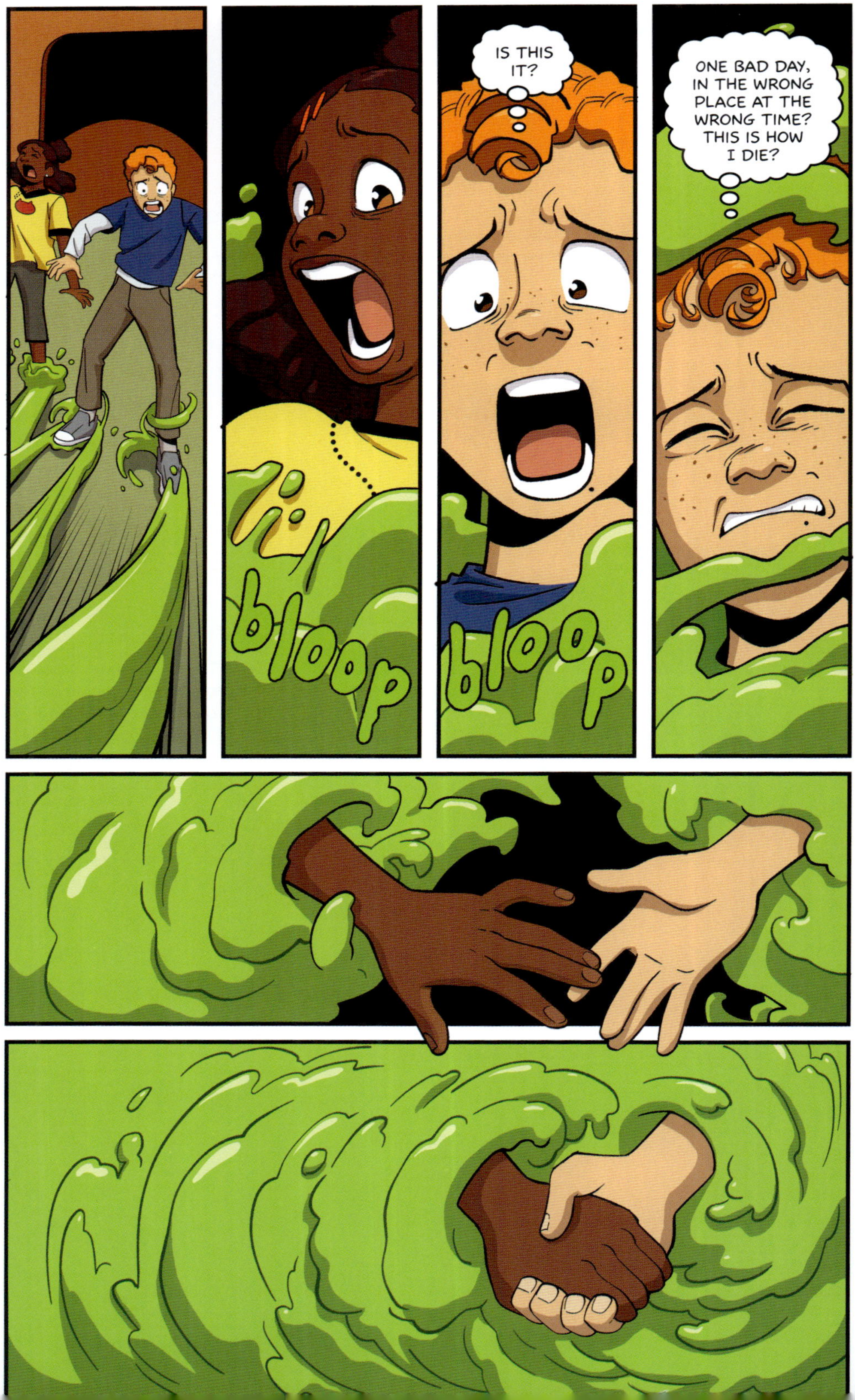
bloop
IS THIS IT?
bloop
ONE BAD DAY, IN THE WRONG PLACE AT THE WRONG TIME? THIS IS HOW I DIE?

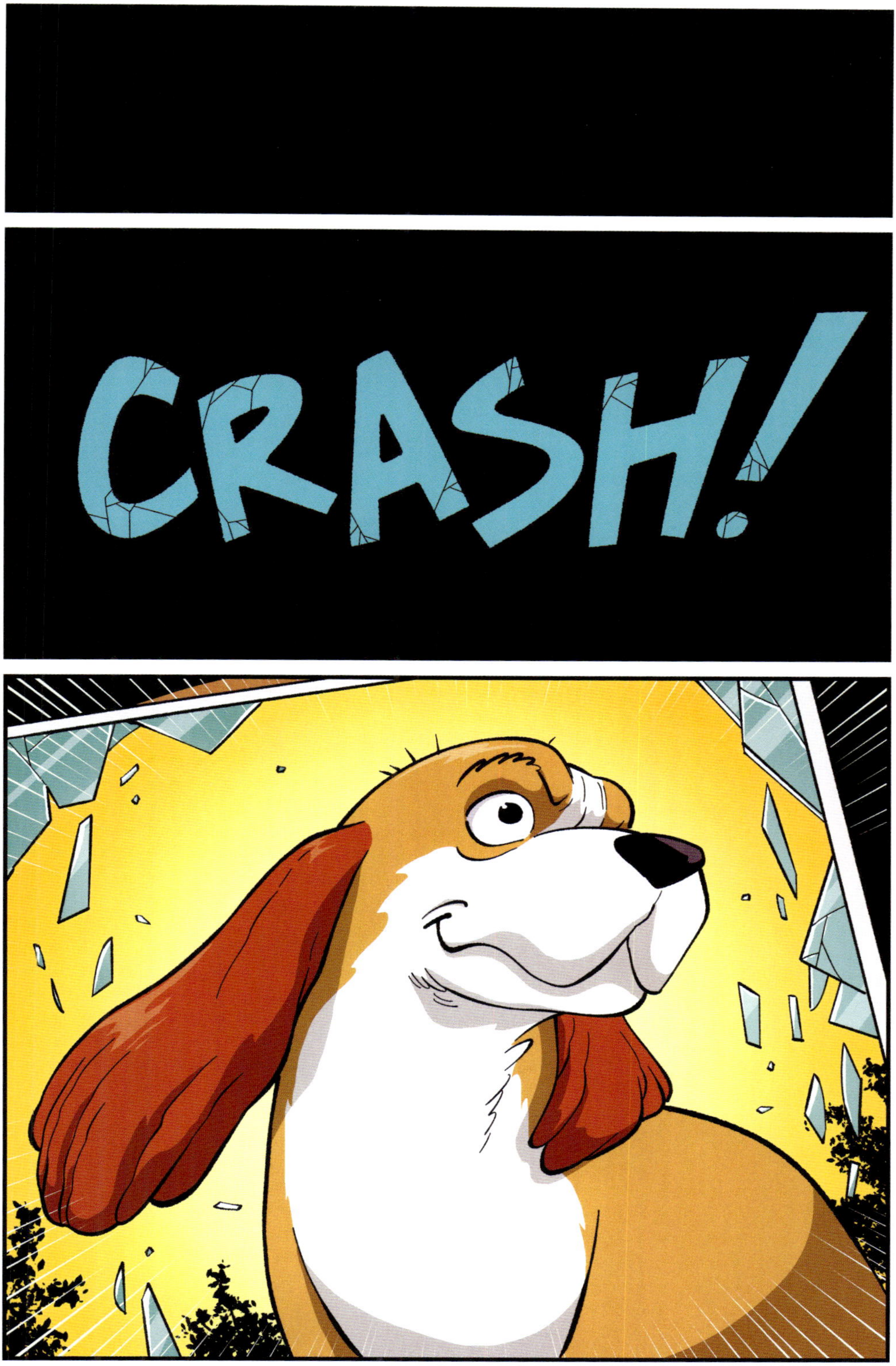
CRASH!

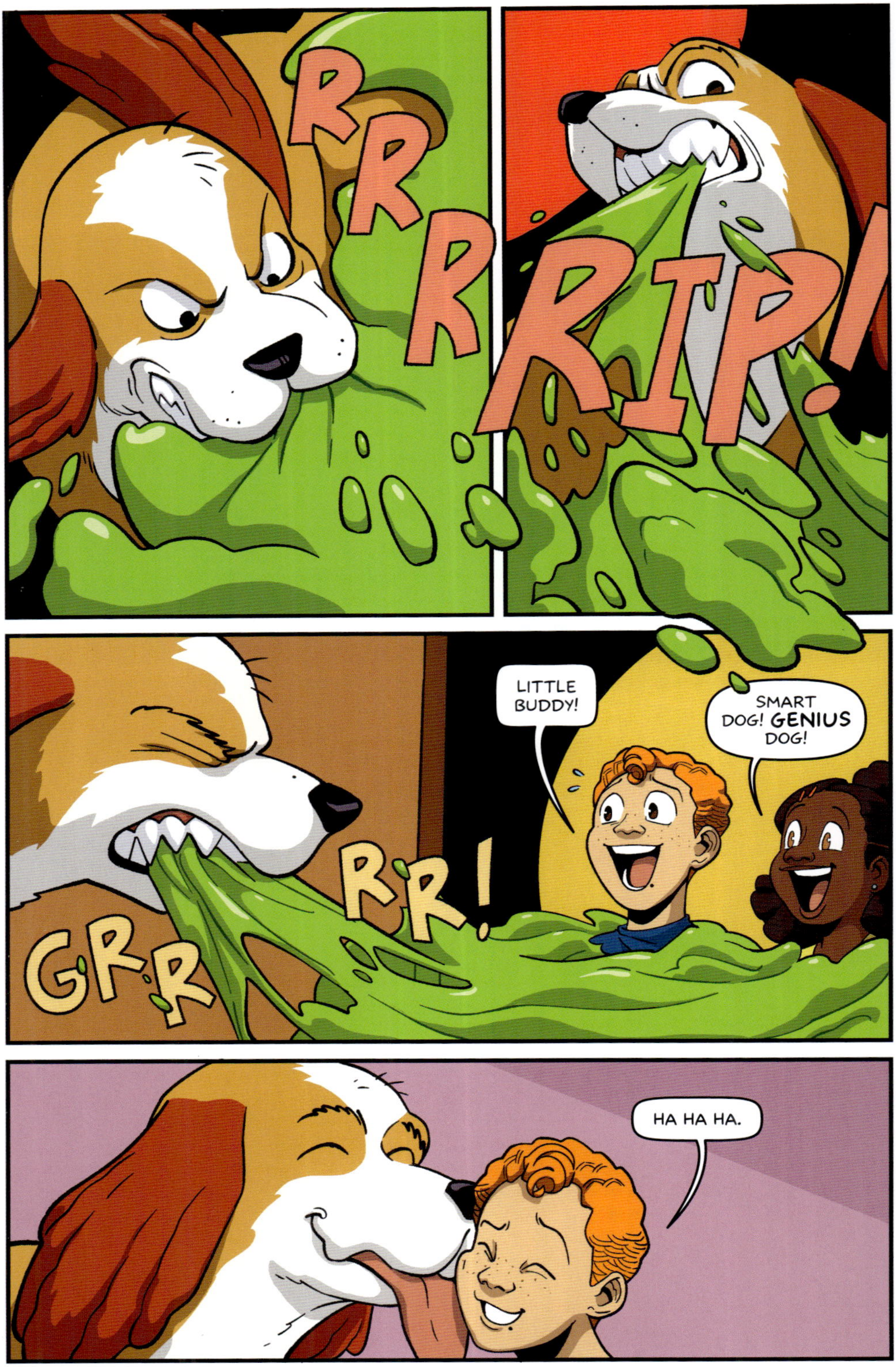
RRRRIP!
LITTLE BUDDY!
SMART DOG! GENIUS DOG!
GRR RR!
HA HA HA.

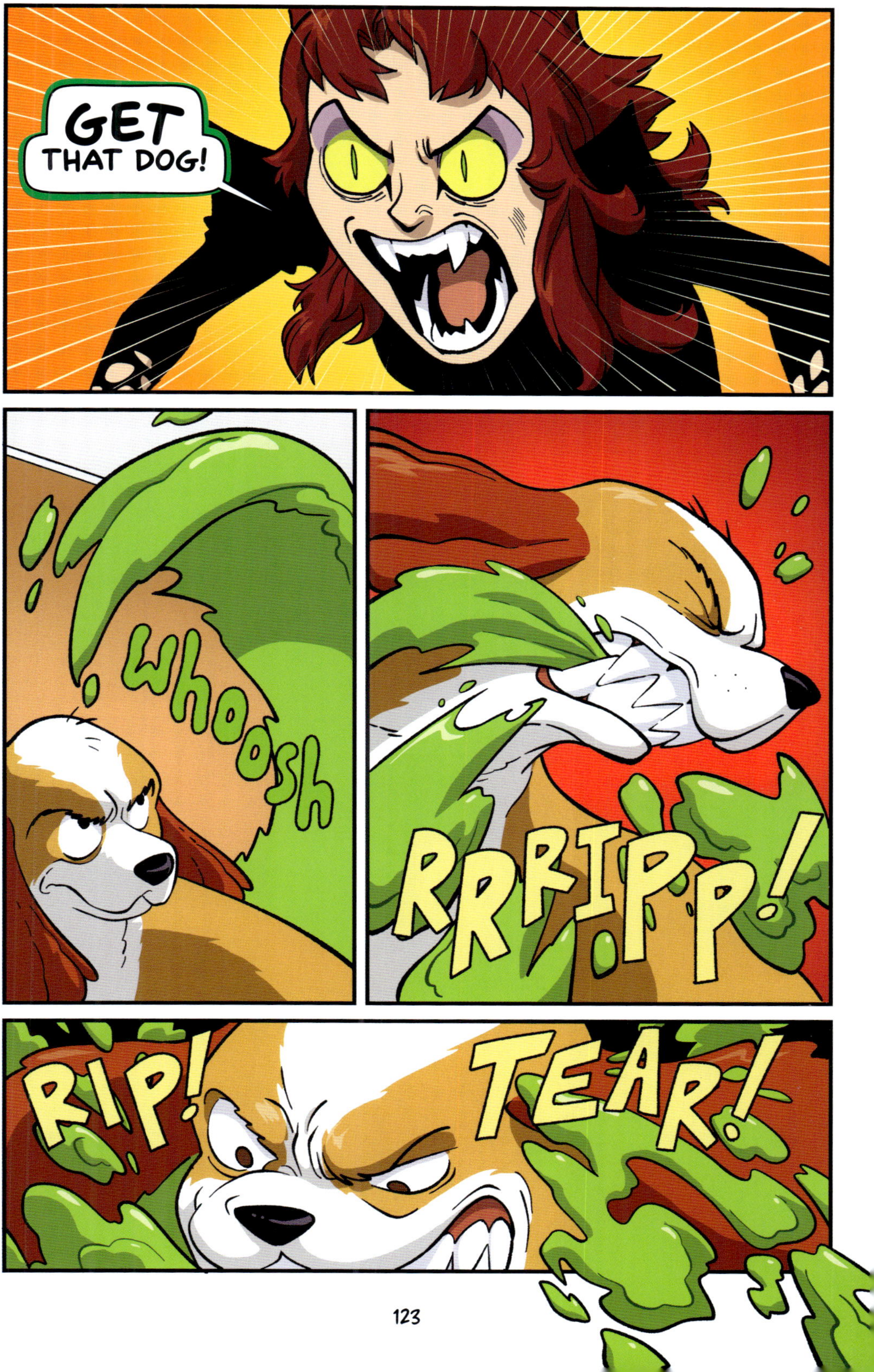
GET THAT DOG!
whoosh
RRRIPPP!
RIP!
TEAR!

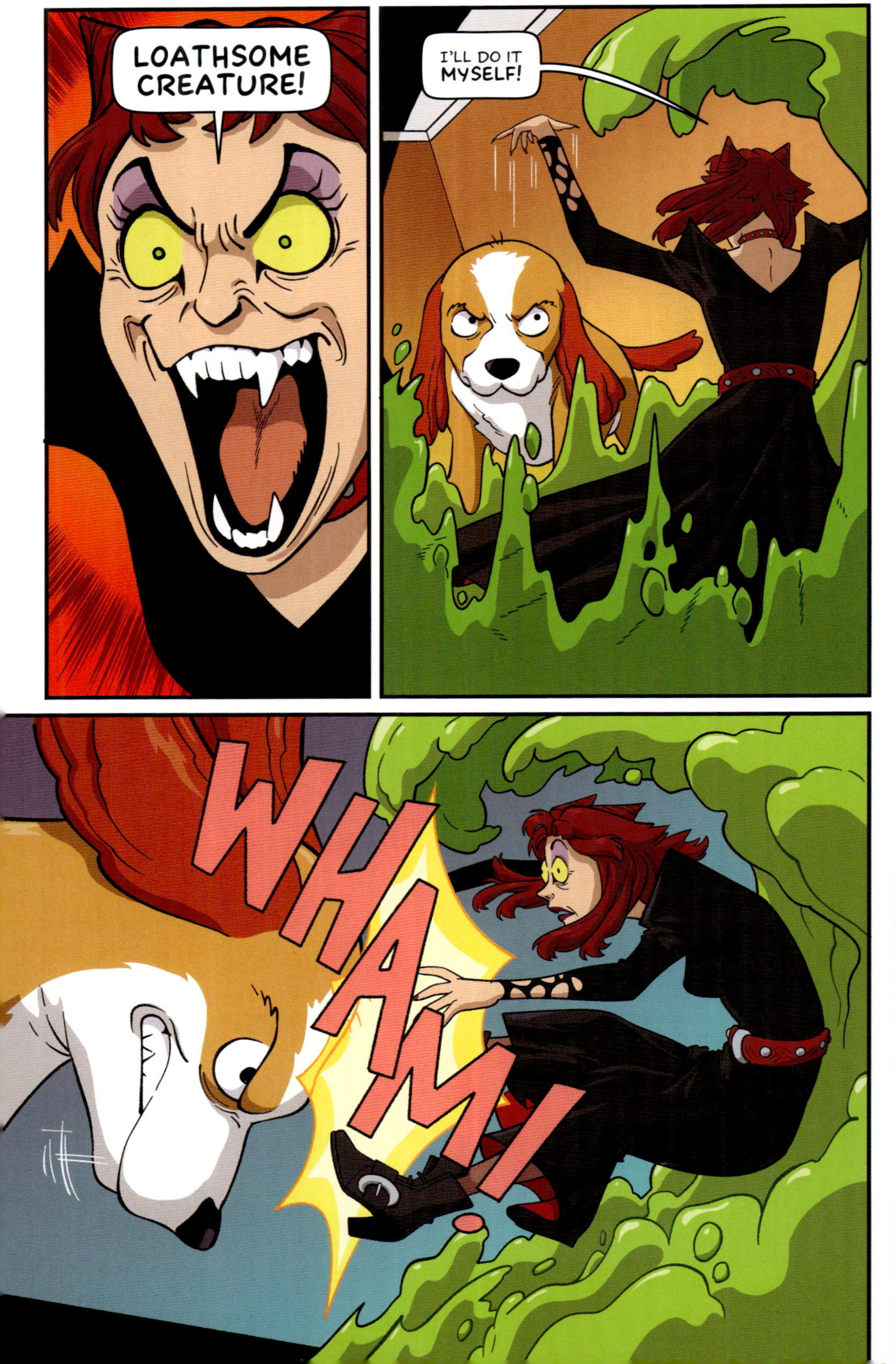
LOATHSOME CREATURE!
I'LL DO IT MYSELF!
WHAM!

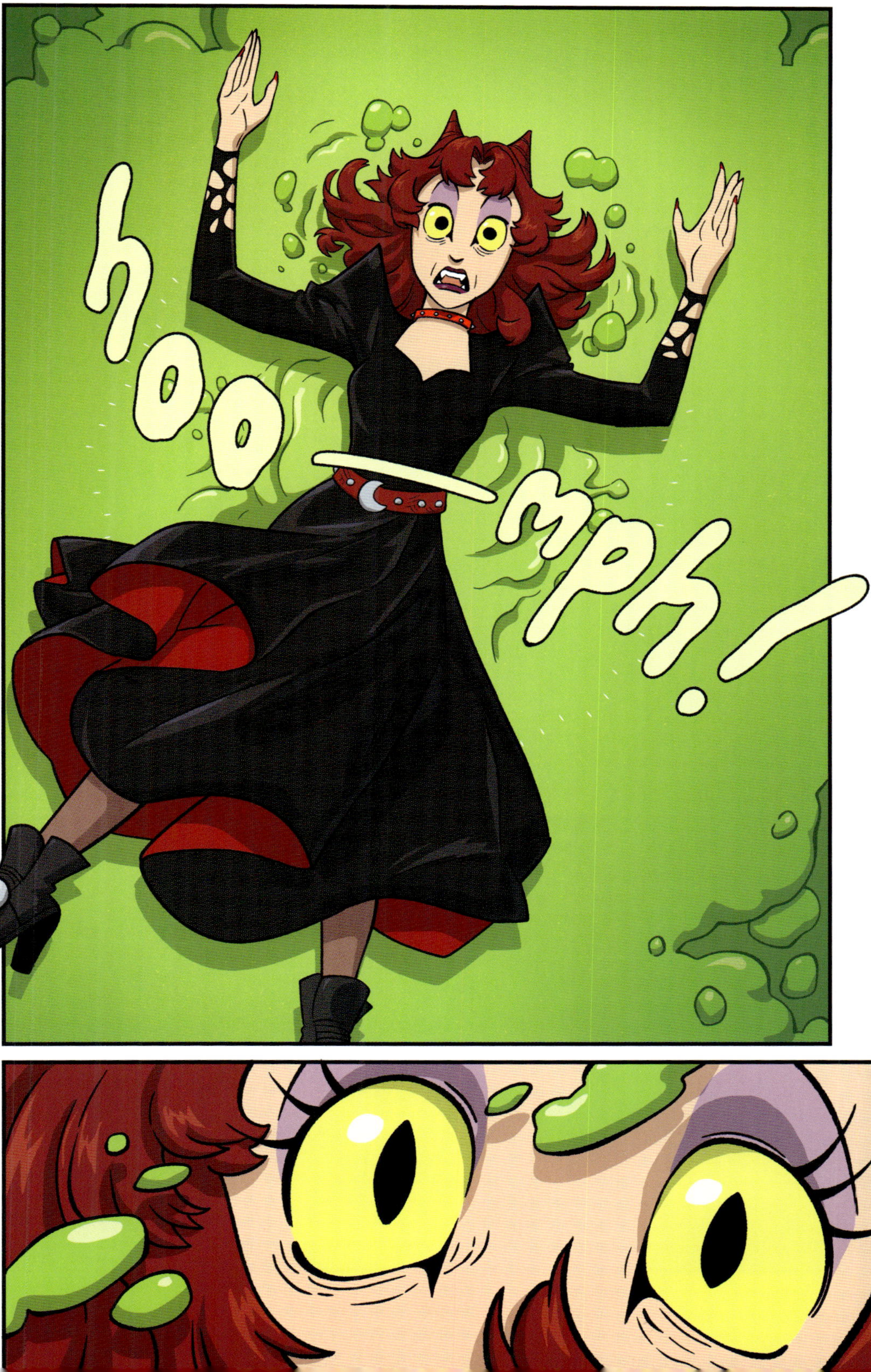
hooo—mph!

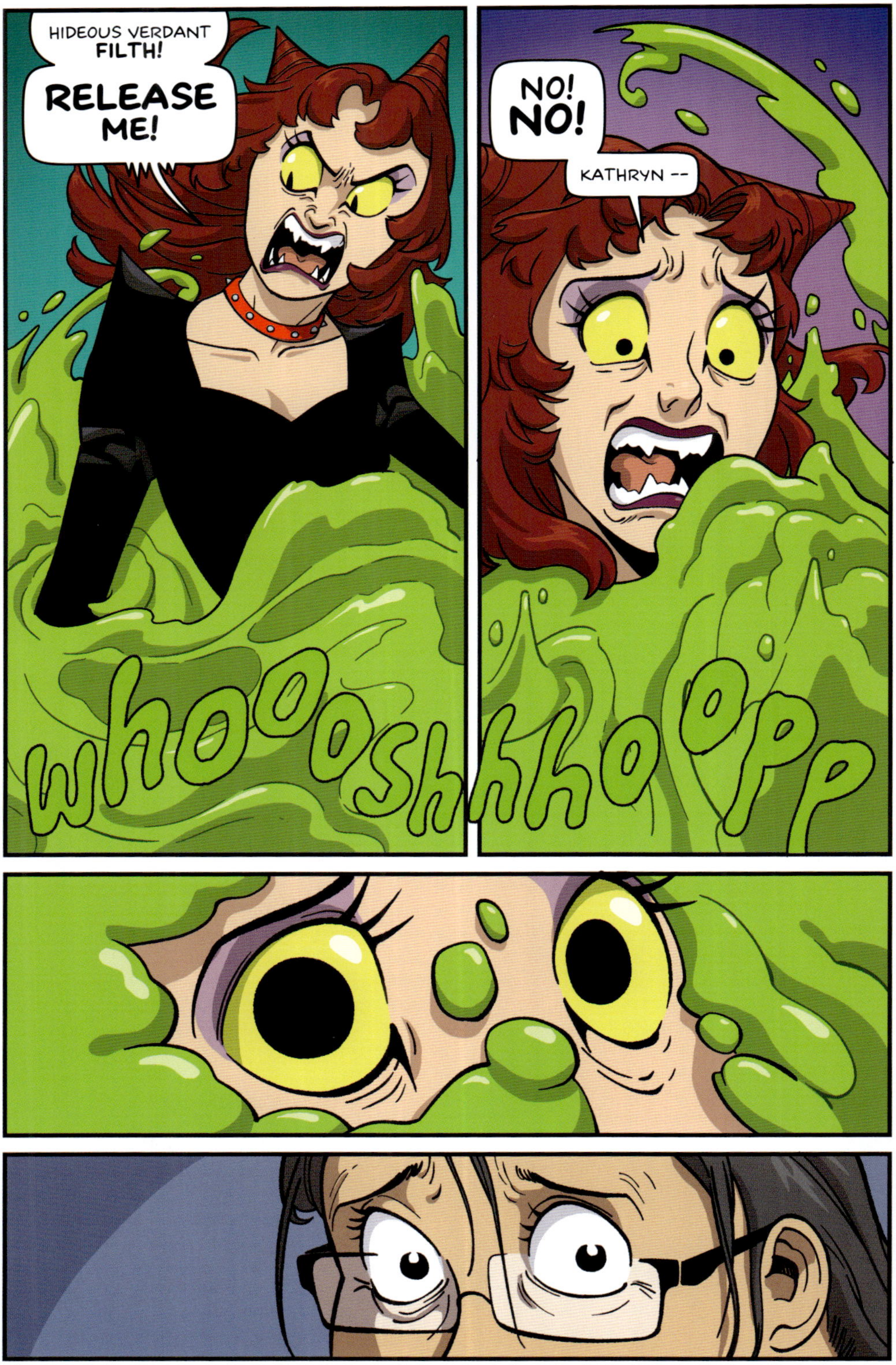
HIDEOUS VERDANT FILTH!
RELEASE ME!
NO! NO!
KATHRYN --
whooooshhhoopp

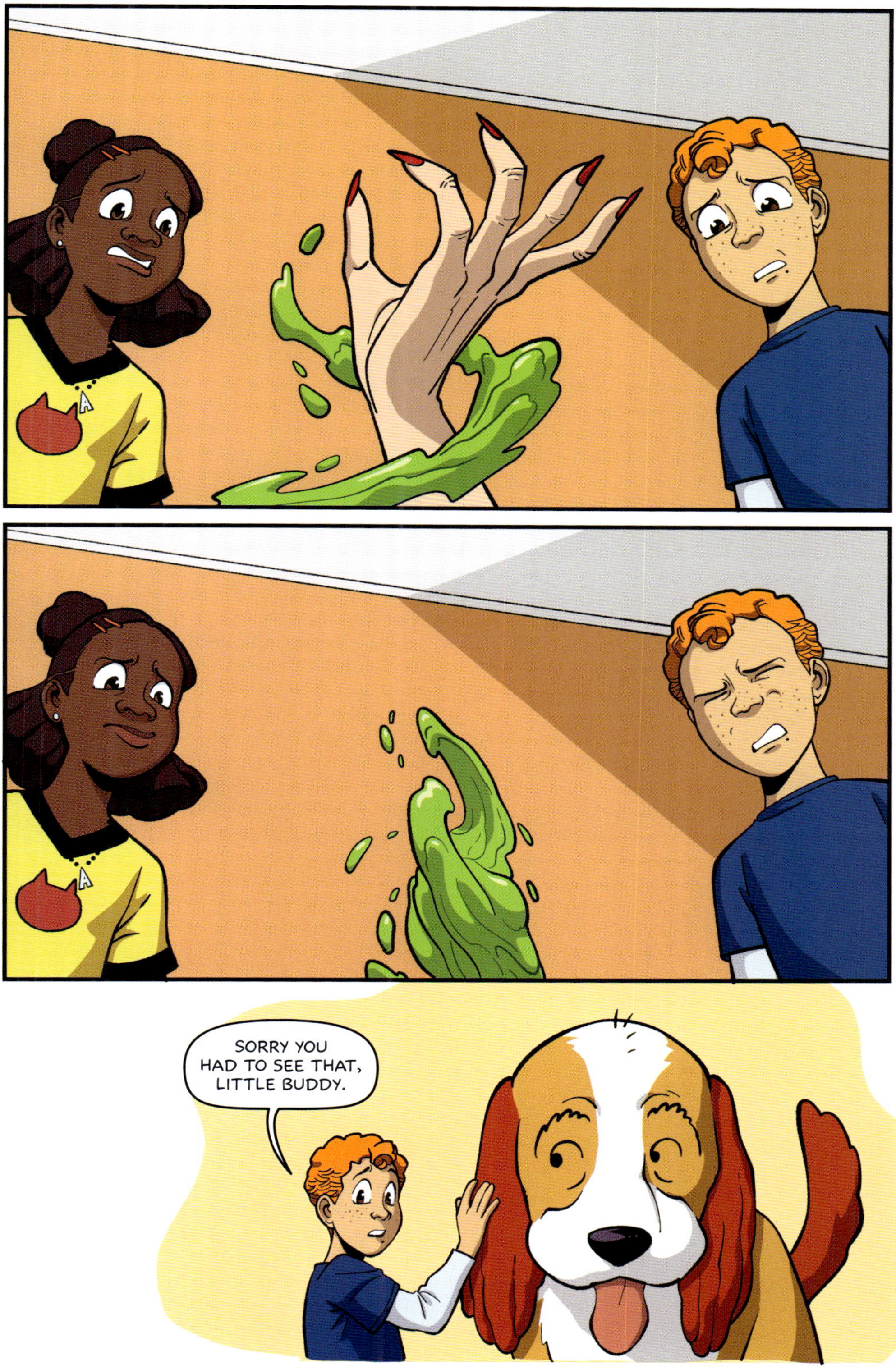
SORRY YOU HAD TO SEE THAT, LITTLE BUDDY.

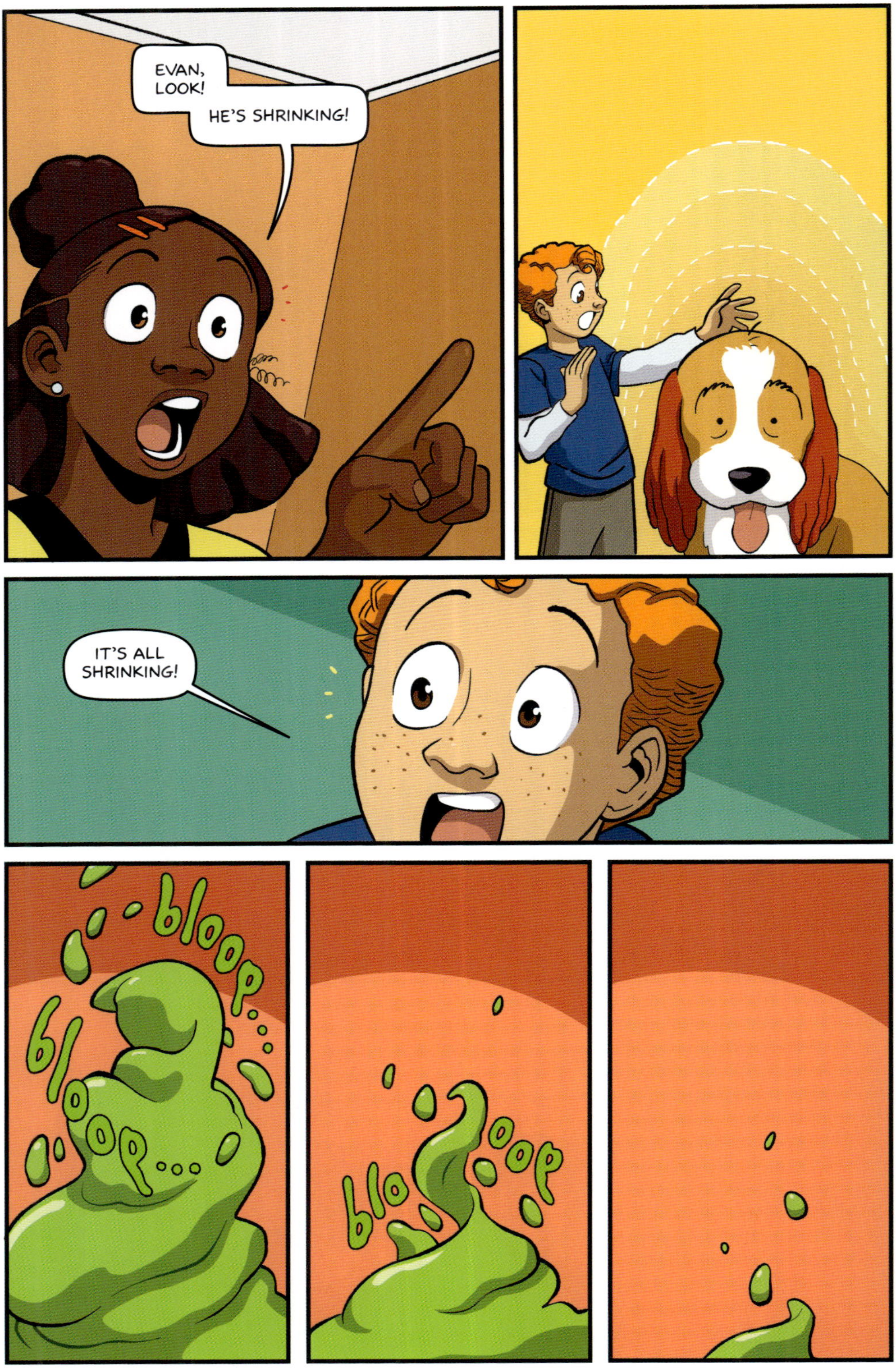
EVAN, LOOK!
HE'S SHRINKING!
IT'S ALL SHRINKING!
bloop
bloop...
bloop

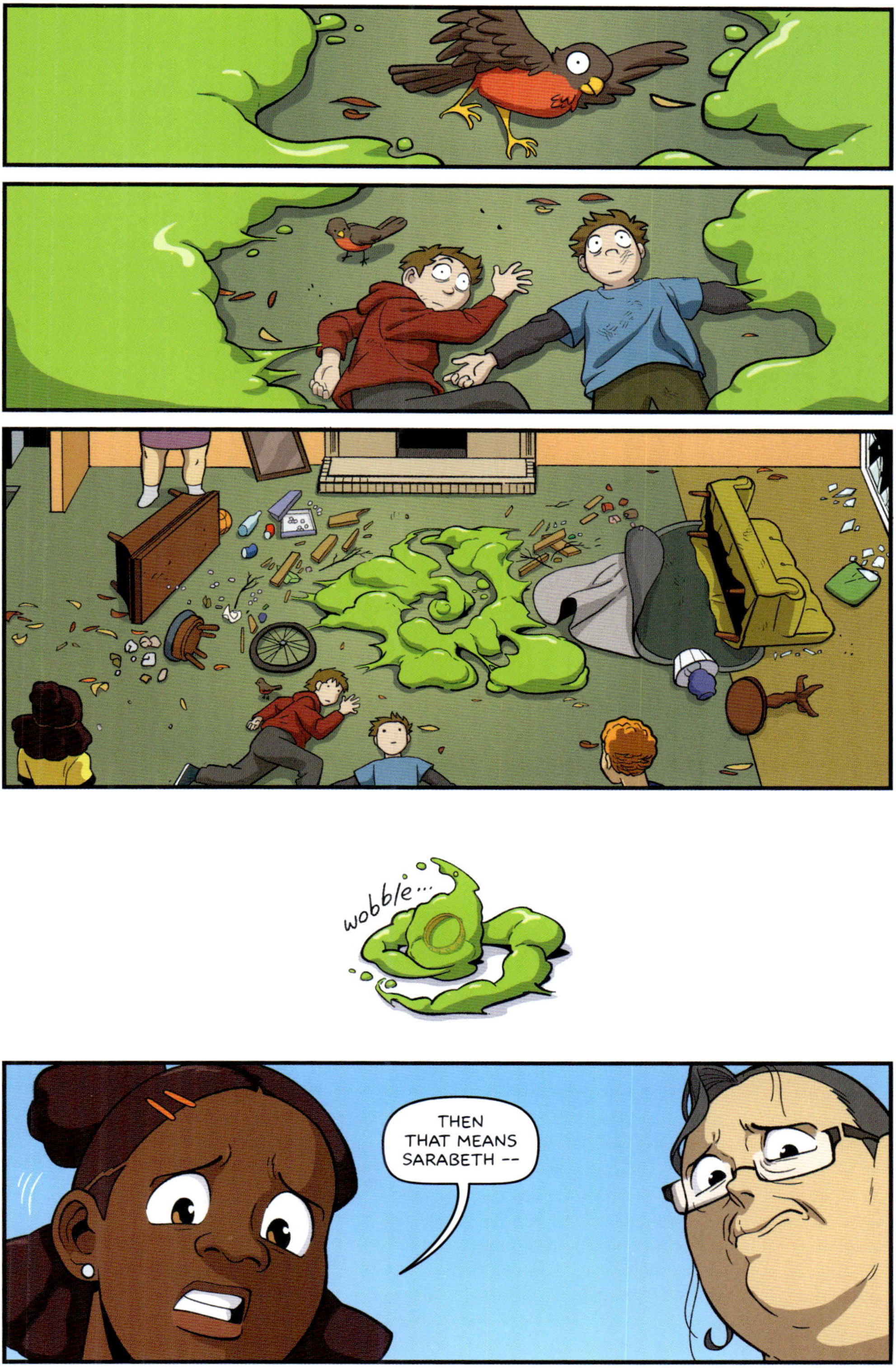
wobble...
THEN THAT MEANS SARABETH --

HER SPELL...
I CAN'T FEEL IT. IT'S GONE.
HER SPELL IS GONE!

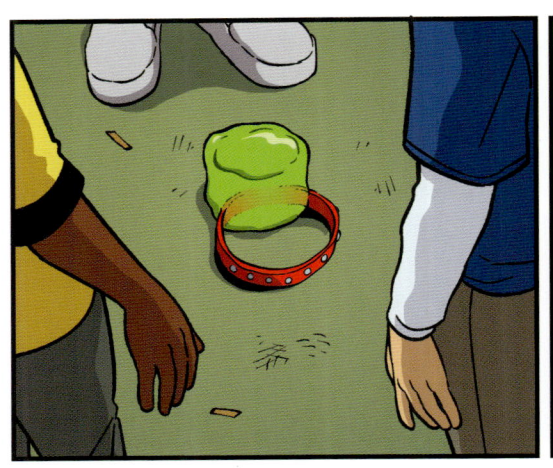

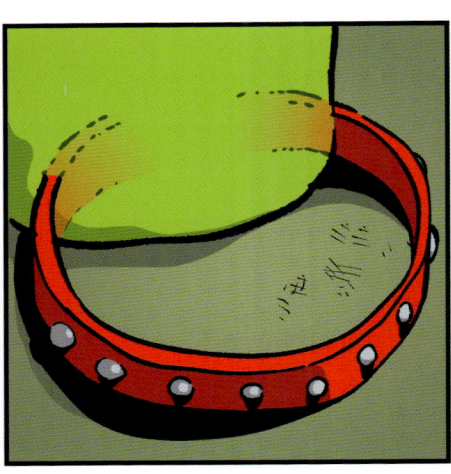

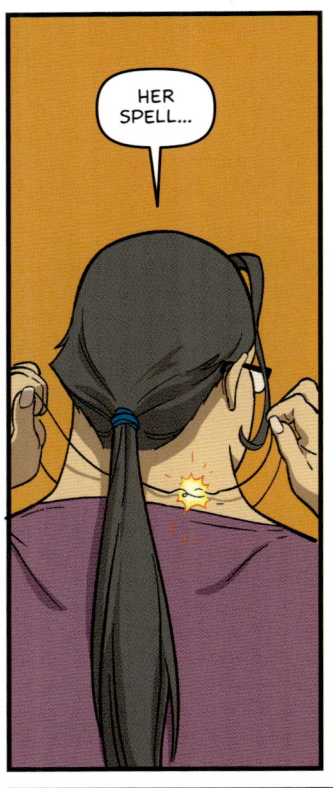

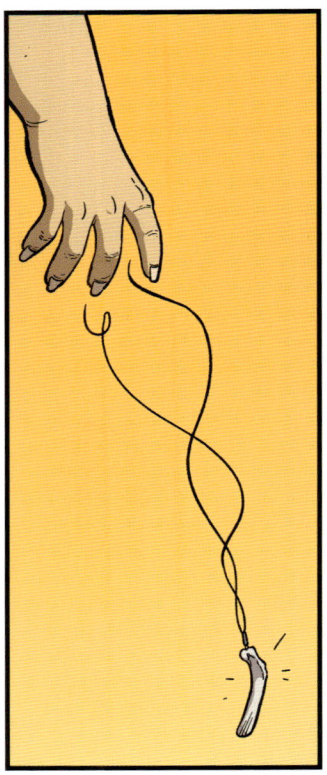

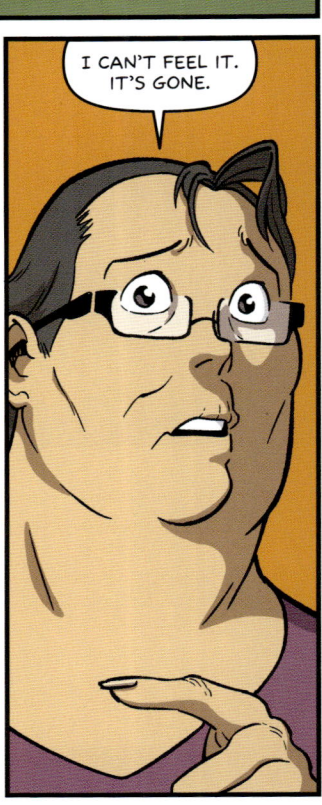

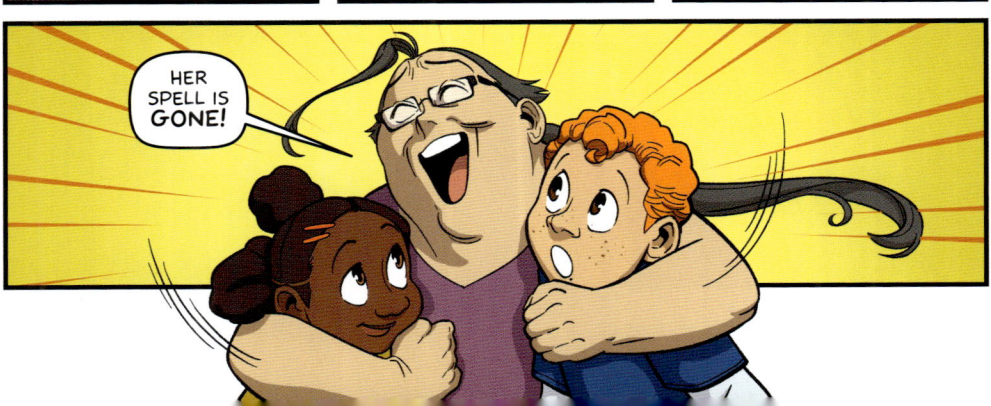

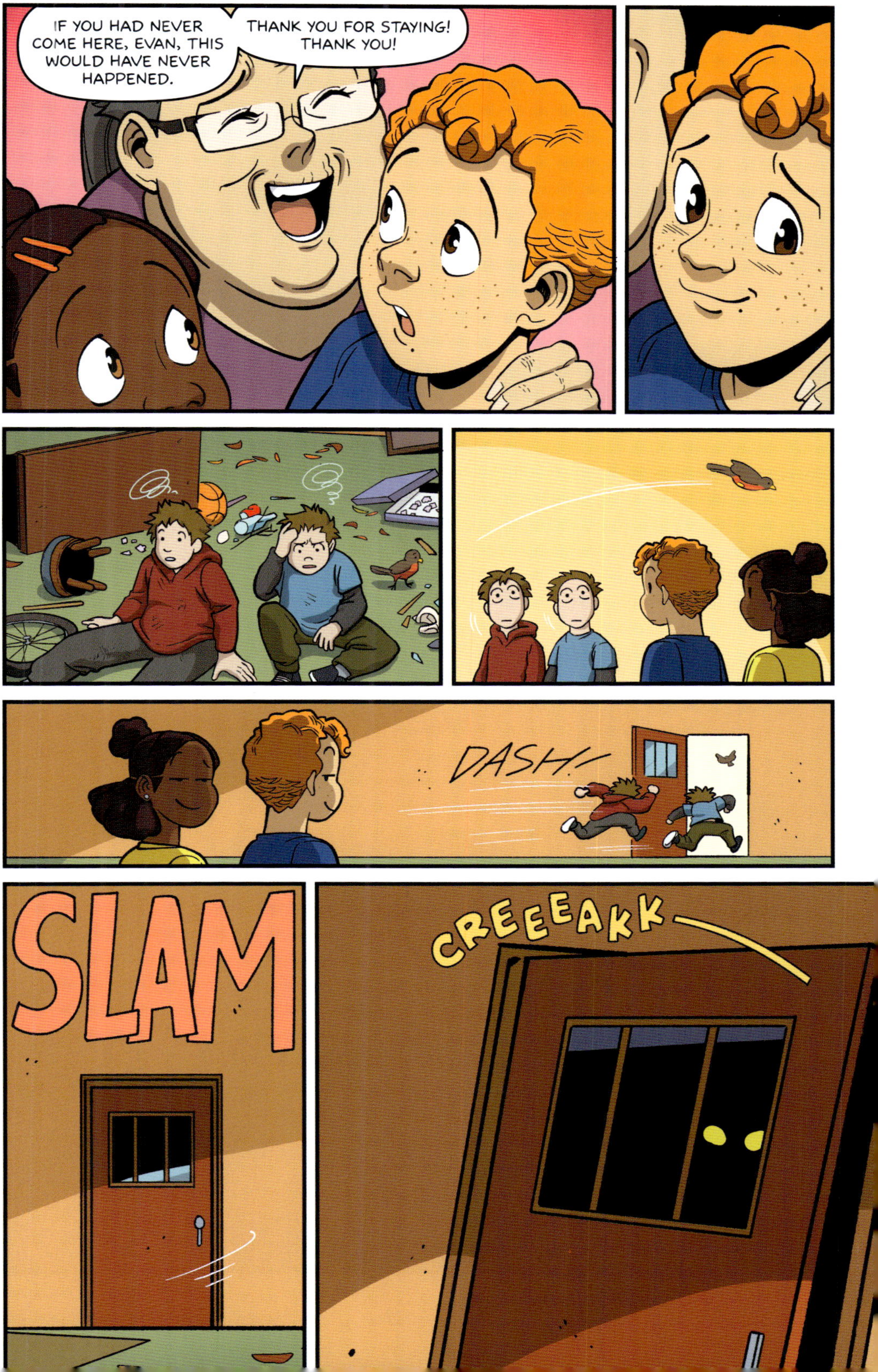
IF YOU HAD NEVER COME HERE, EVAN, THIS WOULD HAVE NEVER HAPPENED.
THANK YOU FOR STAYING! THANK YOU!
DASH!
SLAM
CREEEAKK

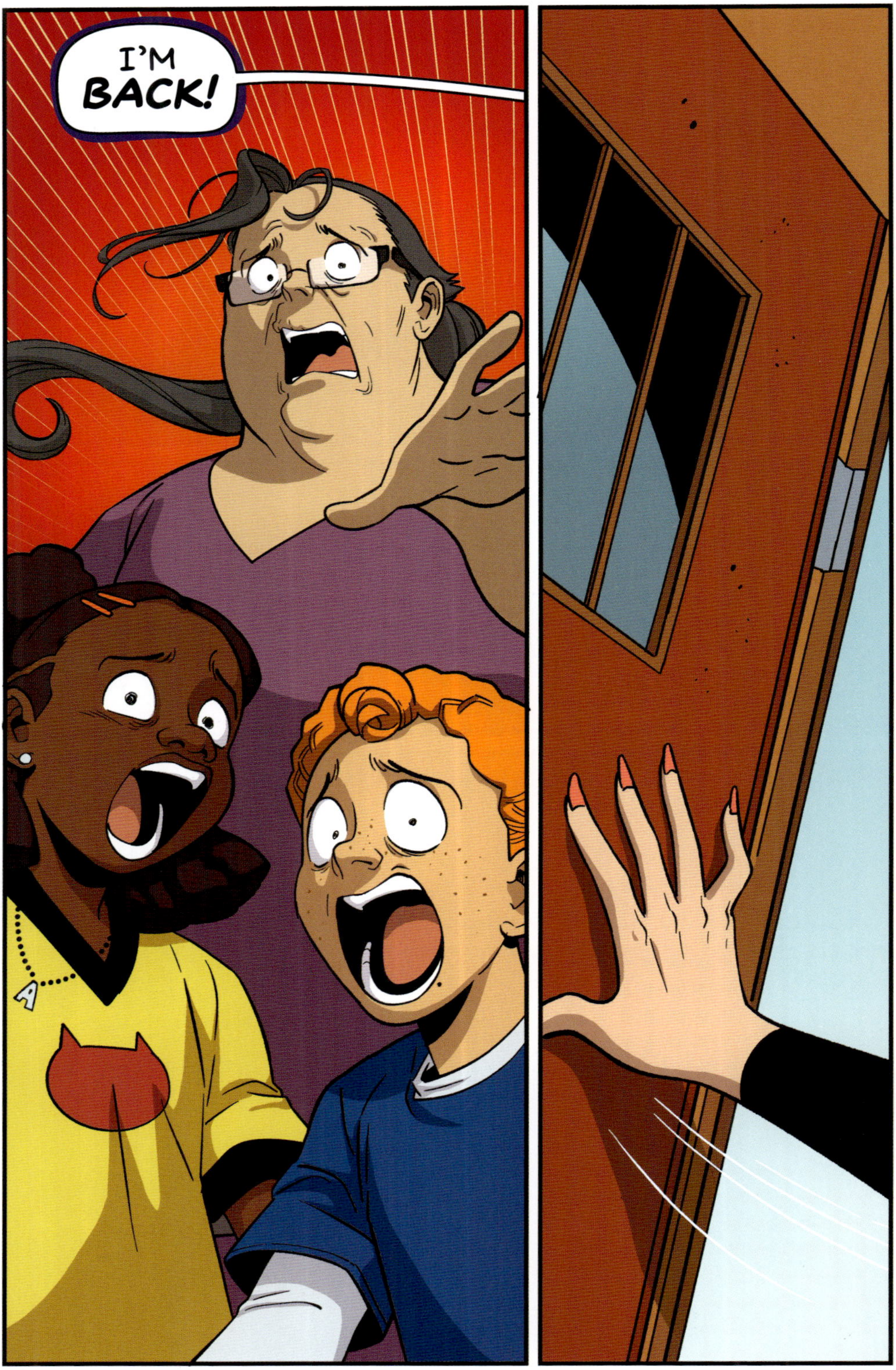
I'M BACK!

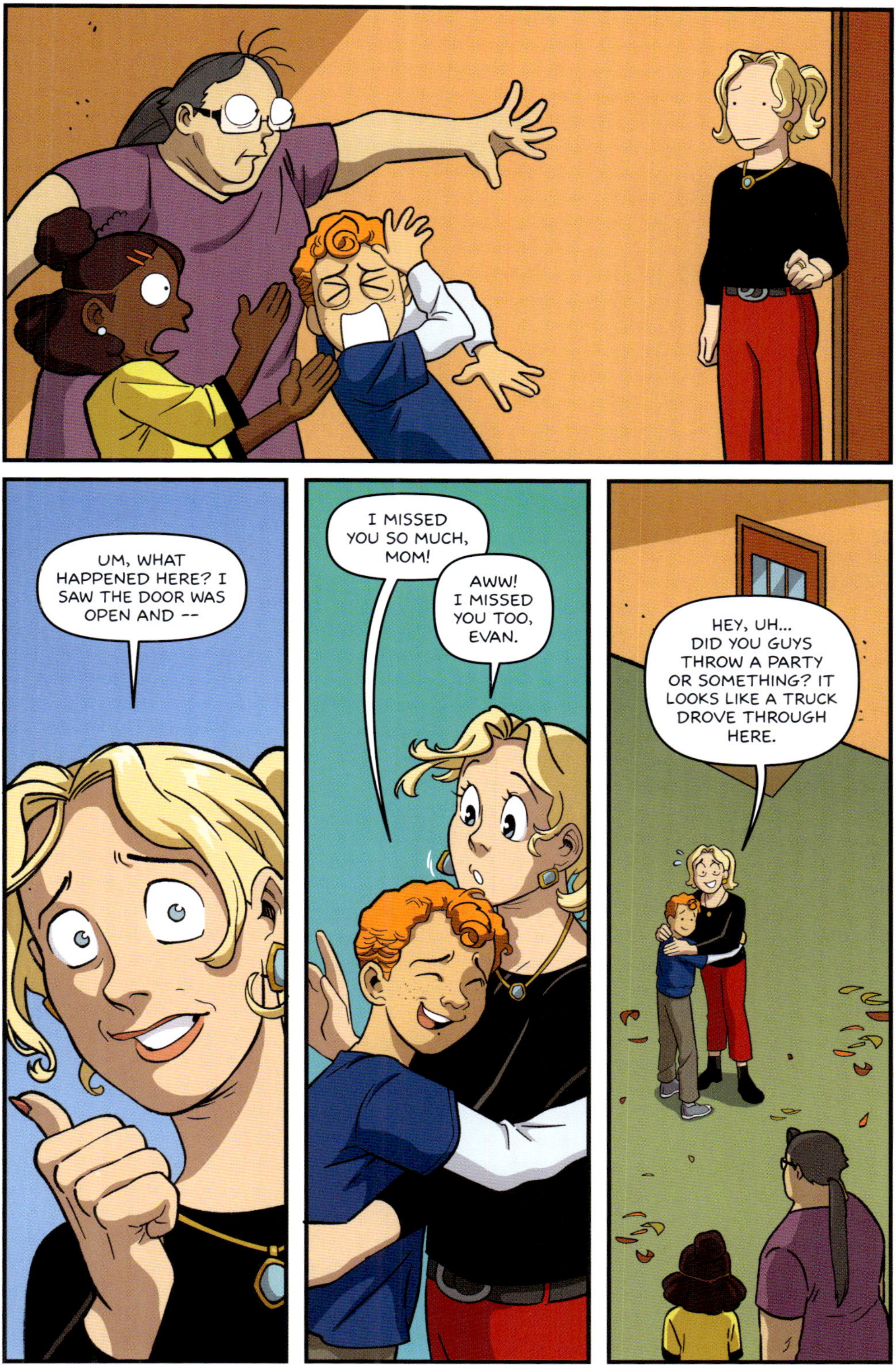
UM, WHAT HAPPENED HERE? I SAW THE DOOR WAS OPEN AND --
I MISSED YOU SO MUCH, MOM!
AWW! I MISSED YOU TOO, EVAN.
HEY, UH... DID YOU GUYS THROW A PARTY OR SOMETHING? IT LOOKS LIKE A TRUCK DROVE THROUGH HERE.

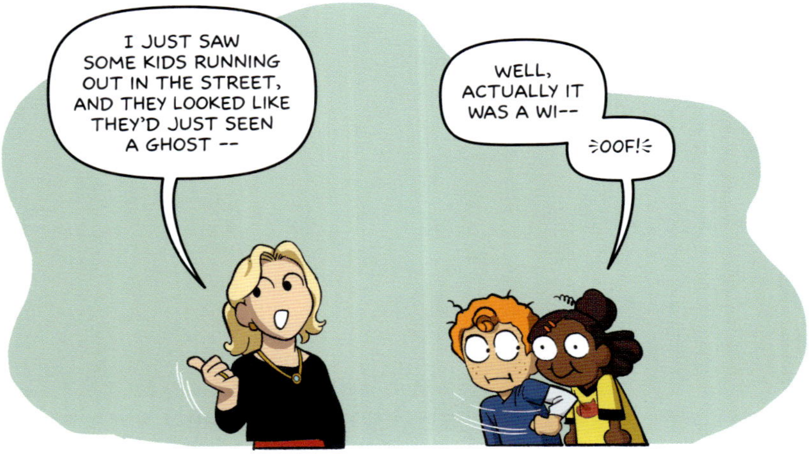
I JUST SAW SOME KIDS RUNNING OUT IN THE STREET, AND THEY LOOKED LIKE THEY'D JUST SEEN A GHOST --
WELL, ACTUALLY IT WAS A WI--
OOF!

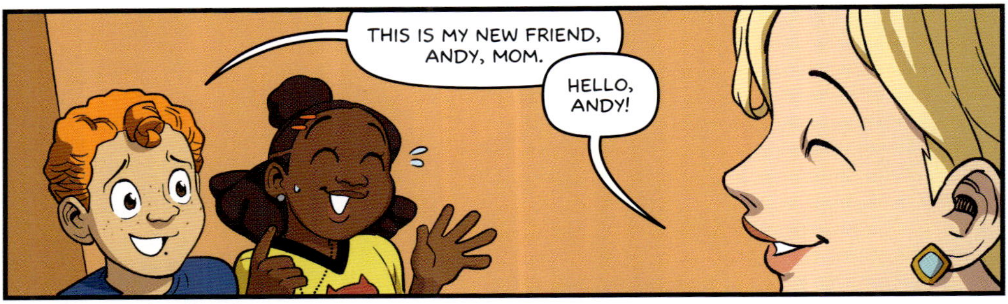
THIS IS MY NEW FRIEND, ANDY, MOM.
HELLO, ANDY!

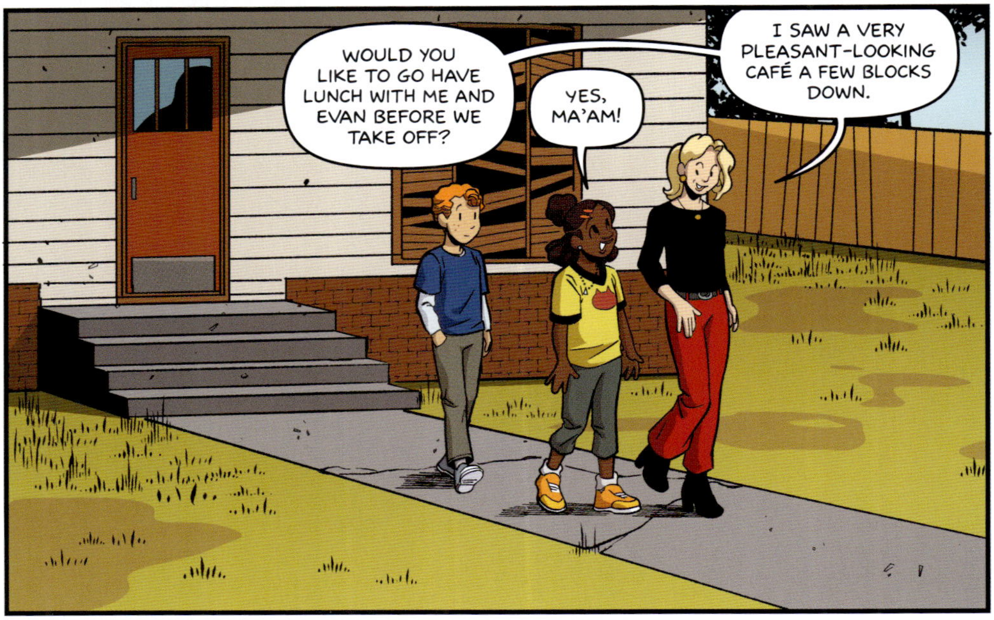
I SAW A VERY PLEASANT-LOOKING CAFÉ A FEW BLOCKS DOWN.
WOULD YOU LIKE TO GO HAVE LUNCH WITH ME AND EVAN BEFORE WE TAKE OFF?
YES, MA'AM!

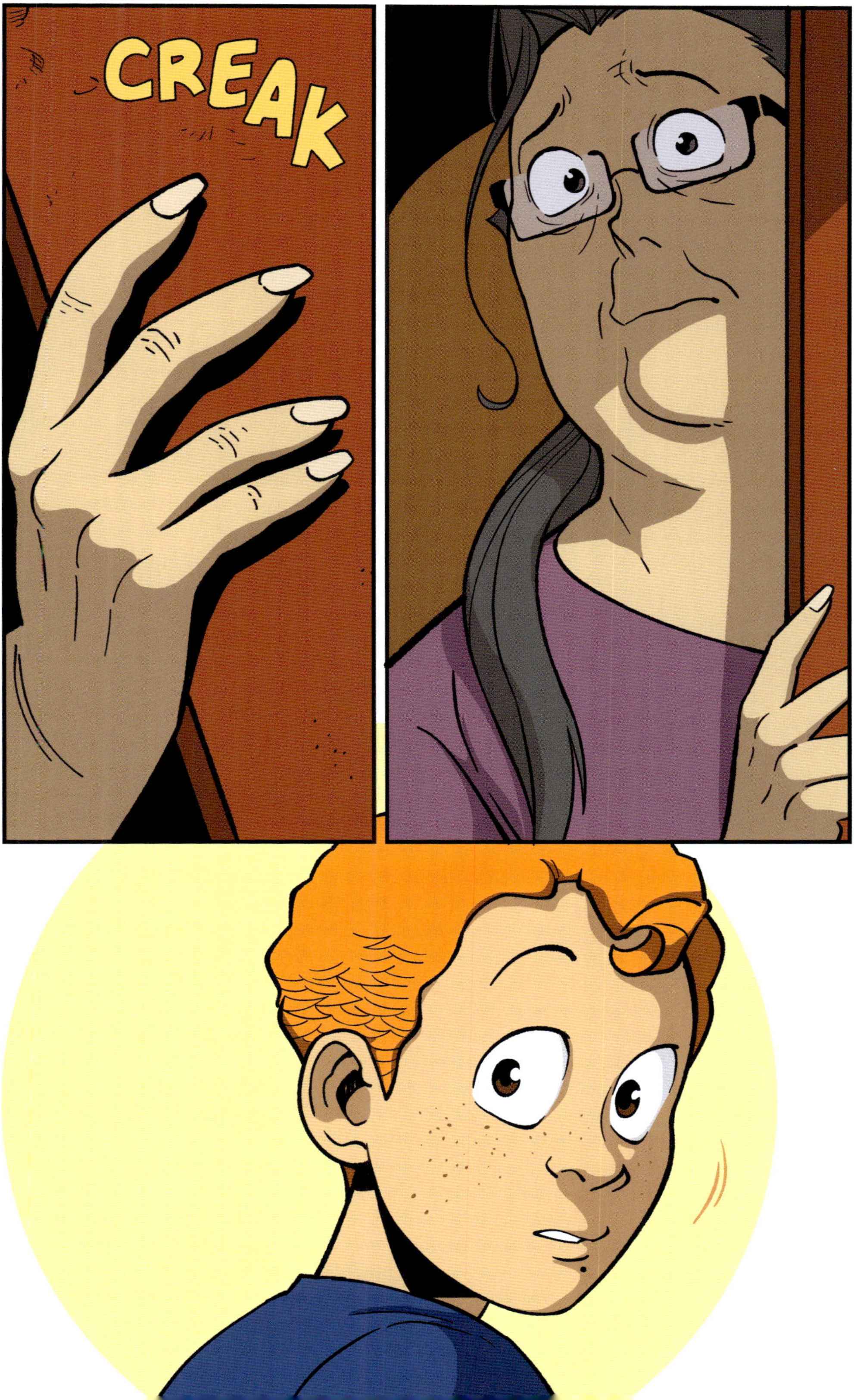
CREAK

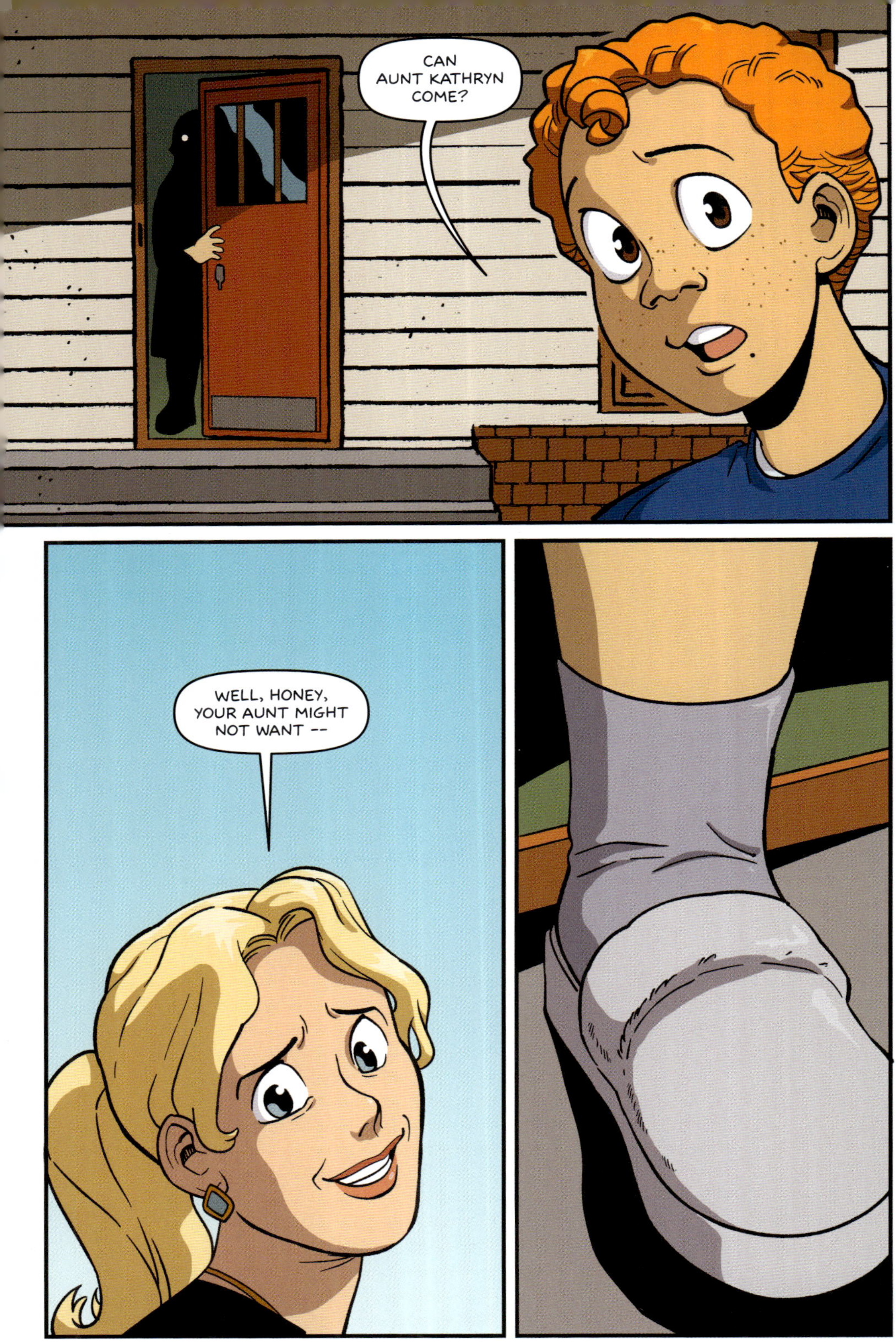
CAN AUNT KATHRYN COME?
WELL, HONEY, YOUR AUNT MIGHT NOT WANT --

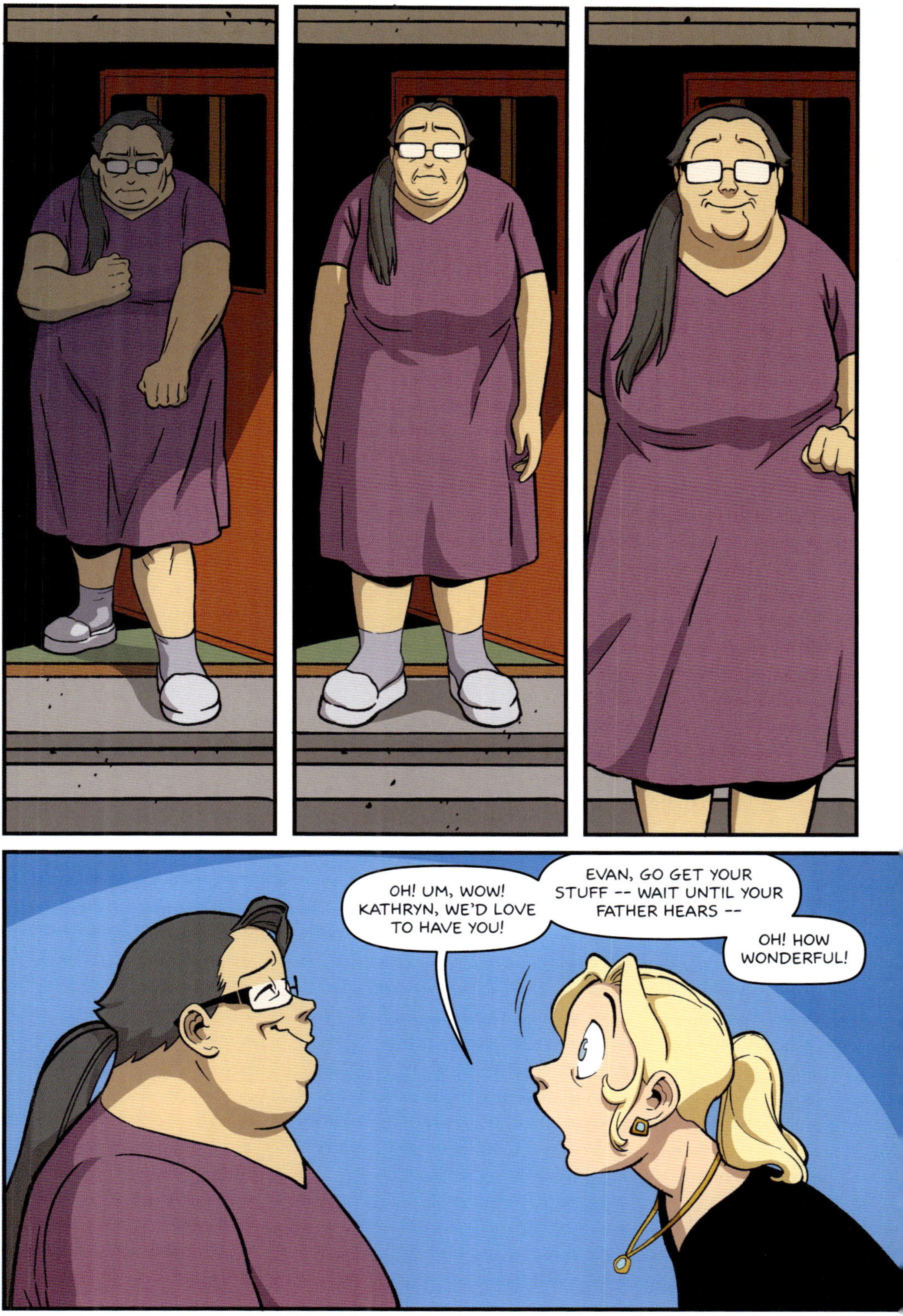
OH! UM, WOW! KATHRYN, WE'D LOVE TO HAVE YOU!
EVAN, GO GET YOUR STUFF -- WAIT UNTIL YOUR FATHER HEARS --
OH! HOW WONDERFUL!

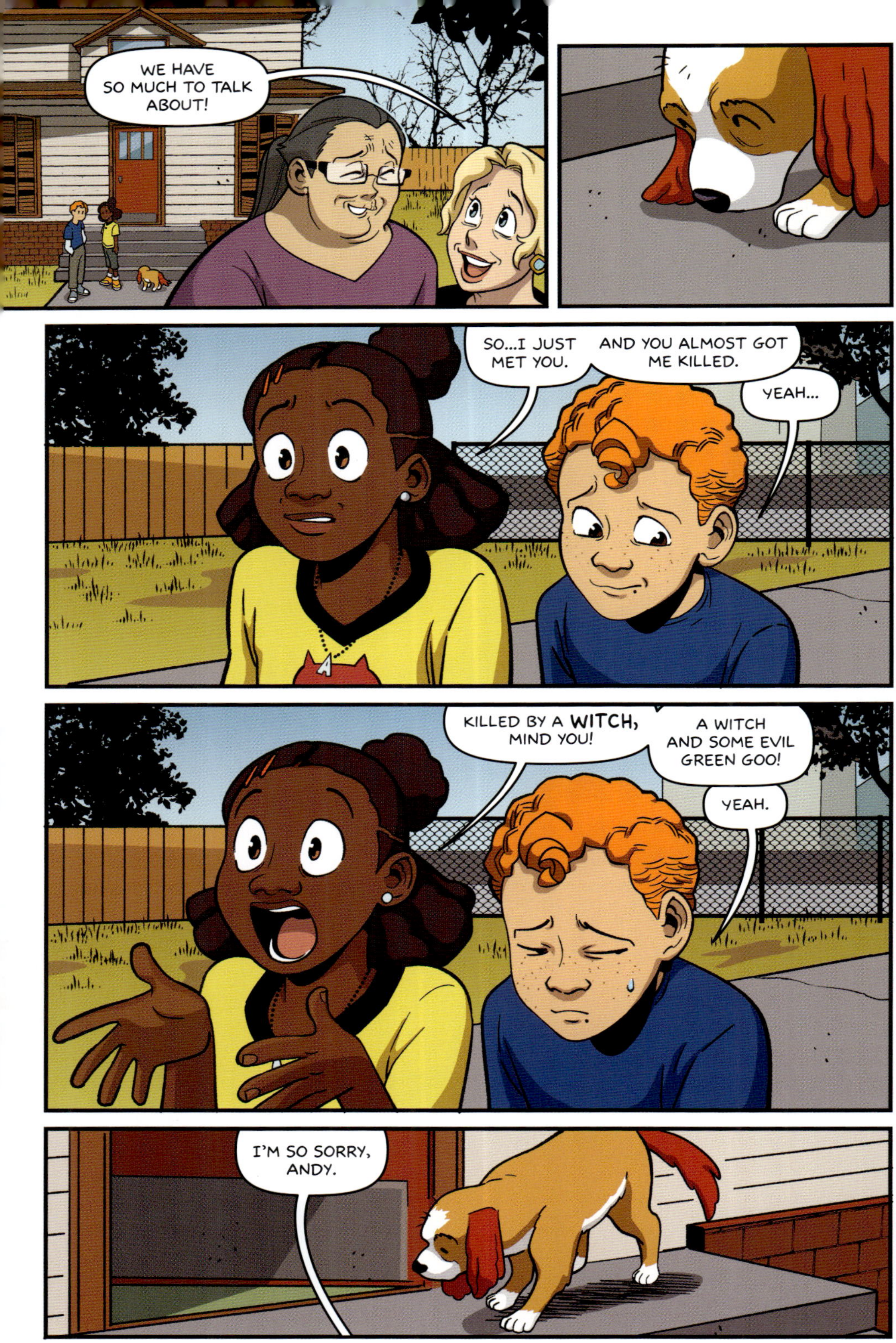
WE HAVE SO MUCH TO TALK ABOUT!
SO...I JUST MET YOU.
AND YOU ALMOST GOT ME KILLED.
YEAH...
KILLED BY A **WITCH**, MIND YOU!
A WITCH AND SOME EVIL GREEN GOO!
YEAH.
I'M SO SORRY, ANDY.

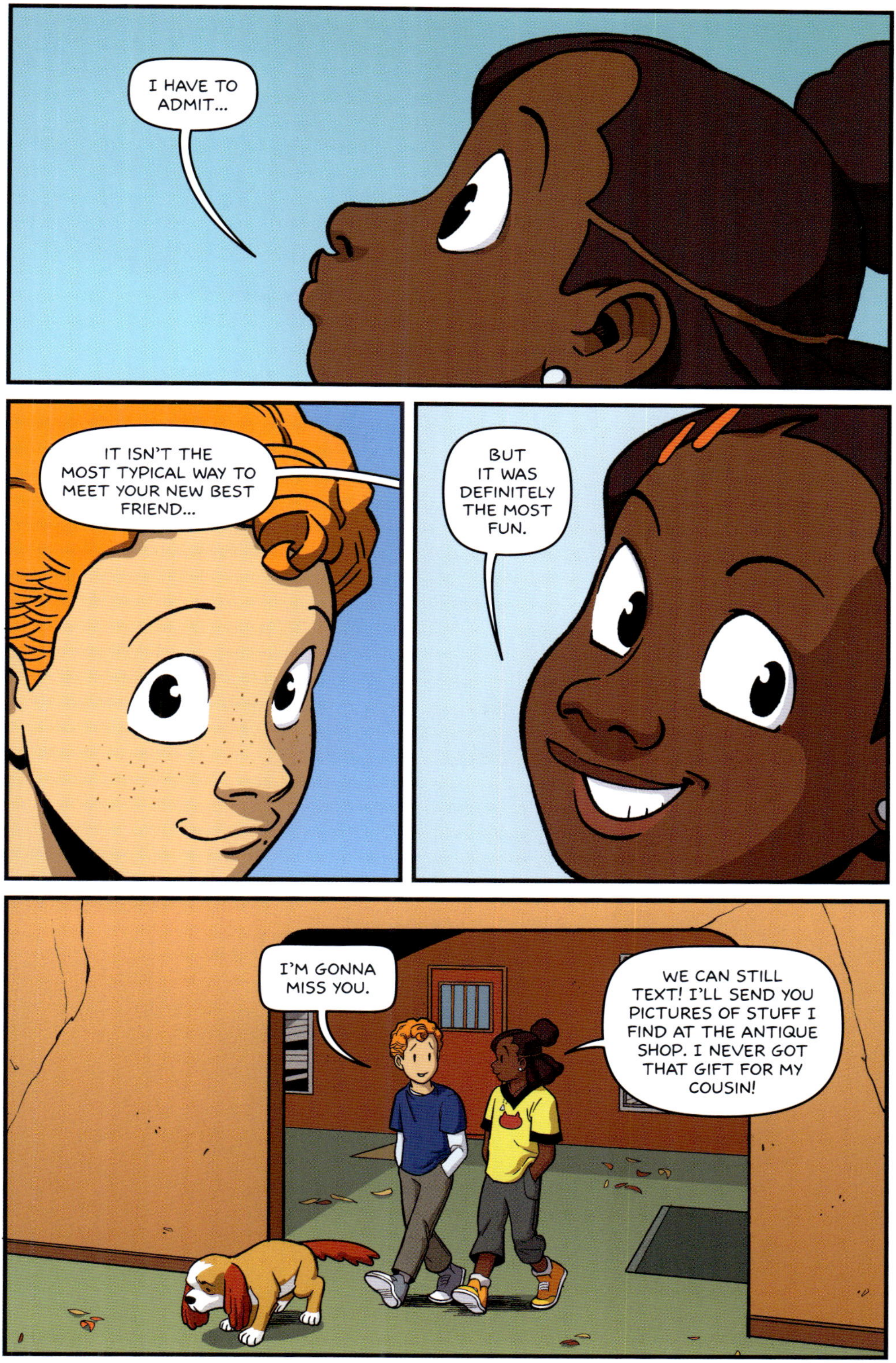

I HAVE TO ADMIT...
IT ISN'T THE MOST TYPICAL WAY TO MEET YOUR NEW BEST FRIEND...
BUT IT WAS DEFINITELY THE MOST FUN.
I'M GONNA MISS YOU.
WE CAN STILL TEXT! I'LL SEND YOU PICTURES OF STUFF I FIND AT THE ANTIQUE SHOP. I NEVER GOT THAT GIFT FOR MY COUSIN!

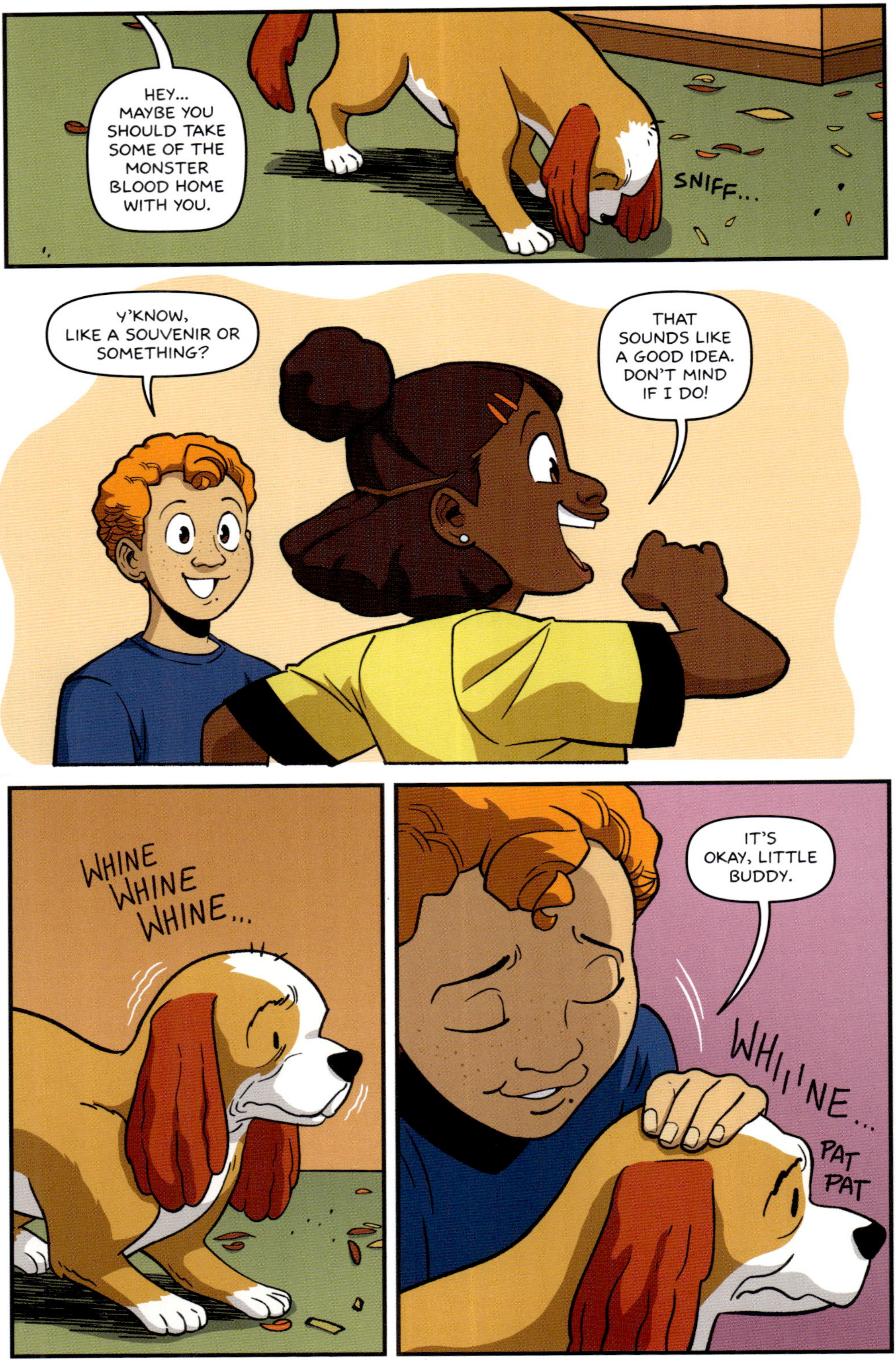
HEY... MAYBE YOU SHOULD TAKE SOME OF THE MONSTER BLOOD HOME WITH YOU.
SNIFF...
Y'KNOW, LIKE A SOUVENIR OR SOMETHING?
THAT SOUNDS LIKE A GOOD IDEA. DON'T MIND IF I DO!
WHINE WHINE WHINE...
IT'S OKAY, LITTLE BUDDY.
WHIIINE...
PAT PAT

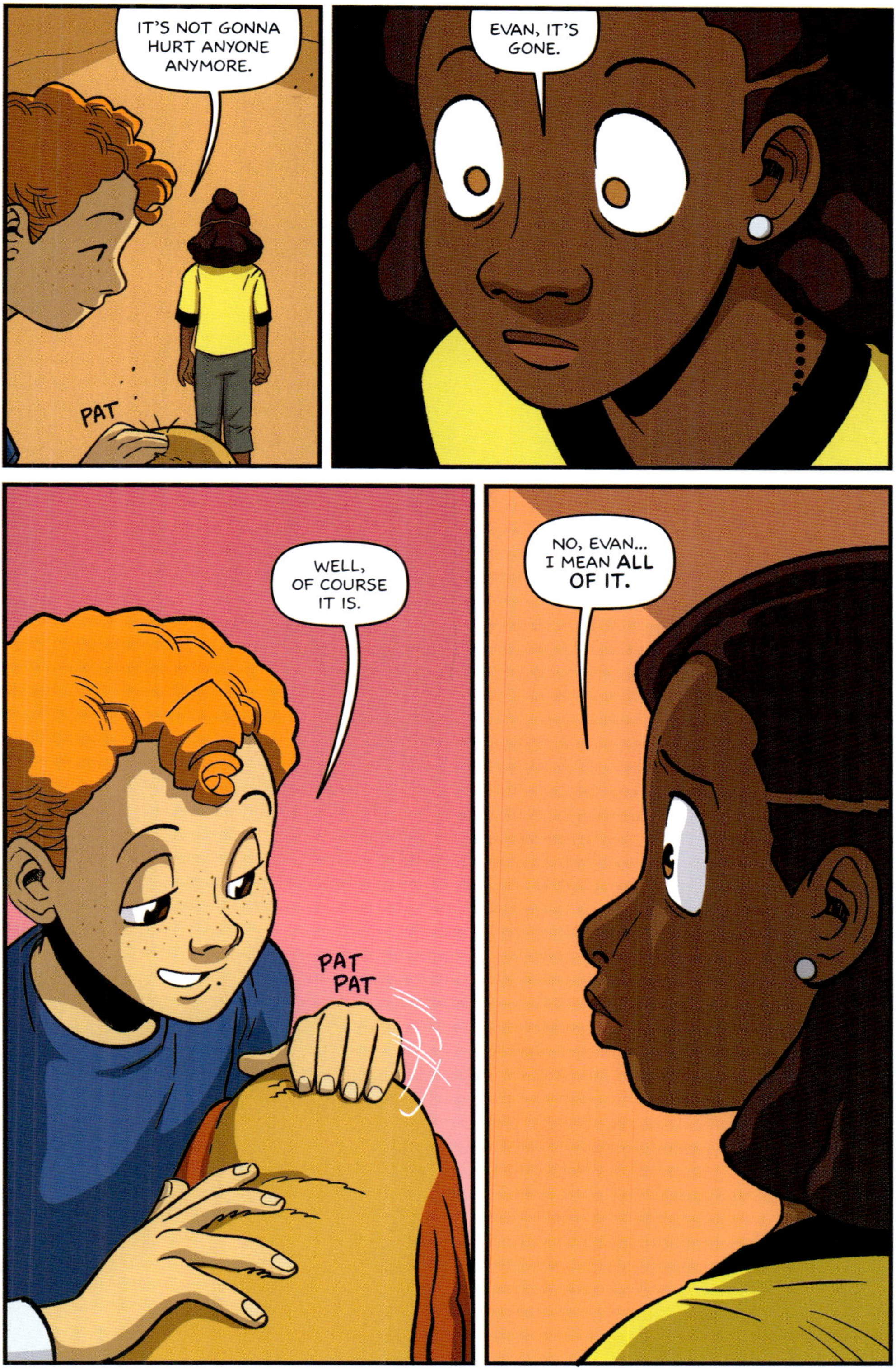
IT'S NOT GONNA HURT ANYONE ANYMORE.
PAT
EVAN, IT'S GONE.
WELL, OF COURSE IT IS.
PAT PAT
NO, EVAN... I MEAN **ALL OF IT.**

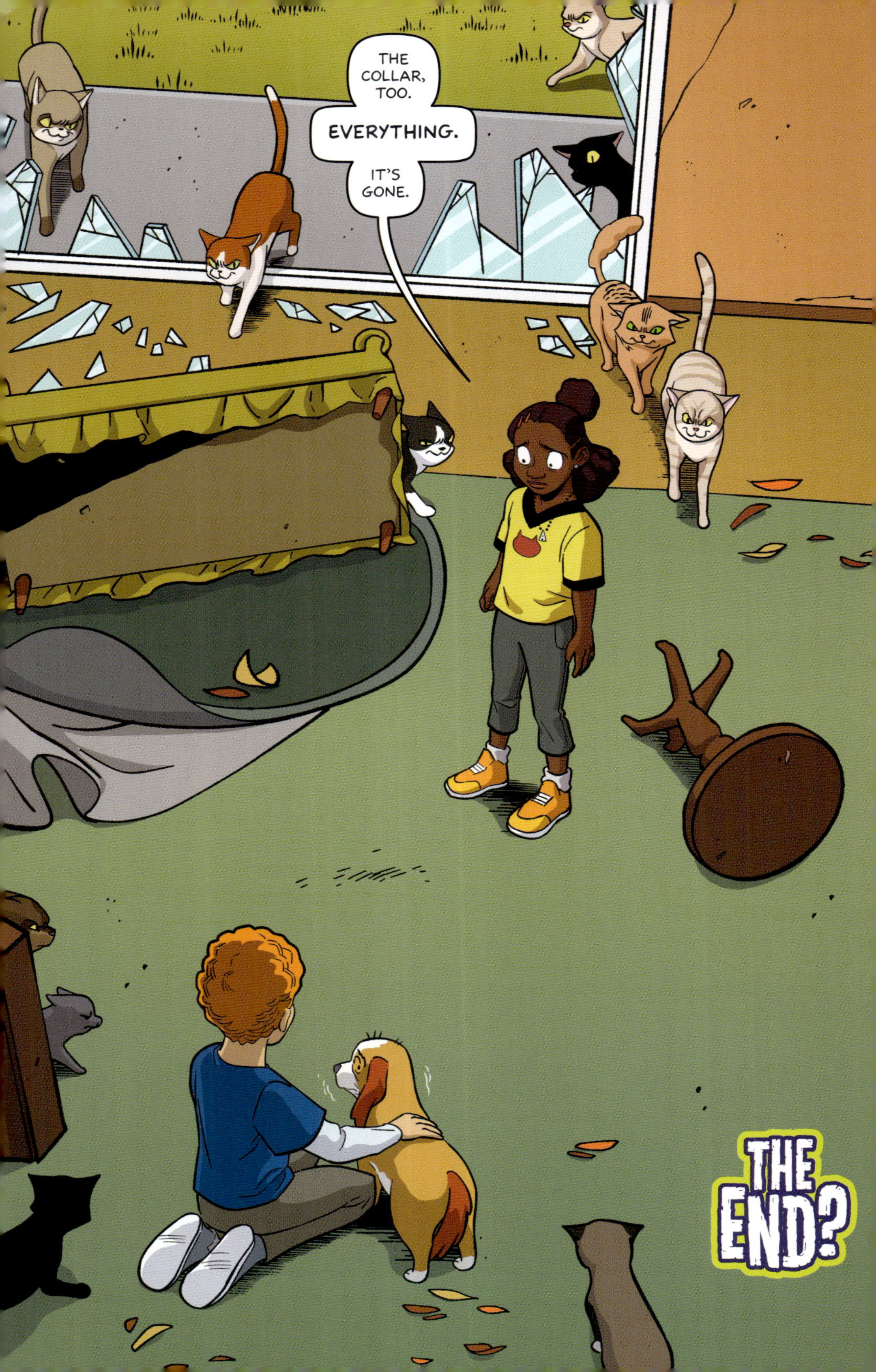
THE COLLAR, TOO.
EVERYTHING.
IT'S GONE.
THE END?

READ ON FOR A SNEAK PEEK OF

Goosebumps
THE GRAPHIC NOVEL

THE HAUNTED MASK

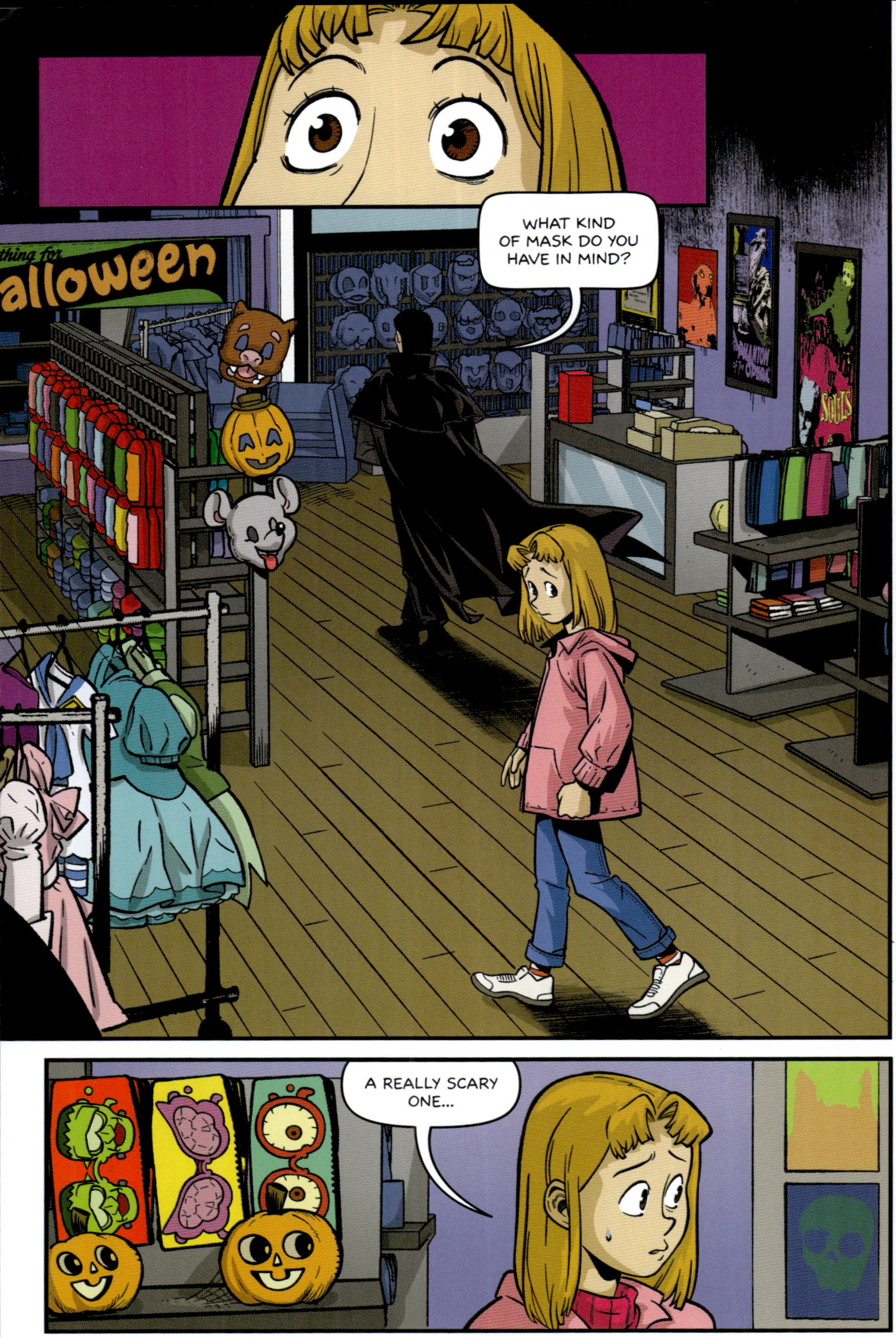
WHAT KIND OF MASK DO YOU HAVE IN MIND?
A REALLY SCARY ONE...

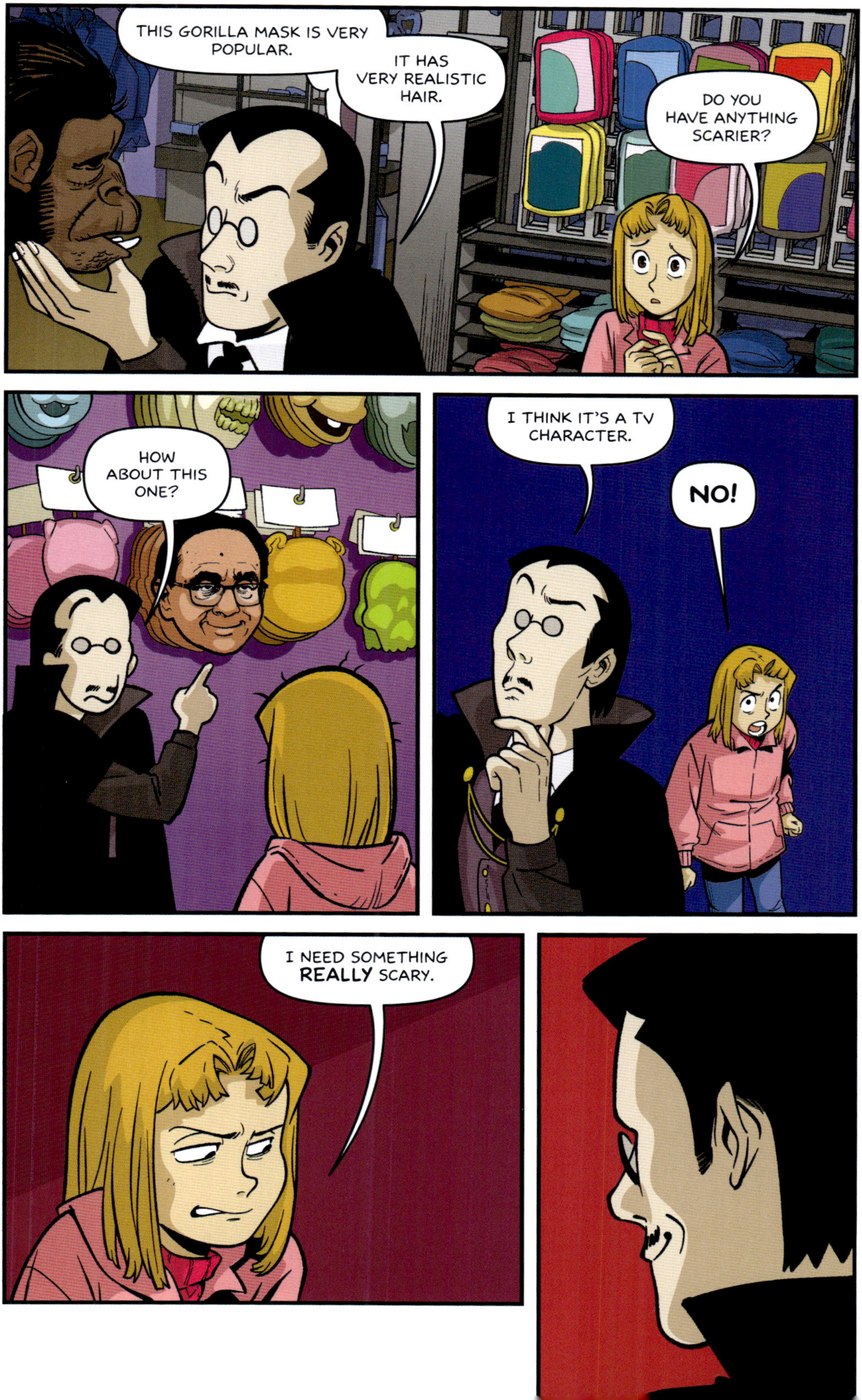
THIS GORILLA MASK IS VERY POPULAR.
IT HAS VERY REALISTIC HAIR.
DO YOU HAVE ANYTHING SCARIER?
HOW ABOUT THIS ONE?
I THINK IT'S A TV CHARACTER.
NO!
I NEED SOMETHING **REALLY** SCARY.

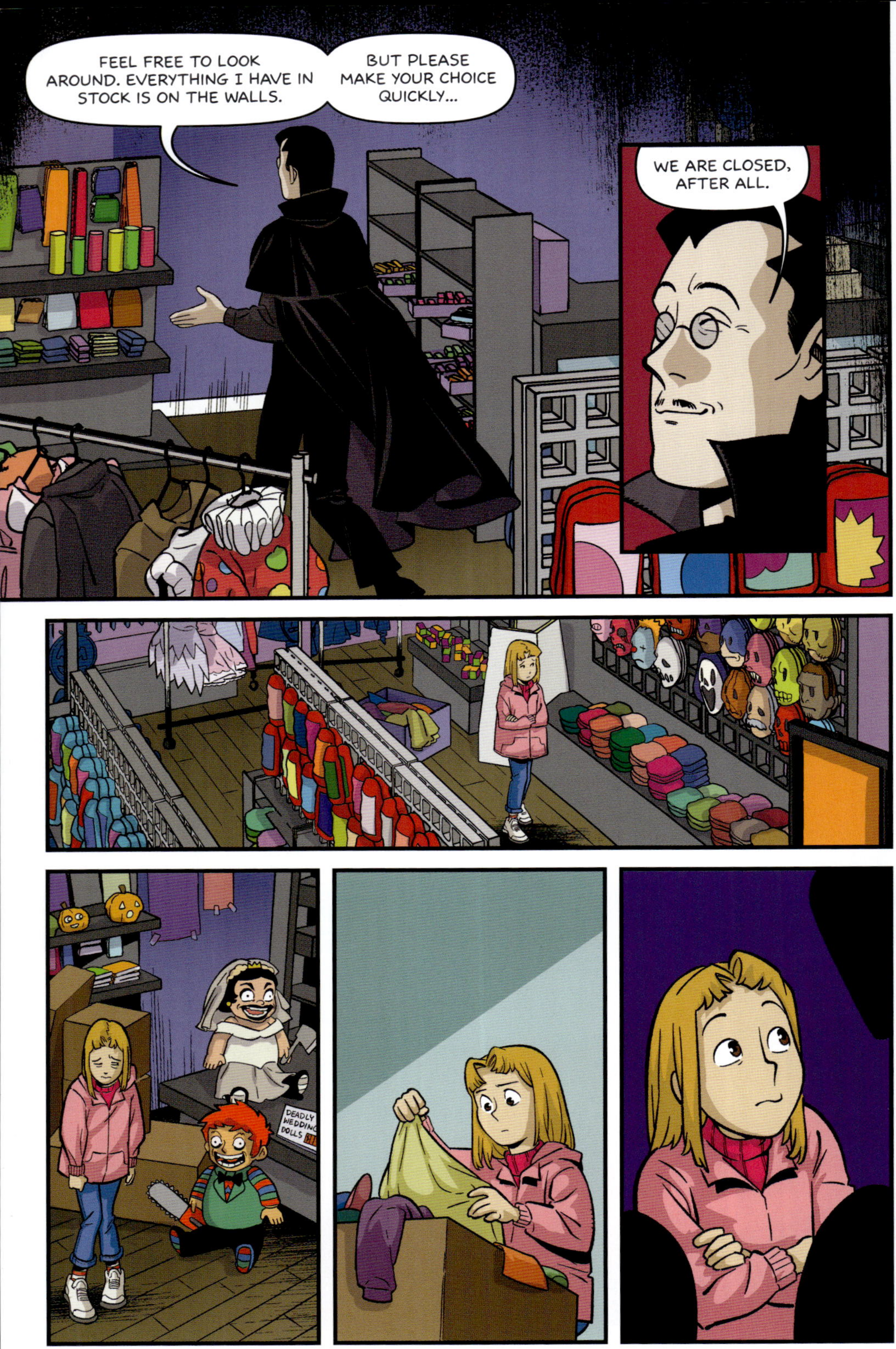
FEEL FREE TO LOOK AROUND. EVERYTHING I HAVE IN STOCK IS ON THE WALLS.
BUT PLEASE MAKE YOUR CHOICE QUICKLY...
WE ARE CLOSED, AFTER ALL.
DEADLY WEDDING DOLLS

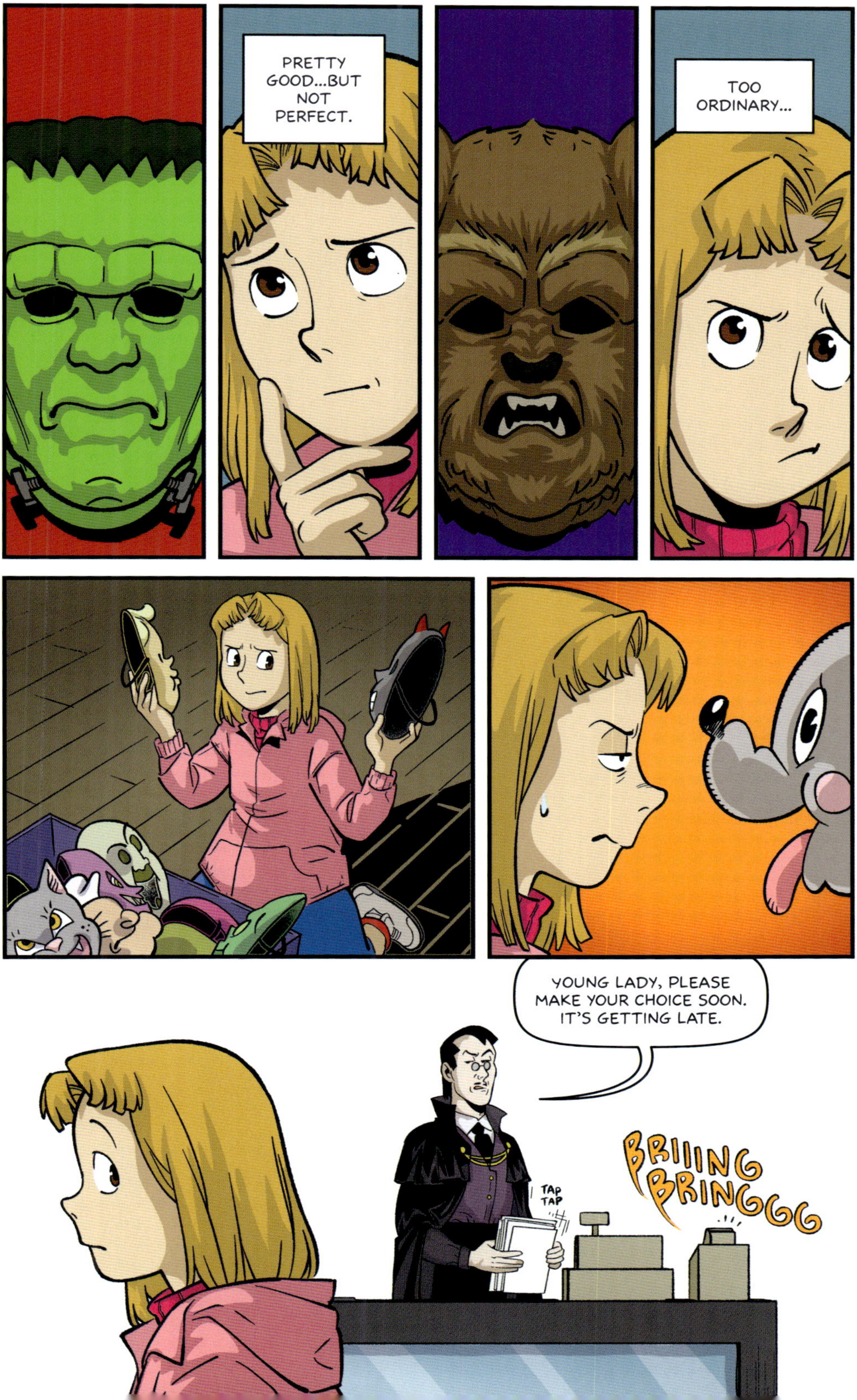

PRETTY GOOD...BUT NOT PERFECT.
TOO ORDINARY...
YOUNG LADY, PLEASE MAKE YOUR CHOICE SOON. IT'S GETTING LATE.
TAP TAP
BRIIING BRINGGG

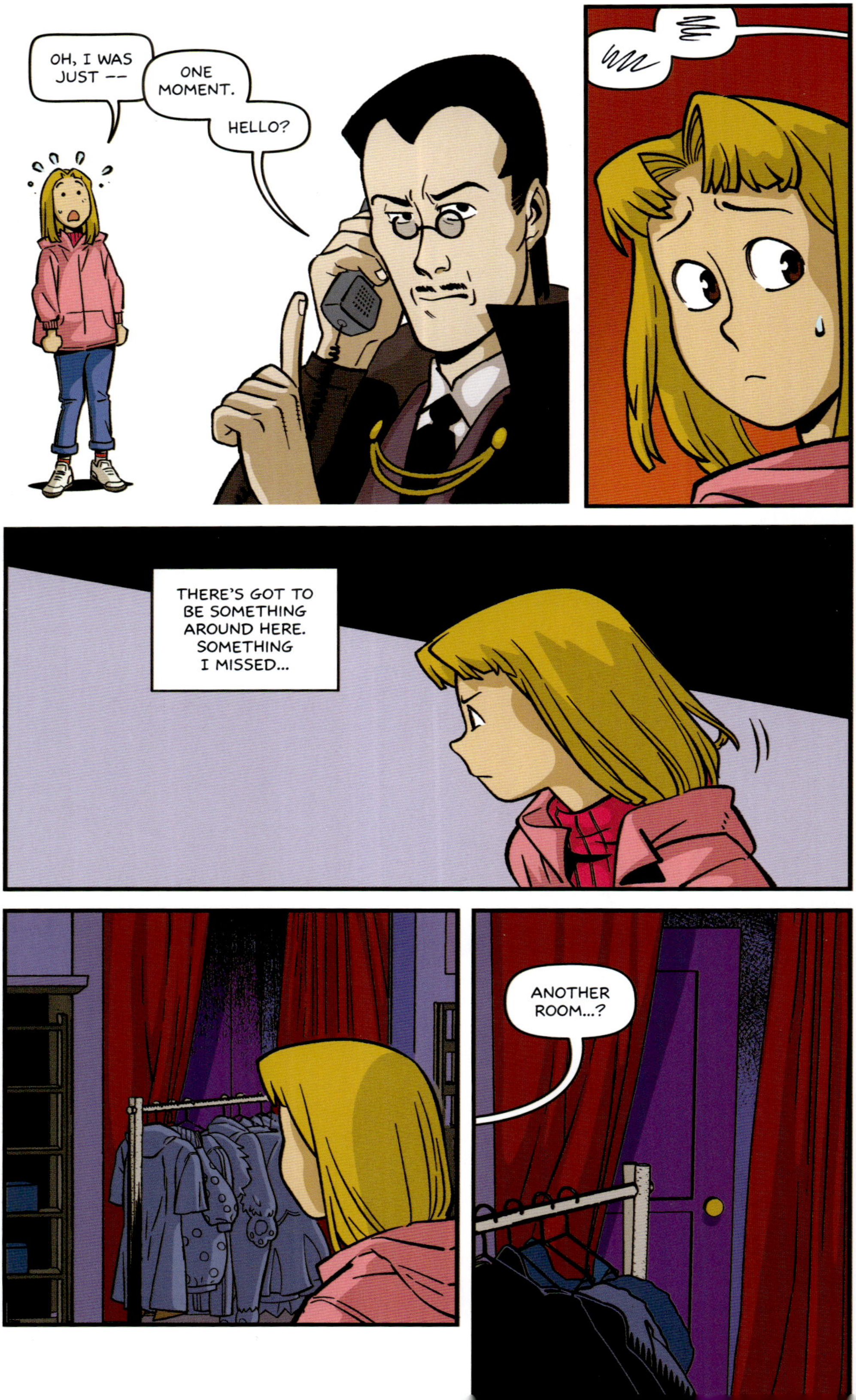
OH, I WAS JUST --
ONE MOMENT.
HELLO?
THERE'S GOT TO BE SOMETHING AROUND HERE. SOMETHING I MISSED...
ANOTHER ROOM...?

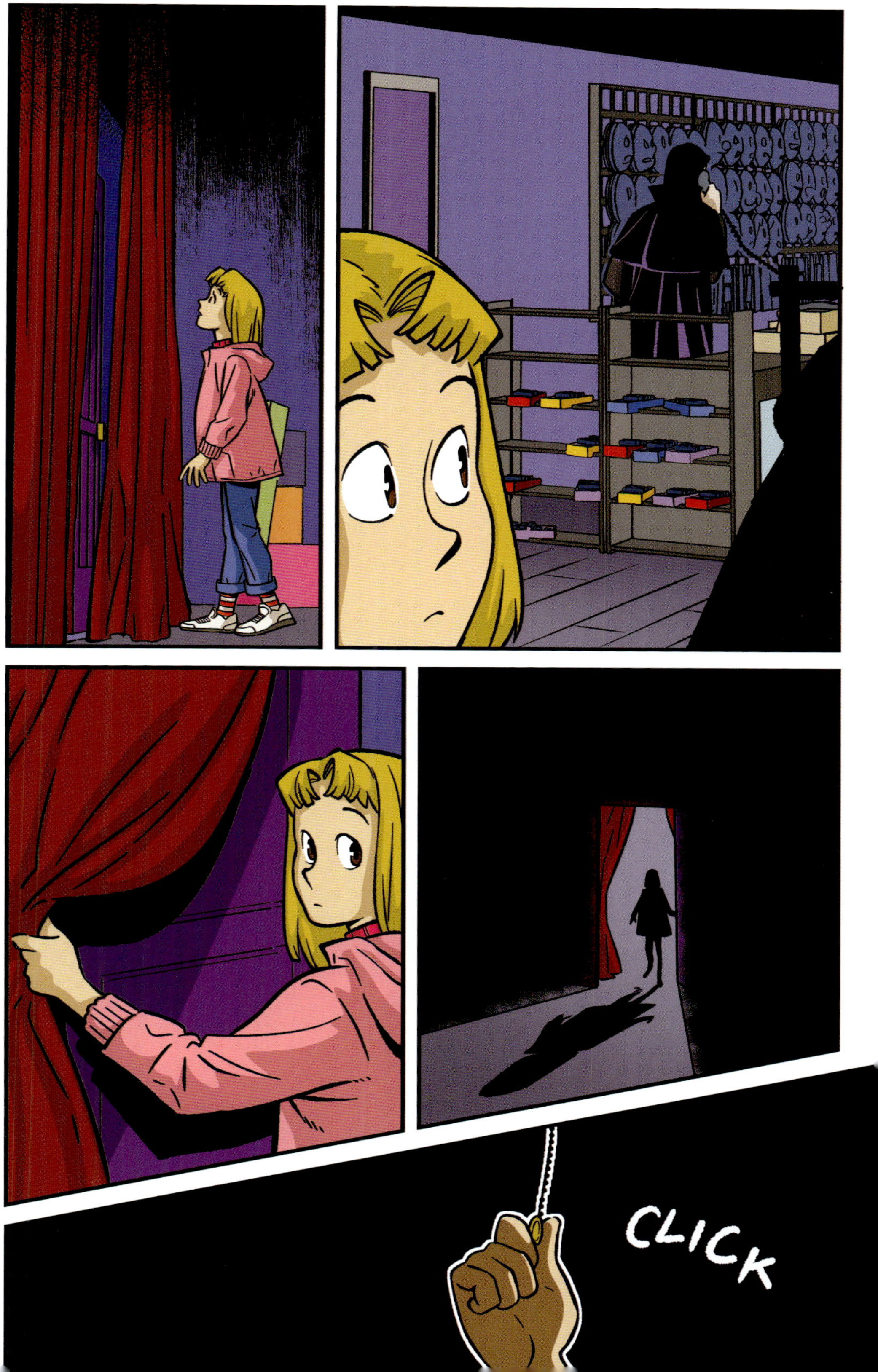
CLICK

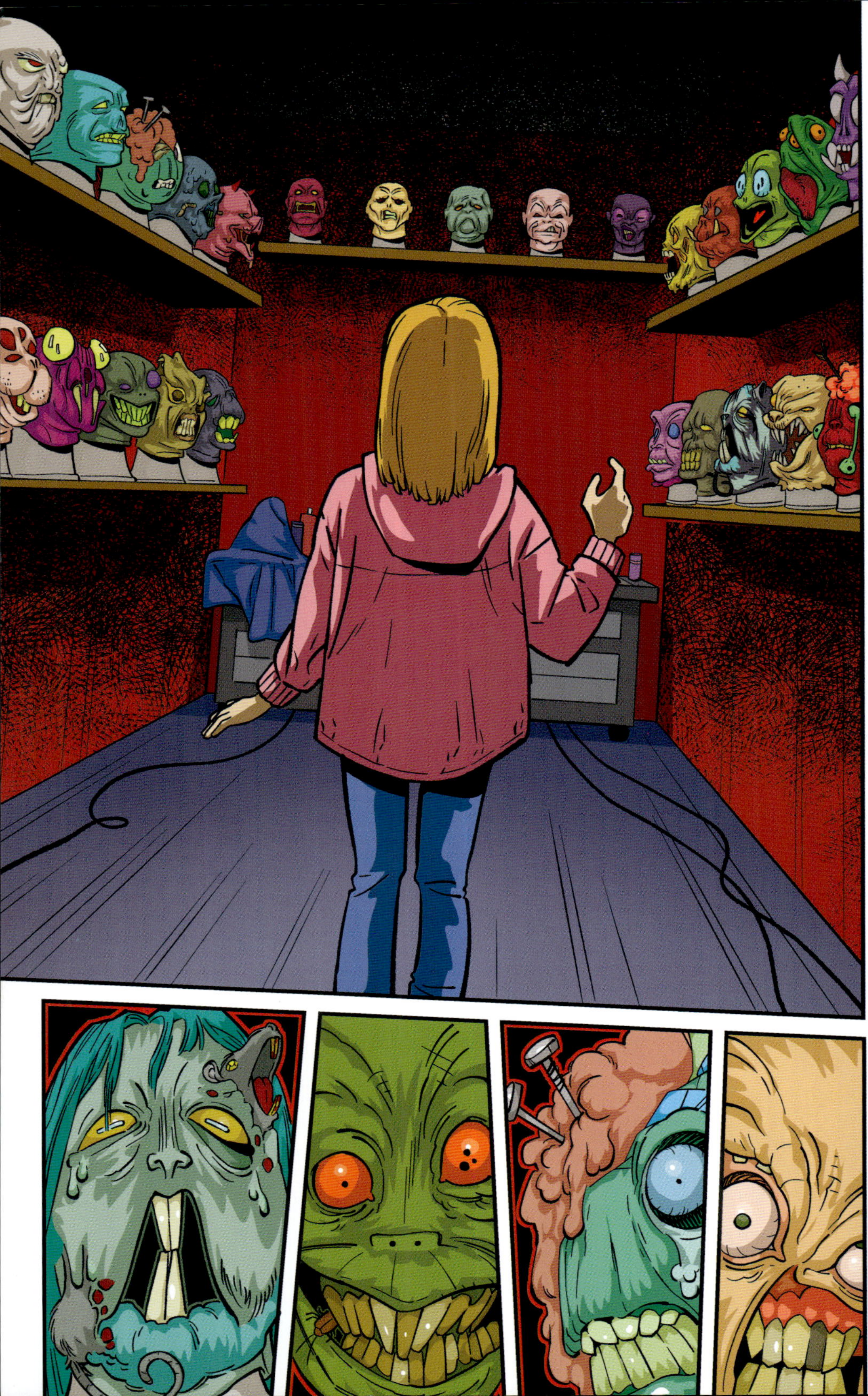

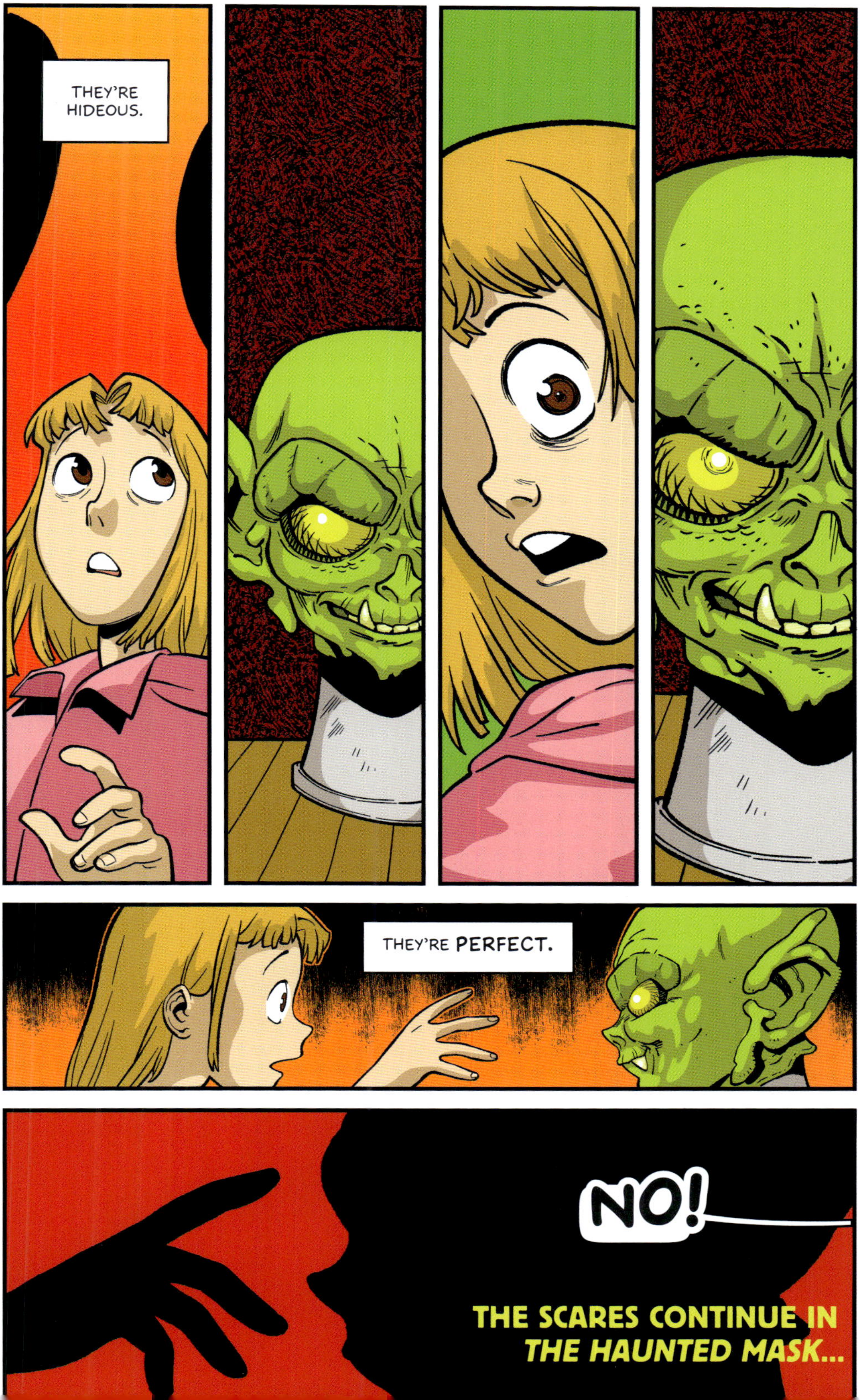
THEY'RE HIDEOUS.
THEY'RE PERFECT.
NO!
THE SCARES CONTINUE IN *THE HAUNTED MASK*...

GET THE ORIGINAL BOOKS—
BEFORE THEY GET YOU!

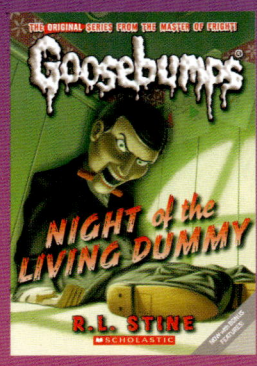 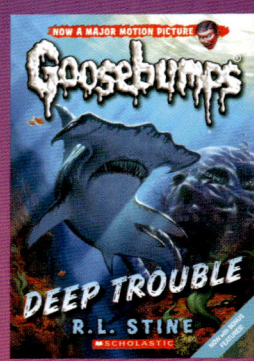 
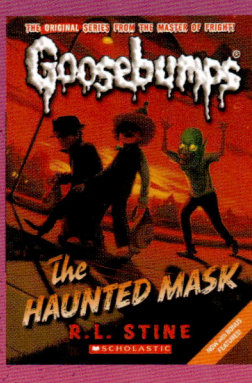 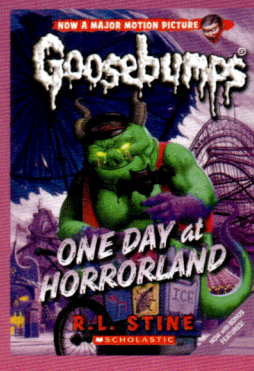 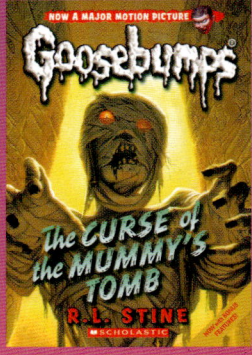
  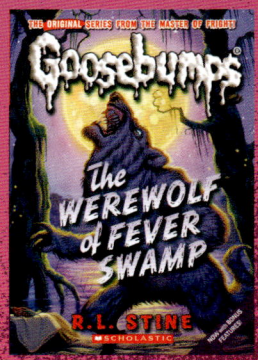

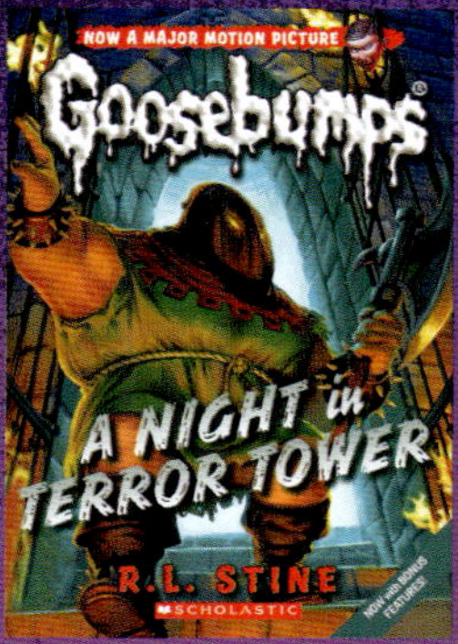
NOW A MAJOR MOTION PICTURE
Goosebumps
A NIGHT in TERROR TOWER
R.L. STINE
SCHOLASTIC
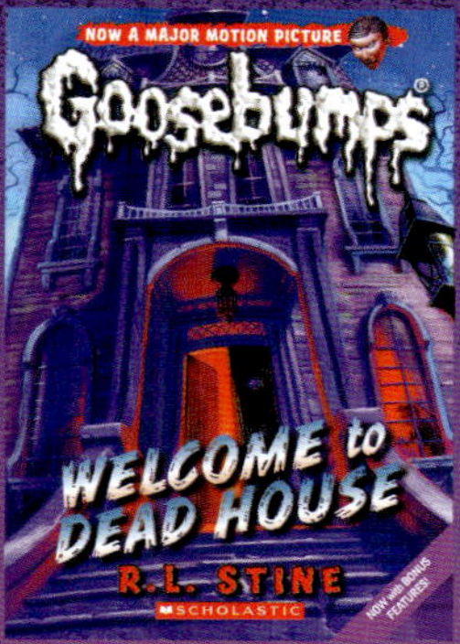
NOW A MAJOR MOTION PICTURE
Goosebumps
WELCOME to DEAD HOUSE
R.L. STINE
SCHOLASTIC
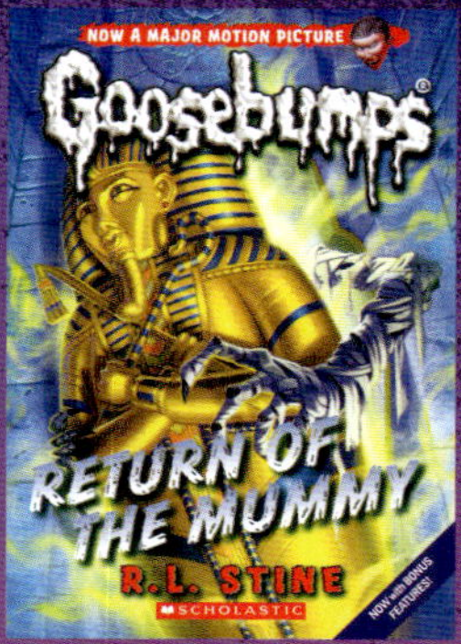
NOW A MAJOR MOTION PICTURE
Goosebumps
RETURN OF THE MUMMY
R.L. STINE
SCHOLASTIC
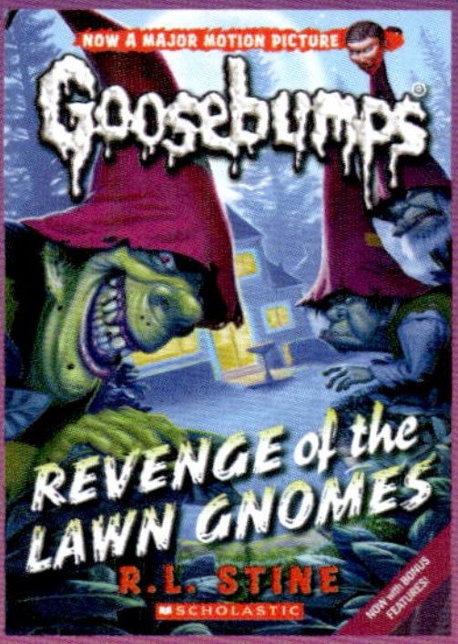
NOW A MAJOR MOTION PICTURE
Goosebumps
REVENGE of the LAWN GNOMES
R.L. STINE
SCHOLASTIC
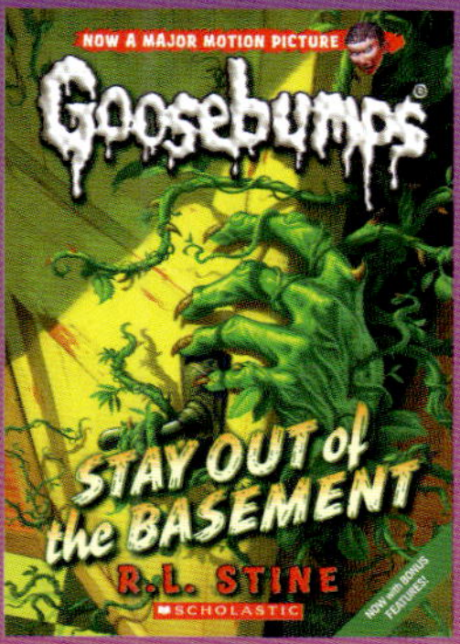
NOW A MAJOR MOTION PICTURE
Goosebumps
STAY OUT of the BASEMENT
R.L. STINE
SCHOLASTIC
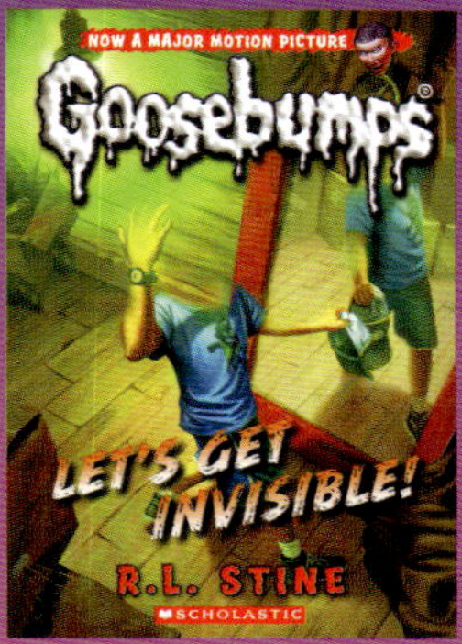
NOW A MAJOR MOTION PICTURE
Goosebumps
LET'S GET INVISIBLE!
R.L. STINE
SCHOLASTIC
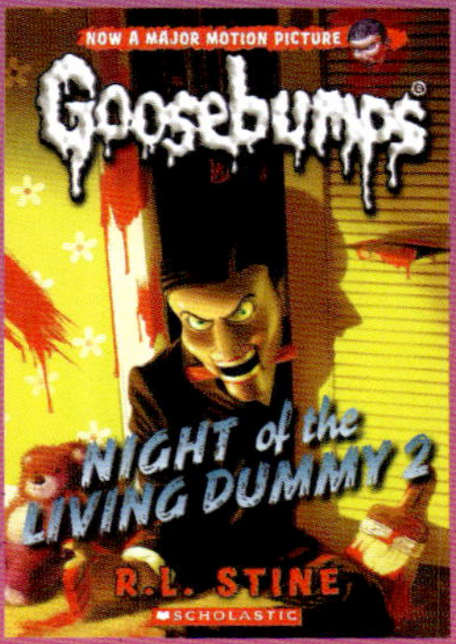
NOW A MAJOR MOTION PICTURE
Goosebumps
NIGHT of the LIVING DUMMY 2
R.L. STINE
SCHOLASTIC
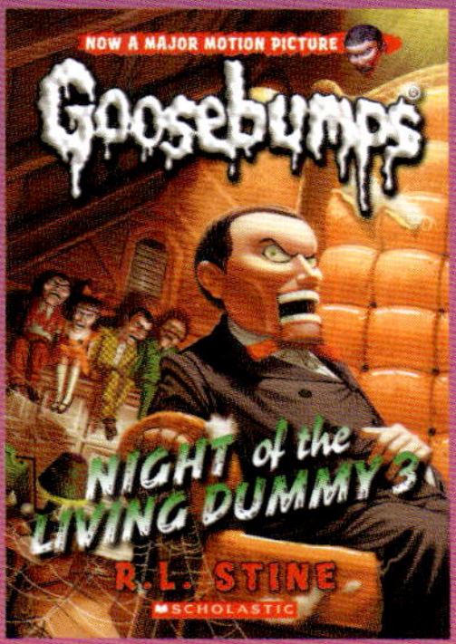
NOW A MAJOR MOTION PICTURE
Goosebumps
NIGHT of the LIVING DUMMY 3
R.L. STINE
SCHOLASTIC
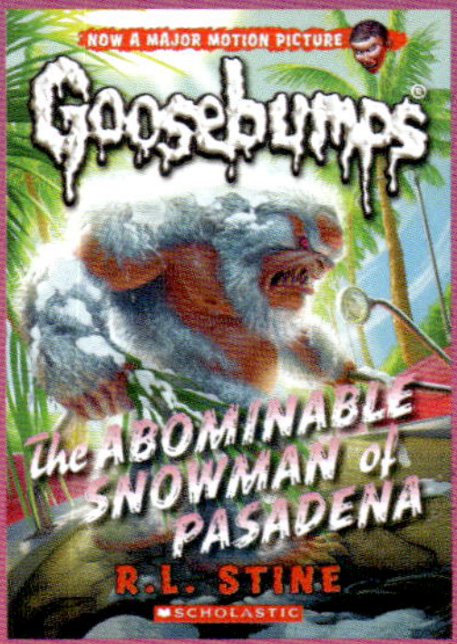
NOW A MAJOR MOTION PICTURE
Goosebumps
The ABOMINABLE SNOWMAN of PASADENA
R.L. STINE
SCHOLASTIC
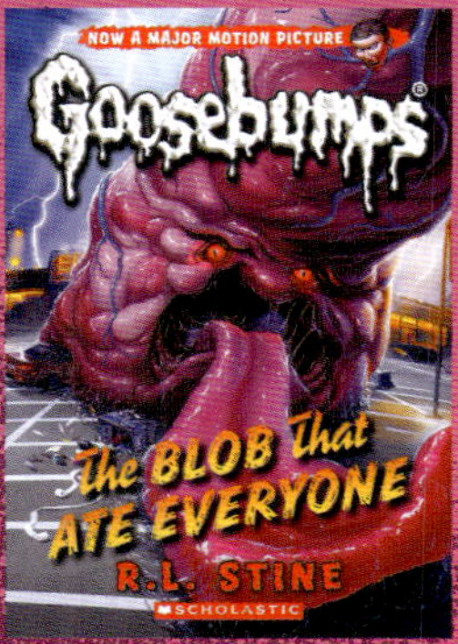
NOW A MAJOR MOTION PICTURE
Goosebumps
The BLOB That ATE EVERYONE
R.L. STINE
SCHOLASTIC
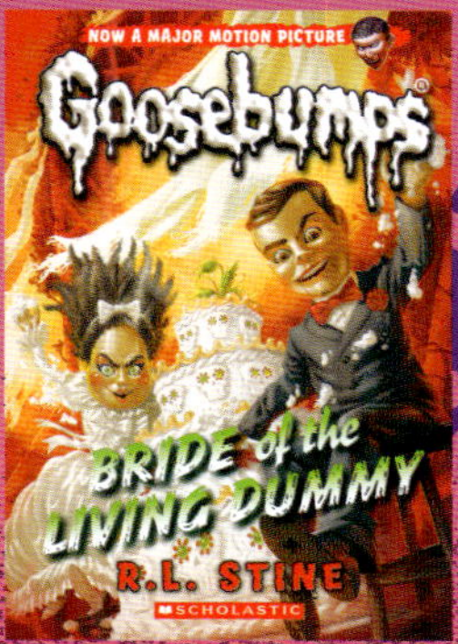
NOW A MAJOR MOTION PICTURE
Goosebumps
BRIDE of the LIVING DUMMY
R.L. STINE
SCHOLASTIC

Goosebumps SlappyWorld

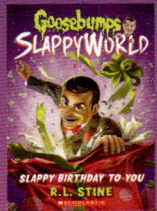 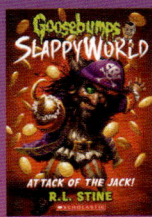 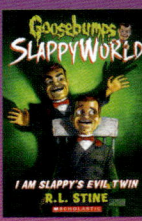 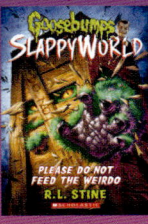 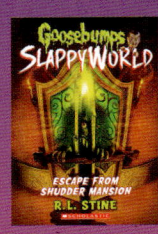
    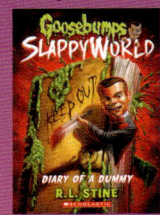
  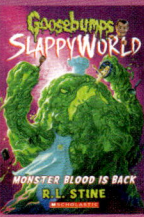 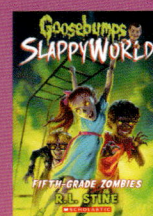 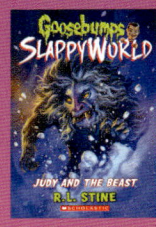
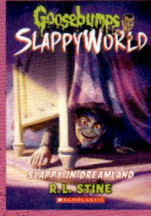 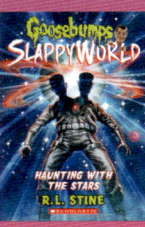  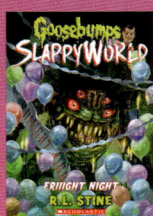

**THIS IS SLAPPY'S WORLD—
YOU ONLY SCREAM IN IT!**

Goosebumps HOUSE OF SHIVERS

THE ONLY THING TO FEAR...
IS EVERYTHING.

Goosebumps
HOUSE OF SHIVERS
SCARIEST. BOOK. EVER.
R.L. STINE
SCHOLASTIC

Goosebumps
HOUSE OF SHIVERS
GOBLIN MONDAY
R.L. STINE
SCHOLASTIC

Goosebumps
HOUSE OF SHIVERS
NIGHT OF THE LIVING MUMMY
R.L. STINE
SCHOLASTIC

Goosebumps
HOUSE OF SHIVERS
SAY MY NAME! SAY MY NAME!
R.L. STINE
SCHOLASTIC

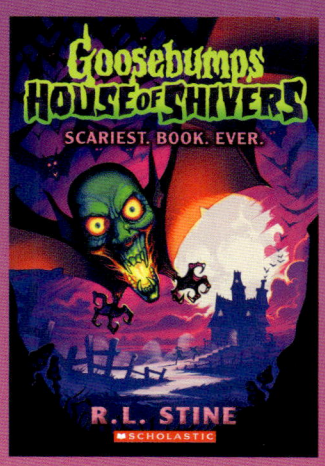

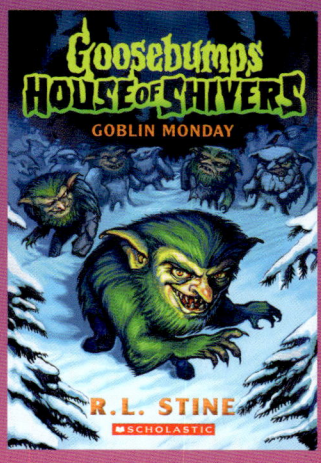

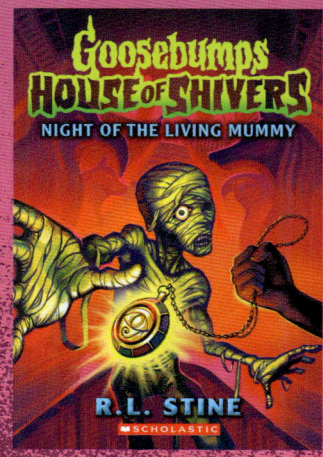

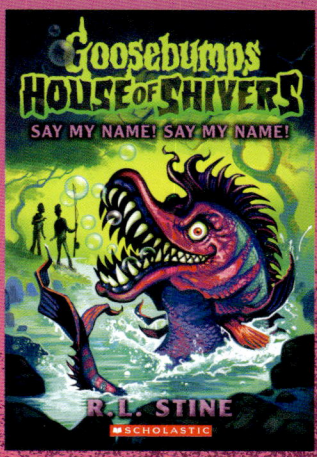

R.L. STINE says he gets to scare people all over the world. So far, his books have sold more than 400 million copies, making him one of the most popular children's authors in history. The Goosebumps series has more than 150 titles and has inspired a TV series and two motion pictures. R.L. Stine himself is a character in the movies! He has also written the teen series Fear Street, which has been adapted into three Netflix movies, as well as other scary book series. His newest picture book for little kids, illustrated by Marc Brown, is titled *Why Did the Monster Cross the Road?* R.L. Stine lives in New York City with his wife, Jane, a former editor and publisher. You can learn more about him at rlstine.com.

MADDI GONZALEZ is a cartoonist from the Rio Grande Valley, Texas. Her Ignatz Award–nominated comic art has a strong focus on humor and horror. Her favorite Goosebumps books are a tie between *The Headless Ghost* and *Stay Out of the Basement*.